Indelible Love — Jake's Story

Copyright © 2012 by DW Cee

All rights reserved. No part of this book may be copied, reproduced, transmitted, or downloaded, whether electronic or mechanical, without the written consent of the author.

This story is a work of fiction. Any similarity to real persons, living or dead, is entirely coincidental.

ISBN: 1491068663
ISBN-13: 9781491068663

Indelible Love — Jake's Story

D W Cee

To Ryan

My Max, My Jake
I love you

CHAPTER 1

Who Is This Girl?

Exhausted! That was the only word that came to my mind after working an eighteen-hour shift. I was sure it was illegal for anyone to work so much, but in these life and death situations I suppose I had no choice. This was the life I had chosen as a heart surgeon. Though, I probably would have been better off working at a different hospital. The chief purposely worked me harder to prove to others that he was not showing any favoritism to his nephew.

Hungry. That was another word that never left my mind when working so much. My stomach grumbled from a lack of food, as I'd had one meal all day and it was almost midnight. What were my options? Drive home and stop by a fast-food joint on the way? If I hit the freeway now, I should be able to reach my house in the Valley in twenty minutes. Or, go to Mom's down the street and hope that she had food in the fridge? I decided to forgo both options and stop by the market to pick up a protein shake before heading home.

Walking into the store, the most beautiful woman walked by, and I couldn't help but follow her from afar. She turned into one of the aisles and started looking for cereal. I paused to stare. She was gazing intently at the boxes in a peculiar way. It was comical how serious this decision was for her. Her long brown hair was pulled back into a ponytail and her porcelain skin would put dermatologists all out of business.

There was something about the way she looked—innocent, angelic, scared? She intrigued me. I decided to stand next to her, pretending to buy cereal as well. She had no clue anyone was watching her even though I stood two feet away. Closer up, she was even more stunning.

What was wrong with me? I was staring at a stranger in the market at midnight. As drawn as I was to her, I decided to go get my protein shake and come back later. It would give me some time to muster up the courage to ask for her number. It had been a few months since I'd been on a date. It'd be nice to meet someone new.

Walking past her, I noticed she had precariously stepped on the bottom shelf to reach for the Captain Crunch box located on the top shelf. I thought about getting it for her when she suddenly fell and knocked us down to the ground. She was embarrassed. I was grateful for the opportunity.

"I'm so sorry!" Her voice sounded almost as sweet as her face. "Are you all right?"

"I'm fine. Are you OK?" Hopefully she had broken something so I could take her to the hospital.

"I think I'm OK. My ankle feels a little weird, but I'm sure it's nothing."

Yes! Here was my chance. I would force her to go with me to the hospital regardless of how minor the injury might be.

"Do you want to try to get up?" I asked while holding her hand and helping her to her feet. Giddy, I felt like a boy holding a girl's hand for the first time. Her fingers were soft.

"Ouch!" She almost fell back to the floor, and I couldn't believe my luck tonight. "I guess it hurts a bit more than I thought it might. It's OK. I'll be all right." She pulled her fingers away while finishing her sentence and tried to walk down the aisle. I didn't know where she thought she was going without me.

"Wait. Let me help you." In two steps I reached her five hobbling steps. "Let me take you to my hospital just down the street and let's X-ray your ankle."

"No, that's so not necessary. I'll just go home and rest it. I knew I shouldn't have been out here this late." It was cute the way she was scolding herself. She was right though. What was she thinking coming out here at this hour?

"Please, let me help you. By the way, my name is Jake, Jake Reid."

"Hi, I'm Emily Logan." Her lips curled up into the most beguiling smile, sucking me into her world. Where had this girl been all my life? Being a cardiac surgeon I knew a thing or two about hearts, but I couldn't explain what was going on in my own. My pulse beat faster, my blood rushed, and my excitement level shot through the roof. We'd barely spoken, and I felt like this was the girl of my dreams—the one I would love the rest of my life. Perhaps I'd lost my mind.

Ignoring her scared look, I forced her to General Hospital and wheeled her into the ER.

"Will you be OK waiting for me here while I get some paperwork filled out?"

She nodded yes like a young schoolgirl. Oddly I sensed through her wide brown eyes that she trusted me to take care of her. My entire being felt this wonderful burden—a loving responsibility—to make sure that this Emily Logan would be OK. I had never felt such a strong desire to take care of someone like I did right now for his girl.

Practically waltzing into the front office, I had to figure out a plan to ask this girl to go out with me.

"Dr. Reid, what are you doing back? Aren't you done for the night?" asked Linda, the head nurse.

"Yeah. I came back in with a patient. She might have sprained her ankle."

I saw all the residents heading my way.

"Who's that hottie you just walked in with?" asked one of the residents.

"Who she is does not concern you. If any of you as much as talk to her, I will make sure you're doing midnight shifts in ER the rest of your stay here at our hospital."

"Oooh! You're so scary, Dr. Reid." Jeffery, our youngest intern at age twenty, attempted a joke. I gave him a be-scared-of-me look, and he backed off.

"I'm going to go back out and stay with her. Take your time calling her in. Treat her like any other patient who comes into this ER. I don't want to be out of here anytime soon." I gave them all my most serious doctor look. I didn't think any of them bought it. Laughter erupted behind me and I followed suit.

"What's so funny?" she asked with curious enthusiasm.

"Um...those residents were harassing me." I smiled at my inside joke. Placing myself as close to Emily as possible, I gingerly elevated her legs and hoped for hours of uninterrupted conversation.

"Do you work here?" Her trusting eyes made me want to tell her my whole life story. "Are you a doctor or a nurse?"

I guess I had forgotten to explain to her who I was. "I'm a doctor here. I work up in the cardiac department."

"Are you working right now? If you're busy, I can stay here by myself. Please don't let me keep you from your job."

I thought to myself, are you kidding me? You would need a crowbar to pry me away from you right now.

"No, I just got off at midnight and I was at the market hoping to pick up a bite to eat when you fell."

"I'm so embarrassed. I can't believe I did that. I'm very sorry." I took a mental snapshot of her beautiful smile and saved it in my memory. "I feel bad you haven't had dinner yet. You must be starving. Please go and get something to eat."

"I'm all right. I'm sure we won't be here long. I told the ER doctors to take good care of you."

"That was really kind of you. I would feel much better if you went and ate something though."

"Would you like to grab a bite to eat with me later?"

"Um..." I heard the hesitation I feared. Before she could answer, those pesky residents called Emily's name already. We had been there less than ten minutes. This had to have been an ER record.

I wheeled Emily into the ER and saw a guffaw in the eyes of each one. Two residents, one intern, and one nurse waited to attend to Emily and waited to see my reaction. The staff was having a good time at my expense.

"Ms. Logan? How does this feel?" Michael began feeling her ankle.

"It doesn't really hurt there...Ow!... That's where it hurts." Tears dotted her eyes as Michael poked into a tender spot. She looked childlike when she hurt. Instinctively my arms went around her shoulders and gave her a light squeeze.

She looked up at me surprised, and I retracted my arms. I could see the staff wanting to howl at my faux pas.

"So, Ms. Logan? How old are you?" Jeffery the intern asked.

"Twenty-four."

"I'm twenty!" I don't know why he sounded so excited revealing his age to Emily.

"Aren't you a bit young to be a doctor?" Emily asked in amazement. Her interest spurred him to continue.

"I'm what you call a genius. I graduated from medical school last year and this is my first year in residency." He had a smug look on his face. I tried to give Jeffery a back-off look, but he purposely avoided my eyes. "Ms. Logan, do you want to go out on a date with me?"

Emily and I both looked at him shocked! I vowed to make Jeffery's life miserable when he got to my department. The other two residents wisely chose not to say anything.

"I don't think it's a good idea for us to go out." Thank God she was turning him down.

"Why not?" he persisted.

"You're really cute, but I don't think it will be possible with our age difference and all."

"We're only four years apart."

"Well you're too young to even go and have a glass of wine with me. Plus, my ego couldn't take people carding me all the time while you got a pass for the next decade."

We all roared in laughter. She had a good sense of humor. I liked that.

"What about me, Ms. Logan? Would you be willing to go on a date with me? I'm off in thirty minutes, and we can go grab a burger and a beer."

"Wow…tempting but I don't drink beer. Sorry!" She gave him an apologetic puppy dog look. Enamored with her, I couldn't even get mad at Al for trying.

All of us stared at Michael to see if he would try.

"I guess I have to throw my name in the hat as well, even though I have a girlfriend," Michael decided.

"Ms. Logan, I'd be honored if you'd like to go out on a date with me." That two-timing jerk!

"Sorry, I definitely don't date two-timers."

"Yes!" I thought. That's exactly what I was thinking.

"Thank you all for your kind offers. I haven't had a date in almost a year and a half. Go figure, I should have hung out in the ER more often." She shrugged her shoulders, and her eyebrows arched up. "But, if you don't mind, I think I need my ankle examined more than I need a date right now."

Fed up and shaking her head, Linda came over and offered to put her in a private room while waiting for the attending doctor to come and take care of her ankle. I was grateful for her help.

"My apologies for those silly doctors. They're here late all the time, and they try to find humor in every situation," she explained.

"No apologies necessary. It was all in fun. I'm flattered more than anything." She was as gracious as she was beautiful. Emily Logan…truly, where have you been all my life?

Linda put us in a nice room and her eyes signaled a good luck sign. I mouthed a thank you. Emily comfortably rested in the hospital bed, and I sat in the recliner next to her.

"So sorry about all those guys…"

She cracked up. "I hope I didn't sound too mean to any of them. You have a bunch of cute young doctors here in the ER. Are all the other departments this fun and lively?"

"No, the rest of us are old and boring."

We laughed together this time.

"So…" I asked nonchalantly, "you really haven't had a date in a year and a half?"

"Uh-huh."

"It's hard for me to believe no man has asked you out. Have you been hiding under a rock all this time?"

She stared at me, probably wondering why I cared. "Well, I've been asked out, but I haven't gone out with anyone."

"May I ask why?" I asked cautiously again. I didn't want to appear too nosy.

"Um…I'm a one-man kind of girl and I haven't found the guy I want to date. Dating around is not my thing." She hesitated, then explained a lot more about herself than I expected to hear. "I was in a serious relationship for four years—all throughout undergrad—and my boyfriend dumped me on the day of our graduation."

I felt bad for her and angry toward this guy as tears flickered in her eyes again. Whoever he was, she must have loved him deeply if she was still hurting.

"Is he why you haven't dated in so long?"

"Um…I don't know if I'd say it was because of Max. It's really more because I haven't met anyone I'd like to get to know. Sorry. You look so tired. Details of my life must be boring you to death." Her eyes perked up again and tried to make humor out of her sadness.

She hadn't responded to my dinner request and I was just about to repeat myself when Linda came back in the room.

"Ms. Logan, I'm sorry but the attending doctor got called away. You'll be in here a bit longer."

"OK, thank you."

"Jake?" Her voice sounded like it was dipped in sugar.

"Yes?"

"Do I really need to stay here? I feel horrible—you've been here so long with me and I'm really tired."

"You should be examined by a doctor." I wasn't ready to let go of her.

"Aren't you a doctor? Do you not know about ankles? Is that too far down south from the heart?" With almost a coquettish grin she was coaxing me and teasing me at the same time.

Chuckling at her humor, I saw the exhaustion in her eyes and had to give in.

"Why didn't I think of helping you, earlier? Let me take you to X-ray then bandage you up if nothing is wrong."

"Would you? Thank you." Her weary eyes filled with relief.

Knowing that this night was coming to an end all too soon, I silently kicked and screamed my protest, while getting someone to X-ray her ankle and confirm my initial theory that nothing was wrong with her. Then I slowly wrapped her ankle with a bandage and hoped she didn't wonder why I hadn't done this the moment we walked into the ER. All the residents came by one last time as I wheeled her to my car.

"Bye, Ms. Logan! Let us know if you change your mind." They all chorused in unison

Emily turned to me as I helped her into the car and shuddered. "That was creepy. Please don't bring me back here ever again."

I couldn't help but laugh one more time. I hadn't had this much fun in a long while.

"Do you want me to drive you home?"

"No, I need to go pick up my car. I'll be OK."

We got to her car and I hated the thought of letting her go. Perhaps it was wishful thinking but as tired as she looked, there seemed to be a part of her that was comfortable with me—that liked being here with me.

"Jake?"

"Yes?" Subtlety not being my forte. I answered her question too quickly.

"Would it be OK if we went to dinner another time? I don't think I can sit through a meal right now."

My heart performed a loop de loop in response to what she said.

As casual as I could be, I answered, "Sure." But of course, much too quickly I added, "How about tomorrow night?"

I saw her hold back a laugh. She leaned over and gave me a light peck on the cheek. Like a schoolboy kissed for the very first time, her lips sent me over the moon.

"Thank you for all your help tonight." With that she hobbled out of the car. Frozen from her embrace, I stupidly let her limp to her car. Running toward her, I encircled my arms around her body and carried her off her feet. In turn, her arms folded around my neck and momentarily, I hoped time could stand still. Bodies close, face-to-face, I struggled to not lock her lips with mine. As I couldn't help staring, she looked away abashed.

"Were you planning on running away without giving me your phone number?" I slowly let her go when her body pushed away.

"Oh, I guess you need that, huh? I have to warn you...I only have a cell phone and I'm not good about answering it. I respond better to texts." She proceeded to rummage through her purse and jotted down ten digits onto a piece of paper.

"Good night or morning." She waved as she closed her car and left the parking lot.

My eyes finally blinked long after her car drove out of sight.

CHAPTER 2

Will You Go Out With Me?

"Good morning, Mom! Good morning, Dad!" I greeted my parents with a cup of coffee at the breakfast table.

"When did you get in? You're unusually chipper this morning. Something good happen at work yesterday?" Leave it to Mom to notice already.

"I met the most amazing woman last night." My grin spanned from ear to ear.

"Oh?" I caught both my parents' attention now. "I don't know that we've ever seen you this excited about a girl," my mom observed. "What's she like?"

"Her name is Emily Logan, she's twenty-four, and she's the most beautiful person. She's beautiful not only on the outside, but on the inside as well."

"How'd you meet her and when do we get to meet her?" my dad joined in.

I explained our ordeal last night from the grocery store to the ER and told them I barely knew her. "For all I know, she might not be interested… although she didn't turn down my dinner offer for tonight." I looked at the clock, and it was almost 8:00 a.m. I'd been up since 6:00 a.m. waiting to call her.

"Why don't you bring her over tonight before going out for dinner? I'd love to meet her." My mom was way ahead of herself.

"Honey," my dad chimed in, "don't you think we'd scare her off before Jake had a chance? That's a bit serious, meeting the parents on the first date."

"Yeah, I guess, but...Jake, where are you off to? We want to hear more," I heard my mom call out as I ran up to my room. I didn't have time to respond. It was 8:00 a.m., and I had a phone call to make.

"Hello?" Tired and weak, Emily's voice sounded like I woke her up.

"Good morning, Emily, how are you feeling?" There were a couple of seconds of very awkward silence. "It's me, Jake."

Still a pause...

"Did you forget me already?"

I heard a groggy giggle.

"How can I forget you when you're the last person I talked to yesterday and the first person I'm speaking with today? You won't allow me to forget you." There was hearty laughter on her part. I didn't find that funny.

"Is that a hint?"

"No. Good morning, Dr. Reid. To what do I owe this very early call?"

"It's 8:00 a.m. already. You call this early?"

"It is when someone kept you at the hospital till three in the morning."

This girl was impossible not to love. I needed to come up with an excuse to go see her this morning.

"I'll ignore that last comment. How's your ankle? Are you in any pain?"

"Now that you mention it, I am in a lot of pain and my ankle looks like a tree trunk."

Perfect. Here was my chance to go see her. "Let me come by and take a look. It shouldn't be so swollen. Can I stop by right now before going to the hospital?"

"Right now?" She sounded horrified.

"Uh-huh. I need to be at work by 9:00 a.m., so if I stop by it has to be now."

"Jake, I'm still in my pajamas. I haven't even brushed my teeth yet." Her whining was even cute.

"Give me your address."

It was like pulling teeth to get her address, but she gave it to me, and I ran down the stairs and jumped in my car before we said good-bye. Her house was within minutes of my parents and the hospital. How could she have been so close to me and yet so far away?

Ding Dong. I counted to thirty before trying again. Ding Dong.

Looking through the window, I saw her hobbling to the door. Between the plush robe and flannel pajamas under it, she was covered from neck down.

"Hi," she answered with her signature shy but angelic smile.

I couldn't answer. Awestruck I walked in and closed the door behind us. Not minding my manners, I placed one arm around her back and the other under her legs and picked her up again. She looked startled.

"You shouldn't be walking on that ankle." That was my lame excuse for carrying her to the sofa.

"Then you shouldn't insist on coming over. You're the one who made me get out of bed." Her biting remark alarmed me until I saw her lips curl up again. I wanted to shower those lips with love as I laid her on the sofa.

"I'm just doing my job as a doctor. Let's see your ankle."

I undid the bandage and saw that it was quite swollen.

"Emily, your ankle doesn't look good. I'm going to take off the bandage and have you rest it on this cushion." I gently put her legs up. "Let me get you some ice. Where do you keep Ziploc bags?"

They're over there." She pointed to a cabinet.

I went into her kitchen and made several ice bags for her and placed most of them in the freezer while bringing one over and placing it on her. Her big brown eyes followed my every move. When I thought about this situation, I wondered why she let me in her house—why she trusted me so much when we had met only a few hours ago. I hoped she didn't do this with everyone.

"Emily?" I sat halfway between her ankle and her erect body.

"Yes?" She stared intently into my eyes.

"Are you always this trusting?"

"What do you mean?"

"Well, it's a bit weird that you've allowed a perfect stranger into your house to take care of you. You don't just allow anyone into your house, do you?" That thought was more than alarming.

"Funny you mention it. I was thinking the same thing. I'm usually a paranoid person. I go around making sure all my windows and doors are locked every night before I go to bed. I don't know why I let you in this morning." She shrugged her shoulders. "But, I suppose you're not a stranger. Aren't you my dinner date tonight? Though, I think dinner is shot. This robe and pajamas will not be coming off today if my ankle persists to stay swollen."

"Does that mean I'm someone you'd like to get to know?"

"Perhaps...or I might be keeping you around only till my ankle gets better, so I don't have to go see those creepy ER doctors again." Her giggle came back.

Whatever the reason, I'll take it.

Her phone rang, and I walked over to get it for her.

"Thanks," she mouthed to me while answering, "Hello? Hey, Sarah."

I probably should have scooted down the sofa and sat in the empty spot at the end, but I didn't want to be so far away.

I listened to her conversation.

"Why are you and Charlie around here at this hour? What? No, I don't want to go to the picnic. I have a legitimate excuse now, I can't go."

She looked at me like she needed my help.

"I'm not kidding. I sprained my ankle and it's really swollen. I can't go anywhere, right, Dr. Reid?" She nodded her head feverishly, so I nodded my head along with her.

"Here." She handed the phone to me. "Tell my best friend I can't go to any picnic with her."

"Hello, Emily's friend," I answered. "Emily wants me to tell you she can't go to any picnic although if you put her in a wheelchair, she would be fine."

"Jake!" She pushed me off the sofa. "I think you're late for work."

It sounded like her girlfriend was asking her who I was. Emily began stammering. "He's a doctor who makes house calls. Anyhow, I'll talk to you when you get here."

"Who was that?"

"My best friend."

"What's with this picnic you're trying to avoid?"

"College reunion of sorts. I don't want to go."

"Could it be because of your ex?"

"Kind of."

"Do you still like him?" Did I really want to know this answer?

"No. I don't like him anymore, but he has a girlfriend already, and I don't really want to see either of them."

"Got it." I would've been happy to escort her if she had asked.

"Jake, it's almost nine. Don't you need to leave?"

"Yeah, I do. I'll come back later with a set of crutches for you. Do you want a wheelchair as well?

"No!"

"OK." I chuckled. "Will you be all right without me?"

"I've been OK the last twenty-four years, so I think I can survive a few more hours," she teased.

"You want to give me a set of house keys so I won't be scolded by someone for making you hobble to the door?"

She didn't even think twice about pointing to her keys.

"Take those. I won't be needing them today." Either she really trusted me or there was something seriously wrong with this girl. She had just handed me the keys to her house and her car.

"Emily." In walked a tall, fairly good looking woman and what looked to be her husband or boyfriend.

"Hey, Sarah. Hi, Charlie."

"Oh my gosh, what happened to you? You weren't kidding when you said you got hurt," Sarah said with a worried tone.

I got up to introduce myself when Emily beat me to it.

"Sarah, Charlie, this is Jake." She turned to me, "Jake, this is my best friend and sometimes mother, Sarah, and her boyfriend since birth, Charlie."

We all said hello, and Sarah gave me a funny look.

"When did you and Emily meet?"

"About nine hours ago." I saw Sarah and Charlie both stare at Emily for an explanation.

"Charlie, can you walk Jake out? He's going to be late for work."

"You'll be OK?" I checked on her one more time. "There are more ice bags in the freezer, and I'll call you from the hospital. I should be done around four." Maybe I sounded too intimate. We really weren't at any stage to be talking this comfortably. "Sarah, will you be taking care of her for a while?"

"Sure." Sarah somewhat slowed her word.

"Bye, Dr. Reid." Emily was trying to shoo me out the door. I walked out with Charlie, disappointed I couldn't stay with her the whole day.

"It was nice meeting you, Charlie. Hope to see you again."

"Well, if you're around Emily, we'll definitely run into you again. Sarah and Emily are like Siamese twins. I think my girlfriend prefers to be with her girlfriend and only comes to me at nights."

We shook hands and I left for the hospital. I wondered the whole way to work what Emily was telling Sarah about me—how she was describing who I was in her life. I wished I didn't have to work today.

As soon as I walked onto the third floor of the hospital, I was besieged with patients. Luckily there were no surgeries this morning, but I had no time to call Emily. I sent a quick text.

It's been a crazy morning. Sorry I haven't been able to call you. Hope you are doing OK. Is Sarah still there taking care of you?

She answered back immediately.

Sarah and Charlie left for the picnic. You have a knack for waking me up. Please let me sleep. See you soon.

People walking by stared as I chuckled to myself. I counted down the minutes till I could leave the hospital and be with her again.

I ran into Chief Henry Reid, my uncle and the chief of staff. The main reason I became a heart surgeon was because my uncle had been such a positive influence in my life. My father, now retired, was an internal medicine doctor, but I was always fascinated with operations. Uncle Henry bought me all kinds of heart books when I was younger and encouraged me to study hard so I could eventually do what he did daily—save lives. Little did I know this job would kill my social life. He never explained the casualties of becoming a surgeon.

"Hey, Chief. Can I leave early today?"

"Why?"

"I've got a date with the most amazing woman."

"If she's so amazing, why would she be going out with you?" The chief had a wicked sense of humor I didn't appreciate today.

"Yes or no?"

"No."

"Chief…Come on, don't you want to see your favorite nephew get married and have kids one day?"

"I'm sure Glen will get married and have kids one day. What's that got to do with you?" he guffawed. "All right. You can leave now but you're on call tonight. Your Aunt Babs and I have a dinner to attend, so I'm putting you in charge."

"No, not tonight. Let me have one night without any interruptions. Please. I beg of you."

"You can have that one night tomorrow."

And just like that, he walked off.

In exchange for a possible interruption tonight, I left the hospital immediately. I drove as fast as I could back to Emily. I was about to ring the doorbell when a happy thought entered my mind—her keys.

"Emily?" I called. I felt like I was home. It felt right. "Where are you?"

"If that's you, Jake, I'm where you last left me."

She hadn't moved.

"You're dressed. Are you feeling better?"

"Well, I thought I should get up and do something, so this is all I got done today." She pointed to her outfit.

"How's your ankle?"

"I think it feels better. I can't tell whether it's getting better or the ice has numbed me to a point where I can't feel my legs anymore. Either way, I'm starving. Can we go eat?"

I tried to pick her up again but she got up and limped toward the door. She locked her arms around mine and we got in the car.

"What do you want to eat? What are some of your favorite foods?"

"Do we have all day? I have a lot of food I like to eat." She laughed to herself. "I'm not picky as long as it tastes good. I'll let you decide."

"I need to be near the hospital because the chief put me on call tonight. Do you mind? There's a slight chance we might get interrupted."

"Do I have a choice?"

"I guess you don't."

We drove to a Mexican restaurant blocks away from the hospital and settled into a booth. I was happy to have this time to ask her questions about her life.

"So Emily Logan, tell me some basic facts about you."

"What do you want to know?"

"Only everything."

Her beautiful smile came back. "Well, I'm twenty-four, and I'm a school teacher. I did my undergraduate and graduate studies at UCLA…"

"Uh-Oh! We've got some problems already."

"What? Oh no! You're not a Trojan are you?"

"Yup. Although, I did go to UCLA med school."

"We're going to have to call off this date now. You can take me back home. I can't be out with a Trojan. My friends would have a heart attack, though I suppose you could be of help if they did have a heart attack."

Her kidding nature kept her smile at bay.

"What kind of doctor are you, by the way?"

"I'm a heart surgeon."

"Wow." She sounded impressed.

A server interrupted us to take our order and since it was early, we ordered a couple of sodas, since Jake was on-call, and a mixture of appetizers to begin.

"So tell me more about you. Where are your parents? Any siblings?"

"No parents, no siblings," she answered with sadness. I wanted to put my hand over hers and console her.

"I'm sorry to hear that." Seeing the sadness in her eyes, I decided not to pursue this aspect of her life.

"Tell me about you and Sarah. How long have you known her?"

Her face lit up again. "Sarah and I met our freshman year at UCLA. We've been best friends since. She has three younger siblings so she can be somewhat motherly."

"And Charlie?"

"They started dating in high school. They're going on eight and a half years now."

"Wow!"

"I know. He'll probably propose any day now. He won't tell me when, because he knows I can't keep a secret from her."

"What about your ex? Did you meet him at UCLA as well?"

"Yeah, Max and I met our freshman year. We lived in the same dorm." My stomach knotted at the thought of them living in the same building, possibly in the same room.

I was about to ask her more about her ex when the pager went off. This was my reality—my nightmare.

"Sorry. I need to call the hospital."

"Not a problem."

I couldn't believe this was happening. The hospital was calling me back in. In the middle of our first date I was going to have to take her home without having fed her any dinner.

"Emily…" I stopped with her name when I returned from the phone call.

"We have to leave." She posed it as a statement rather than a question. Already sliding out of the booth, she not only understood—she was understanding. "Let's go."

I helped her up and placed my arm around her. She leaned into my body.

"I feel terrible I didn't get to feed you anything. Do you want me to pick something up for you before we head back to your house?"

"Don't be silly. You have patients waiting for you. I can go home and fix myself something to eat."

To my chagrin, her house appeared sooner than I'd hoped. Out of habit and desire I took her off her feet and carried her to her house. Her cheeks flushed to a beautiful rose color, and she couldn't look me in the eye. There was something very raw about her.

She got herself down when we arrived at her door and there was that awkward silence again. I wanted to place my lips on hers but thought it was too early to try. Instead, I opened the door for her and asked if I could take her out again.

"Are we talking about another meal?" That was an odd question to ask, I thought.

"Yes. I'd love to try to make up for tonight."

"All right. I'll remember to eat something before you pick me up just in case this is a regular occurrence with you. I guess these are the casualties of going out with a doctor."

"Emily...That's not fair."

"I'm only kidding. We'll try again soon." With that she waved good-bye while I just stood there. "Go. Save a life, Dr. Reid."

Unhappily I said good-bye.

CHAPTER 3

Can Your Lips Be Any Softer?

Sunday, my day off, couldn't come soon enough, as I fastidiously waited for 8:00 a.m. to roll around so I could call Emily again. I had become borderline obsessed with a woman I'd met only a day ago. I couldn't stop thinking about her and wished to be with her right now. I assumed we could spend all day together and thought about what we could do and where I wanted to take her.

"Good morning!" I was my chipper self again.

"Boy, we're seeing a lot of you these days. So you decide to come over only when it's convenient for you?"

"Mom, do you know Emily lives five minutes from you? We could walk to her house."

My mom looked excited. "Where does she live? Maybe I'll take a walk over in her neighborhood."

"Jake, you do know it's Uncle David's birthday today and that we're all having lunch by his house?"

"I know but I was hoping to leave early, so I could spend the day with Emily."

"Why don't you bring her?" Mom looked excited again. "We'd all love to meet her."

"I'll ask. If you'll excuse me, I've got a phone call to make." I hurried up to my room again.

I dialed her number, praying she wasn't sleeping.

"Hello?" A groggy voice greeted me again.

"Did I wake you again?" I couldn't believe it.

"Do you have something against me sleeping in?" She chuckled. "Why are you up so early? Do all doctors get up at the crack of dawn?"

"Emily, it's past eight. This is hardly the crack of dawn."

"It is for me on a Sunday. I like to sleep."

"I've noticed. How's your ankle?"

"Oh, it feels so much better. It's not as swollen either. I was able to gimp around the house yesterday after you dropped me off. Did you have to work late?"

"Only till about eleven." Our conversation sounded so natural—like we'd been dating for months. "What are you doing today? Do you want to have lunch with me? I promise I'm not on call, so we won't be interrupted."

"I don't know…I've lost too much weight since I've met you. Every time I try to get something to eat, somehow you get in my way." Her voice teased.

"That was a joke, right?"

"Partially. I have lost weight since I've met you. Anyhow, I have plans today, sorry. I'm off to Charlie's niece's fourth birthday party. I got a personal invitation from Eunice, so I have to go."

"What time is the party?"

"It's an 11:00 a.m. party but it's out in Oxnard so I'll probably be out there the whole day. Charlie and Sarah are picking me up at ten."

"Will you be back by dinnertime?" Already pathetically whipped and desperate to be with her, I begged for some of her time.

"I don't know. Since Charlie's driving, I kind of have to follow their plan. What will you be doing today? It'll be weird not to see you. I feel like we've spent this entire weekend together."

Her nothing statement encouraged me to believe she too wanted to see me. I proceeded to tell her about my day.

"It's my Uncle David's birthday and our whole family's having lunch out on the Westside. I was hoping to take you with me. After that, I thought we could hang out."

I heard her laugh. "I see. I don't know if I can say I'm sorry to have missed lunch with your entire family, but I am sorry I won't see you today. I guess we'll have to try for next weekend since tomorrow begins another work week."

Her statement sent me to the moon and back.

"Have you had breakfast? You want me to bring over something to eat?"

"I'd love that. Thank you. Can you give me about half an hour to shower and change?"

"Sure. What would you like to eat this morning, Emily? Cereal?"

"No, I don't like cereal. I'm partial toward lattes and croissants—especially almond croissants."

"Almond croissant it is. See you soon."

"Can't wait."

We hung up and I replayed what she'd just said to me. If I heard her correctly, she was sorry that we wouldn't see each other today, and she couldn't wait to see me. That meant she liked spending time with me, which also meant she liked me as well? I didn't know whether to turn this idea into a question or a statement.

Trusting she wanted to spend time with me, I zoomed down the street from my mom's to pick up her croissant and latte. I also picked up a sticky bun, a vegetable frittata, a plain croissant and a scone, just in case she might like any of these items as well. I patiently waited for thirty minutes to be up and walked up her driveway, hoping she was ready to see me.

Ding dong.

Her hobbling turned to gimping. Her walk looked much better.

"Hi," she answered with that sweet smile. "Come in."

"You're walking much better today."

"Yeah. I feel so much better too. I fell asleep soon after you brought me home and even though someone woke me up prematurely, I feel well rested."

"Here." I handed her the box of food and her coffee.

"Thank you." We sat down at the breakfast table and she looked surprised. "Why is there so much food in here?"

"Aren't you the one who accused me of causing you to lose weight? And by the way, what do you mean you don't like cereal? Isn't that why you were at the market so late at night?"

"Yeah. I had this freakish craving for Captain Crunch even though I don't like cereal."

I just stared at her.

"I know…I'm kind of unusual when it comes to food. If I get a craving, I need to satiate it. Have you had breakfast yet?" She got up to get plates and utensils for us and brought out some strawberries as well.

"I've had breakfast already. This is all for you."

"That's no fun. I hate eating by myself," she complained. "Will you eat a little more?" Her voice so sweet, she could have asked me to rob a bank and I would've said yes.

During breakfast, this girl, whom I couldn't get enough of, told me her favorite food was sushi or foie gras—she had expensive taste; she loved to watch sad movies; and her favorite book was *Pride and Prejudice*. Thirty minutes might as well have been thirty seconds. Time flew by as Charlie and Sarah were at her door at 10:00 sharp. They both looked startled to see me here again.

"Jake. Are you here to check on Emily again?" Sarah gave me the third degree.

"No, I came to feed her this time. I was hoping to spend the day with her, but she told me she had plans with you, so I'll get going."

"You're welcome to come with us to the birthday party," Charlie quickly invited.

I nearly ditched my uncle's fiftieth birthday party when I noticed the excitement in Emily's eyes at Charlie's invitation. The Reid family would have disowned me if I did. "Thanks but I have a family function I can't miss. Perhaps next time we can go out, the four of us?"

"That sounds like a date." Charlie and Sarah agreed. "We'll wait for you in the car," Sarah told Emily.

I appreciated Sarah's attempt to give us a few more minutes together.

"I guess I won't see you for a while once work begins?" Surprisingly, Emily was the one who was sad we were parting. "I'll call you when I get back." She actually sighed.

Tension filled the room as we stared at each other, wondering where to go with this moment. Do we just walk out and part? Should I kiss her on the cheek? Do I dare try on the lips? Emily lightly bit down on her lips with some sort of anticipation but I held back. I wanted to smother her with kisses among other things and stay that way the rest of the day, but looking at her wide-eyed countenance, I felt no assurance she would agree to my idea.

"Sarah and Charlie are waiting." Emily broke our silence.

"Sure. Let's go." I locked the door behind us and took her hand in mine, interlocking fingers one by one. A highly charged volt ran through both our hands. I couldn't remember the last time I held a girl's hand and felt such heightened emotions. With her head down, reticence mixed with a smile peered through her beautiful face. We stopped near Charlie's car and I pulled her in for a hug. "I'll miss you today."

"I'll miss you too," she answered back. Since I wasn't expecting this response, her four simple words shot happiness into my heart. I decided to push my luck and leaned in to kiss her. To my dismay she pulled away and explained, "I'm not big on PDA. Can I take a rain check?"

Deciding I didn't care about her not liking PDA, I lightly kissed her lips and answered, "Sure."

It was going to be a long day without her.

"Jake, do you want to drive to the Westside with us?" Mom asked.

"No, I need to stop by and pick up a present for Uncle Dave. I'll meet you at the restaurant."

"What are you going to get him? Do you want me to come with you?"

"Not sure what, but I want to stop by Cartier. I'll walk over to the restaurant from there."

"Cartier? Could it be that you want to pick up something for Emily and not Uncle Dave?" Mom smiled at me. "Isn't it a bit premature to be picking up jewelry for her already? I'm dying to meet this girl."

"Mom, I don't think I've ever felt so strongly about anyone in my life. This is the girl I'm going to marry!"

"Marriage? Already? All right…See you at lunch." Mom sounded skeptical but curious.

Before leaving, I thought it might be too soon to call so I texted her a message.

Call me when you're done. I'll drop by and see you if it's not too late. I miss you very much already.

She sent back another quick response.

How can you miss me already? It's only been ten minutes. I think you are lying. Maybe I am lying too when I tell you that I miss you as well.

I wanted to text back, I love you but thought I should wait on that one.

There were about thirty of us at brunch. Bobby, my father was the oldest of five boys and Uncle Dave was the youngest. All my aunts and most of my cousins were here to celebrate Uncle Dave's fiftieth birthday. Though we cousins didn't get together on our birthdays, we were pretty religious about getting together for all holidays and our uncles' birthdays.

The only ones not present were Gram, who lived in London, Jane, my sister who lived in New York, and Laney, my cousin who was in Japan on an undergraduate student exchange program. We had a lively lunch.

"Hey, Jake," Uncle Dave called, "your gram says she wants to talk to her favorite grandchild."

Of course that would be me. "Hi, Gram. How are you doing?"

"Jakey, when are you getting married so I can have great-grandchildren? What's taking you so long? Why are you so picky?"

"Gram, I promise you within a year, I'll be married. I've met the most incredible woman."

All eyes and ears fixed on me.

"Who is she? Why don't you bring her to London to visit me?"

"I just met her. I'll bring her soon, I promise. I have to warn you though, she's even more beautiful than you are, and I may already love her more than I love you."

"She's no good for you, then. I can't have someone stealing my grandson's love away from me." We both chuckled. "Be good to her, Jakey. Call me often."

"OK, Gram, I love you."

"So who's this girl you've met?" Aunt Barbara, the chief's wife, wanted to know.

"Only the most amazing woman!" I answered.

"You sound pathetic," Uncle Henry replied. "If she's so amazing, why didn't you bring her today and introduce her to all of us?"

"I tried, but she already had plans."

"Hey, bring her to Mom's for Thanksgiving," Doug suggested. "You know Mom throws the craziest theme parties."

"Aunt Babs, what's the theme this year for Thanksgiving?" one of the cousins inquired.

"Pilgrims and Indians—everyone must come in costume." Aunt Babs threw the best theme parties. Each family took turns hosting a holiday. Christmas was always held at our house, Thanksgiving at the chief's, Easter at Uncle Billy and Aunt Sandra's, Mother's Day at Uncle Dave's and Aunt Debbie's, and Father's Day was at Uncle Roy and Aunt Pattie's home. We had a good relationship with one another.

"Can I bring Emily this Thanksgiving?"

"We'd worry if you didn't," Aunt Babs reassured me.

Several times during our meal I texted Emily but got no response. Once our meal was over, I called to find out how her day was going.

She picked up on the first ring.

"Hi, Jake." She sounded happy to hear my voice.

"Hi. Are you busy?"

"Um...kind of. How was lunch? Is your whole family still there?"

"Lunch was good. You would have enjoyed it. Have you had lunch?"

"Not really."

I heard her saying no thank you to some guy who kept asking her if he could get her a drink. I hoped she had not been spending the day with another guy.

"Who are you talking to?"

"Oh...you don't want to know."

"I think I do. Is he the reason why you haven't responded to any of my texts today?"

"Uh huh. Let's just say he reminds me of those ER doctors I met on Friday."

That wasn't good news for me. That probably meant he hit on her. He probably had her cornered since she couldn't move around too well.

"Do you want me to come get you right now?"

"I'd like to say yes but I need to stay. I'll call you when we're done. I hope it's soon. I'm hungry."

"Why haven't you eaten?"

"I don't do hot dogs at kids' parties." With that she gave me a cute giggle and said good-bye.

My cousins and my brother, Nick, wanted to catch a movie so I decided to tag along. I thought it would be a good way to kill some time while I waited for Emily to get back. Of course I couldn't concentrate on the movie when I thought about the creep who had Emily cornered. I was on edge since my conversation with Emily.

Nick, Doug, and I decided to go have dinner in Venice, and Emily still hadn't called. It took every ounce of self-control for me not to call her again.

"Who is this girl who has you in knots right now? Why do you keep looking at your phone?" Nick shook his head in disbelief.

The phone rang as I was explaining to Nick about Emily. "Sorry, Nick, I need to get this."

"Emily?"

"Hi. Are you still on the Westside right now? Sarah, Charlie, and I want to go out to dinner. Do you want to meet us?"

"I'm in Venice with my brother, Nick, and my cousin Doug. Where will you be?"

"I'll text you the address. Bring both of them. I want to meet them."

"I'll ask. See you soon."

"Was that my future sister?"

"Yup. We're meeting right now. She invited you guys to come but I'm uninviting you. I don't need a third and fourth wheel. See you later." I ran out the door.

When I got to the restaurant, Charlie and Sarah were seated at the bar.

"Where's Emily?"

"She's answering a call. You didn't see her outside?" Sarah asked.

"No."

"I'm sure she'll be right in."

"So, Jake...Did you and Emily really just meet on Friday?" Charlie asked.

"Why do you both have such a surprised look on your face? Is something wrong?"

Sarah and Charlie kept looking at each other like they were wondering whether or not to tell me what was already on the tip of their tongue. "Well, we're just a bit shocked at how comfortable you two seem to be already. Emily hasn't dated anyone in a while, and even when she was with Max, I never saw her so...what would be the right word, Charlie?" Her conversation started with me and ended with Charlie.

"At ease? Relaxed? Let loose? Are those the right words?"

"Do you like our Emily?"

I found it comforting that Sarah and Charlie both protected this girl whom I was so fond of.

"I like her enough to want to be able to call her my Emily."

They both gave me an approving nod. "Please be good to her," Sarah pleaded. "She's been through a lot in her short twenty-four years of life. No one deserves more happiness than she does."

Charlie sensed my alarm. "Don't be so melodramatic, Sarah. Underneath that pretty face, Emily's a tough girl."

I felt someone tap me from behind, and I quickly turned the stool around.

"Boo!" Emily attempted a scare.

"Hi, Beautiful!" I grabbed and kissed her, catching her off guard.

She unconvincingly nudged me away. "I told you, I don't like PDA," she whispered.

"You asked for a rain check," I whispered back.

"Not here and not in front of those two who are staring at us." Sarah and Charlie laughed.

"Who were you talking to for so long?" Sarah beat me to the question.

"Charlie! Your sister gave that creepy guy my number. He wouldn't let me get off the phone. Please tell Janice I won't ever go back to her house if Dr. Erickson is around."

"Who's Dr. Erickson?" Though this probably wasn't a story I wanted to hear, Emily's mad face was darling.

"This appears to be my weekend for attracting creepy doctors." She quickly added, "Not you, of course."

"Thanks...?"

"Charlie's sister, Janice, wanted to set me up with her neighbor, Dr. Tom Erickson. He insisted I address him by his title the whole day. Then he followed me around from room to room, chair to chair, and wouldn't stop talking to me. He also had the gall to try to feed me a hot dog and spiked punch when he saw that I wasn't eating. He was so gross."

Our laughs encouraged her to elaborate.

"He was bald and short and had a six-month-pregnant belly. What was your sister thinking?"

"I think she thought it would be nice to set you up with an established doctor," Charlie said, weakly defending his sister.

"He's a podiatrist. All day long he talked about calluses and bunions. Eew! He asked me to go away with him next weekend. If I had eaten anything at all today, I would have barfed on him."

Sarah and Charlie continued to laugh, but I put my lips over hers and kissed her again. Her shocked look was worth another try.

"Why do you keep doing that?" Though she complained, she kissed me back each time.

"I don't want to hear about the podiatrist anymore. Can we talk about something else?" I leaned in closer.

"What do you want to talk about?" Coquettishly, her lips came dangerously close to mine.

"How about us?"

"What about us?"

"Since you haven't had anything to eat yet, I thought I'd attempt to ask you to go away with me. Do you want to go to Bacara next weekend?"

"Didn't we just meet yesterday? How are you any different than Dr. Erickson?"

"Would you allow Dr. Erickson to do this?" Before she could react, I grabbed the back of her neck and rushed my mouth onto hers. She initially tried to pull away but quickly gave up and enjoyed our deep kiss.

"I can't believe I'm making out in public with a man I just met. What's gotten into me, Sarah?"

"I don't know. You're definitely not the Emily I know."

Charlie added, "I prefer the new you."

Emily shook her head.

"Why are you shaking your head?"

"It's in response to your invitation. I can't go away with you."

"Will you go if Sarah and Charlie come along?" I hoped this would encourage her to spend some uninterrupted time with me.

"Well…only if I get to room with Sarah and you room with Charlie."

"Deal. You two OK with Bacara next weekend?"

"We can't next weekend but the weekend after that is OK," Charlie answered.

My phone buzzed while Emily ordered herself some dinner.

"Hey, Nick, what's going on?"

As I started talking to Nick, Sarah began whispering to Emily, and my attention was on them rather than my brother.

"Emily, what's going on with you?"

"What do you mean, Sarah?"

"Don't you think you're taking this a little too fast? Jake seems nice and all, but you just met him. You're going to go away with him for the weekend?"

"Sarah. I only said yes after you and Charlie agreed. You know I wouldn't have gone by myself."

"Emily, I'm worried. It's unlike you to take things so fast with a guy. You barely know him."

"I know. I'm a little worried too. There's something about Jake…I trust him. I feel safe with him."

"Jake…Jake! Are you listening?" Nick interrupted my eavesdropping.

"Sorry, Nick. Say that one more time."

"Jake, I'm sorry to bother you, but Doug left me here to meet some girl and I'm stranded. Do you think you can give me a ride back to school?"

"Nick! All right. I got it." I was going to have to leave her again. Frustrated, I told him, "I'll be there in twenty minutes."

I was hoping to hear more, but Nick hung up, and I didn't have any more excuses to eavesdrop.

"You have to leave, huh? Do you have something against watching me eat dinner? Why do you always bail on me when dinner is about to be served?" I didn't know she could pout. There was no expression I didn't love on this girl's face.

"Nick got stranded by our cousin so I need to go get him and drop him off at school. I'd ask you to come with me but I brought my two-seater so that's not a possibility."

"Well, I wouldn't have thought too highly of you if you had decided to leave your brother stranded for some girl you met only yesterday. I'll see you again soon."

"Trust me, I was very tempted to leave him stranded, but I didn't think my mother would have been too happy with me. I have to go to my house in the Valley tonight so I can't stop by. I'll call you from the hospital tomorrow."

"OK. You want me to walk you out?"

"No, you go ahead and eat." With that, I asked Charlie and Sarah to take good care of Emily for me, and I gave her a peck on the cheek good-bye."

CHAPTER 4

Can You All Just Leave Us Alone?

Once the week began, it wasn't easy seeing Emily. She went to work earlier than I expected, and I always worked later than she expected. Her phone was off until school was done at three, then every time I attempted to call, I got a page sending me to the next patient.

Can we do dinner tonight?

It drove me mad we hadn't seen each other since Sunday and it was already Thursday.

I don't know, can we? It's always up to you.

I'll call around seven and let you know. I miss you.

I can't remember what you look like so I don't know who it is that I miss. Call me soon before I forget what you sound like as well.

What a sense of humor this girl had. Having visited all my patients, I called Emily the first chance I got.

"Hi, Emily. Are you ready for dinner?"

"Dr. Reid, do you know what time it is?"

"Isn't it around seven?"

"It's 9:30 p.m.! It's long past dinnertime. Have you not eaten yet?"

"You're kidding, right?"

"I wish I were. I've never been stood up so many times in one week. My ego is beyond bruised."

"I can't believe I did this to you again. Did you eat?"

"Uh-huh. I assume you didn't? Come over. I have dinner for you."

Luck was on my side as I hit every green light from the hospital to Emily's house. I got there in record time.

"Did you fly here?" she asked opening the door.

I got in and held her in my arms for a while. "I've really missed you. It's been a long four days without you."

"I've missed you too. Come and eat. I have dinner on the table for you."

Emily had grilled a steak along with a variety of vegetables. It looked and tasted scrumptious. With the knowledge that I had purchased a ring for her, I was tempted to get on one knee and propose to her right now. Seeing how she could hardly stand kissing me in public, I didn't think she was ready for any lifelong commitment.

"You can cook?" I had eaten half my meal before looking up to talk to her. She sat in front of me and enjoyed watching me eat.

"I can. Tonight's meal was easy. The grill did most of the work."

"What's this mealy yellow stuff I'm eating?" I shoved some in my mouth.

"It's polenta. I pan-fried it. Do you not like it?" She looked at me with a curious face.

"No. There's not much flavor and it has a weird texture. Do you eat like this all the time? I thought you said you didn't like eating by yourself?" The meal was so good, I was already done.

"I cook like this once or twice a week. The problem with me is that when I eat a meal, I need to eat a complete meal. I can't eat random foods that don't go with one another." We took our wine and sat on the sofa. "Whether I'm at home or maybe one day eating at a place like French Laundry, my food has to have order and meaning. Way too complicated, huh?"

"It's fascinating. You're fascinating." She looked embarrassed by my last comment. "So what do you eat the rest of the week if you only cook once or twice a week? Leftovers?"

"That's the other terrible thing about me. I hate leftovers. I really dislike eating the same thing twice. Many times, I just don't eat dinner. It's lonely eating by myself. I'll just have a big lunch and be done for the day."

An image of Emily eating by herself made my heart feel a sense of pain I'd never felt before. I hurt for this beautiful girl who was by herself without any family. I wanted to be her family—to come home to her daily, to have dinner with her nightly, and to love her eternally.

"Jake... as much as I enjoy you being here, I have to get to bed. I have an early conference tomorrow morning and a meeting till late. My students don't like me when I'm tired. I become psycho teacher." That was my cue to leave. I guess we weren't at the point where she was going to ask me to spend the night. Maybe a week of dating was a bit early for that.

My body didn't want to leave. My movements were slow and my heart couldn't fathom her absence.

"Where are you sleeping tonight? Are you at your mom's or at your place?"

"I might stay in town to be near you." I still hadn't gotten off the couch. She pulled me up with her. "Can't I stay just a bit longer?"

"No. If you stay any longer, I may not allow you to leave." She flashed a sly grin. "You need to leave now."

"Emily," I whined but followed obediently. "I have Saturday off. You want to go have brunch and watch a movie?"

"Yes, now leave," she commanded.

I got to Emily's house early on Saturday, eager to start our official second date. When I rang the doorbell, Emily, of course, was still in her pajamas.

"Perhaps I should invest in a set of keys for you so you won't wake me up every Saturday and Sunday morning." Emily looked groggy. I had woken her up with my text around 3:00 a.m. saying good night to her. She heard the text and jokingly scolded me.

"I'd love a set of keys. Does that mean I can come and go as I please?"

"No. It was a joke."

"Maybe later?" I hoped.

"Probably not." She smiled and hopped in the shower.

I walked around her house staring at pictures and books that decorated her home. Sometime during our date today I wanted to ask her about her parents and why she was living alone in this home. Possibly today, I could give her this eternity band and formally ask her to be my girlfriend. I wanted the world to know that she was exclusively mine. I didn't want any Dr. Ericksons attempting to ask her out again.

Giving her a ring hopefully wouldn't scare her off. I'd never given any girl something so serious before. In all the years I dated Kelley, I'd never given her a present with so much commitment attached to it. Kelley probably would've been happier if I had committed more but she couldn't grab my heart the way Emily did from the moment I saw her.

Thinking back, I guess I had dated a lot of girls. Kelley was my longest relationship but we were so on and off. She and I couldn't make up our minds. We didn't know where we wanted our relationship to head. Then there were the few doctors and nurses I dated at the hospital. What a mistake that was. I watched and worked with my mistake daily. Most recently there was Allison. Talk about a mistake. That was the biggest.

Allison was Jane's roommate when Jane was living up north. She wasn't shy about wanting to date me. She constantly called me and sent me gifts. She had moved down to LA a few months ago and showed up at my doorstep one night. Though Emily was the most beautiful woman I'd ever laid eyes on, Allison, the fashion model, was tempting.

Having fallen into temptation, we went out on a few dates. Actually, we didn't go out much. We spent many nights together but soon I ended our so-called relationship. She wasn't happy, but I was relieved. I wondered how many men Emily had dated. If she dated this Max for four years, there couldn't have been too many other men in her life. That thought was even more troublesome.

I knew little about Emily. She told me she didn't date around, and she liked being with one man. This probably meant she was deeply in love with Max. He probably devastated her when he dumped her. What an idiot. I couldn't wait to see what he looked like. I was sure our paths would cross one day. I couldn't imagine letting go of someone as special as Emily, especially not after four years with her. It upset me to think of Emily being with another man.

"What are you sighing about?" Emily walked out looking stunning in a yellow sundress.

"I was wondering how much longer you were going to take."

"Jake? Do you think we can invite Charlie and Sarah to join us today?"

Though I was a bit disappointed we wouldn't spend this day alone, I was happy to oblige. "Sure."

"I know you want us to be alone and we will...there will be plenty more time for that. Charlie and Sarah have always invited me to spend some part of the weekend with them. They know how much I hate being alone. You would think I'd be used to it by now, but it still bothers me. They've really been like parents to me, taking care of me when they can."

I appreciated them for taking care of Emily for me. I would prove to them that they can be at peace about passing the torch on to me.

"I'd like to invite them to spend a weekend with me...I mean us. Would that be OK?"

"Of course. Give them a call."

"Good because I already did." They're meeting us in an hour." She looked pleased. "Let's head out. We can walk around the marina before we meet them."

We got in my car, and her face lit up when she heard the *Carmen* opera CD I had picked up after a performance at the Met Opera House in New York a few months ago. This was the second time I noticed this wistful look in her eyes. The first time she showed it was when talking about French Laundry. It occurred to me, these must be places she wanted to visit or activities she wanted to do.

So far, I'd uncovered Emily's three faces. The first and most appealing was her angelic face. She was kind and funny and gracious. From the day I met her, her concern was for others first, and then herself. Next was the sad face that appeared whenever she talked about being alone. Though she didn't show this face too often, whenever it appeared, I wanted to tell her I would be the one to erase her loneliness. The last was this wistful look. This look made me sad knowing there were so many opportunities she didn't have being alone in this world—but happy knowing I could be the one to show her these experiences. That's what I wanted to do—help fulfill all of her wishes.

"You're not on call today, are you?"

"Does going out with me make you paranoid?"

"Kind of. I mean, it's OK if you are. I know it's your work and you save lives on a daily basis. A date with me is no comparison to the important work you do."

"Emily, being with you has become the most important part of my life these days. I could give up saving lives but I don't know that I can give up spending time with you."

Her head tilted downward again. Maybe it was a little too serious? I basically told her she was the most important person in my life. Her eyes looked excited by my confession, yet I sensed hesitation in her face.

"Jake, look. Sarah and Charlie are here early too." I grabbed her hand before she could run off to them. "Hi, guys!"

"Hi, Emily. Hi, Jake," Sarah greeted us.

"Hey. Let's sit and grab drinks before we start our meal," I suggested.

We sat, and Charlie turned to Emily with a chuckle in his eyes. "My sister keeps calling to tell me that Tom Erickson wants to take you out." Charlie started laughing.

"Eew! You can tell him I said get lost! I've been screening all his calls."

"Jake, you need to watch out or Emily's going to get snatched out from under you." Charlie sounded like he was about to warn me about Emily's appeal to men.

"Huh? What does that mean?"

"Oh, only that she gets asked out by men everywhere we go. No matter where we are or who she's with, some man will come up and ask her for her number. It's her innocent look. Men seem to love it," Sarah explained.

"You two are so exaggerating the truth. They only ask me out because they see you guys attached at the hips, or lips, and I'm always by myself."

"Max used to get furious! We'd be on a double date and somehow some man would corner Emily and ask her out before Max realized what was going on."

"Charlie, that only happened once."

"You know, I think Charlie and Sarah are right. The first night I met you, all three guys in the ER asked you out. Then the next day, you got asked out at the birthday party. Do I need to keep you locked up in your house?"

"Let's move on to another topic. What did you and Charlie do last night?" Emily and Sarah started their own conversation while Charlie explained to me about his job at the architecture firm.

"Oh, we went out with…" I heard Sarah hesitate. "Charlie ran into Peter, and they decided to go out for drinks, which led to dinner for all of us—Charlie, me, Peter, Max, and Jennifer."

There was a mixture of sadness and discomfort in Emily's disposition. I tried not to let her notice my stare, but it disturbed me that her ex had such a hold on her.

"How's Peter doing? He must be very mad at me. I haven't called him since last June. What am I going to do when I see him again?"

Charlie leaned over to explain that Peter was Max's best friend and loved Emily like a sister.

"Yeah, he's livid with you." The intonation of Sarah's voice sounded like he wasn't mad at all. "You should call him, he misses you."

"Yeah, I miss him too." I waited for the next obvious question. "How's Max?" she meekly asked.

"I don't know. I didn't talk to him or her the whole night," Sarah huffed.

"Sarah, he's your friend. Just because he broke up with me doesn't mean you can't be friends with him. And why are you being mean to Jennifer? She's done nothing wrong."

"Emily, how can you think anything nice about him after what he's done to you?"

Now I was really curious as to what this guy had done that was so wrong.

"Sarah, let's not get into this now." Charlie gave Sarah a look of warning, probably because of me, which made Sarah stop immediately.

I put my hand over Emily's, and she gazed at me and smiled. There was a broken heart in that smile.

"Shall we go eat?" Emily asked.

"Sure, let's go," I answered, hoping to change the mood.

We walked through the garden toward the dining area when unexpectedly my pager went off. Emily looked at me, disappointed.

"I'm not on call today. There's no reason for the pager to go off." I immediately looked at the phone number. "It's the chief. He must have some personal issue he needs to talk about. Grab your food and I'll meet you back at the table."

"Is it OK if I stay with you?"

"Of course," I answered stealing a kiss from her. She smiled and brought her body close to mine. Happily she put her arms around my waist and leaned into my chest.

"Hey, Chief. Why are you bothering me on my day off?"

"Jake, I'm sorry to do this to you but you're going to have to fly to Atlanta for me today."

"What? Why?"

"The president of the hospital board just got hospitalized after having a heart attack. I need to go into surgery right now. I'm sending you my keynote address. You will have to present it for me at the conference. My assistant emailed your plane ticket and everything else you need. I'm sorry,

Jake. I know you're with Emily, but there's no one else I can trust to give this address but you."

"All right." Another date interrupted. What was I going to tell Emily?

"You need to leave." Again a statement rather than a question—she knew the drill. I feared she may never want to go out with me again.

While checking my email, I held her tight and couldn't look her in the eye. "How will I prove to you this is not what it will always be like? I have to leave you again. The chief needs me to go to Atlanta for him. I'm sorry." I begged for understanding.

"What time is your flight?"

"It's at 1:00 p.m."

"I guess we'll have to leave now." She wasn't angry, she wasn't happy, she was matter-of-fact.

"Why don't you stay with Sarah and Charlie?"

"Can I go with you? We can be together a bit longer. I'll bring your car to my house then pick you up from the airport when you get back. When do you think you'll be back?"

"Possibly tomorrow if all goes well with Chief's surgery."

"All right, let's go."

I apologized to Sarah and Charlie, and we rushed to the airport. Mom called while we were in the car and asked me to put her on speakerphone, so she could converse with Emily.

"Hi, Emily! I'm thrilled to finally meet you. Jake talks about you constantly."

"Hello, Mrs. Reid. It's very nice to meet you too."

"Please, call me Sandy. You must be upset your date got interrupted again."

"Yeah. I'm beginning to think Jake starts the day thinking he wants to go out with me, but then has the hospital page him when he realizes I'm not much fun."

"Emily..." I complained.

"I apologize for my son."

"Let me talk now." Aunt Barbara sounded like she was running from the other side of the room.

"Hi, Emily. I'm Jake's Aunt Barbara."

"Hi, Aunt Barbara. It's nice to meet you."

"When will you be visiting Sandy's house? We're all dying to see what you look like. Jake has put you on a very high pedestal. Will we see you before Thanksgiving?"

"Thanksgiving?" Emily asked, confused.

"I forgot to tell you I'm taking you to Aunt Babs' for Thanksgiving."

"Uh-oh. I'm sorry, Aunt Barbara, but Jake never told me about Thanksgiving. I have plans already to go back East to my best friend's parents' house. We just made all the arrangements yesterday."

Both my mom and Aunt Babs scolded me. "Jake!"

"Really? You're not spending Thanksgiving with me?" That bummed me out.

"You never mentioned Thanksgiving. I didn't want to presume." Did this girl still not get how much I liked her?

I hung up on my mom and Aunt Babs without saying good-bye.

"Why didn't you ask me before making plans with Sarah?" I was a bit upset with her. This was my chance to show her off to my family. I had only told all of them this was the girl I was going to marry.

"What was I to ask? Um…will you be taking me to your aunt's home for Thanksgiving? Jake, we've seen each other a handful of times in the last three weeks, and most of those times were interrupted by your pager. I'm not going to make any assumptions about us. If you wanted to take me to meet your family, you should have asked." Everything she said made complete sense, but I was still upset. I stopped talking so I could clear my head. I did this whenever something made me mad. If I continued to talk, hurtful words generally came out of my mouth that would get me into trouble later. If I stopped talking, at least I wouldn't say anything stupid. Emily stayed quiet as well.

I had so little time to spend with this girl and I wasted our ride to the airport keeping my mouth shut. I regretted my action the entire ride but couldn't break the silence. Without asking, I parked the car in the lot so Emily could walk in with me.

"What will you do about clothes and toiletries? Do you need me to send you anything if you end up staying longer than a day?" She was always looking out for me. The selfish being that I was, all I thought about was how I felt. I didn't stop to wonder how she was feeling right now.

Timidly, she leaned against my car wondering where my mood would take us. Holding her hands I caught a glimpse of fear in her eyes. That look gave me a swift kick in the gut.

"I'm very sorry for getting upset with you earlier. You were right. I had no right to assume you were coming with me, and I had no right to assume you needed to ask my permission before doing anything. And most of all, I'm sorry I wasted our precious time in silence."

Emily continued to stay quiet. I held her hand all the way to the boarding area in silence.

"Are you OK?" She still didn't look at me. "Did I make you mad?"

"No, I'm not mad." She said this, but I couldn't trust the tone in which she said it.

"What are you thinking about?"

"You and me." I definitely didn't like the way she said you and me instead of us.

"What about us?" I needed to get this answer from her before boarding the plane. It would drive me crazy the whole flight to Atlanta if I didn't get a satisfactory answer.

"I was just contemplating if there can be an us." That did it. We needed to talk.

Last call for passengers boarding flight #1311 heading to Atlanta. Please board Gate A. Last call. The flight attendant called.

"You better go in. Let me know when you're coming back. I'll come pick you up."

"We need to have a talk as soon as I get back, OK?"

She nodded her head yes but shied away from my kiss.

Frustrated, I left Emily for Atlanta.

CHAPTER 5

Who Is This Keeping Us Apart?

Chief never made it to Atlanta and the conference kept me busier than expected. Emily and I tried to communicate but she had an unusually busy week as well. I had hoped to be home on Wednesday, but Chief asked me to stay till Friday so my flight would land me back at LAX early Saturday morning.

Finally, Emily was calling. "Hi, Sweetheart!"

"Hi. I was calling to see if I should cancel Bacara. We don't have to go this weekend and Sarah and Charlie won't care either way."

"No. I want to spend some time with you before you go on your trip with Sarah. When do you leave, and when do you get back?"

"Sunday to Sunday."

"Is Charlie going too?"

"No, it's just us."

"That's an awful long time."

"Not any longer than your trip to Atlanta." Of course she had to add this. "Sarah and I are spending Sunday through Wednesday in New York then going over to her parents' in New Jersey."

I was going to have to spend another week without her. With the ending we had at the airport, I was worried about being away from her for so long.

"Do you want to stay at Jane's apartment while you're in New York? She comes home Monday, but you can use the apartment if you want. I'll have my mom bring over a set of keys."

"No, that's OK. We have a hotel reserved. When do you come home, Jake?"

"Early Saturday morning."

"What time? I'll come pick you up." Though our conversation was more formal than I would've liked, it made me feel good to know that she wanted to pick me up.

"I'll grab a cab home and come pick you up for Bacara first thing Saturday morning. I need you ready early, OK?"

"Sure." She paused and my heart dipped, as I wondered what she was thinking. "I miss you, Jake."

Relieved with this last comment, I told her, "I can't even begin to explain to you how much I miss you. See you tomorrow, Beautiful."

Perhaps I overreacted to our conversation back at the airport. I'd be with her soon and that was all that mattered.

The sun was barely out when the plane landed at LAX. Thinking that Emily might have called, I checked my phone, and there was an ominous message from the chief telling me to come to the hospital first thing in the morning. After a week in Atlanta, he couldn't possibly have me working, or so I hoped. I got to Mom's, slept a few hours, then went in to see him.

"What's going on, Chief? I'm going away with Emily this morning to Santa Barbara. You don't have me working, do you?"

"No, but Roger passed away yesterday, and they are having a viewing today and a memorial service tomorrow. I'm sorry, but you're going to have to attend."

I gave Chief an incredulous look.

"I'm sorry, Jake. I want to let you go, but he was the president of the hospital, and he died while under our care. Though it wasn't our fault, we need to show our respect and support his family."

"Well, can I leave after the viewing then come back tomorrow for the memorial?"

"That would be fine. Just stick around and help out where you can."

I contemplated going over to Emily's to explain what was going on but then decided to call her instead.

"Jake! Are you back?" I loved how excited she sounded knowing I was home.

"Hi, Beautiful. Did I wake you?"

"No. I've been awake waiting for you to call. When can we leave?"

"Sweetheart, can you go with Sarah and Charlie? I'm going to have to meet you there."

Though she didn't make a sound, I heard the sigh and envisioned the frown that marked her face as well.

"OK. What time do you think you'll come?"

"I need to attend a viewing that begins sometime in the afternoon, then I'll drive straight up there. I'm..."

"Don't worry about it.." She cut me off before I could apologize. "I'm going to leave your car key on my kitchen counter. There's a spare key to the house under the mat by the back door. Use it to get in the house. I guess I'll see you later." She sounded skeptical. I hated not being able to keep my promises, especially to her.

"I'll see you soon."

I got back to the cardiac ward and everyone was in a somber mood. Continually checking my watch, I went about my day waiting for the viewing to begin.

Hi, Sweetheart. How's Bacara?

Her responses were always quick.

Lonely.

I don't think she realized how affected I got whenever she told me she was lonely, especially since this was strictly my fault.

I'll be there soon. Will you be lonely enough to allow me to kiss you in public?

Perhaps. You will never know till you get here.

Do we still have the same roommates?

We do but if you show any signs of not showing up, Sarah will bolt to the other room. Which means... I will be even more alone. It's all up to you. Come soon.

Will do.

It was dinnertime and there was no sign of a viewing. I asked the chief if I could leave, and he informed me that Rebecca Stein, Roger's widow, had just been hospitalized and their family requested the chief and I be her attending doctors. Someone was out there doing his best to keep Emily away from me. I dreaded this next phone call.

"Are you on your way?" She didn't even say hello.

I couldn't answer.

"Oh no. You're not coming." Once again, it wasn't a question, it was a statement. "Sarah, you can move next door," I heard her lament.

"Sweetheart, I don't know how I'm going to make this up to you. I probably won't get up there at all now."

"I don't know either. It's going to take you many tries to make things right." Being her understanding self, she tried to sound chipper.

"I'll be happy to make it up to you the rest of my life."

Silence. I felt like I was performing a monologue.

"Emily?"

Silence again.

"Emily!" I tried to illicit a response.

"Yes?"

"Why are you so quiet?"

"Well... I wish you wouldn't make me any promises you won't be able to keep. The rest of your life is a very long time from now."

I knew I deserved this but it stung to hear her say it. "Wow. I think those are the most hurtful words you've said to me. How can you disregard my sincerity?"

"Jake..." Simultaneously she started and stopped her thought.

"Yes?" I needed to finish this conversation with her. This was an extension of our LAX conversation. "Emily, what's on your mind?"

"I know you mean well but you can barely keep a dinner date with me. I can't think much beyond what we have right now."

"Emily, that's not fair. You know I want to be there with you. These are circumstances beyond my control."

"I know and I don't blame you for these circumstances."

"Then why can't you believe me? Why can't you see much of a future for us? This is what you said at the airport too." I knew she had some reason she wasn't willing to spit out. She had been so understanding up until now. It couldn't be my schedule holding her back. "What is it you're not telling me?"

"Jake, even after four years of believing I would spend the rest of my life with someone, this someone woke up one morning and stopped loving me. I can't believe after four weeks, your mind could be made up so easily."

Anger. Rage. Frustration. All these emotions ran up and down my body but came to a screeching halt as soon as I heard whimpering on the other end.

"I'll talk to you later," she said and quickly hung up.

I wanted to call back but decided against it. She probably needed some time alone. I would try calling later.

Thinking through our conversation, this girl, whom I loved dearly, had loved another man dearly. Though I didn't think she still loved him, the hurt was far from being gone. Not having any family most likely compounded the hurt when he left her so suddenly. Whenever I got a reprieve from this job, I vowed to shower her with love and erase the hurt that lingered.

The next morning I woke up to a kind text.

I'm sorry for hanging up on you. I didn't mean to sound so doubtful. I really miss you and am frustrated I won't see you for another week. I leave on the 8:30 p.m. flight out of LAX. Do you think you can come see me before I leave for New York?"

I'll be there. I really miss you too.

She texted back a smile.

After a long surgery on Rebecca Stein, I made a mad dash to LAX. It was nearly 11:00 p.m., and I was hoping Emily's flight got postponed and that she would still be there. It wasn't a good sign since she wasn't answering her phone, but I wanted to go check just in case. I sprinted to her boarding area and frantically searched for her and Sarah. Not seeing either of them, I only confirmed Emily's theory that I couldn't keep my promise and that there really was no future for us.

With hope lost, I turned to leave when I saw my angel curled up in a fetal position, asleep on one of the chairs. Her face looked like she had been crying with a tear drop still fresh on her cheek. There weren't enough days for me to make this girl happy and all I'd done to her this weekend was made her cry. I knelt down and wiped away her tear.

Startled, she jumped. "Jake!" She hugged me and confirmed my belief or perhaps my hope—that she loved me too. "I'm so happy to see you, I've missed you so much." Tears rolled down her pale cheeks.

"I've missed you too, Beautiful." I pulled away from her to look at her face. She was a mess. "Don't cry. I'm sorry I keep breaking my promises to you. You know I want to be with you, right?"

Her face looked hesitant.

"And you know when you're not with me, I miss you more than anyone I've missed in my life?"

Her face looked like she wanted to say yes but her head shook no.

"How could you not know all this? Do you still not understand how I feel about you?"

"I thought...I thought maybe you were using work as an excuse to end what we have."

"Emily, you crazy girl, what would make you think such a thing? Do I not make myself clear when I tell you how much I like you?"

"I just have a hard time believing. I was so sad thinking it was over. I don't know if I like this effect you have on me. You have this way of making me feel amazing when we're together but when we're apart I feel lonelier than I've ever felt. No one has affected me like this before. I know we can't be together all the time, and I don't want to sound so needy. I know how important your job is to you and how important you are to your job."

Funny how just a few minutes ago I thought she was going to break up with me. Who knew she was thinking the same thing about me. Tonight I realized buried inside this beautiful person was a fragile girl who needed stability—something I haven't been able to provide for her with my hectic schedule.

"Should I be thrilled I make you feel amazing, or should I be upset I make you feel lonely?" I chuckled despite her teary disposition.

She laughed along with me.

"Emily, I'm sorry I keep breaking my promises to you. I want you to promise me though that you'll tell me whenever I make you feel sad or lonely, OK?"

She nodded her head again and I pulled her back into my body.

"How am I going to let you go away for a week now? I'm going to miss you so much. Are you sure you don't want to stay at Jane's just in case I come to see you?"

"I'm sure. Sarah and I have a hotel in midtown."

"Where is Sarah, by the way?"

"She got on the original flight. She had to meet her sister at JFK but I waited for you. Barring any more emergencies, I knew you'd come for me. I really wanted to see you."

"Oh, Emily." *I really will make this up to you the rest of my life. I love you.* "When is the last flight out?"

"They've started calling us. I need to board soon."

"Let me see your ticket." Horrified at the thought of Emily trying to sleep sitting up, I went up to the desk and changed her seat. Starting now, I would do everything in my power to take care of this girl. She would never second-guess my intentions or my love. I would love her unconditionally. Without a doubt, this was the girl I wanted to be with the rest of my life.

"Emi, I changed your seat so you can sleep on the plane. Have a wonderful trip and call me often."

"Jake. It's only a five-hour flight. Why did you spend so much money? It's unnecessary."

"Sweetheart, I've only just begun making up for all my broken promises. Believe me when I tell you I'll take care of you from now on."

She nodded her head one last time. Before I let her go I kissed her in public in front of a horde of people boarding the plane. She didn't pull away, but she did turn her usual rosy color.

"So for the record, I am asking you a month in advance, you are spending Christmas with me and my family?"

"Are you asking me or telling me?"

"Both. It is at my parents' house, and if you don't show up this time, my whole family will think I've made up some phantom woman."

"Christmas it is. I'll call when I land. I'll miss you."

"I'll miss you too. Have a good flight."

I watched her walk in and left the airport satisfied. I knew we were headed in the right direction. Now if only I could get a decent length of time with her so I could get a commitment out of her with this ring. Only then would I be relieved, knowing she was wholly mine.

CHAPTER 6

How Much Do I Love Thee?

My phone rang right on cue.
"Good morning, Beautiful. Did you have a good flight?"
Without answering my question, she started with her own.
"Jake, did you send me a driver? Who is this gentleman holding my name on a piece of cardboard?"

"Yup. The driver is there for you. He's going to take you to your hotel. Just tell him which hotel you're staying at."

"Jake!" There was disapproval in her voice. "I'm not that helpless. I like taking the subway."

"Emily, who really likes taking the subway? It's too much of a hassle from the airport. You'd have to take the AirTrain, then transfer to a subway, or take the train into Penn, then get on a subway. Just get in the car. He'll take you straight to your destination."

"OK, but no more of these unnecessary luxuries, OK? It's a bit too easy to get used to this." It sounded like she was holding back a giggle.

"Get used to it. I'm going to dote on you for a very long time. Enjoy your day and call me with updates."

"Thank you. I'll text, you call."

The rest of my day went slowly. Of course since Emily was out of town, there wasn't much going on at the hospital. I was tempted to buy myself a ticket and go visit her in New York. A phone call was a more realistic choice.

"Hi, Jake!" Never could I tire of the excitement I heard in her voice when she answered my call.

"What are you and Sarah up to?"

"Hi, Jake!" I heard Sarah call out.

"Tell her I said hi."

"He says, hi," she whispered over to her best friend.

"I'm going to have to have a talk with Charlie. He has yet to call while Jake sat you in first class, sent you a driver, plus has called already," Sarah grumbled to herself.

Emily proceeded to tell me about her morning. "Since you were kind enough to send me a driver, I asked him to stop by the Doughnut Plant and I picked up a dozen donuts for me, Sarah, and Lily, her sister."

"Oh, I like that place. Jane doesn't live too far from there."

"I had three donuts this morning. I ate two tres leche and one blackout. I might be a bit heavier next time you see me," she confessed like a schoolgirl.

"That's gross to eat three donuts."

"I know. I also went next door and had a bialy."

"Emily. Did you not eat up at Bacara?"

"No, I waited for you the whole time, remember? I couldn't eat because I missed you so much."

"Eew!" I heard someone shout. I assumed it was Sarah's sister, Lily.

"Well, since it's my fault you didn't eat well up in Santa Barbara, I made reservations for you at Le Bernardin tomorrow night. Do you and Sarah have plans already?"

"Le Bernardin?" The foodie in her couldn't hide her excitement. "I tried for weeks to get a reservation. How did you do it so easily? I wonder if Eric Ripert will be in the kitchen."

"He'll be there. I checked. Sweetheart, I'm being paged. I'll call again later. I miss you."

"Bye. Have a good day."

I went about having a nice day, as it was a short one. The chief let me off early, since I did double duty out in Atlanta. Attempting to be a nice big brother, I surprised Jane and picked her up from the airport. She looked stunned to see me. I didn't know why she was so surprised. Wasn't I the poster boy for an ideal older brother?

"What on earth are you doing here? Are you here for me?" She still wore a shocked expression.

"You want to catch the van home? Should I leave? Some thanks I get for trying to be nice."

"Why aren't you at work? Hey, I hear you have a new girlfriend. When do I get to meet her? Tell me about her."

"Her name is Emily and she's a school teacher. She's the same age as you. She's actually in New York right now. I wish I could be there with her." In my mind, I pictured what she and Sarah might be doing. There were six more days of this drudgery till I could see her again. "Hey, Jane. Can you try this on for me?" I took out the eternity band from my glove compartment.

"What's with the monster ring?"

"I bought it to give to Emily when I ask her to be my girlfriend but I'm unsure about her size."

"A bit sappy for you…I've never seen you this enamored with a girl. All those years with Kelley, had you given her anything like this?"

I ignored her commentary on my past love life. "Jane, this girl is it. She's the sister you've been wanting your whole life. It drives me crazy I can't progress as quickly as I would like to. I don't think she's thinking marriage just yet."

Jane put the ring on her finger and it looked stunning. Goosebumps ran through my body thinking about Emily wearing this ring.

"Jake, it's beautiful but can I give you a piece of advice?"

"What?" I wasn't going to listen if she said anything negative.

"This is too serious if you just started dating. Get a necklace and have her wear it as a pendant. I can't see any girl wanting to put this on her finger after one month of courtship."

"You think?"

"I know. Where'd you get the ring?"

"Cartier."

"Let's stop by. I'll help you pick out a necklace. I have to say, I'm impressed. This ring is gorgeous. I think Emily will like it."

Not able to hold off any longer, my fingers dialed Emily's number again. Her excited voice loomed over the speaker phone.

"Hi, Dr. Reid. Are you not working today?"

"No. Apparently you took all the patients with you when you left. The hospital is empty and I'm done for the day."

"You've got to be kidding me! You're done for the day already? How come this doesn't happen when I'm in town? I'm beginning to think you don't really want to be with me." She began her many bouts of giggling.

"Oh here we go again. Did we not work this all out at the airport?"

"We did, but I can't let you forget so easily how many times you've left me in the middle of a meal or just plain stood me up."

At this point, Jane started cracking up.

"Who's that?" Emily sounded surprised.

"Are you jealous I have another woman in the car?"

"Not as jealous as you'll be if I tell you how many guys have asked me for my number this morning."

"Seriously? Did someone ask you out already? I really have to lock you up."

"I'm kidding." She tried to play it off.

"No she's not," Sarah and Lily chimed into the phone.

"Aw, Emi, how many?"

"You first, who's in the car?"

"No, you first," I argued.

We got into an information tug of war. I lost, thanks to Jane.

"Hi, Emily. This is Jane, Jake's sister."

"Hi, Jane! Did your sweet brother come pick you up at the airport?"

"No, Nick's at school, the mean one came instead."

Two of the three women in my life howled at my expense. My mother would have joined in the guffaw if she were here.

"I'm sorry we missed each other. I would have loved to meet you. Will you be in town long?"

"I leave on Sunday but I'll be back in two weeks. We should get together then. I'll tell you all about my brother." Jane gave me a dark be-nice-to-me look.

"That's a date. We'll definitely meet the next time you're in town. Since he won't give me more than an hour of his time, you'll have to fill in all the blanks. Trust me; there are more blanks than bubbles filled in. I think he's trying to hide something." I'm sure Emily's lips were forming into a smile.

"Enough about me. Emi, I want you to stay away from any strange-looking men."

"Then, do I have permission to talk to the good-looking ones?"

"Emily!"

"OK, Dr. Reid. I have to go. I'll call you tonight when I get back to the hotel. Sarah and Lily are both extremely annoyed with me. I'm having too much fun on the phone. We're trying to have lunch."

"Where are you eating?" I didn't want to let her go.

She whispered, "I'll tell you tonight. They're both staring at me right now."

"Should I fly in to see you?"

"No," she continued to whisper. "Spend time with your family. Your sister is in town. Bye. I miss you." She hung up before I could say another word.

Jane's eyes mocked me. "You're pathetic! What happened to Dr. Jake Reid, the man every woman wanted to date? How did you become such a fool in love? Have Mom and Dad seen you lately?"

"Yup, this is what I've become. Mom's talked to Emily as well. She likes her and can't wait to meet her."

"She does sound sweet. Set up a time for us to meet when I get back. So what else has been going on?"

Jane and I had lunch and picked up a necklace for Emily. Though my body was with Jane, my mind was with Emily. Since Sarah and Lily thought I called too often, this time I sent her a text instead.

Which hotel are you staying at?

The W at Times Square. Why? Are you coming to see me? Lily already has dibs on the rollaway.

Why there? The rooms are so tiny? How are the three of you staying in one room?

Don't knock it. Sarah and I scrounged up all our points to stay there for three nights. Most of us can't fly first class and stay at the Plaza. Plus, we like the Bliss products.

OK. Call me when your day is done.

With the five of us in town, we went for sushi, and the whole family noticed how I anxiously awaited Emily's phone call. Nick and Jane tormented me the whole night playing doomsday naysayers.

"She's not calling tonight. It's already past midnight her time and your phone has yet to ring." Nick started the harassment.

"Trust me, she will call," I reassured.

"Why is my sister-in-law out so late without you? You think she met another guy? Didn't you say she was hot?" Nick continued. It did make me nervous she was out past midnight.

"Mom, this Emily must be a future Reid. I've never seen Jake wait around for any girl. She actually had to tell him to stop calling her today. Remember how Kelley used to complain all the time about Jake's indifference toward her? She used to call me and lament how he paid little attention to her. I'm so curious to meet her."

"Me too. She sounds delightful," Mom added.

Ring ring—there it was, the call I'd been waiting for since lunch. Not wanting to appear so desperate, I let it ring a few times before I answered.

"Hello?" I answered nonchalantly. My entire family burst into laughter.

"Hello?" Emily questioned. "Jake?" She sounded unsure.

"Hi, Sweetheart." I was back to my jovial self.

"Hi. You sound so different. Who are all those people in the background? You're having way too much fun without me," she said, probably pouting.

"It's my family. We're having sushi right now."

"Bummer! I wish I could've been there. You know I'm weak to sushi. Jake. What's with the suite?" I knew she would call to complain about her new room. "You can't go around upgrading my life. I told you, it's too easy to get used to this."

"The three of you can't stay in that tiny room. This way, you'll be able to sleep comfortably. Plus I told you to get used to the doting."

"No, I don't want to get used to this. It's not my reality. We'll stay tonight but since Lily is going back to Jersey tomorrow, Sarah and I are going back to our regular room."

Lily grabbed the phone from her. "Hi, Jake. I'm Sarah's youngest sister Lily. Thank you for the fantastic room. Don't listen to Emily. Sarah and I will convince her to stay here. It is so much better than the cubicle they were in. I hear you have a younger brother. Is he as wonderful as you are?"

She sounded cute. "I do have a younger brother. If you're ever out here, I'll introduce you to him. And no, he's not as wonderful as I am."

"Who's that?" Nick grabbed the phone from me. "Hello? Hi, Emily. This is Nick. When will we see you? We're all really curious to know what you look like. Yeah, Jake's been going around talking about you to everyone. Ha! Ha! Ha! You're funny. All right, I'll let everyone know you're an urban legend."

"Give me that!" I grabbed the phone from Nick. "Emily, why are you out so late?"

"Oh my gosh, you're not serious are you? Aren't you still out yourself?"

"But it's past midnight your time and…"

"Jake."

"All right. Tell me what you did today." As I started my long conversation with Emily, we all got back in the car and headed home. Nick drove for me.

"We went to this little pizza joint in Brooklyn run by a cute seventy-five-year-old gentleman. We waited almost two hours for a pie. This man makes all his own dough and tomato sauce, then grates mozzarella straight onto each pie. When the pie is done he reaches into a hot pizza oven and pulls it out with his bare hands. Can you believe that? To top it off, he grabs a bunch of basil and oregano with a pair of scissors and snips them right onto the pizza. How much more homemade can you get than that? My new favorite vegetable is rapini. It's wonderful on pizza. How come we don't top our pizzas with rapini in LA?"

I loved listening to her talk about food. This had to be her biggest passion. Hopefully one day, I would take over as her biggest passion. It was going to be a tough fight. There was no guarantee I would come out the winner.

"After lunch, we had a slice of red velvet cake and walked it off in Soho."

"Did you buy anything?"

"Nope. Nothing today. After Soho, we went to Babbo for dinner and I ate more carbs. I'm stuffed. I'm definitely coming back to you heavier."

I liked the way she told me she was coming back to me. Our conversation at the airport must have solidified her feelings for me.

"We also saw some weird off-Broadway show. It wasn't very good. That was my day. What did you do?"

"After I picked up Jane, we had lunch, then Jane helped me pick out a present for you that goes with another present I bought earlier for you…"

"You bought me a present? What is it?"

"It wouldn't be a surprise if I told you. Then we all had sushi, and now we're all going home. Emi, do you have to stay out there till Sunday?"

"Yes."

"Can I fly in to see you tomorrow if the hospital is slow?"

"No." Her answers were so blunt I shut down again. "Jake. I'm sorry if I hurt your feelings. I miss you very much, but I need to explain something to you." Emily was quick to catch on but I stayed silent.

"Are you listening?"

"Yeah," I grumbled.

"Since Max and I broke up last June, Sarah and Charlie have purposely stayed apart from each other on Thanksgiving and Christmas so I wouldn't feel alone. Sarah planned this trip with me months ago, even though she could have been with Charlie's family this week. I'm not going to abandon her because I met someone I really like. Do you get it now?"

"But, why can't I come visit you for a few days?" I couldn't help my five-year-old rant.

"Because Charlie could have been here too, but Sarah made it so it would just be us. Are you OK?"

"Yeah," I lamented. "I guess I'll see you when I pick you up from the airport. By the way, I still have your house key. What do you want me to do with it?"

"Keep it for a while. If I lose my keys, I'll know who to turn to. Good night." On that note, I ended my first long day without Emily.

Tuesday was much the same except for the many pictures and texts I received from Emily while she was at Le Bernardin. She sent a food blog for each course she had from this Michelin three-starred restaurant.

The first picture she sent was of herself eating.

Here I am eating my first course. It's layers of thinly pounded tuna with foie gras on a toasted baguette. It's so delicious! The aperitif goes nicely.

Second is a poached egg swimming in Osetra caviar with a wickedly delicious bubbly. Did I ever tell you how much I like caviar?

My third course is a salad. I generally don't like salads but could eat this one every day. It's topped with seared langoustines, wild mushrooms, shaved foie gras and sprinkled with a vinaigrette. We drank a German Riesling. Oh Jake, I wish you were here with me.

Fourth dish—Pan-roasted monkfish in a sake broth. It's amazing how they cooked this fish so perfectly. I don't know what I'm drinking with it. I think it's some French wine.

Fifth course was the most interesting pairing of crispy black bass in an Iberico ham and peppercorn sauce. The salty and spicy sauce played nicely against the buttery sweetness of the fish. We had a Spanish red wine with this course.

My sixth course was my favorite course! It was baked lobster on a bed of truffled foie gras stuffing. This course has three of my favorite gastronomic words—lobster, truffle, and foie gras. I know it's hard to believe I would have such taste buds on a teacher's salary.

Next course was my least favorite—the cheese course. I couldn't get beyond the smell so I opted not to have it. Sarah enjoyed it.

Last but not least was dessert. It was a caramelized custard with hazelnut praline and brown butter ice cream. We topped it off with a Guatemalan rum.

Jake, this experience could have only been made better if you were here. As much as I enjoyed Sarah's company tonight, I wish you could have been with me. Thank you for my most special gastronomic experience! We will catch a cab back to the hotel and crash. We are full from all the food and sloshy from all the wine. Sarah says, "Thank you!" as well. I will call you in the morning. I miss you dearly.

Though I hadn't had dinner yet, I felt full just reading how satisfied Emily was with her meal tonight. I too wished I could have been there with her. In the future there would be other restaurants we would enjoy together. For now, a heap of contentment filled my soul.

Thanksgiving came and went, and I felt a loneliness I had never felt before. There was this gap in my life that couldn't be filled no matter who I was with. Emptiness followed me all day. Even with a room full of family, people I have loved all my life, I couldn't shake this feeling that something—no I guess I should say someone—was missing. If this is what Emily was talking about when she told me how alone she felt, it made me sick to my stomach I made her feel this way.

Sunday couldn't come fast enough. Emily's plane would land at 8:00 p.m. so I rushed to go get her. Giddy and nervous about seeing her, I paced near the arrival gate. No matter what I tried, this bundle of nerves wouldn't disappear. The sight of Charlie was a happy respite from my hyperactive senses.

"Hi, Charlie. Did you have a good Thanksgiving?"

"Yeah, it was great. How was yours?"

"Mine was long. I couldn't wait to see Emily."

"So I heard. I got an earful from Sarah on how attentive you were all week."

I guess I needed to apologize to Charlie. Maybe I had put him in an awkward situation.

"Sorry, but I had to make up for all our botched dates. I think Emily was ready to stop seeing me when I didn't make it up to Bacara."

"Yeah. She wasn't happy up there." Charlie shook his head. "I want you to know Sarah and I are glad to see Emily so happy again. We haven't seen her this lit up in a long time. You've been really good to her and for her."

"Thanks. I have to tell you, whatever good I've been for her is miniscule compared to the joy she's brought to my life. I was telling my sister the other day I've never loved any girl as much as I love Emily. I'd marry her today if I knew she felt the same way."

Charlie looked somewhat uneasy. "Take it slow with Emily. She's been through a lot, and though I think she's healed now, I don't know if she's ready to jump into a serious relationship so quickly." He must have seen the uneasy look on my face. "I don't mean to worry you. She'll come around. I will admit, I've never seen her show so much emotion toward anyone as she's done with you. You've brought out a whole new side of Emily. I can tell she really likes you too."

I appreciated Charlie's efforts to try to make me feel better. We were chatting about our holiday when I heard my name being called and saw Emily running toward me. She placed herself wholly into my chest, and my arms molded around her naturally. Seeing her, solidified my knowledge that she had permanently tattooed herself into my heart. Her presence felt like an immutable fixture never to be removed.

"I'm so happy to finally be with you, Jake."

"And I'm very happy you feel that way. I've missed you, Sweetheart."

"Not as much as I've missed you," she declared.

Stunningly, her blazing kiss in the middle of the airport surprised me even more than how much she missed me. I felt self-conscious for her, making out in public as many eyes were staring. When we both came up for air, Charlie looked at me to say, "Maybe I was wrong. She might be ready after all."

Embarrassed to show her face after her attack, Emily buried her head in my chest. I kept both my arms around her and kissed the top of her head.

"Let's go home, Beautiful." I only wished this home was our home. I didn't know if I could part from her tonight.

CHAPTER 7
Why Is He Still in Your Heart?

Another couple of long weeks passed without being able to spend much time with one another. Nothing made me happier these days than being with Emily.

"Hello, Sweetheart. Are you done with school?" I called her on her cell.

"Yeah, it's almost vacation so there's not much for me to do. I came home early. Do you want to come over for dinner?"

"It might not be till late," I answered.

"Was it ever early?" she laughed. "Come whenever you can. Call me right before you leave."

Early for my standards, I left the hospital around eight and stopped by the flower shop before going to Emily's. Not knowing what flowers she liked, I picked a vase filled with a large array of flowers. I drove like a madman, toppling the vase a couple of times, to see her as quickly as possible. Rather than ringing the doorbell, I used my set of keys. I tiptoed in quietly, put the flowers on the dining table, and crept up right behind her and kissed her neck.

She hollered in fright.

I frightened her even more by forcing a kiss to stop the hollering.

She broke off much too soon. "JAKE! You scared me to death. I need my key back if you're going to do this again."

"I'm not giving it back." I kissed her some more. "What are you making? It smells good."

"I'm trying to make a paella. It's almost done. Will you set the table?"

Searching through every drawer, I took out all the necessary utensils and opened a bottle of wine. Without a doubt, this felt like home.

"Jake, I want to ask you something." She brought over our meal.

"What is it?" I took the large spoon and served both of us. "Emi, this is delicious!" I said after taking the first bite.

"Well, there's this Christmas Ball I attend every year and I was wondering if you'd like to go with me this year?"

I looked up from my bite. "Of course! When is it?"

"Tomorrow."

"Tomorrow? How come you're asking me now? What if I'm working tomorrow night?"

"If you're working, we don't have to go. I didn't go last year either. Sarah and Charlie are forcing me to go this year, because they are involved with the planning."

"Will your ex and his girlfriend be there? Is that why you don't want to go?"

"Kind of…I'm such a chicken, huh? I'm still not mentally ready to see him or his new girl. I'd be totally fine if you didn't want to go."

"Emily, let's go and get this over with. I'm perturbed that you're still bothered by your ex. Maybe you're not over him." I put down my utensils and confronted Emily, though this was not my intention. She looked startled.

"I am over him! I just don't want to see him," was Emily's defense.

"If you don't like him anymore, why is it so hard for you to see him again?"

"I don't know. I'm afraid to see him. I don't want to remember the hurtful memories of our last day." Emily's eyes watered and this angered me further. Here was a girl I wanted to marry and she was still crying at the memory of her ex-boyfriend. I knew she hurt easily and teared readily and I should have been more understanding but this only fueled my frustration.

"Emily. From the day I met you, every time Max's name came up, your expression turned gloomy and your eyes flooded with water. How are we to progress if you can't let go of your past?" I regretted my words as soon as they came out.

"Have you never loved someone so much that when it was over you felt like your life was over too? Well, that was me with Max. He broke my heart into so many pieces it's still not back together again. Honestly, I don't love him anymore, but I can't say I don't still hurt. I don't know when this hurt will stop."

Her response borderline enraged me. I couldn't believe what I'd just heard. "What about me? What about us?" My tone was harsh.

"Jake, I like you very much but we just started getting to know each other. You really do have a way with making me feel so special. And I was telling you the truth when I said I feel empty when you're not with me. But please understand, Max was with me every day for four years. All those memories are hard to erase so quickly."

"So quickly? It's been a year and a half already. Emily, I don't think you want to forget. If that's the case, what am I doing here?" I got up to leave mid-dinner.

"Jake, please don't go." She held my hand and followed me to the door. "Can't we talk this through? I'm not in love with him anymore, I have no desire to be with Max, and I'm working on letting go of all the hurt. Can't you give me a little more time? You and I met suddenly and whatever it is that we have right now blossomed much quicker than I expected."

"What do you mean whatever it is that we have? Are we not in a relationship?"

She looked at me with tears flowing in her eyes again. This time the tears were a result of my words. This had nothing to do with her ex. "I don't know what we are in. We've never sat down to talk about us. Every time I think it might happen, you get called away."

"So, it's back to being my fault. Emily, I can't win with you. Let's talk later. I'm going to leave." I let go of her hand and walked out the door. As I peeked in her window while driving the car around I saw that she hadn't left her spot. I shouldn't have said all those things to her. She was right. We hadn't talked about our relationship. That was the reason for the ring—to solidify our commitment. I thought about going back to her and telling her how much I loved her, but the damage had been done.

I got home and found her text waiting for me.

I'm very sorry. I wish you hadn't left. I miss you.

Terrible was an understatement for what I felt before reading her text and now I felt even worse. Why had I done this to her? She was only being honest telling me where her heart was at. I couldn't blame her for not feeling as strongly as I did. Needing to make things right, I called her immediately. There was no answer. A minute later I called again. She still didn't answer.

Emily, where are you? Why aren't you answering your phone?

She took much longer than usual to answer her text.

I'm home.

Why aren't you answering your phone?

Because…

My heart broke and my stomach turned. I had made her cry again. This was probably why she wasn't answering her phone.

Emily, are you crying?

There was no answer again.

Emily, I'm sorry too. I shouldn't have walked out on you. Do you want me to come over right now? Can we talk?

I think I'm going to turn in for the night. I'll talk to you tomorrow. You don't have to go with me tomorrow night if you are busy. I will go by myself. You were right. I need to face Max at some point and move on with my life. I'm sure the first time is the hardest.

I will come pick you up around six. Can I shower and get ready at your place?

Sure, but you really don't have to take me. I promise. I will attend with or without you.

Goodnight, Sweetheart. I'm sorry I left you alone. I miss you too.

Good night.

Right on time I parked outside her house to find the lights off and her car absent. My texts and calls went unreturned, so I worried that she was still hurt by my actions last night. Wanting to wait for her inside but holding off a few more minutes I replayed last night's conversation. Tonight we would discuss our relationship, and I would get this ring on her and show her where I would like for us to head.

Finally, her car pulled into the driveway, and she almost stumbled out of her car in excitement. She beamed a most stunning smile when our eyes met. Beautiful!—The only word that aptly described this woman in my life. Trusting she wasn't upset anymore I walked over to greet her.

"Hi, Jake. I'm so happy to see you. Have you been waiting long? I wish you would have called me," was her welcome.

"Hi, Beautiful. You look stunning." I didn't think it could be possible for her to look any better. "Do you not have your phone on you? I called and texted all day but you never answered. You had me worried."

"Sorry. I guess I forgot my phone at home. I'm so happy you're here." She stopped to hug me. It made me feel wanted and appreciated but a little guilty that she was so happy to see me. "Let's go in. You can use the guest room to get ready."

"Did you not believe me last night when I said I was coming to pick you up at six?"

A peculiar smile donned my beauty's face. It looked like she didn't believe me but was trying to play it off.

"Well?" I pushed a little harder for a truthful answer.

"Go in and get dressed," was all I got as she pointed to the guest bathroom. I let it go for now.

We both walked out at the same time, and my date was a picture of perfection. "You look amazing," I declared, putting my arms around her. She had a funny guilt-ridden look on her face. Maybe she felt bad about last night's conversation. We needed to work through last night's argument once this evening was done. Tonight, I really needed to give her this ring and have us commit to one another.

"You look pretty amazing yourself. I'm going to have to fight off all the ladies in the ballroom," she teased. With Max attending this event, there was not a chance I would be with anyone but Emily. My eyes would not let this beautiful girl out of my sight.

We walked to my car, and I caught Emily staring at me in the most loving way. I'd not seen this look before. This look gave me a sense of hope that we would make it to the very end. I loved this girl immensely but she frustrated me with her response. Some days she responded as though she loved me just as much as I loved her, and some days I wondered if we would make it through the day.

We got to the hotel and walked into a large ballroom. "Emily!" was all I heard when, in the blink of an eye, I had lost my date to a group of ladies. Three women had pulled Emily away and they were whispering and giggling together. Emily looked my way and pulled me back to her side.

"Jake, this is Becca, Lizzy, and Christie. We have all been roommates at some point throughout my four years in undergrad.

"Ladies, this is Jake," Emily introduced us.

"Hello, Jake!" they all chorused in unison like those ER residents did to Emily. She was right. It was creepy.

"Hi." I smiled and nodded politely.

"Jake, I'm going to go see Sarah and Charlie and get us checked in. Hang here with all the gals, will ya?" Emily said with a wink. Helpless, I had no choice but to talk to these women as Emily quickly walked away with a smirk on her face.

"So, Jake…what do you do for a living?" The girl with the red hair asked. I think she was Christie.

"I'm a doctor."

"Ooh, what kind of doctor?" This time it was the blond girl who asked. Becca, possibly?

"I'm a heart surgeon."

"Wow!" they chorused again.

"So how did you and Emily meet? When did you meet? Have you been dating long? Are you just friends? Are you two serious? Which hospital do you work at? I'd love to give you my number if you and Emily aren't an item." I got whiplash going back and forth listening to the onslaught of questions. Even if I wanted to, I couldn't say a word.

As they kept asking more questions, I realized these women were no different than those ER interns. Emily knew exactly what she was doing when she left me here alone. That was why she had that smirk on her face. I'd have to get her back for this one.

"Excuse me, ladies. I need to get back to my Emily." With that I walked away and hurried toward Emily, who was talking to a group of people.

Rudely interrupting her conversation, I grabbed her from behind and forced my lips on hers. Stupefied, Emily tried to push me away as her cheeks turned many shades darker. Her eyes stayed wide open.

"Oh geez, Charlie, look. Those two are at it again," Sarah responded with a happy sigh.

When I thought she'd had enough, I let go. Her ragged breath and flustered cast had Charlie, Sarah, and me in stitches.

"What was that?" she whispered, embarrassed to show her face.

"Payback." I playfully threatened her. "Why did you run away and leave me with those women? If I have to spend any more time with those women, I'm going to take you back to the ER tonight."

Emily understood and started cracking up. "You didn't like my friends? I'm sure they liked you!"

"I missed you. Don't leave my side tonight. I don't want to be apart from you, OK?"

She nodded her head.

I realized many eyes were staring at us. "I'm sorry," I said to Emily and her friends, "was I interrupting something?"

Emily now looked rattled. By the way she started stammering, I knew who this guy was.

"No...This is Max. Max...this is Jake."

I put out my hand. "Hi, it's nice to meet you, Max."

"Nice meeting you too." Max sounded agitated. "And this is my girlfriend, Jennifer."

Emily was not included as Max introduced Jennifer to the people around him. I felt Emily grab my hand and stand slightly behind me. I knew she was hurting, thinking about Jennifer, who took over her position so soon after Emily had vacated it. Timidly she stayed behind me. She wanted to be protected, and I would be her protector.

"Let's go see where we're sitting. We'll see you all later," I called out and took Emily away from the spotlight. Stepping away from the crowd, I wanted to make sure Emily wasn't tearing as she so easily does.

"Emily, are you OK?" Attempting to sound more comforting than annoyed, I saw her crinkled face change into a weak grin.

"Yes. I'm OK. Are you sorry you came tonight? Isn't this what you didn't want to see—me being rattled by the sight of Max and his new girlfriend?"

"You seemed more rattled by watching the rest of our reactions. Emily, seeing you anxious doesn't make me happy, and I have to apologize to you for my behavior last night. There was no reason for me to be so angry, and I definitely shouldn't have walked out on you and our dinner. I'm all right seeing you and Max together. Can we let this go for now and have a long overdue talk when this function is over?"

I assumed her responsive kiss was a yes.

"Let's go meet some of my friends. I see them at our table." She sounded happy again. "One more thing, Max and Jennifer are at our table. I hope you don't mind. Sarah and Charlie thought it would be funny to have us all together. I'm sorry." I didn't care who we sat with but Emily sounded annoyed.

In my meanest tone I told her, "I'll have a talk with them later tonight."

She giggled.

We went on to meet more friends. Emily let go of my hand and hugged one of her friends longingly. I could tell by her face that this was her dear friend, Peter. He too seemed to have missed my Emily very much. She tugged me over toward him.

"Peter, I want you to meet my date. This is Jake. Jake, this is Peter, my friend, my quasi brother."

"It's nice meeting you, Jake. When did you and Emily start dating? She never told us she was seeing someone." He ended our conversation aiming the question at Emily. She answered with an innocent smile.

"Emily and I started dating a couple of months ago," I answered.

"Oh, that's not very long." The way he said these words was a bit peculiar. I couldn't grasp his hidden meaning.

"No, I wish we could see more of each other but due to my work schedule we date when possible. If I could, I'd spend every day with her." I looked over at Emily and winked.

She shook her head and mouthed, "I don't believe you!"

I forced another public display of affection on her and answered back, "I'd spend every waking and sleeping moment with you if it were possible."

Peter looked uncomfortable. Emily turned red again and walked to the next table to talk to her friends, probably fearful of any more sudden attacks.

I found out tonight that Peter was a second-year med student, and Max was in his first year. We enthusiastically talked about the classes he was taking and the hardships of medical school. His bemoaning reminded me of those arduous years with no end in sight. Medical school faired easy when compared to residency. Looking at my life now, residency faired even easier when I thought about the long hours I worked—especially the hours that kept me away from Emily. Peter had no idea what he was in for after med school was done.

The emcee called for a first dance so I excused myself and went over to pick up my love. Charlie and Sarah waltzed over to us immediately.

"Hey, Jake!"

"I don't know if I should be saying hello to both of you for putting us at the same table as Max and Jennifer. Are you trying to help us or tear us apart?" Of course I was kidding.

"We are only trying to show you off to Max," Sarah answered. "I want him to know Emily is doing very well without him."

"Sounds great to me!" I answered enthusiastically.

Emily didn't sound as happy as she squinted her eyes at her best friend and said, "Great. Thanks!" She then moved us away calling out, "See you later."

With no one else to bother us, I pulled Emily into my body as close as possible. Six weeks of dating coupled with my hectic schedule and Emily's demure nature, I hadn't done more than kissed this girl. Bewildered, I couldn't figure out whether our lack of physical progress was due to Emily's innocence, her lack of desire, or maybe even her lack of experience. She and Max had dated for four years so it couldn't have been a lack of experience. I shuddered at the image of her and Max. Possibly we could talk about this tonight as well.

My lips started on her ear, slowly nibbling their way to the back of her neck, then across the cheek, and to her jaw. When I stopped at her lips she let out a quiet moan and her lips quivered as I covered them with my own. This was the passion I'd wanted to share with Emily and the reaction I'd been looking for. I showed her my plan of attack. She did not retreat. Enjoying her complete participation, our kiss deepened when my pager went off and broke our embrace.

"Damn! Not again!" I declared.

I looked guilty; she looked critical, but soon started to laugh. "Don't worry about it. I'll meet you back at the table," she spoke, shaking her head. As she walked away I noticed Peter taking her back to the dance floor.

"Hey, Linda, did you page me?" I prayed Linda wouldn't tell me I had to return.

"Dr. Reid, I thought I'd let you know your patient, Adam Chen, who got discharged this morning, came back in with chest pains."

"Has Dr. Carter seen him?"

"Yes, but Mr. Chen has been asking for you. What shall I say?"

"Call me if the situation gets more serious. Otherwise, he'll be in good care with Carter."

"Will do."

Hopefully I wouldn't be needed anymore tonight. I walked back into the ballroom and found Emily in Max's arms. Hurt and angry, I had to calm myself before going back to Emily. I couldn't understand why she would be dancing with him. Last I saw, she was with Peter. What had happened? I needed to go to her and get an explanation.

"Ahem. May I cut in?" Max jerked away and Emily panicked. Instead of a guilty look, she had a look of fear in her eyes I had never seen before. My heart sank. She was afraid of me.

Her words faltering and her face filled with anxiety, she tried to explain herself. "Peter danced with me after you left and made me switch partners and told us to talk it out and...and..."

At this point I didn't care if Emily still had feelings for her ex. I just wanted to comfort her and let her know I wasn't upset with her.

"It's OK, Emily. You don't have to explain," I answered pulling her into my chest.

"I promise I wasn't trying..."

I cut her off. "Shh. Emily. It's all right."

She still couldn't let it go. I saw the tears swell. She looked like a little girl caught with her hand in the cookie jar. Even this look was lovable.

"Nothing happened, I promise. I'm sorry." Her voice was defeated.

"Emily. I wish I didn't make you so anxious. It's OK. I'm OK. You don't need to apologize. Let's go back to the table." I did my best to reassure her but she didn't look comforted. I couldn't tell whether her sadness was caused by me or Max. I didn't know which would be worse. I needed to let her know that there was a possibility I might have to leave. That's the last thing I wanted to do, but it was my reality.

"What will happen if I have to leave you early tonight?" I feared her answer.

"Do you have to leave?" Her visible disappointment was a happy response this time.

"No, not yet. There's a chance."

We were about to sit down when the pager went off again. I kissed Emily on the forehead and walked out to make my call.

"Dr. Reid, I think you need to come back. Your patient needs you."

"All right. I'll be there soon."

I made a quick call to Uncle Henry. "Chief?"

"Yes, Jake."

"I'm being called back into the hospital right now even though I'm not on call. I need you to give me the rest of this weekend off. "

"I got it. I'll make sure nobody looks for you this weekend. Now go see your patient. Obviously they really need you or else they wouldn't have contacted you."

"I'm holding you to it." I trusted Uncle Henry would keep his word. Next I needed to call Uncle Dave.

"Uncle Dave? This is Jake."

"Hey, Jake. What's going on?"

"I have a favor to ask of you." I prayed he could help.

"What do you need?"

"Can you get me a table for two at French Laundry, tomorrow?"

"Tomorrow? Do you think I'm a miracle worker?"

"Please, Uncle Dave. I'd like to take Emily tomorrow for lunch. Please!"

"I'll try. I won't know till tomorrow morning. I'll be in touch."

"Thank you."

"When do we get to meet this girl, Jake? You've said a whole lot but haven't shown us anyone."

"Christmas. You'll meet her then. Thanks again."

So far, all has gone according to plan. I needed to go back to Emily with a plan. Using my phone I booked two seats on the 8:30 a.m. flight out of Burbank, then I called Jane.

"Jane, do me a favor."

"Well, hello to you too, big brother." I ignored her sarcasm.

"Are you still up North?"

"Yeah. What do you need?"

"I'm bringing Emily up tomorrow and I need you to get me seats at the Opera House. I believe they're doing *Carmen*. I'll give you my credit card number. Reserve the best seats you can. Also, can you go out and get her something to wear? If you're busy, I can have concierge do all this for me."

"No, I'd love to do it for you. Can I come too? I can't wait to meet her." Jane had always wanted a sister. Knowing how lonely Emily had been for a good part of her life, she and Jane would grow to love each other like sisters. They complemented each other well.

"That would be nice. Emily has been asking about you too. Make dinner reservations also. We'll probably get to the apartment around three."

"I've got plans all day tomorrow but will meet you and Emily for dinner. I'll email you all the information. I can't wait to meet her, Jake. By the way, what size dress and shoes do I get for her?"

"I'm not quite sure but you and Emily are about the same size. She's a bit thinner and much prettier."

"Great, thanks. You're always so encouraging."

I chuckled and got off the phone. Now it was time to face Emily. I walked in the ballroom hoping not to find her in Max's arms again. The sight before me made me laugh. This time she was talking to Jennifer, Max's girlfriend. What a night for Emily. I was only about to make it worse.

My sweetheart looked at me with hope and jitters. "Hi. Done with your call?"

I confirmed her fears as I let my sentence trail. "Yeah..."

"Oh, that doesn't sound good." She let out her cute whine.

"Well, I've got some good news and some bad news. Which do you want first?"

"The bad." She was always the pessimist.

"I have to go back to the hospital," I said as quickly as possible.

"No!" she protested. "Not again. I thought you had the whole night off. Jake, we hardly ever get to see each other. I think I've seen you once a week in the last couple of months." Her protest was completely founded and I had stood her up too many times. I also didn't want to leave her tonight of all nights, as she appeared so fragile, so unprotected—like a raw wound flinching at the sight of pain.

As an apology, I uttered, "I know, and I'm sorry. I thought we'd be together tonight but my patient came back with complications, and I might have to go back into surgery."

She unhappily shrugged her shoulders and submitted to our reality. "Save another life tonight, Dr. Reid. I want to stop you but I can't...I won't."

I loved this girl for always understanding my crazy work schedule. Tonight would not be the easiest night for her but she was letting me go without much fuss.

"But," I told her, "the good news! Chief gave me the whole weekend off so I'm taking you on a surprise trip. We're going somewhere far where no one can call me back to the hospital. Can you be ready by 7:00 a.m.? I'll pick you up at your house."

"Sure..." She still sounded glum. "Where are we going?" I was taken aback that she didn't sound more excited. "How shall I dress? Is it going to be very cold?"

"It's always cold up there," I slipped, hoping to generate more excitement.

"Up there?" I got her attention. "When will we be back? I assume we will be back tomorrow night?"

The enthusiasm in her voice gave me hope that we could finally spend a night together. Two months and very little intimacy, this was long overdue.

"Do we have options? Can we stay the weekend?"

Her silence was uncomfortably long. Maybe she felt self-conscious answering in front of eight pairs of eyes waiting for her to speak. They all appeared way too interested in our conversation. Max definitely couldn't hide his interest.

"Um..."

I didn't like the sound of this...

"No. I don't think it's wise for us to spend the night."

No matter. I would convince her otherwise when we got up there. Excited to spend an entire day with her, I gave her an intense kiss while my pager beeped endlessly.

"Bye, I'll miss you." I then added, "And please, don't fall back into your ex's arms after I leave." We both got a good laugh.

With Emily being alone, I hoped Sarah and Charlie would take care of her. Peter would drive my girl home, so that was one thing off my mind, but I wasn't sure what frame of mind or better yet, what her heart would look like when I picked her up tomorrow morning. After seeing Max tonight, I hoped she'd put everything behind her and start new with me without any baggage.

CHAPTER 8

You're a What?

Even with only three hours of sleep, the thought of being with Emily all day woke me with a frenetic energy. I showered and went to pick up breakfast for my girl and got to her door exactly at seven. I rang the doorbell.

She opened the door wearing a knitted dress with knee-high boots. The dress clung to her body, and as always she looked stunning. I leaned in to kiss her lips.

"Good morning. Are you ready to leave?"

"Not quite. Come in."

I handed her a croissant and latte while surveying the house. "Whoa, what happened here? Slumber party?" Peter and Jeff were asleep on the floor.

Emily explained that these guys drank too much to drive home, and they ended up sleeping here.

"I think they're getting up now." She looked over at them. "Good morning. Did you sleep well? Are your backs OK?" While she talked to them I could only think that I hadn't even spent the night here yet, and these random guys were lucky enough to be with her, though they weren't exactly with her.

"Jake? Do you still have my spare keys? Can I have them back?" She held out her hand. I didn't want to give them back, but I had no choice.

I watched her throw my keys at Peter, so I picked up her coffee with one hand and held out the other for Emily so we could leave. A guilty look dawned on Emily's face, and I quickly followed her eyes to see Max come out of the guest bedroom. He had spent the night as well. Outraged but trying to keep composure for Emily's sake, I didn't say a word. Emily looked worried again.

Peter broke my angry mood and asked about going on a road trip with Emily and all of her friends. Knowing Max would be there with her, I didn't want her to go alone, but I knew I couldn't get any more time off after Hawaii.

Hawaii. I forgot to tell Emily about Hawaii.

"Emily, what are you doing next Monday through Thursday?" Emily's rattled look turned into a blank stare. "My mom called this morning to tell me we are all going to Hawaii right before Christmas, and she wants me to bring you along. You know my family's been dying to meet you. She's reserved a seat for you on the plane, and you can room with my sister, Jane."

Flustered, but with a smile, she asked, "With your whole family?" She thought about it some more and then questioned, "How did you get four days off?" This one really stumped her.

I guess I had never told her about Uncle Henry. "Well, the chief of staff at the hospital is my dad's brother. Mom reminded Uncle Henry that I haven't had a vacation since I got there. It also didn't hurt that she promised him four tickets to the Rose Bowl game."

"I see. Are you sure you want me there for four days with your family?"

How could she possibly ask this after my many heartfelt confessions to her? I suppose another reassurance was in order. "I couldn't think of a better Christmas present than to have you spend four days with me and my family."

There was a glint in her eyes. "OK, then. Tell your mother I said thank you and that I'd love to go."

Emily grabbed a coat, said good-bye, and we headed out the door. No more than a few steps out, she stopped me.

"Jake, I'd like to explain about the guys you saw this morning, especially Max. I know that was really uncomfortable, and I'm sorry." It wasn't so much guilt I saw in her face; it was more a voice of penitence. She feared hurting me.

"Emily, you don't have to explain anything." I tried but couldn't hide the awkwardness.

"I do. Peter and Jeff went out to the bar with our friend and they got so drunk, they couldn't drive home. We found them lying on my doorstep and they asked to spend the night."

"Can I ask where you and Max were at this time? I assume you weren't with them?"

Now this answer scared me more than everything she'd told me about her and Max combined. After seeing them together last night, this relationship wasn't completely over for either one of them.

"No. We went out for a bite to eat. I didn't have any dinner, and Max suggested we grab a bite to eat before we met up with the rest of the gang. Our dinner took longer than expected, and when we got back to my house, Peter and Jeff were comatose on my front porch."

"Dinner?" I asked in a frightened tone.

Emily's face broke into a chuckle. I couldn't understand how she found humor in this situation. "It was literally dinner," she answered, grabbing the hand I let go. "We also had a good talk, which I'd like to share with you whenever you'd like to hear about it. Are we good? Can we go on with this day without us being uncomfortable with one another?" She now softened into her beautiful smile. "I told Max last night that I was really looking forward to spending a whole day with you. Even though we've been dating a few months, I don't think we know each other very well."

What? How could she think this?

"What do you mean we don't know each other very well?" While I held her door, she held back her grin. "Get in. We need to get going or we're going to miss our flight."

I couldn't even last a few seconds into the drive, before demanding, "How can you say we don't really know each other?" I was still flabbergasted at her last statement. This woman, whom I wanted to spend the rest of my life with, complained that we were almost strangers. We had a long ways to go before I could even broach the topic of marriage.

"Jake." She sounded slightly piqued this time. "When was the last time...better yet, has there ever been a time when we spent an entire date without being interrupted? Our first date at the Mexican restaurant—what happened? You got paged and went in to perform some surgery. Our second date, brunch—what happened? The chief sent you to some conference in Atlanta. That's also when we got into our first argument and couldn't even talk it through because you had to leave."

Perhaps I shouldn't have brought this up. She was making a strong argument in her favor.

"Don't get me going on our third date to Santa Barbara that ended before it even started. We didn't see each other for almost two weeks."

"But, I came to see you at the airport, we worked everything out, and I told you how much you mean to me," I defended myself.

"Only after I postponed my flight twice, hoping you would show up. My flight was at 8:00 p.m. You showed up sometime after eleven."

"Didn't I make up for it in New York?"

Emily leaned over and kissed my cheek. "You did. But I would've given up all the luxuries in New York to have spent one full day with you."

This time, I leaned over and she met my lips.

"You would've given up the first class seat?"

"In a heartbeat."

"The driver?"

"Without a doubt."

"The suite at the W?"

"Of course!"

"Le Bernardin?" I was truly curious to hear this answer.

"Absolutely...not." She burst into a cackle. "I told you, as much as I enjoyed Sarah's company, I wished you would've been there with me that night. None of this means much if you're not with me."

Heaven. Her answer put me in a state of bliss. How could I not love this sweet girl?

"Your answers might have earned you an unforgettable lunch," I hinted. "So are you done with your argument?"

"Nope. Let's not forget last night. You left me stranded before dinner was served. Although I think we managed to spend an entire three hours together. That's a record, you know."

"But what about all the times I come by, call, or text you?"

"Are you kidding me? The last time you came by my house you got mad at me and left in the middle of dinner. You call from the hospital and have to hang up within minutes. Your texts look like an hour-by-hour hospital itinerary. How did you ever have a relationship with this schedule? Does your hospital have no other doctors but yourself?"

She shook her head in disbelief and laughed. "So, you see why I'm so excited to spend this whole day with you?"

Sweetly she smiled and put her hand over mine.

"I suppose I get your point." I could marry her today, but she obviously didn't think she knew me well enough. "I already feel very close to you, but you apparently need more convincing. That will be my mission today. Ask me whatever you like. I'll answer all your questions."

"First question—where are we going? Burbank Airport? Could we be flying to San Francisco? It couldn't be Seattle, that's a bit too far for a day trip. Any hints?"

"Not a chance. You'll have to wait until we get there." Happy to keep her guessing, I didn't give her a clue, even though she told me how she didn't like surprises. What girl didn't like surprises? Emily could be a bit odd at times.

Out of nowhere, Emily leaned over and my body froze. Her lips slowly grazed my neck and went up to nibble my ear.

"Are you sure you can't give me a hint?" she whispered.

My foot stepped off the pedal and the car went on autopilot. Though I enjoyed the coaxing, I was forced to ask her to stop before we got into an accident.

When we got on the plane Emily stopped us from sitting in our seats and asked, "You don't have to go into work today, do you? They can't make you come back from San Francisco or worse yet, find you an operation to perform up in San Francisco?"

I had to laugh at her paranoia. "Does my job make you that nervous?"

"Yup!" she immediately answered. "I think I'm going to reconsider dating a doctor, or at least I'm going to date a doctor who doesn't ever have any emergencies."

I knew where she was taking this conversation. My expression stayed nonchalant. I didn't want to give her the satisfaction. "Yeah? What kind of doctor would that be?"

"Maybe a dermatologist or a podiatrist," she answered with a smirk on her face.

With her ring in my jacket pocket, I knew she would be solely mine after lunch today. "Trust me, after today, you're not going anywhere from me."

She retorted, "Very confident there, Dr. Reid. We'll see about that."

My words didn't carry as much weight as I thought they should.

We landed at SFO and I had two texts waiting for me.

Confirmed 11:00 a.m. lunch for two. Have a great time. Can't wait to meet the future Mrs. Jake Reid.—Uncle Dave

A box at the opera house confirmed. Dinner at 6:00 p.m. at Quince reserved. I will send over clothes and shoes sometime in the afternoon. I'm really excited to meet my future sister. See you at dinner.—Jane

Yes! I knew Uncle Dave and Jane would pull through for me. We got a car and drove up the 101 freeway. Taking in the scenery, Emily rambled about some of her dreams—one of which was wanting to hear Andrea Bocelli sing in an open meadow in Tuscany. I would be more than happy to whisk her off to Tuscany. When we got back, I would look into taking her. Even better, I would ask her to give me a list of places she wanted to go and activities she wanted to do. She was in a deep muse.

"A kiss for your thoughts?"

She just stared at me.

"Well?" I prompted.

"Where's the promised kiss?"

As much as I wanted to give her an open-mouth kiss, this road was not conducive to such action. Instead, I placed a chaste kiss on her hand.

"I was admiring all the unique architecture." By the dreamy look on her face, there was something she wasn't telling me.

"That's it?"

"My answer was about as exciting as that kiss you just gave me."

That was challenge enough. I pulled her neck as close to me as possible and gave her the torrid kiss she asked for without getting us both killed. She looked embarrassed but still stayed quiet.

"Well? Shouldn't that kiss elicit a better answer?"

"I thought it would be nice to go back to Tuscany..."

Now, she was being a tease. I pulled the car over and placed my mouth over hers deeply, intensely, lustfully. How will you react to this, Emily Logan?

"...with you when I'm old and gray..."

YES! I couldn't have dreamed of a better answer.

"It's so beautiful up here. Are we spending the whole day here?" With her cheeks a bright pink, she was trying to change to a safer topic.

"Would you like to?" I asked. Perhaps I should have considered letting her decide what to do today.

"Sure. But I don't really care where as long as we're together. I'm really happy to be here with you," she whispered and gave me her version of a lustful kiss.

From the onset of our day, Emily's attitude had changed. Her words and her actions proved she was ready to move forward with our relationship. She was heading where I was waiting. Something about her time with Max last night freed her from his last grip. Hopeful and excited, I parked in front of our first destination.

Emily's face broke into sheer excitement. "How did you get us a table here on such short notice?"

Of course she would know where we were. Being the foodie that she was, this had to have been one of the restaurants she wanted to visit. I wanted to be the first one to bring her here.

"How did you know this was my dream restaurant destination? I can't believe we're here! Thank you, Jake." Elated, she hugged me.

She began asking questions about my family while noshing on the first course. As I told her about my immediate family first, then about all of my uncles and aunts and cousins, she looked delighted that I had a big family. While outlining my family tree, Emily devoured her two amuse bouche, the oysters and caviar—which she thoroughly enjoyed, the cured hamachi belly, and the seared duck foie gras. There was sheer happiness on her face as she ate her food as there was on mine watching her eat.

Next came risotto with white truffle, and pure bliss fell on her face again. Somewhere along the way she had told me how much she liked white—not black—truffles. Like a child in a candy shop, she thoroughly enjoyed herself.

I finally got to ask her about her family. I felt almost negligent not knowing anything about her parents or siblings and why they weren't around. My heart broke when she told me that her dad died when she was in middle school and her mom followed her dad when Emily was in high school. Her only relatives, her maternal grandparents, passed away sometime during her college years.

She teared when she spoke of her parents. I wished I could've been her comfort during those lonely years. Our family would have overwhelmed her with love. I longed to tell her that my love would be sufficient to make up for the loss of her father, mother, and grandparents. Oh, Emily. My heart was heavy.

Another question I had for her was how she paid for college and living expenses, and how she had bought a house already. In the cutest way, she eyed the whole roasted turbot, watching the servers fillet it and place it on each plate with a burnt lemon. She was fascinated by this lemon. She smelled it, tasted it, squeezed some on her fish, then quickly chewed a bite before answering my questions.

"Underneath this weak frame, I have a survival mentality." She then told me how she had worked since high school as a tutor, supported herself through college, and bought her current home with her earnings plus money from the sale of a condo her grandparents bequeathed her. What an amazing woman she was. Behind the pretty face and tender heart, she was a true fighter. I didn't realize she had so much strength in her. It didn't seem possible to love her any more than I already did, but my admiration for her grew deeper with each passing course.

Naturally, I had to pose the most important question. "Can I ask about your relationship with Max? Do you mind telling me? I'd also like to know what happened with you and Max last night, if you don't mind."

She looked hesitant but began dissecting their relationship. "Max and I met our freshman year and it was absolute love at first sight."

"Lucky guy." I was jealous already. "So what about him did you like so much?"

She made me feel insecure as she laughed at my question. "You guys are both so funny," she explained.

I gave her a why look and she answered, "Max asked me the same question last night."

It made me feel good to know that they were talking about me and not about themselves.

"So what did you tell him?" I hoped it was something great.

"I think I'll keep you guessing on that one." She gave me an adorable wink and I couldn't help but be even more enamored.

She continued with her wonderful years with Max, how they spent every waking moment together, and how she believed they would get married. Emily talking about marriage with another guy didn't settle well with me. She couldn't talk beyond today with me, but she had thought about the rest of her life with Max. It disturbed me.

"I'm sorry, Jake!" she quickly apologized. My face must have told her what my heart told me. "You didn't need to hear all of that. I got a bit carried away." She kept apologizing.

Stupidly, I asked her to continue though she appeared hesitant. I chuckled, wondering if she was hesitant to talk for fear of hurting my feelings or because she wanted to eat her well-marbled Japanese beef sirloin. She eyed her meat several times and without looking, there was no doubt her mouth was watering. I watched to see what she would pick—satisfying my curiosity concerning the state of her heart, or satisfying her curiosity of the palate. Happily surprised, I won. Conceivably I was overtaking food as her biggest passion.

She continued at my prodding. "Well, there's not much more to say. On graduation day, Max appeared nervous all day and tried to avoid me so I thought he was going to ask me to marry him. Instead, after the ceremony, he broke up with me, giving me some excuse about not being ready for a serious commitment. Just like that he let go of four years; the bond I thought could never be broken...broke."

There was sadness in her voice and possibly tears in her eyes. I didn't want to look at her. Today, she confirmed my fears. She had been deeply in love with Max and their breakup shattered her heart and her trust in love. Because she had believed all those years she would marry a guy, who eventually left her, she was afraid to think about marriage with me for fear that I would leave her as well. Our mood had turned dark. I attempted to change it.

"So I'm still wondering how you answered Max last night about your feelings for me."

She showed a loving smile and answered, "Well, I told Max how comfortable I feel with you. I feel protected and secure and I can be myself with you. Although I've only known you for a short while, it's like you've been with me my whole life."

Emily spoke aloud exactly what I felt. I too felt that comfortable with her, like she was meant to be in my life forever.

"I don't know," she continued. "It's a bit strange but you're the only person aside from my parents who makes me feel entirely comfortable. I can't quite explain this. Max got very angry with me last night when I told him this."

"You mean you've never felt entirely comfortable with Max?" I finally had one up on this guy—and a big one it was.

"With Max, I was always trying to please him. I think I was infatuated with him. Max appeared at a time in my life when I had nobody but my grandparents. My parents were gone and I didn't have any siblings to share my pain. Max not only became my boyfriend, but he also became my only family. I think I smothered him with my love. Maybe I was a borderline stalker. That's probably why he eventually broke up with me."

I had to laugh at this statement or I'd want to cry thinking about the hold Max had on my Emily. She considered him much more than a man to love; she had thought of him as her only family. No wonder he'd had such a profound impact on her. This was probably why she couldn't completely let go. Who can let go of a family member? But, he was not her family, and I needed her to realize he was no longer a part of her life. I would like to be her boyfriend, and I would like to be her family. My immediate and extended family would all welcome her with the same love I had. This was the life I wanted to show her.

"You want to know the hardest part about this breakup?" she asked me.

Did I want to know? Nope. But she was going to tell me anyway.

"All the loves in my life left me without any warning—my dad, mom, and Max. I don't think I loved anyone as much as I loved these three people and I felt abandoned by all of them." She held back those pesky tears. "I had a tough year and a half of letting go. Four years wasted..."

At this point, I wanted to stop talking about Max and give her the ring and ask her to be my girlfriend. But there was a nagging question that had to be asked. Terrified of the answer, I held off until I couldn't any longer. "Are you sure you're over Max? Do I want to know?"

She started talking about how Max had apologized to her last night and how she had finally found closure. She said, "Yes, I am over him, but four years is hard to erase." This statement didn't reassure my uneasy feelings. She'd given me more of herself during lunch than she had the last couple of months, but I still needed more.

She caught me off guard and asked me about my relationships. Not wanting to explain everyone I'd dated since—there were many more than her one Max—talking about Kelley was the only solution. My most recent "girl," Allison, needed to be kept top secret. Though I talked about Kelley, Emily was so engrossed in her chocolate cake and cinnamon ice cream, I didn't know how much she'd heard or maybe even cared.

To both our delight Uncle Dave had asked Thomas Keller to stop by and say hello. Emily's face lit up. I'd have to talk to her about how she never looked this excited when I entered the room. He asked her about her favorite dishes and her answers cracked me up. Of course she picked all the dishes that were supplemental charges on top of the hefty pre fixe tab. This girl was going to be expensive to court.

Nine courses of fine food, an intimate talk with my love, a meeting with Thomas Keller, and a kitchen tour later, we drove back down to the city. Without any explanation, I took her to our apartment near the Ferry Building and hoped to rest before starting the next half of our day.

Emily had a bewildered stare and wondered where we were. Since she told me she didn't like surprises, I'd have to continue surprising her till she got used to it—at least for the rest of our lives together. When I opened the door to our apartment, Emily walked in and studied the place silently. Ending the surprise, I explained that this apartment belonged to our family and that we were here to rest before dinner and the show.

"Dinner? Show? How can you eat again after French Laundry?" She shook her head no. "There's no way I can eat again today. I am so full. Besides, I have nothing to wear to attend any shows up here. What are we going to watch?"

She looked stunning in her dress, but I knew Jane had gone out and picked out something nice for her. I wanted to delight her again. We both headed to the sofa, hoping to hang out for a few hours. Relaxing in front of the TV and maybe even taking a nap sounded like the perfect remedy to all our libations.

I brought her as close to me as possible and the next thing I knew, she was dead asleep against my arms. Carefully, I laid her with me on the large sofa. She was nestled between me and the back of the sofa. My arms cradled her neck and she used my chest as a pillow. This was how I imagined our life to be—a lazy nap together on a weekend afternoon. With both my arms curled around her body, I dozed off with her.

Happily, I woke up to Emily's arm sprawled across my chest. She slept like an angel—my angel—while my lips grazed the top of her head and my hand worked the remote.

"Oh, my gosh." She awoke sooner than I would have liked. "How long have I been asleep?"

"A couple of hours, I think."

"I'm so sorry, Jake. I can't believe I fell asleep on you. I don't think I've ever fallen asleep on a date before."

"It was nice. I rather liked it. You appeared quite cozy." I kissed her again and wrapped both my arms around her tight.

"Um...I didn't drool on you, did I?"

Her face turned a cute shade of red. "Do you normally?" I asked, laughing at her flustered look.

"I don't think so but of course the first time I fall asleep with a man, I would make a fool of myself."

I pondered her statement. What could she have meant about this being the first time she fell asleep with a guy? She broke my thought by trying to get up and get away from me.

There was no way we were changing this perfect position. Instead, I pulled her body up to my eyes. Not aware whose lips reached first, they joined excitedly together. She had wanted this as much as I had. Excited to share in an embrace, I couldn't keep my mouth in one place. There were too many parts of her body I wanted to explore, but with the position that we were in, I couldn't reach beyond her face and neck. She responded to my every touch.

Right as I was about to get up and carry her into my room, there was a knock on the door that was far worse than any pager. I got up and opened the door to the doorman delivering all of Emily's clothes for tonight. Perusing through the stack, Jane had done a nice job.

"What's all this?" Emily looked through the rolling rack. "How did this all get here?"

"Jane's in San Francisco right now, and she helped me. She offered to go out and get all this for you. I hope you don't mind. Jane's the only girl in the family and she's always wanted a sister. She's more than excited to meet you and become your friend. Is that OK?"

"Jane, your sister? Oh, I can't wait to meet her!" She had that childlike excitement on her face and in her voice.

"Jane is quite an opera buff and I remembered you talking about *Carmen*. So Jane helped out again and got us seats at the opera house, and that's the final half of our date. We are meeting her for dinner so you have to eat again."

Her face turned into one of sincere appreciation. I'd never seen such tenderness in her eyes before. Something I just said or did made her look at me like I was her answer to love. I didn't know what I had done, but I enjoyed the admiration.

"Jake, this has been one of the most amazing dates. Lunch was a gastronomic feast. Meeting the chef owner was almost as phenomenal as lunch and I'm really touched you figured out how much I like opera. I guess you do listen during our dates even though they're always cut short. You are an amazing man." She came to me and put her arms around my body.

"I love you, Emily," was on the tip of my tongue but I held off just a bit longer.

She and I both went into separate rooms and got dressed for dinner. I got out before Emily, waiting with one more surprise. Finally, this was our time to commit to one another. I feared Emily's response to the ring, but I knew today we had made huge progress. I held in my hand a box—like the kind a girl would receive when a man was down on one knee about to propose to the woman he loved. This was a tempting thought. I didn't think she would agree to marriage—yet.

Emily walked out looking dazzling in a formal gown. She curiously eyed my hand.

"I want to ask you something." I started my thought process with these words. "This is for you." I opened up her hand and placed the box. "Please don't be scared. It's not as serious as it looks."

She did look scared. Carefully unwrapping the bow and opening the box, she looked back and forth between the ring and my face. "Um…it's stunning but could you explain this ring to me?"

Maybe a quarter-inch band with hundreds of diamonds was a bit serious when asking her to be my girlfriend. I just hoped it would fit on one of her fingers.

"It's not an engagement ring. I wish it were, though I'd probably buy a bigger diamond if I were proposing, nor a wedding band as you might fear. I wanted to give you a ring that symbolized our commitment to one another." I didn't like the way that sounded. I deleted that statement and held her hands. "Emily, we've dated a couple of months now and I know you're not quite sure where we stand in the formal sense. This talk is long overdue. I actually bought this ring for you after our first date. Even back then, I knew I wanted to be with you. I mean, date only you." I babbled a few more incoherent thoughts then got straight to the point. "Um…I would like for us to date…exclusively date. What I mean is…Will you be my girlfriend?" This was a lot harder to ask than originally thought.

Emily eyed me curiously then giggled. I couldn't believe I had a ring in my hand, a serious question of commitment out of my mouth, and all she could do was giggle.

"Are you going to answer? You're making me nervous."

"OK, so let me get this straight. You spend thousands of dollars to ask my permission to do what we are already doing now? Dating?" Now that she put it this way, the ring did seem a little over the top.

I reminded her that she was the one who needed clarity and a title to what we were doing.

"Aren't we already exclusively dating? Have you been seeing other girls as well? Is that why it's so hard to spend any time with you?" This joke I neither got nor wanted to laugh at. She saw the annoyance on my face.

"I haven't had a desire or need to see anyone else. I feel blessed to be with you," she reassured me. "I trust you and feel most secure when we're together. You are the only man I want to be with." These choice words melted my heart.

"What about Max?" I needed an answer to clear my doubts once and for all.

As much as I appreciated her words, I thought about the two of them last night and felt insecure again. Could there be a possibility she would want to get back together with him again? As she had said earlier, four years was hard to erase. She studied my face again and knew she needed to reassure me even more.

"I'm sorry you had to witness my first encounter with Max and his new girlfriend. Being such an awkward moment, I didn't react the way I would have liked. I guess it hurt me more than I thought it would, even with you by my side."

This was not what I wanted to hear, but she continued anyway. "But you and our relationship add so much joy to my life. I wasn't lying when I said you're the only person who makes me feel entirely comfortable. I'm elated when we're together and lonely when we're apart. Will this answer do? I would be honored to be your girlfriend."

The second half of her statement definitely made up for the first half. I contemplated telling her how much I loved her. Not wanting anything close to a rejection after her confession just now, I decided to wait again.

Jane and Emily needed no introduction when they met at Quince. They instantly bonded. They began their conversation talking about New York. I didn't realize how much Emily liked New York. She told Jane she wished she'd lived there at some point in her life. This was also something I'd have to try to do for her.

"Jake was so miserable when you were in New York." Jane started talking about me. Emily smiled and squeezed my hand. "You should have seen him at Thanksgiving. We were all seated at a large table and we noticed Jake constantly looking down at his lap. Finally, Uncle Henry went over and grabbed what was in his lap—his phone, of course—and took it away from him. It drove him nuts that he was texting you, but you wouldn't respond."

"Well, by the time you all sat down for dinner, we were toward the end of ours and Sarah's grandma was telling us stories of her childhood. I couldn't get up from the table, nor could I text in secret, so I didn't respond. I got so many texts that Sarah, my best friend, was really annoyed. She told me to go back home if we were constantly going to be on the phone with each other."

"Yeah, well Jake got into trouble with Uncle Henry, but he didn't care. He got his phone back and kept waiting for your response."

"In all honesty, I was pretty miserable too. Apparently Sarah and her boyfriend, Charlie, had a bet going that week." From the insane kiss she gave me at the airport, miserable was an understatement.

"Really? What bet was that?" I jumped into their conversation.

"Sarah believed I would come crying, begging to go home because I missed you. And Charlie believed I would feel too guilty to say so but instead, you would come to see me in New York."

"So who won the bet?" Jane asked. "Who was more correct?"

"That's hard to say. Sarah was right because that's exactly what I wanted to do, but Charlie was also correct knowing I couldn't do that to my best friend. Also, if I hadn't stopped him, your brother would have spent Thanksgiving with us in New Jersey. I guess they both know me too well."

After today and Emily's many confessions, I felt like I knew her quite well. She appeared comfortable talking about her feelings concerning me as well as her past feelings concerning Max. We had made huge progress today as I had hoped.

"The whole family can't wait to meet you," Jane said, rolling her eyes. "Jake couldn't stop talking about you at Thanksgiving. Supposedly he did the same at Uncle Dave's birthday, one day after meeting you."

"I'm nervous I'll disappoint. I think Jake's gone around telling too many exaggerated stories."

"I have not," I said. "The family's only expecting the most beautiful and gracious woman, which would be you."

"Great!" This time Emily rolled her eyes. "Now I'll absolutely disappoint."

Unnecessarily, Jane retold many stories about me and Kelley, and she started telling Emily about my temperament. Like a typical younger sister, she explained only the bad side of her older brother. Emily joined the bandwagon and complained about me being a workaholic. Jane had asked her what she liked about me, and Emily was being coy with her answer.

"Tell her, Emi," I encouraged.

Her eyes glowed when she finally professed. "Jake has this amazing way of making me feel like I'm the only person in this world who matters to him. I feel incredibly special. Not only is he attentive, he's a caring and loving person."

She got it! That's exactly how I felt about her and how I'd wanted her to feel. She was the one who mattered to me. Leaning over to kiss her I whispered, "That's how I want you to feel, always."

"Thank you. I do," she responded with her own embrace.

Then I explained what I loved about my Emily. There weren't too many things I didn't love about her, but Jane reminded me we only had so much time before the opera started.

"If I had to sum up what I love most about Emily, it would be her honesty. Even though she knows it's not to her benefit, she'll still tell you what's in her heart. I know way too much about her last relationship." I shook my head in displeasure.

Emily looked mildly alarmed. "Was my honesty at lunch not to my benefit? Am I in trouble?"

It never ceased to amaze me how easily I could make her feel loved and anxious all within the same breath. Even after today, my girlfriend still couldn't convince herself that I cared for her deeply. Once again I reassured her.

"I appreciate your honesty whether or not I appreciate your answers."

Jane asked many questions about how we met and I went into our long story of the first night at the ER and the next two days we spent together.

"By the way, why are you guys going back down tonight? Jake, didn't you ask Emily if she wanted to stay the weekend?" Jane posed a question that earned her whatever she wanted for Christmas. She turned to Emily, "You should stay with us in the apartment and go down tomorrow night. We could spend another day together. Are you uncomfortable with me being in the apartment? Do you want to be alone with Jake?"

I remained quiet and deferred all answers to Emily. Tongue-tied and flustered, Emily paused...turned to me for help—I didn't help at all—then answered Jane. "Oh, no, Jane...I don't feel uncomfortable with you. Jake didn't fully explain what was happening today."

"Then you'll stay the night?" Jane sounded excited, but not nearly as excited as I was at the prospect of spending a night with Emily.

"I'd love that, Jane," Emily relented.

Reaching over to hold Emily's hand, she appeared nervous and in deep thought about something. I just tried to hold back my humongous smile, relishing spending two full days plus a night with my girlfriend.

"So, Jake, anything else you want to tell me about Emily?" Jane startled both of us.

Emily excused herself to go to the restroom, and I hugged and kissed my sister. She pushed me away with a disgusted look.

"What was that for?"

"That was my way of thanking you for getting Emily to stay the night. I asked her on Friday and she flat-out turned me down. What do you want for Christmas? I'll get you whatever you ask for." My grin traveled from ear to ear.

"You're so lame! I didn't do it for you. I want to get to know my future sister. I did it for me."

"You could see her as a part of our family too, huh? Isn't she fantastic?"

"Yeah, she's pretty great. She's so genuine and kind and very charming. I don't know why she likes someone as selfish as you."

"That's not all she is. Let me tell you some other qualities you don't know about my Emily. I love her strength. I've never met any girl who is such a survivor. She's been on her own since high school, put herself through college, and then bought and created a home all by herself. She has worked for everything she has. Nothing has been handed to her. And yet she smiles and enjoys life. Her attitude is amazing."

From the corner of my eyes, I saw Emily stop, waiting for me to finish, but also listening to what I had to say. Her once flustered composure turned dreamy, and I could see her lips curling the way only she could smile. I continued with a vow just loud enough so she could finally understand how much I loved her.

"But as strong as she appears, she's terribly tenderhearted. I think this is what makes me so enamored with her. She hurts easily, cries readily, but loves deeply. She makes me want to care for her and shelter her from anything that may harm her. I've never felt such a strong desire to protect someone as I do for Emily."

"Wow, Jake. I didn't know you had it in you to love anyone so selflessly. I'm impressed and shocked. You're not the Jake Reid I grew up with. Maybe Emily forced you to grow up." Jane chuckled.

Emily chose to ride with Jane over to the Opera House only on the condition she would ride home with me. They were going to stop by some of the stores in Union Square to pick up bare necessities for the overnight. In the meantime, I got to the venue early and thought about renting binoculars when I saw these cool binoculars with built-in extendable handles for sale. I purchased one for Emily and, after a second thought, one for Jane too.

Sitting and waiting patiently in the box, a pair of hands covered my eyes and whispered, "Guess who?"

Always playful, I matched her surprise by grappling her arms around my side and pulling her onto my lap. My lips instantaneously landed on hers to stop her loud whoop from disturbing others in their boxes. Jane made some cheeky comment but smiled watching us have fun. Emily pulled away the second I let go of my grip.

"How many times do I need to tell you I don't like PDA? It's embarrassing!" she whispered, moving to her seat.

I put my arms around her as she sat down and leaned in to her ear. "OK. We'll continue when we get home." I felt her body stiffen as I gave her one last kiss on the back of her neck.

Several times during the opera I looked over at my love to see her engrossed in the performance. When we got back to LA, I'd have to look into getting season tickets to the opera. Mesmerized and moved by the show, I waited for the tears but surprisingly, there were none. No different than the supermarket; she had no idea I was watching her more than I watched the show. Jane glanced over at us a few times and gave me an encouraging smile.

"How did you like *Carmen?*" I asked Emily on the way home.

"I loved it. Never did I think I would enjoy opera this much. It stirred my emotions in so many directions. I was sad to see it end. Most of these are stories of unrequited love, huh?"

"I guess. I've never thought of it that way. You were completely absorbed in the performance. You didn't even notice me the whole night."

"Yeah, I did. I saw you watching me more than you watched the performance. I notice a lot more than you think I do, especially where you are concerned."

I didn't mind the sound of that. She paid more attention to me than she led on.

"Did you know I was staring at you the night we met at the market?"

"Kind of, but I thought you were looking at me, not out of interest, but because you thought I was weird for staring at cereal boxes at midnight."

We both laughed. "That's not wholly incorrect."

Back at the apartment, we changed and met back in the living room. Without any prodding, Jane excused herself to make a phone call, and Emily looked tense, possibly because I looked so excited.

"So...where will you sleep tonight?" I asked. "My room, Jane's room, or alone behind door number three?" I pointed showing her where each room was located.

There was a long, unbearable silence.

"Jake, I need to tell you something."

I didn't like where this was going already. What could she possibly want to tell me in the middle of this conversation? She knew where I was headed. All she needed to do was follow.

"I guess it's time to confess since we're at this juncture. Maybe I should have told you before accepting your ring. You might have had second thoughts about wanting me as your girlfriend."

She sounded like a schoolgirl at confession again. This was definitely not going as I'd planned. "You're making me nervous; what's wrong?"

"Nothing is wrong," she kept reassuring me, but I couldn't trust her. "I want you to know that I've never, um…"

Yes? The suspense almost killed me.

"Well…I've never slept with a man before. You are literally the first man I fell asleep with earlier today, though nothing happened. I'm not planning on being with you or any man till I get married."

I processed everything she had just told me. Relieved to know I hadn't done anything wrong; confused as to how she and Max had held off for so long; happy that she had been with no one else; but chagrined realizing that she would not be with me tonight—these ideas all flashed through my head.

"You mean you and Max have never…"

"No, we've never been together in that sense."

"But how? You dated for four years." I needed to know! After this revelation, I respected Max a lot more. It couldn't have been easy watching your girlfriend hold out on you for four years.

"It was hard, but I really wanted to save myself for whomever I might end up marrying. My mom was old-fashioned and she wanted me to wait till I got married. This was a promise I made to her before she died, and I'd like to honor her wishes. Also, watching my parents love each other, I thought it would be most special with the man I'd spend the rest of my life with."

"What if that man isn't as pure as you are?" Though there weren't that many, I definitely couldn't say she would be my first. Listening to Emily's reasoning, perhaps I would have liked for her to have been my first love in that sense as well.

"That's all right. It would be most perfect if we were each other's first, but I can't expect everyone to have the same beliefs. Are you OK with my confession? I'm sorry I didn't bring it up earlier. I didn't quite know how to approach this subject. Are you upset?"

Her head fell downward, and she worried again about being in trouble. I must have done something wrong during our short relationship to cause her such alarm so easily. This needed to change somehow.

"Disappointed, yes, most definitely yes; upset, no. I guess this happily speeds up our timetable," I answered aloud. I was disappointed for tonight but glad thinking this was one more reason to ask her to marry me as soon as possible.

I kissed her good night and watched her walk into Jane's room. Frustrated, I stayed in the living room and watched ESPN. The same highlights aired half-hourly, and conversation, coupled with bouts of laughter echoed through the night from Jane's room. Somewhere between bouts of angst and frustration, I must have fallen asleep on the sofa. Darkness and the flashing of infomercials greeted my weary eyes. It was probably close to 5:00 a.m., but I washed up and decided to go for a bike ride to get rid of all this curbed energy.

Was our conversation last night a nightmare or was it a reality, I had to ask myself. Was I really to wait until we got married? I didn't want to think about this right now. I needed some fresh air. Browsing through the newspaper, I skimmed to see what was going on in the world.

"Good morning," I heard my girlfriend whisper.

"Good morning, Beautiful. Why are you up so early?"

"I can't ever sleep well outside my own bed. Are you going somewhere?" She had noticed my biking attire.

You had no problems sleeping in my arms yesterday, was what I wanted to say, but I held back. Scared but willing, Emily agreed to ride with me through the city. I didn't know if having her next to me was the best solution to relieving this tension, but knowing that she was up, I wanted to be with her.

"What do you want to eat?" Of course I knew Emily's answer.

"How about a greasy donut or an almond croissant and a latte?"

I led her out with our bikes and we headed south into the Mission District. She would love Dynamo Donuts and their Four Barrel coffee and Tartine. Who wouldn't love Tartine?

"Wait," she hollered. "You're not thinking of riding all the way into the Mission District, are you?"

"Yup, you know this town better than I thought."

"Yeah, I've been around the block a few times in this city."

Considering my angst-filled night, this was not the right euphemism to use. "Apparently you don't go all the way around the block in any city," I answered sarcastically and rode off.

Her cackle echoed half a block down as she huffed to catch up to me. Emily's response to my bitter pill fared lighthearted, as she coaxed her way toward a warmer response. I didn't know if I was capable of giving it to her. I knew I was being childish but I didn't want to accept the answer she gave me last night.

Dynamo Donuts looked like a bike-a-thon as all the cyclists had the same idea this morning. We locked up our bikes and stood in line to order.

"Which one is your favorite, Jake?" It cracked me up how excited she got over the simplest things.

"I like the maple-glazed apple bacon."

"Eew! That's my least favorite. Let's look at the chart. I wonder if they'll have banana de leche." She was too busy reading the wooden menu plaques to notice my piqued expression. "What a bummer, they don't have caramel de sel. I love that sweet and salty combo." Now she was just talking to herself. "Jake?"

"Yes?"

"Can we order one of every donut?" Her eyes popped open at the thought.

"I guess…" I answered unenthusiastically. "Go grab us a table. I'll bring everything over."

"Thank you." She beamed and kissed my cheeks.

After eating way too many donuts, we biked several blocks over to Tartine. I needed to help Emily get her almond croissant fix. Standing in line, I pouted at her confession again. In a sour tone I asked, "Do I need to buy one of everything here too?"

Emily glared at me without her usual smile. She was tired of my pouting. I could tell I was going to be in trouble.

"Jake, are you going to be upset with me every time we're in an overnight situation?"

"If I say yes, will you do something about it?" Let's see how you're going to answer that.

"Yup, I will."

"You will?" Maybe my pouting worked. She sounded like she was going to give in. YES!

"I'm going to have to make sure we are not in this situation ever again. You'll have to apologize to your parents for me and tell them I can't go to Hawaii with you."

You have got to be kidding! I put myself in a worse situation.

"Emily..." I whined. I had lost. The white flag was up.

Emily got close and gave my lips a quick peck. "Will you be OK with Hawaii or should I stay home?" She was grinning. She saw my invisible flag waving with the San Francisco wind.

Annoyed, I tried to shake free of her hands. Uncharacteristically, she grabbed me and kissed me amorously in front of a long line of people. I couldn't help it. I was a sucker for her affection. I caved and smiled.

"Jane was wrong about you. I find you adorable when you're mad." And she kissed me once more.

After taking bites of more food—a morning roll, frangipane croissant, bread pudding, and Croque Monsieur—we needed to ride off our full stomachs. I picked a long route back to the apartment and Emily bravely rode along. She didn't complain. As usual, she was a trooper. We dropped off all the food and bikes in the apartment, and I held Emily's hand over to the Ferry Building.

"Where are we going now?" She sounded tired.

"The Ferry Building—I need to buy something for today."

During my sleepless night I contemplated what I would like to do for Emily today. A picnic made the perfect sense. Watching her enjoy the oysters yesterday I thought she would like to go up to Point Reyes and eat at an oyster farm. Hopefully this would be another first for her.

"Where's the farmers' market? They have one of the best ones here."

"They don't open on Sundays," I answered.

"What a bummer."

The shopping spree began at Sur la Table with a picnic basket.

Her eyes twinkled. She looked thrilled, not to mention darling. "Are we going on a picnic?"

"Maybe you are not a part of the 'we.' Didn't you prefer Jane's company last night? I'm taking someone else on a picnic today." Regret surfaced quicker than the last two sentences. She and I both thought I had lost my five-year-old attitude back at Tartine—wrong! I needed to get back in her favor.

She quietly followed me to Miette while I bought two of every Parisian macaroon they had. Her eyes lit up immediately at the sight of this bakery when we first walked into the building. It was their featured baked good, Parisian macaron, that most likely caught her eye. I also purchased condiments for the oysters such as caviar, hot sauce, and mignonette; and other picnic items such as wine, cheese, crackers, and deli meat. Of course I couldn't forget the coffee to go with dessert.

Emily stayed uncommunicative—absolutely no expression shown—and I tried not to let this worry me as we went back to the apartment.

Jane was finally up. "Why did you guys ride this far?" she asked while noshing on all the food we brought back.

"I don't know. Ask your brother," Emily responded with a hint of anger.

Uh-oh. She was upset. I ran after Emily and grabbed her hand before she could walk into the shower.

"Are you mad?" I asked.

"Yes." Though her voice was mad, her face looked happy—almost a giggly kind of happy. I couldn't tell which one was the real Emily.

I apologized then tried to kiss her, but she moved away. I gave her a hurt expression.

"Jake. I can't be in a relationship with you if you continue to stay angry with me for not having sex with you. Here, let me give you back this ring."

She started fumbling with the lock. I guess she was serious about not having sex till she got married. Holding her hands hostage behind her back, I kissed her long and hard. We both needed air but I wouldn't let her go. Her struggles began and ended within seconds. She willingly and enthusiastically participated.

"OK, I'm sorry. I won't be upset anymore," I said in between more kisses. "But I'm still going to try to get you in bed every chance I get."

"I'd be worried if you didn't," she responded with a heavy kiss of her own.

I gave in to her purity demands...for now.

Since my "ablutions" took half the time of my girlfriend's, I packed up our picnic basket and got us ready to leave. Tenderly, Emily came up behind me, encircling her arms around my waist. Without looking, we knew each other had a smile.

"Thank you for this special weekend. You have made many of my dreams come true. You are too wonderful!"

I wanted to embrace her but Jane walked out and Emily turned to ask her if she was joining us today.

"No," Jane and I answered simultaneously. Jane didn't look happy. I didn't invite her. I didn't care.

"My old roommate, Allison, is coming over and we're going out for lunch."

"Allison?" I asked, wondering why she would be up here hanging out with Jane. I hoped I didn't have a look of guilt when I asked this question.

Emily looked at me with an inquisitive stare, and Jane gave me a peculiar one. Please, Jane, if you've figured out our connection, don't give it away to Emily, I begged in my mind.

Too late as Jane shouted, "Oh, my gosh. You didn't finally succumb to her wiles, did you? Jake! Did you two date? Did you sleep with her? You're such an idiot! No wonder she kept asking about you."

Whatever Christmas present I promised Jane—canceled! I couldn't believe she revealed my past to Emily. What would Emily think now, especially after she told me how she wanted to save herself for someone special? She might believe I went around sleeping with every girl I dated. Crap!

I kept mum to all questions and rushed Emily out the door. Aargh! There was Allison, rushing over to see me. Even with my one hand on the picnic basket and the other holding Emily's hand, Allison came and hugged me a little too longingly for comfort. If panic had yet to set in, it went into overdrive when Allison kissed me on the mouth in front of my girlfriend. Emily abruptly let go of my hand and stepped aside. My heart did a nosedive, and my sense of alarm sped out of control.

"Hello." Allison introduced herself to Emily. "I'm Allison, Jake's friend."

"Nice to meet you. I'm Emily, Jake's girlfriend." Even in the midst of this scary situation, I chuckled to myself. Emily actually had a mean side to her. She most surely told Allison who was in charge here.

"Jake. I rushed over here because I need to talk to you. Can you spare a few minutes for an old flame?" She sounded desperate.

I was about to say no when Emily whispered, "I'll see you at the car." She was graciously walking away, allowing us to talk and helping me out of this so very unnecessary ménage à trois.

As my love walked away, I turned to Allison and asked, "What is it?"

"Jake, I'm moving back to LA and was wondering if I could stay with you at your house. Would you want to be with me again?" Her tone was a lot more suggestive than her words.

"No!" I had to cut off the oxygen supply to her hope. "I'm in love with Emily. She's the girl I plan to marry, so if you'll excuse me…" With that, I left Allison and ran to the car.

I prayed Emily wasn't crying. Very slowly I opened the car door, and Emily was sitting there calmly listening to music. Her face was unreadable and her body language, unapproachable.

"I'm sorry about…"

"Don't worry about it," she cut me off.

"Don't you want to know why she was here?"

"I prefer not to know, if that's OK with you. I know you didn't live under a rock before you met me. You're thirty. I'm sure you've dated many girls before I came along. I prefer not to know what you did before us."

She sounded hurt and I too was a bit hurt she wouldn't let me explain that nothing happened. I understood what she said but the many girls I dated couldn't compare to the one man she loved enough to want to marry. I drove without saying a word.

Emily must have sensed my disappointment. She put her hand on mine. "Jake?" She tried to start up a conversation.

"Hmm?" My mood, glum, I didn't really want to talk.

"Why are you so quiet? Did I do something wrong again?"

I couldn't understand why she always thought she was in trouble with me. "Emily, why would you think you did anything wrong?" It shouldn't have, but it sounded like I was accusing her of some wrongdoing.

"Well, generally when someone stops talking to you, it's because they're upset with you. All right…let me explain why I don't want to hear about that vile woman."

That was funny. My laughter broke our solemn mood.

She started by telling me about all the disturbing thoughts that went through her mind as she was waiting for me in the car. "Watching her kiss you unsettled me to a point where my mind raced in all directions jumping to conclusions about your relationship with her, past and present. Unpleasant would be a mild way of explaining what I felt."

"This doesn't make me feel any less guilty," I told her.

"But then I thought about what you had to witness on Friday with me and Max, and I decided whatever I felt this morning couldn't have compared to what you must have felt meeting my only boyfriend of four years. So, I thought it only fair to let everything go and enjoy the rest of the day."

As expected she was thoughtful and insightful. She knew exactly how I felt when she wouldn't let me explain my side of the story. Perhaps she would understand soon how deeply I loved her and how much I wanted her to know every part of my life. Very possibly, I would confess this to her soon.

We spent a brilliant afternoon picnicking. We bought a bag of oysters, and I shucked while Emily assembled them with all the condiments we bought. We thought of Charlie and Sarah, as more than half the food we bought went uneaten. When we were done, Emily lazily sprawled out on our blanket. She looked radiant gazing at the scenery.

"What's on your mind, Beautiful?"

"Um…I was wondering whether I should kiss you."

What an odd thought. "Why would you wonder that? What's stopping you?"

"Because you kissed another woman—a vile but stunning woman—this morning."

"But I didn't kiss her! She kissed me."

"It doesn't matter. Your lips touched. They've been defiled as far as I'm concerned." She fell to her back and started laughing.

I pounced on her and covered her mouth with mine regardless of how she felt about Allison or PDA. Locked in our embrace she didn't resist. Our closeness lasted longer than I would have ever anticipated in public.

"Jake?" Eventually pulling away she called out my name with gentleness. "How did you know Parisian macarons are my favorite dessert? I don't think I ever told you this, did I?"

A bit of a random question, but I could tell this was important to her. So many times she fell into a childlike awe and wonder about my attitude and feelings for her. She still didn't get her place in my life. There was none higher than Emily on my scale of importance—apologies to my parents and siblings.

"You have this almost wistful look in your eyes when you talk about or see something you like." She looked excited when I told her this.

"That's exactly what my mom used to tell me. While you call it wistful, she called it covetous. How boring and predictable am I when you've figured me out this easily and so quickly." She sighed.

"On the contrary, I find you to be the most interesting and desirable woman I've ever met. I can't get enough of you!" I declared.

"That's only because I'm the one girl who hasn't jumped into bed with you on the first date." With that she proceeded to take a bite of each of the macarons and finish only the ones she liked.

This weekend had come and gone far too quickly, and to my chagrin, reality awaited my return to LA. Paused on the tarmac, Emily couldn't keep her eyes open. I pulled her into me and held her to sleep. While she dozed off, I finally professed what I'd been wanting to tell her all weekend.

"I love you, Emily," I whispered and kissed her off to sleep.

CHAPTER 9

Do You Love Me?

After an entire weekend with my love I got up early to visit her before heading to work. Today would probably be an insane day since the hospital left me alone all weekend. I figured Emily would be asleep and would jokingly scold me for waking her up. With a croissant and a latte, I sped to her doorstep.

Ding dong. The door opened immediately.

"Good morning, Beautiful." I planted a longing kiss on her, as it had been a whole six hours since we last saw each other. I continued my kiss even though I heard Sarah's annoying attempt to break us up.

"Hello!" Sarah demanded.

"Hey, Sarah. What are you doing here so early?"

"I was going to ask you the same thing."

"What are you both doing here at this hour?" was Emily's attempt to join in our conversation as the phone rang, and Sarah ran to answer it.

Emily wondered why I was here so soon after a date. She knew it would be a crazy day for me as well. I asked her to come by the hospital to have lunch with me since I probably wouldn't see sunlight today.

She laughed. "Oh? What time should I come by for lunch?"

I was about to give her a random time when Sarah yelled over to tell her that Max and Peter wanted to have lunch with Emily. My sour look reappeared.

With a wicked smile, Emily asked, "Well, Dr. Reid? Lunch today? I've got another offer on the table. Can you match that?"

I knew I couldn't. "No. Go ahead and have lunch with your ex. I don't know when I'll get out of surgery." After spending a wonderful weekend together, the thought of Emily being with Max bugged me.

Emily made some snide remark about not kissing Max like I had kissed Allison and sent me off for the day. My mood spiraled south.

My day at the hospital was worse than expected. I was thrown into surgery then went to assist the chief with his operation. When I got out, it was almost 1:00 p.m. Work kept me so busy, I actually forgot about Emily. I wondered if she was still at lunch. I texted her.

Are you done with lunch yet? You did keep your promise with Max?

She answered immediately.

What promise? I didn't make you or Max any promises, did I?

She loved toying with my emotions. I was definitely the weaker link.

Yes, you did! You weren't going to allow him anywhere near you.

Well, he picked me up, drove me to lunch, and is now sitting next to me. Does that break my promise to you?

Are you kidding me? was what I wanted to write. Instead I wrote,

Emily! This isn't funny. You're torturing me.

I'm not the one who kissed another woman in the middle of our weekend together.

I would live to hear this story the rest of my life.

I thought you said you're going to let that one go. I promise! I didn't kiss her back. When will lunch be over? You want to come visit me at the hospital?

I don't know when lunch will be over and, no, I don't want to go to the hospital anymore. After the ER incident, I'm afraid of doctors now. Everyone at my table is giving me an unpleasant look because I'm ignoring them while texting you. Come over tonight and I will consider whether I want to kiss you since you've now reminded me of Allison. I have to go. Bye.

"Jake." I turned to see the chief calling me. "David is coming by in a few minutes. You want to have lunch with us?"

"Sure. Where are we going?"

The chief's phone rang. "Let's go," he said, "David's outside."

Uncle Dave picked us up and we arrived at the dim sum restaurant and found Mom and Dad waiting for us as well.

"Hi, Mom. Hi, Dad."

"Hello, Son, long time no see. How was your weekend?" Mom asked with a knowing smile.

"You didn't talk to Jane yet?" I answered.

"We talked to her last night, but I thought I'd get your version as well." Mom smiled again.

"I heard you dropped a pretty penny at French Laundry," Uncle Dave added to our conversation. "Thomas Keller told me you added every supplemental item to your meal. I assume you enjoyed it?" He too had a knowing smile.

"So obviously, you all know I had a good weekend. What answers are you exactly looking for?"

The chief also joined in. "So is she still the one after two full days together? You've never once spoken of marriage till this Emily came along."

"She is most definitely the one! This weekend only solidified what I already knew."

The dim sum cart started coming around and everyone began picking their favorites. I saw my mom choose the shrimp and scallop har gow; Uncle Dave picked out the pan-fried dumplings; Dad decided on the siu mai, and the chief picked Chinese broccoli and shrimp rolls. I picked a deep-fried pork dumpling, and I thought of how much Emily would have enjoyed having lunch with us. There wouldn't have been anything she didn't like at our table.

"So what makes her the one? After years with Kelley, you never mentioned marrying her. Were you too young back then?" This time my dad wanted to know.

Considering how close we were as a family, it was only fitting that every Reid expressed not only curiosity, but also concern about my relationships.

"Dad, when you meet her, you'll understand. She is such a sweet person. She's honest and open and down to earth. She's had a tough life. Her dad died when she was thirteen and her mom followed him when Emily was only seventeen. At times, I see signs of loneliness and sadness, but rather than being down on life, she's playful and affectionate and heartfelt. I can't get enough of this girl."

"Does she feel as strongly about you?" That was a legitimate question from Uncle Henry.

"Not yet, I don't think. Because she's been alone for so long, I think she wants to lean on someone entirely but is also afraid to do so. She told me this weekend she felt abandoned by her parents for leaving her so early." I decided to leave out the part about Max and their four years together. This wasn't something I wanted anyone to know since it wasn't important to her or me.

I saw my mom start to tear. "How heartbreaking to lose not just one parent but both of them so early in life. I will definitely dote on her when I meet her in Hawaii." Knowing Mom, she would most assuredly do so. "Jane called to say Emily was wonderful. She told me they made a pact to be sisters regardless of what happens to your relationship."

"I guess we have a new Reid in the family. We can't wait to meet her next week," Uncle Dave declared as we finished up lunch.

The rest of the day flashed by. When I got to Emily's doorstep it was already midnight. The lights were off but I couldn't resist seeing her. I had missed her all day.

Ding dong. The lights turned on like a domino effect—the family room, the kitchen, the dining room to the living room.

Incredibly excited to see my love, I wanted to hug and kiss her the moment I saw her. Instead I was shocked to see Emily's face.

"What's the matter, Emily? Have you been crying?"

"How'd you know?" Her face looked even more surprised than mine.

"Your eyes are puffier than a marshmallow. Why were you crying?" We walked hand in hand, and while I went off to the couch, she went to look at her eyes in the mirror.

"Does this have something to do with your lunch with Max today?" I knew her meeting with Max would be a bad idea. I hoped he didn't undo all our progress this weekend. "Do you mind telling me what happened?"

Without missing any detail, she told me Max regretted breaking up with my girlfriend when she was his girlfriend. When I asked her how she felt about Max's regret, she gave me all the right answers, but I still couldn't understand why she had cried.

"If you don't want a relationship with Max and it is me you want, why were you crying?"

She was at a loss for words. Thinking about this for a few seconds, she answered, "I cried because a lot of the pain I felt after we broke up resurfaced. Those were the words I wanted to hear eighteen months ago, not now. Maybe I was angry at him for…"

"Waiting this long?" I finished her sentence. "Do you want to get back together with him but can't because of me? Am I in your way?"

What possessed me to ask these questions and leave the balance of our relationship up to her was beyond me. I guess I needed to know her answer.

"No! I want to be with you, Jake." She hugged me tenaciously, body shaking. "Please don't think that. Please, please believe me when I tell you how much I cherish our relationship."

With such ardor, I was happy to have asked my questions. I brought her close to me and attempted to understand her.

"Emily, explain to me what's on your mind. There must be something lingering in your heart for Max for you to be in such anguish."

"To be honest, I don't exactly know what hold Max still has on me, if any. I know there's no more connection between us, but why I still hurt so much when he brings up the past, I can't explain." She looked guilty again. "I'm sorry I'm such a mess. This is the kind of stuff I don't want you to see. What I do know is that in the short while we've been together, you're the one I want to be with, not Max."

I decided at this point it was time to tell her how deeply I felt. I'd held back as long as I could. "Emily, I'm not letting you go anywhere. We are not separating for any reason. I can't imagine my life without you anymore and I hope you feel the same way about me. You must know by now how much I love you. I can't believe I've waited this long to tell you."

I saw more signs of hesitation.

"And by the look on your face you don't quite reciprocate?" I asked to be sure.

"Jake, I'm not there just yet," she answered half shrugging her shoulders.

"Emily, are you really not there? I think you're just afraid to admit it."

"To me, when I tell someone I love them, it's a forever kind of word. I can't take it lightly. Forever is not in my vocabulary just yet with us."

I got angry again. "Why do you keep saying that? Didn't you tell Max you loved him? Why are you so negative about us all the time? Do you think I take the words 'I love you' lightly? The words 'love' and 'flippant' do not coexist in my vocabulary either. This appears to be a weekly argument with us."

"I'm sorry, Jake." She had a coquettish but apologetic smile as she sat on my lap and put her arms around my neck. "Can we not argue about this again? Just give me a little more time? Please?" She had perfected the art of flirting with my hope.

"You can't admit you love me and you refuse to have sex with me. Why am I still here with you?"

"Because you love me." She answered before propositioning my lips.

The next day I stopped by with breakfast but had to leave within minutes when I got paged. I came back fairly late in the evening to find dinner waiting for me.

"What's for dinner?"

"Spaghetti, chopped salad, and garlic toast."

"That smells good! I brought a cheesecake for dessert." I held up the bag to show her. "Should I put it in the fridge?"

"Uh-huh. Can you get out the iced tea I put in there? Dinner's ready. Let's eat."

"How was your day?" Emily asked nonchalantly not realizing how much she sounded like a wife asking her husband about his day.

I delighted in her question and forgot to answer.

"Are we not talking tonight?" She stared at me.

"My day started off intense but slowed down after lunch. What did you to all day?"

"I did just about nothing. I read a book, went grocery shopping and made dinner. I think I could live like this for a while."

"Me too," I answered but she didn't understand my comment.

"Jake…" It was never a good sign when she dragged my name. Either I was in trouble, or she needed to confess something. "Can I ask you something that's been bothering me since I saw Allison this weekend?"

"You're not going to bring up the kiss again, are you?"

"No, not this time."

"Then what's bothering you?" I tried to think through all the things Allison said and did while Emily was present. There wasn't much else that happened, I didn't think.

"Well…"

"Emi, just spit it out."

"Well…when I met Allison, I noticed she had a similar…never mind. I'm being silly. Finish your dinner. Let's talk about something else."

I dropped my fork. "I'm not eating anymore till you finish your thought. What is it?"

She hesitated for a long while then tried again. "I noticed Allison had a similar ring as mine and I wondered if you had given that to her." Her head dropped immediately. I just hoped she wasn't crying.

"Emily, what ring? I didn't give her any ring." Furiously I searched my brain for a mental picture of Allison's finger that morning. I also did a quick jog through my memory to make sure I hadn't given her anything that significant.

My girlfriend didn't look convinced.

"It's OK if you have." She tried to backpedal. "I don't mind." Obviously she did. "I shouldn't have asked. Sorry…"

"Emi, I promise you, I haven't given her any gifts. I don't know what ring she had on, but it wasn't from me."

"OK." She answered and took a big awkward bite of her spaghetti.

"You don't believe me, huh? I promise, it wasn't from me."

Emily didn't say anything but continued eating.

"All right, let me tell you about all the girls I've dated and what I've given to each one of them so you will believe me when I tell you I've given no girl a ring in my life but you. You are the only one."

Comically, Emily's eye bulged and she cringed at the can of worms she'd opened. Purposely and tediously I named every girl I'd "dated," even the ones I had a crush on in elementary school, and told Emily about each and every gift a girl or woman got from me. It started with the girl in first grade who received a pink pencil from me all the way to Kelley who received several Tiffany trinkets, to books to a trip to Mexico. I gave the names of all the other women I'd gone on a date with and where we went and what we did, to the best of my memory. For the sake of our relationship, I didn't outline all that I had done on my dates and filled in the blanks to some I really couldn't remember.

"OK! OK! I'm sorry. I believe you. I don't need to hear any more. It's not that I didn't believe you the first time, I felt stupid having asked that question. I was jealous."

"No, I think you need to hear more." I punished her with copious details, many of which were unnecessary but made my adventures even more drawn out. Toward the end of the story, all Emi could do was laugh. I had made my point. She conceded a loss.

"You can be so mean sometimes," she accused.

"Oh, you charge me with giving Allison the same ring you have on and tell me I'm the one who's being mean?"

"I'm sorry. How can I make this up to you?" The banter began again.

"Will you let me stay the night?"

She gave me a "seriously" look.

"I'll sleep in the guest room. Just let me stay here tonight."

"I think it's time for you to leave." Emily got up and started clearing the dishes. "We'll have the cheesecake tomorrow night. Will you be back?"

"Can I stay tomorrow night?" I didn't let up.

She shook her head no again then grabbed my hand and led me to the door.

"What time is your surgery tomorrow morning?"

"Early. I won't stop by in the morning but I'll be home early as well." I wondered if she caught the word home as I referred to it as our home. I was sure she did but pretended not to have heard it.

"Good night." She tiptoed to give me a peck on the lips.

I caught the peck and responded with lust of my own.

The day started before the sun was up and I didn't get to communicate with Emily till about noon. I called but she didn't pick up her phone so I sent her a text.

Hello, Beautiful. What are you up to?

I could never understand why she texted back so quickly but wouldn't pick up the phone.

I'm having lunch with Sarah. What time will you come over tonight?

Probably around 4:00. Tell Sarah I said hello. I miss you.

Will do. If you get there before I do use the spare key by the back door. Miss you too.

I got to Emily's earlier than expected and found her car but no one to open the door. Possibly Sarah had picked her up and they weren't back from lunch yet. I went around back and walked in using her spare key. Setting the key on her coffee table, I looked into Emily's bedroom and found her taking a nap. Unable to resist, I gingerly walked over and crawled into bed with her. She didn't feel my weight on the bed but quickly froze in fear when I curved my arm around her waist from behind.

"It's only me," I answered with kisses to the back of her head.

"You scared me," she complained turning around.

Rather than pushing me off the bed as I had expected, she curled herself into my body and fell back asleep. We napped till the sun had long gone down and our stomachs started grumbling.

"You want to go out and grab a bite to eat?" I asked her as she stayed comfortably in my arms.

"No. Let me make us dinner." I was sorry I asked. She got up, went into the kitchen and in the blink of an eye, pulled together a salad.

"What did you make so quickly?"

"It's a shrimp and crab Louie salad. I had all the ingredients prepared. I just needed to assemble it." She poured Thousand Island dressing on both our salads and I happily ate.

"Should we go watch a movie tonight?" I asked.

"What time to do you need to get into the hospital tomorrow?"

"I got in early today. I don't start till 9:00 tomorrow. We can hang out tonight."

"OK, but no movie. Maybe we can go rent a movie instead. I feel lazy. I don't want to go anywhere. Let's just hang out here."

"Sounds good. How was lunch with Sarah? What did you eat today?"

"Sarah had some project near downtown so we ate at Langers. I had a pastrami sandwich craving."

These cravings had helped us meet so I was always happy to hear about them. I got up and cleared our dishes and we sat comfortably in her living room without any agenda. As always, I enjoyed my time with her.

"Emily, I'd love to hear more about your parents. Will you tell me about them?"

"You want to hear about them?" She sounded thrilled. I would have asked sooner if I'd known it would make her this happy.

She ran over to get photo albums, and she plopped on the floor ready to begin her journey. She started with pictures of her parents when they were in college.

"Your mom was stunning!" I blurted out.

"I know, isn't she beautiful?" she answered wistfully. "When I was younger, I used to hate it when people told me how pretty she was. Unfortunately I didn't really appreciate her till I got older."

"Why would you hate someone telling you your mom was beautiful?"

"Because I was jealous. No one ever said anything remotely complimentary about me. The comment I got repeatedly was, 'I hope you grow up to look just like your mom.' It bugged me. Plus, my mom had such a vibrant personality, and I was so shy. She was always the life of the party and I was the wallflower in the corner."

"Love, girls don't come much prettier than you...even your mom," I reassured her.

"You wouldn't be saying that if you'd seen my mom in person."

"I'd say it regardless. So how'd your dad get so lucky?"

Emily started cracking up. "Oh, my gosh, that's such a funny story. My dad told me when Mom got to college, she was the talk of her Texas campus. Every guy wanted to date her. She was in some sorority and every frat and non-frat guy had visited her house to ask her out."

"So did your parents meet at a frat party?"

"No, my dad was the antithesis of my mom. He was awkward and extremely shy. He was a senior when Mom was a freshman, and they only became friends because she needed help in calculus and he was her school-appointed tutor. He tutored my mom her entire freshman year."

Emily flipped through many more pages of the photo album. "She was really beautiful, huh?" She spoke rhetorically and sadly touched her mother's face.

"So my mom was dating some hotshot guy on campus but spending loads of time with my dad, because her math skills were so pathetic, and they developed a friendship during these tutorial sessions. My dad was probably one of the very few men who was more attracted to my mom's heart than her face. Do you know what he told me he loved most about her?"

"What did he love most about her?" How could he choose just one or two qualities? I could sit here all day and count the ways I loved my Emily.

"My dad said that Mom was the most caring and attentive person he'd ever met. Every time they were together, she'd bring him a little something to thank him for working with her. She'd bring him lunch if it was lunchtime or a piece of chocolate she knew he liked, or she'd buy him poetry books. My dad was a bit of a poet. He devoured the attention. Oh my gosh…"

"What?" She looked like she'd just had an epiphany.

"I'm dating my mother. You remind me exactly of my mom. You're both attentive and outgoing and exceedingly sure of yourselves. Oh gosh…" She trailed and went into her own thoughts one more time.

"What?" I asked again.

"Max was the epitome of my dad—shy, reserved, and gentle. How sad. I miss my parents so badly, I need to date people who remind me of them." Emily shook herself out of her thought and continued with her story.

"So all this time, my dad loved my mother but didn't do anything about it."

"Was your mom into your dad also?"

"I asked that same question, and they both said no. She was dating someone else, but she said she always thought of my dad as a dear friend."

"So how did they get together if she was dating someone else?"

"When school ended, my mom was driving home to LA and about an hour away from school, she got a flat tire. She said the first and only person she thought to call was not her boyfriend but my dad. She knew then he was the man she loved and trusted to take care of her. Of course my dad came to her immediately upon receiving the call."

"And that's how they got together?"

"Kind of…remember how I told you my dad was terribly shy?"

"Uh-huh."

"Well, Mom knew he liked her but wouldn't admit it unless something extreme happened. So when he got to my mom, she ran to him and hugged him as if he had rescued her from death." Emily proceeded to guffaw. I watched and waited for her laughter to die down. "She embraced him dearly and started confessing her feelings. My dad, being in a state of shock, didn't say a word but tried to pry her body off him."

She looked at me and added, "You know, they were in the middle of the 10 freeway and cars were honking everywhere."

"Did she let go of him?"

"Nope. My mom told me she held onto him till he was forced to confess his feelings for her. You want to know what else she forced him to do?"

I shook my head no.

"He was about to go off to grad school, and she didn't want to be separated from him, so she got him to propose to her and tied him down all within the same hug. Isn't that insane?"

"Lucky guy! Could something like that happen with you?"

"I doubt it. I'm not brave like my mom. She always knew what she wanted and she went after it till it was hers. Strong and secure would be the two words I'd use to describe her. She rarely wavered. I, on the other hand, take too much after my dad. I'm introverted and insecure. Even if I want something, I probably won't out right tell anyone. It can be a bit of a guessing game with me."

"So when did your parents get married?"

"They got married that summer. Mom transferred schools and finished undergrad while she was married to my dad."

"You mean she got married when she was eighteen?"

"Just about...I think she turned nineteen right before her wedding day. Here are their wedding photos."

Emily's mom looked radiant in her wedding dress. I imagined us in this photo and how beautiful my bride would be on our wedding day. I only needed to convince her that this was our future together.

"That's a great story. So when were you born?"

"The day after my mom graduated from college. She was a balloon at her graduation. Look at her." Emily pointed to her pregnant mom with her cap and gown.

"When I was young, I was painfully shy just like my dad. My mom thought she could turn me into a mini-me but failed miserably. She couldn't understand why I didn't want people giving me any attention or why I couldn't speak my mind. The only person who really understood me was my dad. He knew exactly how I felt, because he felt the same way."

"But you're not shy now, although I suppose you get embarrassed easily."

"That only happened after my dad died. My dad and I were really close. When I was younger, I was probably closer to my dad than my mom. I was unusually small for my age and my dad carried me around like a little child till I was seven. He understood my need to be alone and my fear of unwanted attention. He showered me with love and affection and protected me from all my insecurities."

The tears finally appeared. I'd expected them much earlier. She had held off a long while, for her standards.

"Then he died when I was in eighth grade, and his death devastated me. My mom and I had both lost the love of our lives and our best friend. This was also when I started to finally grow and develop physically. I was a mess in every way when I got to my grandparents' home in LA."

She worked to hold back her tears so she could finish her story.

"When we got to LA, my mom went through bouts of depression and it terrified me. I forced myself to come out of my shell and tried to be everything my mom wanted me to be—cheerful, lively, and strong. She did her best to stay content, and this was when she and I bonded. Even with my grandparents around, we felt like we had no one but each other. Rather than spending time with friends after school, I spent time with my mom. She told me everything she could about Dad up to when my memory clicked and I shared about all my days with Dad when it was just the two of us. She had become my love and my new best friend. Then she died the end of my junior year a few days before my birthday."

At this point Emily couldn't hold back. I held her and let her cry. Her body convulsed, she wailed painfully then sobbed softly. There was no way I could erase this pain for her. I realized tonight no matter how much love I gave her, this pain would never go away.

"A year later, Max came into my life and soon became my best friend, my love, and my only family. Four years later, I lost him too. My heart's been severely broken three times. I don't think I can stand another heartbreak. That's why I'm so cautious with us. I'm sorry I frustrate you, but do you think you can be even more understanding of me than you've already been and allow me to move at my own pace? I know I'm being unfair to you, but this is the only way I can be in a relationship right now."

What could I say to her? I finally understood her. It really wasn't me, it was her.

"Emily, I love you regardless of how fast or slow our relationship has progressed. I am happy to do what you've asked if you will promise to do one thing for me."

She looked up at me, wondering what that one thing would be.

"Promise me you will stop looking at me as the one who will break your heart but try to accept me as your new best friend, your eternal love, and the one who wants to create a family with you. That's what I want to be for you."

She nodded her head and agreed.

"By the way," I added, "when's your birthday?" How ridiculous I didn't even know my girlfriend's birth date.

"May twentieth," she answered.

"No way!" I said in amazement. "My birthday is May nineteenth."

"Are you kidding me? We have almost the same birthday. How fun!" So childlike, her mood changed from crying to laughing within a sentence.

"We'll celebrate our birthdays together and for two full days, OK?"

She shook her head yes again.

It was time for me to leave my tenderhearted girlfriend. As usual, my entire being wanted to settle right here in her house for good.

"Can I stay tonight?"

Emily shook her head no.

"Please? I want to be with you tonight. We don't have to do anything. Let me just hold you."

Her head shook no, but I saw hesitation written all over her face. Her guard was coming down and she was falling my way.

"Jake, it's never been so hard for me to say no but I have to do it. This is a promise I made to myself as well as to my mom."

"But we won't do anything but sleep." I started building my case.

"It may start off that way, but you know that's not where it will end. I'm not as strong as you think I am. Look at me earlier today. With you already in my bed, I happily curled up in your arms and slept. I shouldn't have done that."

"But, Emily...I'll be strong for both of us."

She laughed. "Yeah, right! Like you'll be able to fight me off if I decide to take advantage of you." She cackled at the thought. "I'm going to the movies with Sarah tomorrow night so I won't see you unless it's really late."

"All right. I'll call when I'm done and we can decide what to do. Goodbye, My Love."

"Good night, Jake."

Thursday proved to be a difficult day to see each other.

Good morning, Love. Would you like me to stop by with breakfast?

Good morning. No, I'm still sleeping. Sarah called after you left and we talked till very late last night or better said, early this morning. I don't want to get out of bed.

What did you talk about for so long?

You.

What about me?

Aren't you late for work? We'll talk later. I want to sleep.

Can't I stop by?

Then I have to get out of bed and be somewhat ready to see you. I'll see you later. Have a wonderful day. I'll be thinking of you in my sleep.

That could be construed in a naughty way.

Only by you…good-bye!

    I got to another full day at work. The chief and I lunched together in the cafeteria and quickly got back to a couple of afternoon surgeries. The second surgery I assisted for the chief took much longer than expected, and by the time I got out of the hospital, it was way past midnight. As much I wanted to see Emily, I had to go home and pick up more clothes to bring back to Mom's. With no basic clothing left, laundry was calling my name.

I just got out of work and need to stop by my house in the Valley to pick up some clothes. What are you doing?

I got in about an hour ago from dinner and a movie with Sarah. Does someone live in your house in the Valley?

Yup, I have roommates who haven't seen me in a couple of months because of you.

These roommates aren't women, are they? Is that why we always hang out at my house? You've never taken me to your house. Should I be worried? Allison doesn't live there, does she?

Oh there it was again. I thought we had gone a few days without talking about Allison.

Think what you like. I'm not going to answer any of your questions.

You can be so mean! I guess I won't see you for a while. I'm not letting you into my house till I get an explanation on your house.

I love you!

Oh like I believe that now. Good night.

Friday and Saturday, Emily and I didn't see each other because the chief decided to take a few days off before I went on my vacation. Being so busy, I didn't see much beyond the hospital walls. I texted Emily when I could but even that wasn't very often.

Hi, Sweetheart, what are you up to? I miss you.

Hi! I'm having dinner with Sarah, Charlie, and Peter.

Oh? What did you do all day?

Waited around for you to call or possibly stop by. I thought maybe we could have lunch together.

Why didn't you send me a message? I would have come over for a short while. I thought you were busy today since I didn't hear from you.

You seemed so busy. I didn't want to bother you. When are you done tonight? Can you stop by? I miss you a lot.

I won't be done till really late but I'm off as of tomorrow. I'll stop by after checking on my patients. We'll have tomorrow till Thursday together. I can't wait.

Me neither. I have to go. My friends are upset again. They're so sensitive, huh? By the way, the answer to the question you're dying to ask but haven't is no. Max is with his family tonight. Bye.

I love you!

My vacation officially began Sunday. Since the chief wasn't around, I still stopped by the hospital and checked on all the patients before going by Emily's home. No surprise, she opened her door dressed in pajamas looking groggy.

"How do you function on so little sleep?" Emily asked while getting ready for our day.

"I've never needed much sleep. I can do fine on three to four hours a day." I comfortably sprawled on her bed and watched TV. "What shall we do today?"

Emily pondered what to do.

"Emi? What are some things you've always wanted to do?"

"What do you mean?" she sounded confused.

"You know, like if money were no object or in your wildest dreams you'd like to…"

"Like a bucket list? Aren't I a little too young for a bucket list?"

I gave her a stern look. "Emily Logan, your list."

After a few minutes she answered.

"#1—I want to hear Andrea Bocelli sing in some outdoor stadium in the hills of Tuscany.

#2—I want to take a series of cooking classes in Italy, France, or Japan.

#3—I want to climb all the steps of Machu Picchu.

#4—I want to eat a formal Kaiseki meal in Japan.

#5—I also want to go on a dining spree in Spain.

#6—I want to live in New York City for a while.

#7—I want to spend a few nights in a hut in the middle of some island—like the ones you see in travel magazines.

#8—I want to learn to ballroom dance,
#9—I want to go on one of those trips with that chef Anthony Bourdain.
#10—I want to be a judge on Iron Chef."

None of those seemed too difficult for me to do for her except for #9 and 10.

"I have one more; #11, I want to picnic at the Tuileries Garden with someone I'm madly in love with."

Another wish that could easily be granted. Now that I knew all the things she wanted to accomplish, I would start going down her list. First, I'd take her to Europe and we could cross off numbers 1, 2, 5, and 11. That was half the list. After Hawaii, I'd beg the chief to let me off for a couple of weeks in late spring and surprise my love with a European trip. Maybe I could propose to her there.

"Jake...Jake!"

"Huh?"

"What are you thinking about? I was asking you if we can go shopping today. I still haven't bought your mom a gift. You have to help me buy something for her."

I told Emily about Mom's obsession with clocks. No matter where we traveled, Mom always came back with a clock. It was a good thing her house was big; otherwise, it would look like a clock museum.

We walked through a flea market and Emily was on a mission to find the perfect clock for Mom. Mom would be touched Emily cared enough to buy her a present. Jane's glowing report of Emily compounded with my confessions of love, Mom and Dad already loved this girl as their own daughter. I couldn't wait to introduce them.

"I just realized, the two months we've been dating, you've never met my parents or Nick."

"Nope, I haven't."

"How did that happen? Why didn't I take you over to meet my parents? You live minutes from their house."

"I don't know. I thought perhaps you were embarrassed to introduce me to them." She tried to keep her face still but couldn't help a mischievous grin. "You've never taken me out for sushi either, and that's my favorite meal. I had to go with Sarah the other night because I craved it."

"Let's go have sushi and meet my parents."

At dinner I asked Emily to tell me more about her years with her family. Though I knew it was a sad topic for her, I was curious about the family I would never meet. Coming from such a large family, I couldn't imagine being completely alone. I figured Emily would have some aunts and uncles or at least cousins her age. Sadly, she told me her parents were only children and since her grandparents' death four and five years ago, she'd been alone every holiday.

"So after your mom and grandparents died, who did you spend your holidays with?"

She stared at me, not with tears, but with a wondrous look of love and appreciation. She understood why I was asking these questions, and she tried her best to placate my hurt for her.

"I spent a few holidays with Max's family and a few with Sarah's family. One Christmas, both Max and Sarah were out of town visiting relatives, so I spent it alone. That was a sad Christmas."

My heart broke. Loneliness marked her big brown eyes, yet her concern was still for me. She smiled and made light of her situation. "I sound so pathetic, huh?"

She fed me a bite of her dessert—a feeble attempt to gloss over both our sadness. I couldn't believe she had gone through so many painful days before we met. I reached over and held her hand.

"Oh, my sweet Emily...My Love...I hate thinking about you being alone. I wish we could've met earlier. I would've filled your void." I vowed to her and myself, "I won't ever let you be alone again."

After dinner, we called my parents but they weren't around so I dropped off Emily at home and we separated, knowing we would be back together for four straight days.

CHAPTER 10

Is This Heaven on Earth?

"I'm around the corner…" I said on the phone to Emily.

"Great!" She sounded extra cheerful.

Right as I got to her house, she was waiting on the sidewalk with one compact suitcase.

"Hi, Beautiful." Greeting her with my usual enthusiasm, she reached up and kissed me hello in return. "You're in a good mood."

"Why wouldn't I be? I get to spend four days with you and your family. After Christmas who knows when I'll see you again? It may be months before we get another chance like this."

She wasn't completely incorrect.

At the airport, without any prompting, Emily went and hugged Mom, Dad, and Nick, introduced herself during the embrace, and thanked them for inviting her on our trip. By my family's huge grins, I could tell they welcomed her immediately.

Nick came over to me while grabbing our bags and whispered, "You weren't kidding when you said she was hot. She's gorgeous."

"I know, isn't she? She's just as beautiful on the inside too. I think Mom and Dad like her already."

We looked over to see the three of them talking and laughing about something. Emily glanced over at me and winked.

We landed in Maui and met Jane at the hotel. Jane and Emily went to get settled in their room, and I stopped by their room after Nick and I had unpacked.

"Are you ready for our first excursion?"

Emily nodded her head. "Where are we going?"

"You'll see." I grinned. "Let's go."

Emily's eyes popped at the sight of the helicopter waiting to take us on a tour of Maui.

"I've never been on a helicopter before. I've actually never been to Hawaii. This is so exciting," she whispered into my ear.

On the helicopter, no different from the opera, I enjoyed watching Emily's wide-eyed expression more than the view itself. She seemed most in awe with all the waterfalls we passed over. We'd have to go swim near a waterfall, if that was what she enjoyed the most. I held her close to me the whole ride, and I could sense Mom watching us with a smile. Knowing my abundant love for this girl, Mom couldn't help but love her as well.

Emily took off her headset and pushed mine back to whisper another message into my ear. "Watch the view...you see me all the time."

I kissed her and confessed, "I'd rather watch you."

She smiled.

At lunch, Emily sat next to Mom and Jane and they talked feverishly about taking a girls' ski trip up to Mammoth before Emily's and Jane's vacations were done. I thought about protesting a girls-only trip but let it alone, as I'm sure Mom and Jane both wanted to get closer to my love.

"Emily, Jake tells me you're a foodie. Do you want to pick out some restaurants with me to try out during our stay here? We can't eat hotel food the whole time." Nick brought up Emily's favorite conversation.

"I'd love to! Did you bring any guides or should we look it up online?"

"Let's stop by a bookstore and do some research."

"Sounds great. I'll talk to the hotel concierge as well. That sounds like fun. What's next on the agenda?" Emily asked Mom.

"We have a tour guide waiting for us to take us on a hike. Did you bring walking shoes?"

"Yes. I'll go change into them right now."

We walked to Emily's room and she couldn't stop smiling.

"Why are you so happy today? Is there something other than what you told me this morning?"

She shook her head no. "I'm happy to be a part of a family, especially your family." That statement should have made me happy but instead it grieved my heart thinking about Emily's not having had a family for so long.

"What's the matter?" she asked, seeing the change of expression on my face.

"Nothing. You should hurry. Everyone's waiting for us."

We went on a long hike that led to a dormant volcano, then went snorkeling for half of us and scuba diving for the other half. I got scuba lessons for Emily so she could eventually dive with me on our next water vacation. By the end of her lesson, she looked exhausted.

"I need a nap," she lamented in the ocean.

"We can go back and take one—your bed, my bed or the cabana?"

"At this point, I'll take anything. I never exercise so today was too strenuous for me. Can we rest before dinner?"

I was thrilled to take a nap with her—assuming it was her plan to sleep with me. We ran into Mom and Jane at the hotel, and they talked Emily into going to yoga with them. There was regret in her eyes when we parted. I ended up surfing with Nick and Dad.

"Your mom and I really like Emily. You weren't exaggerating one bit about her." Dad was always on the encouraging side. He tried to find the positive in every situation and the good in every person.

"Thanks, Dad. I can't explain how much I love this girl. I could spend every day, all day with her and it still wouldn't be enough. Would you and Mom be fine with having Emily as a daughter-in-law?"

"Son, if you love her, we love her too. We would welcome her as a daughter."

"Me too, I'd take Emily as a sister any day. She's so cool not to mention drop-dead gorgeous."

"I'm going to go meet Emily. She should be done with yoga. What time is the luau?

"It's at eight," Dad answered.

"See you there."

I chuckled to see Emily walking out of the yoga room completely drained. She fell into my arms, and I took her back to her room.

"I'm so tired," she complained falling onto the sofa. "What time is dinner?"

"You have an hour. Do you want to take a nap?"

"No, it's not long enough. I need to get ready for dinner. My body is salty from the ocean and gross from all the sweat. Will you come back for me in thirty minutes? I'm going to try to take a shower if I don't fall asleep right here."

"Sure. I'll shower and get dressed as well."

Jane opened the door for me when I got back and Emily was lying on the sofa watching TV.

"I think she's asleep," Jane whispered.

"I'm not," Emily whispered back. "I haven't moved since you left me, Jake."

I sat and placed her head on my lap. "Do you want to skip the luau? I'll let everyone know you're too tired."

"No, I want to be there. I'll get up and change. Just give me a few more minutes. Jane, aren't you tired?"

"A little sore from yoga but I feel fine."

"You must be in great shape. My body will not function properly tomorrow at the rate I'm going."

Always the trooper, Emily smiled through dinner, answered everyone's questions, and participated happily.

"Hey, Emily, do you like the food here?" Nick started his food conversation again.

She shook her head no. "There are lots of choices but nothing to really choose. Everything tastes mediocre."

"I agree. What should we eat for lunch tomorrow?"

"Do you think we can go out of the hotel and eat?" Emily addressed both of us.

"Let's do that. Hotel food is so boring. I'll see what my parents have planned for tomorrow and I'll let you know at breakfast."

"That sounds great." Then she turned to me and spoke softly, "I think I need to go sleep. Is it all right if I leave now? The show is over, right?"

"I'll go with you, Love."

"I can go by myself. Why don't you stay with your family a bit longer?" She tried to encourage me.

"Are you kidding? I'm just as wiped out as you are. Nick made me go surfing while you were at yoga."

Emily went over to Mom and Dad and thanked them for today's activities and hugged them good night. I hastily told Jane to go grab her stuff out of her room and sleep with Nick.

"Does Emily know about this? I don't think she's planning on being your roommate tonight."

"Just do as I tell you. She's going to be too tired to fight me tonight." I grinned.

"You're pathetic!" she answered and left to do as I asked.

I had an elaborate plan of all the reasons why we should spend the night together and rehearsed my argument while Emily was in the shower. Next thing I knew, I woke up to light kisses on my lips. This was my chance. I abandoned my speech and pulled her into bed with me.

"Jake. Please get up and go to bed."

"I am in bed."

"No, your own bed!"

I held her tighter and knew she was accepting the inevitable. Her body didn't put up any resistance.

"Love, let's just sleep like this." I started kissing her lips so she couldn't argue.

"My hair is still wet, and your sister will be here any minute now," she answered when my lips traveled down.

I sent Jane a text signaling a thumbs-up and told Emily, "It's done. Now sleep here with me just the way you are and let's talk tomorrow morning. I am very tired." Her verbal fight ended, and we spent a wonderful night together—though all we did was sleep.

My eyes rudely opened when I felt Emily pull herself away from my body, so I complained. "Emi...come back to bed. It was amazing being in bed with you the whole night. Let's stay a little longer."

She wouldn't fall for the complaint or the begging that came after. She forced me to go get ready and within minutes, we went downstairs to breakfast. I saw my family's smiling faces and Emily's embarrassed one. I smiled right along with my family to Emily's annoyance. I'd have to try spending the next two nights with her as well.

Breakfast, a basketball game—one where Emily couldn't let herself root for our team—lunch, scuba diving, and surfing, I had to take my girlfriend away or she would collapse. I rented a cabana and took her in to take a nap.

"I thought you were going to let me take a nap," Emily complained when I scooted her to the edge of her lounge chair to lay down with her.

"I'm helping you take a nap." I grinned mischievously, letting her use my arm as a pillow.

Before she could answer, I showered her face with a barrage of kisses. Her weak complaints only encouraged me to take our intimacy further. I slid my hand under the cover-up and untied her bikini top. My hands flew to touch parts of her body that had never been explored.

Aroused by her soft moaning, I pulled her body on top of mine and attempted to pull down her bikini bottom. I couldn't believe Emily was allowing me to get this far. Her complaints completely stopped and her lips dared not part from mine. Just when I was thinking I didn't want Emily's first time to be in a cabana on a lounge chair, we fell off the narrow chair. Emily laughed, turned around and swiftly covered herself. Great! I thought. Though I got to touch briefly, I still hadn't seen enough of Emily.

"Let's go out and enjoy the rest of the day," she said, smiling apologetically.

"OK…" I mumbled. Having gotten that far, I had to try again tonight. With a little encouragement, Emily looked ready to show and tell her love.

Dinner took longer than anyone thought it would so we canceled our night excursions around town. Emily and Nick talked about all the restaurants they would visit tomorrow, and I told Jane to move her stuff out of her room and to bring my suitcase into her room.

"Did you get very far last night?" Jane asked. "Emily told me she had no plans to have sex with you."

"We got nowhere but sleep last night. But, plans are meant to be changed. Stop asking personal questions. I don't ask you who you're sleeping with," I admonished her playfully.

"I won't ask either since I know you won't be 'sleeping' with anyone either. Good luck. You'll need it." Thankfully she did as she was told.

I took Emily back to her room and she picked out a video but fell asleep on my lap five minutes into the movie. I attempted to carry her to her bed but Emily woke up and asked about Jane.

"Where's Jane?"

"She's with Nick. They're at the movies."

"Why didn't we go with them or why didn't they come here with us?"

"Sweetheart, they're trying to give us some privacy." The moment these words parted from my lips Emily looked around the room and realized what was going on.

"Why is your stuff here? And where are Jane's belongings?"

I nervously explained we had switched rooms and that I planned to be with her the rest of the trip.

She scolded me and went into her long speech about wanting to stay pure.

"Come on, Emi. Wasn't last night wonderful? Let me stay here with you."

She cut me off and said no.

"Just one more night, please? I'll switch back with Jane tomorrow."

"No." She was way too adamant on this issue. "Will you please ask Jane to come back into this room?"

Did I have a choice? I called Jane, and she laughed at me. "I told you so," she jeered.

Like a child, I pulled my arms away from Emily's shoulder and sat on the other side of the sofa. She held back her smile and put her head sweetly on my lap and placed my hand on her cheek. Whatever grudge I tried to hold dissipated faster than it formed.

With half the trip already done, Mom and Dad told us to spend Wednesday without them. They were committed to some alumni activity. Without looking, I knew Emily was ecstatic there would be no more strenuous activities. She and Jane talked about a spa day until I interrupted their plans.

"You are not planning to leave me alone and go to the spa all day, are you?" I accused Emily.

She and Jane both shook their heads yes.

Rather than scold my girlfriend, I got mad at Jane. "What am I to do if you take Emi away from me?"

"I don't know. You and Nick find something to do. Go watch another basketball game." Jane fought back.

"No way, Emi's with me. You find your own friend."

Nick got into this argument too. "I thought we were going to go find local food?" He looked over at Emily.

"I have a solution." Emily stepped in. "How about if Jane and I do a half day at the spa while you boys go watch the morning matches? We'll meet for lunch around one, and we can go into town and find yummy food." Jane and Nick loved the idea. Emily knew I wouldn't go for this without a fight.

To shut me up, she began kissing my lips. "My body hurts badly from all the exercise. I need a massage to unwind me. Would you be OK with that?" She pursued my lips till I gave in. What could I say to her but OK? Jane and Nick laughed at me, knowing my biggest weakness was my girlfriend.

Nick and I took the car and drove to the stadium but I only had the patience to watch one match. After two full days together, it was hard being away from Emily.

"Hey, Nick. Let's go shopping. I haven't finished my Christmas shopping yet."

"Great. I still have a few people to buy presents for as well."

We went to a mall and on the way to buying the chief a gift, I saw a solitaire engagement ring that caught my eye. Visions of this ring on Emily's finger and us at home with kids running around, filled my mind. I wanted to propose to a woman who couldn't yet admit she loved me. But judging by her actions, I knew she too wanted to spend the rest of her life with me. No longer would Emily be lonely on holidays or wondering who would love her the rest of her life. There would be no more fears about me breaking her heart, because we would commit to one another forever. I would most definitely be her best friend, her love, and the one to create a family with her. Telling myself to hold off proposing till Emily was ready, the salesgirl was ecstatic with my huge, spur-of-the-moment purchase. I, in turn, walked out content with my purchase and excited about our future together.

Nick came over and found me. "Hey, it's almost one. Let's get back."

"Is it time, already? Did you get your shopping done?" I asked.

"Not really. I hope some of the shops are open on Christmas. I have several people to buy for."

"If you're not done here, I'll go with you when we get home. I'm sure some of the stores will be open."

My love looked happy and relaxed when I picked her up.

"Hi!" She beamed and gave me a hug. "I'm hungry. Let's eat."

Hungry she was. She and Nick forced us to eat three lunches along with ice cream to top it off. Only after Jane and I begged, did she and Nick show us mercy. After lunch, we went back in our cabana but it wasn't nearly as much fun as yesterday. Emily took a nap, and I read a book. Many times I looked over and desired to pounce on her but I gave her a respite from my advances and let her sleep.

Thursday brought more eating in town along with a peaceful day with just the two of us. Mom, Dad, and Jane went exploring, and Nick, after lunch, decided to go surfing one last time. We went back to the shops, and Emily bought presents for the rest of my family; I walked around content as her bag boy. We picked up Nick, and after one last trip to the ice-cream store, headed to the airport.

CHAPTER 11
Will You Marry Me? Part 1

We got into LA early Christmas morning, and we all went our separate ways. Emily walked on cloud nine talking about my family. It felt wonderful to know they all got along so well.

"I had such a wonderful time with your family, Jake. Thank you! Though I just met them, I cherish them like my own. Your mom and dad did an amazing job raising you three. I see why you turned out to be such a caring person. I'm really glad I came on this trip. I feel much closer to you and your family."

If she loved my family as her own, she must love me as well. And since love to her is an eternal word, then she must want to be with me forever. After making such deductions, I pulled the car to the side of the road and decided to propose...now!

"Why are we stopping?"

I went to the trunk and pulled out the engagement ring from my suitcase and handed it to Emily. She looked shocked.

"Merry Christmas, Sweetheart."

"Jake. I left your present at home. Let's exchange gifts when we get back to my house."

"No, I want you to open this now."

She slowly unwrapped the present and looked frightened the moment she opened the box.

"Emi, don't be scared," I tried to convince her. "I bought this thinking I could hold off till you were ready but after this trip, I realize I don't want to be without you." I took a deep breath.

"Emily Anne Logan, I know it's only been a short two months, but I want to be with you forever. I love you more than any man could love a woman, and I promise to love you this way for the rest of my life. Will you marry me?"

Yes! I did it!

There was a long silence. Emily stared blankly. She looked like she was thinking about our situation. I leaned over and kissed her a few times to try to break her confused glare.

"Jake. You know how much I like you..." This was not the way I thought her answer would begin. "After meeting your family and spending time with you in Hawaii, I know your family is just about as perfect as a family can be. But, I'm not ready for a lifelong commitment. It's too soon. You can't mean this already. I am committed to you as a girlfriend, and that's where I'd like to stay for a while. I hope this is OK. I'm sorry, but my answer is no."

Rejected. She had outright rejected my proposal even though I'd asked her to think about it. I begged her not to say no but just to consider it. She did none of that. Her answer was a flat-out no. Was I wrong thinking that this girl wanted to be with me the rest of her life? She always appeared so complete when we were together. There was no way I was wrong in thinking that no matter what she could or could not admit, she loved me as much as I loved her. We were perfect for each other.

With a guilty face she said, "I'm sorry. Are you hurt by my response?" She kept repeating "I'm sorry" as though I hadn't heard it the first, second, or third time.

Was I hurt by her answer? Was she kidding me? Angry, I turned the car back on and started driving her home.

"Jake, we just started dating. Why do we need to move so fast? Can't we just enjoy ourselves?"

I was going to keep quiet but I couldn't hold back. "Emily, why can't you even consider the proposal? Why do you need to reject it so quickly? I've known since the day we met at the grocery store I wanted to marry you. Can't you see how much I love you? Why are you so scared all the time?"

I became more upset than I would've liked. "Hurt?" she asked. I was devastated. But, broken up as I was, I didn't want to unnecessarily scare Emily. I knew she walked on eggshells when I went into my tirade.

"Jake, it's been two months. How do you know already? How do you know a few months down the road you will still desire forever with me? Maybe we were both caught up in the bliss of Hawaii."

The bliss of Hawaii? Now I was furious. "Why do you always doubt my love for you? Is it because of Max? Just because he callously dumped you rather than marry you doesn't mean I'm going to do the same thing to you. Don't compare us! Are you still not over him? Is this what your rejection is all about? Would you have said no to him if he had asked you to marry him?" I yelled loudly enough hoping that Emily didn't catch my name immediately changing from Jake to Ass. I would have to do some serious groveling to get back in her good graces for all the accusations I had just thrown at her.

"Why are you bringing Max into this?" Emily yelled back. She went straight from penitent to angry.

"Forget it, Emily! Forget I just proposed. Let's forget everything."

Those were not choice words, but they were what I blurted out. I saw Emily turn her head toward the window and she went silent as well. My ears strained, listening for muffled cries but my eyes were too fearful to go searching for proof. I drove as fast as I could to her house. When I pulled up to her driveway, she got out of the car and fearfully asked, "Do you want to come in and talk?"

My eyes swiftly averted from the drops of tears that dotted her every eyelash. "No. Let's just forget this whole ordeal...just forget everything. I'll see you later," was all I said.

The light in her eyes extinguished faster than I could finish my sentence, and the roar of her pain was deafening. If my legs were long enough to reach my rear end I would have used one to give myself a life-threatening kick. Nevertheless, I ignored her pain and dwelled on my need to placate my hurt feelings and my bruised ego. Did this girl not comprehend I had never loved another enough to want marriage? What about my attentiveness and loving kindness would possess her to refuse me? She was an enigma!

Half a block down from Emily's house, I sat in the car berating myself. You *are a world class idiot! Loser! Moron!* I did exactly what I told her I would never do—break her heart and leave her. As much as I denied it, my girlfriend and almost fiancée was crying as she left my car. Who was I kidding? She cried the whole ride home. Aargh! How did this vacation go so wrong?

Proposing after only two months; yelling at her for turning down my proposal; taunting her about a proposal that never happened, one that I knew broke her heart—what an ass I was!

I definitely shouldn't have brought up Max. I knew he wasn't the reason she turned me down. Knowing Emily, she was probably scared again. She couldn't let herself believe I loved her enough to want to take care of her the rest of her life. She was right. It was too soon for her. I would give her more time and ask again when I saw that she was ready.

Bravely, I walked up her driveway and rang the doorbell.

It felt like someone was stabbing me in the heart with an ice pick when I saw Emily greet me with that painful look of dejection.

"Hi," I whispered, unsure whether she would take me back. "Can I come in? Can we talk?"

In silence, she stepped away from the door and away from me. Reaching for her arm, I pulled her into my body and held her as if my life depended on it. I couldn't lose her now, or ever.

"I'm sorry! I'm so sorry! It killed me to see you walk away, so hurt by all the things I said to you."

Before she could reject me I feverishly spewed out everything that was on my mind.

"I knew you'd be hurt, I knew you'd be crying, but my ego got the better of me and I couldn't stay to work this out. My head needed my mind to be clear before I could come back and find a resolution. I'm sorry I yelled at you. I'm sorry I was so angry with you. And I'm really sorry that I brought up Max and said all those asinine words to you." There was only a dead silence. "Emi?" I kissed the tears from her eyes. "Why are you so quiet? Talk to me," I begged.

"Where does this leave us now?" she asked, her voice shattered.

"What do you mean?" Was this her way of breaking up with me?

"You told me twice, 'let's just forget everything.' Does everything include us? If so, I'd like for you to be honest with me. Since I turned down your proposal, I get it if you want to break up with me."

"Unbelievable!" Did I hear this girl correctly? She was crying because she thought I was breaking up with her? Oh, Emily. I really needed to have a talk with her.

But, before any talk…I grabbed her beautiful face and kissed her like she'd never been kissed before.

"Does that answer your question?"

Not surprisingly, she shook her head no.

Emily! I sighed to myself. Obviously the first kiss hadn't convinced her. She was issuing a challenge that I gladly accepted. Practically swallowing her mouth we disengaged only when it was obvious we would soon pass out from a lack of air.

Her big brown eyes were unconvinced...still!

Before bringing my head down for another round, I exclaimed, "I can do this all day until you get it."

"Wait!" She stepped away, breathing hard. "Let's talk."

I waited for her to make the first move. Little by little she moved away from me to the other end of the couch and sat there for a while reassessing.

"What did you mean when you said you wanted to forget everything?"

"Emi...I just wanted to undo the mess I had gotten myself into. I'd said so many careless words to you. I didn't mean to bring up your heartache with Max. I know you don't love him anymore. In some ways, I was mad, hurt, jealous—there were so many emotions going through my head, and I said everything that came to mind. There was neither discretion nor discernment, and I'm sorry."

"Why would you be jealous? Of what? Of whom?"

"Of Max, I suppose. There was a time you wanted him to propose to you. I thought maybe you'd want the same from me..."

"Jake. I know I haven't made myself very clear on this subject, but I am absolutely in love with you."

I KNEW IT! She loved me! Happy days were here again.

"Say that again," I issued my own command while creeping closer to her.

Her face finally broke into a smile. "Which part? That I haven't been too clear with you or that..."

Tease.

Our bodies formed a straight and perfect lower case L on the couch with me on top.

"You love me?" I questioned while necking my way back from perdition.

"I am irrevocably in love with you, but I'm not ready to marry you. Can you deal with that?"

"Do I have a choice?" I murmured still unable to take my lips off her face. "This just means I have to work harder to get a yes out of you on both accounts."

"Huh?" She giggled as I sucked on her neck.

"Sex and marriage! In that order, starting now, if possible."

That's when I got kicked out of the house.

I left Emily's to go home and unpack before dinner. I tried to convince her to come with me but she decided to stay home, rest, and get ready to meet all my relatives tonight. As soon as I got home, Nick asked me to go shopping with him, so we left for the few specialty shops we knew would still be open.

"Jake? Nick?" Mom called out. "Can you guys stop by the caterer's and pick up some more place settings? I don't think they sent enough."

"Sure. Can you call me the moment Emily gets here?"

"Will do, Son."

Several hours into our shopping I called home to see if Emily had come by.

"Dad. Has Emily arrived?"

"Oh yeah. She's been here for a few hours now."

"What? How come no one called to tell me? Nick, hurry it up. Let's go home. Emily's there already."

We zoomed home and I raced upstairs looking for Emily.

"Here you are. I searched all over the house for you." I came over to embrace my girlfriend.

She shied away from me and asked, "Why?"

I gave her an incredulous look. Apparently the two women in my life were planning another New York trip without me. I protested heavily and told Emi I needed to be there with her. That's when Jane protested even more heavily and tried to get me to stay home. Knowing how much Emily loved New York, there was no way I was going to let her experience it again without me.

In the end, Emily came up with a peaceful solution and had the four of us, Nick included, travel to the Big Apple. It wasn't quite what I had in mind but as long as Emily would be there, I was happy. Using Emily as bait Jane got me to agree to a dinner at Masa for all four of us. Emily might not see me the week prior, as I'd have to work extra hours to pay for this meal.

I was dying to get Emily alone in my room. I pulled her away from Jane and toward my room even before they got to say a proper good-bye. Emily was amazed at the size of my room. I never thought it was that large until she kept mentioning how grand it was.

"So..." I hesitated to bring up this morning, "are we OK?"

"Shouldn't I be asking you that? You were the one upset. Here lies a scar on my heart," she pointed to what I saw as her left breast rather than her heart, "because of your asinine actions this morning! Jane was right. You can be really nasty when life doesn't go your way."

Dear God. "This is going to be another Allison situation, huh? You're going to use my folly against me for the next month."

"A month? Are you kidding me? This is worth at least a year."

Enough with the talk, I picked her up and dropped her on my bed.

"Jake…your parents…your entire family is in this house, she whimpered while we made out like it was our last kiss."

"I don't care," I responded in between my lips staying busy on her body and my hands trying to undo all the buttons on her dress. Today of all days, she had to wear a complicated dress. I had half her dress undone and Emily stopped protesting and started participating. Almost done, victory was only a few buttons away.

Then there was a loud knock on the door.

"Jake…Oh, Jake…" It was Nick, my own brother, keeping me from the finish line.

"GO AWAY!" I yelled at him.

"Mom told me to come and get you and Emily. Everybody's waiting. Dinner's about to begin. Come out soon, or I'm going to have the chief come up and get you," Nick started bellowing. He knew I was irritated.

"Nick, I'm going to remember this next time you have a girl up in your room," I threatened.

Emily jumped out of bed as soon as I got off of her body. She laughed though I knew she too was sorry it ended.

"Jake…" I heard Emily call my name but was in such a foul mood I didn't answer her. "Jake. Can I give you your Christmas present before we go down?"

Like a child, my face lit up at the talk of a present. Emily walked over to her purse and brought out a book that was nicely tied together with ribbons and a bow.

"What is that, Emi?"

"You have to promise me one thing," she said before giving me the present.

"OK. I promise." Without even hearing what it was that I was promising to, my head bobbed yes.

"This is a journal I started writing soon after we met. I wrote in it after every date or conversation or even a fight. My initial intention was to journal my feelings and thoughts. This wasn't written for anyone to read but me. When I thought about what I wanted to give you for Christmas, I knew you would most appreciate my heart. Whatever I felt during our time together… it's all in here."

My mind was in a state of shock. She was actually going to open herself up completely to me and show me all that was in her heart. This was huge progress. I would have to propose again very soon. She was almost there—ready to take that last step. I loved this girl infinitely, and now I knew for sure she loved me just as much.

"I'm sorry I'm so frustrating. You're a patient man to deal with someone so indecisive. This journal will hopefully answer all your questions and take away any doubt you might still have about us."

She left me speechless.

"So back to the promise." She pulled away from my embrace. "You can't read this till after I leave."

"Why not? If you wrote it you know everything that's in there."

"It's embarrassing. You can enjoy it when I'm not around. I also don't want to see your ego blowing up page by page. Your head might burst."

"Can I take a peek before dinner?"

"No! I'm taking this back if you don't keep your promise."

"All right. I promise. I can't wait to read it." I had an eager smile. I would have to start tonight.

"I'll leave it over here on your bookcase."

Halfway down the hall, Emily stopped me again. "I love you, Jake, and I'm really happy to be here with you," she professed.

I swept her off her feet again and tried to take her back to bed, but she forced us downstairs.

My poor Emily greeted the entire family and tried to memorize all their names. Mom had hors d'oeuvres laid all around the living room, and I saw Emily's attempt to eat fail each time as she got accosted by an aunt or uncle or cousin.

"She's super hot!" Doug came up to me and whispered. "Where did you say you met her? Does she have a sister? Isn't she more my age than yours?"

I whacked him on the back of his head. "Don't even think about it. She will soon be your cousin, not a possible date."

Aunt Barbara also came up to me to rave about Emily. "She's so sweet. I approve of her wholeheartedly."

"Thanks, Aunt Babs."

Mom sat us in the middle of the table so Emily could converse with as many people as possible.

"Jake," Emily whispered.

"Yes, Love?"

"Who is sitting across from you? I can't remember her name."

"That's Susan, and next to her is Glen; they are with Uncle David and Aunt Deborah."

"I feel like I'm in school and there's going to be a pop quiz on names and faces." She sounded a bit worried.

"You're doing great. No one expects you to know everyone's name tonight."

"Stay near me tonight. I might need you to keep reminding me who is who."

"You don't ever have to tell me to stay near you." I leaned in to kiss her, but of course Emily moved away with a frantic please-no-PDA look on her face. I laughed and kissed her anyhow. I hadn't seen her face turn rosy in a long while.

The chief monopolized my Emily from the onset of dinner. While the soup was being served he told her many unnecessary stories of all the staff members I'd dated. Though, I didn't mind him telling her stories of all the women who wanted to date me.

"Jake told me about many of these women. He sure did date a lot of girls..." She let out a cute sigh.

"You must have had your share of dates, Emily. You're absolutely beautiful. Men must follow you around all the time." Uncle Henry said with a wink.

"Thank you for the compliment, but no, I didn't date much. I was never as popular with men as your nephew has been with the ladies."

"You mean guys weren't lined up to ask you out?" Sadie asked.

Emily shook her head no. "Stupid me...I met a guy my first day in undergrad and I dated him all four years. Then, a year and a half and no dates later, I met your cousin and now I'm stuck again." Her lips spread slightly and she had a devilish look in her eyes. "Maybe I should stop seeing your cousin and date around a bit, huh? Do you think I've missed out?"

All my cousins shook their heads yes.

"There are so many men in this world. Why commit to one for so long? How will you compare who's the best if you haven't dated other guys?" Susan asked.

"Hey, let's not give Emily any unnecessary ideas. And, Emi, you are kidding, right? Don't blame your college years on me. That's when you should've dated around, not now."

Uncle Henry changed subjects and asked, "So, Emily, are you coming to the pre-party and football game with all of us on New Year's Day?"

"Um, I don't think so," she answered. "I wasn't invited. Plus, I'm a Bruin."

Every head turned our way, and Emily got an ovation of boos.

"Maybe I should leave," she whispered in my ear. "They don't like me here anymore."

I put my arms around her and kissed her head. "I love you, and that's all that matters."

She gazed into my eyes and whispered, "I love you too."

While we were enjoying our dinner, Gram called and asked to talk to her favorite grandchild.

I gladly answered the call. "Hi, Gram!"

"Jakey, is Emily there?"

"Uh-huh."

"Let me talk to her."

"What about me?" I asked, but she insisted on talking to Emily. "She wants to talk to you," I said, handing over the phone.

Emily quietly asked, "You have a grandmother?"

I nodded yes.

"Why didn't you tell me? How shall I address her?"

"I forgot and you can call her Gram."

Emily got on the phone and proceeded to have a long conversation with Gram.

"Hello, Gram, this is Emily. It's very nice to meet you."

A frantic look appeared on Emily's face as she answered, "I'm very sorry, Gram, but Jake never told me I was supposed to call you. But I'm thrilled to meet you! I lived with my grandmother since I was thirteen. Talking to you makes me miss her very much."

Gram must have asked if Emily's maternal grandma was still alive, because the tears flickered as she answered, "No. She passed away a few years ago. Gram, why aren't you here with the family? I wish I could have met you too."

What kind words my girlfriend shared with Gram. I was sure Gram liked Emily a lot. I went back to eating my prime rib when all of a sudden Emily gave me a horrified look.

"Oh, Gram." She sounded so sweet. "Jake can be silly at times. How can he possibly think he loves anyone more than his grandmother? Plus, I'm not that pretty. It's only in Jake's eyes."

Women—no matter how old or young—their feelings got hurt so easily. Gram must have been complaining about the remark I made at Uncle Dave's birthday. I turned to talk to the chief about a patient when all of a sudden I heard Emily say, "He was treating me very well till this morning. He was mean to me, and he made me cry."

That sounded an awful lot like her telling my entire family I had made her cry today. Clank, clank, clank…every forked dropped and all eyes glared at me.

"Oh my gosh, Emily! I can't believe you just told everyone I made you cry this morning."

"But you did," she answered sadly. I didn't realize I was dating an actress. Laughter was in her eyes but melancholy choked her voice.

While Emily talked away with Gram, I defended myself against the women. They all ganged up on me and took Emily's side.

"How can you take the word of a person you just met tonight over your own flesh and blood? I promise, it was me who should have been crying, not her. Ask her."

I turned to Emily for some help. She shrugged her shoulders, winked, and mouthed "I love you," before she went back to eating her Chilean sea bass. I would have to get her back for this act of treason.

With the meal over, we all sat around in the living room watching Mom get ready for our white elephant game. Emily sat on the couch with Doug and Nick, noshing on her mini cheesecake square. I tried to squish between them but the sofa wasn't large enough for the four of us and no one would move.

"Go find your own seat," Nick told me.

"This love seat is meant for those in love. Why don't you two get lost? Let me sit here comfortably with my love."

"Whatever," Doug answered and didn't budge.

Refusing to sit on my lap, she offered to sit on the ground so I could sit next to my cousins. I sat on the ground instead as the game began. Emily was in for a treat, as this was the only time the Reid family fought, cheated, and stole from one another.

"What gift did you bring, Emily?" I heard Nick ask.

"I brought a movie gift card. What did you bring?"

"I brought literally a white elephant statue."

"Eew! Which one is yours so I don't pick it?"

"I'm not telling." He started to laugh.

We all picked numbers and both of us got numbers toward the end. We had a good chance of ending up with decent prizes. Doug had the last number. He was excited.

"Do you want to trade numbers, Doug?" I saw Emily try to work her charm.

"Not a chance…well, maybe if you dump my cousin and agree to go on a date with me—then I'd be willing to trade numbers."

"Not a chance!" she mimicked him. That's my girl!

The first person to pick was Aunt Babs and she opened up an elaborate box. We all died laughing when we found an 8x10 autographed picture of the chief in that box. Next was Nick and he picked a smaller box. In it was a box of chocolate from Fauchon in Paris. We all envied the gift until Nick followed the "open me" instruction on the box and found that each chocolate had been bitten into. That was another funny gift. Next was Glen. He opened a tiny box, and there he found the golden ticket. There was always a "grand prize" Mom added to the pot, and this year they were two floor seats to a Laker game.

Emily's eyes lit up. "Honey, can you get that for me? That's what I want."

"You like basketball?"

"I love basketball! Help me get those tickets."

"Of course!" Who knew my girlfriend liked basketball? I guess there were still many things I didn't know about her.

With the game done, everyone left content with their meal and happy to have spent time with one another. All my aunts and uncles came by to tell me how much they enjoyed meeting Emily, and Emily said good-bye to all the cousins first, then to every aunt and uncle. By now, she knew everyone's name and had memorized a mini bio of each person.

My immediate family went upstairs tired from Hawaii and tonight's dinner. Emily was the last one to leave. I still hadn't come up with a good enough retribution for what she had done to me at dinner. She came to me with her arms open, and purposely I stepped away. Surprised, she couldn't understand what was going on. I'd never rejected any of her advances.

"I can't believe you threw me under the bus today. You're so lucky I didn't tell my whole family how you chopped up my proposal and my heart into pieces."

She knew she was in trouble. In her most tempting voice, she snuggled up to me and asked, "What can I do to make things better? I'll make it up to you."

Although I knew this was not said in any suggestive way, I thought I'd push my luck. "Stay the night with me." I demanded. Pause. Pause. Pause. I couldn't believe it. She didn't reject my demand.

Before she could change her mind, I picked her up and hurried her up the stairs and into my room. Every room I passed—my parents' room, Jane's room, Nick's room, and even up till I got to my room, I expected Emily to protest and beg me to let her go home. Instead she wrapped both her arms around me and laid her head against my own. Her consent spoke loudly through her silence.

I laid her gently on my bed and looked into her eyes for any sign of hesitation. Without a doubt she desired to be with me tonight. Wanting tonight to be perfect, I didn't rush anything. I wanted her to remember each kiss, each touch, each moment's embrace. I wanted tonight to be as memorable for her as it would be for me.

Unbuttoning her dress, I looked into her eyes one more time. She gazed back at me, but this time her thoughts went elsewhere. Her resolved fortitude briefly turned to doubt. I knew I had to stop. She was not ready to give up what she had fought so hard to keep all these years. Thirty years from now when she thought about her first night, I wanted her memories to be filled only with joy—without any regret. My fingers grudgingly placed the buttons back where they belonged.

"Jake?" she quietly called my name. "What's the matter?"

It pained me to answer her. I wanted to be with her tonight in every way. "Emily, I'm content to just hold you tonight. We don't have to do anything else."

"Why? What's wrong?"

"Sweetheart, as difficult as this is for me, I want to keep you as you are until we get married—and trust me, we will get married," I promised her.

She did her best to change my mind but we both knew she was grateful for my decision. Relief marked her face.

"Jake…I'm fine. I want to do this for you…with you. I'd like to be with you tonight."

I appreciated her efforts to give me what I wanted. I'd made my intentions clear from the onset that I desired to be with her. I loved her for choosing me to give the gift she's been holding on to all these years. But since this was a gift she could never retrieve, I didn't want her to ever regret who this gift was given to. Only after she was married would she feel confident she had given this gift to the right person. It was only a matter of time before this gift came to me.

CHAPTER 12

What Have I Done?

We spent a beautiful night together. I woke up several times watching Emily sleep in my arms and I cherished her more this night than I had our entire two months together. I pulled her in as close to me as possible and hoped for more nights like these to come soon.

Way too early, Emily woke up frantic. She pulled away, telling me she had to go home and pack for her road trip.

"What?" Where was she going without me? I thought. "You're going somewhere?"

"I'm going to Vegas with my college friends, remember? I have to leave right now." She tried to get up.

"Don't go. Stay a little longer. I'll fly you out to Vegas later today." This would give me another hour with her before I had to go into the hospital.

She wouldn't go for it since everyone was supposed to meet at her house. She jumped out of bed the first chance she got and hurried out the door.

"I'll call you later. I love you," she whispered and left the house.

Whenever she told me she loved me, it sent shivers down my spine. I couldn't believe she was finally admitting it. Those precious words lingered long after they were said. I too jumped out of bed and got ready to go see Emily before she left me for three days in Vegas with all her friends and one ex-boyfriend.

"Where are you off to so early? Do you have an early surgery?" Dad asked as I ran straight for the front door without even noticing my parents at the breakfast table.

"I'm off to see Emily before she leaves for Vegas with her college friends. Why are you both up so early? You must be tired from last night. It was a wonderful dinner, Mom. Emily and I enjoyed it very much, thank you."

"You're welcome, Son. Everyone seemed to enjoy meeting Emily. Compliments were overflowing last night on how sweet she was and how you two made a lovely couple." Mom's words were encouraging.

"Gram called not too long ago and told us how pleased she was with Emily as well," Dad said. "She mentioned Emily sounded lovely and would take good care of her favorite grandson. She told me to make sure you treat her well, and she wants you to bring her to London soon. End of March is too late, she says."

I'd have to talk to Emily and see if she could take a few days off and go for a long weekend to see Gram in the next month. Once Gram decided she wanted something, it had to be done soon.

"I'll do what I can, Dad. I'll talk to Emily today and let her know. We'll try to go see Gram within the month."

I drove to pick up breakfast for my love and got to her house right at 6:30. I didn't see any cars outside so I assumed no one had arrived yet. Perfect. I'd have some alone time with her before she left. Walking up to her house, my phone rang.

"A bit early to be calling me, don't you think, Chief?"

"Then shall I take back this trip to Paris I was going to offer you and Emily this February?"

"What? What trip to Paris?"

"There's a conference in Paris I was going to attend but can't. Since you were kind enough to fill in for me in Atlanta, I thought I'd give you the opportunity to spend a week in Paris with that lovely girlfriend of yours. I can't believe someone that sweet and beautiful wants to be your girlfriend." The chief laughed. "Anyhow, I transferred my plane ticket to your name, a hotel has already been booked, and there's even an expense account for meals for a week. You just need to buy a ticket for Emily."

"Fantastic! Finally, you're compensating us for all our interrupted dates. We'll take it. I'll let Emily know. I'm about to walk into her house now. Thanks, Chief."

"You're welcome. Don't be late to work."

This was turning out better than I expected. We could go to Paris for the conference then go see Gram in London. I nearly skipped to Emily's door. I rang the doorbell and it opened to a surprised Emily. She obviously wasn't expecting me.

"Good morning, My Love. I wanted to stop by and see your face before you left." I closed the door and couldn't part from her lips, knowing we'd be separated for a while. "Love, I've never slept as well as I did last night. We're going to have to have more slumber parties. How did you sleep?"

Taking her breakfast off my hands, Emily slyly grinned. She wouldn't answer me, but I knew she slept well. I supposed she didn't have to answer me as I watched her sleep throughout the night. She slept like an angel.

I told her about the conference in Paris and my wish to go with her. She looked reluctant until I told her that Gram wanted to see her sooner than March. Her qualm abandoned, she said she would work it out with her principal to get a week off in February. I took that as a yes and mentally began planning my trip to Europe with my girlfriend. A proposal in Paris was definitely high on the priority list. A month and a half should be plenty of time for her to sort out her feelings.

When it came time for both of us to leave, I took her bag and carried it out for her. As I reached for her hand, I noticed she was wearing the eternity band on her finger—the fourth, ring finger!

"You're wearing the ring...on your finger?" My spirits were flying high.

"You noticed finally?" She kidded that the ring was too heavy on her neck and that she wanted to see if it would be any better on her finger. Lucky for me, it fit only on her ring finger. Then, she turned to me to reveal, "I am committed to you as your loving girlfriend. When I see us heading toward that last step, you'll be the first to know."

I saw cars pull up and her friends get out. I knew this would embarrass Emily, but I couldn't help myself, especially not after that kind of confession.

"I love you Emily," I declared before grabbing her and kissing her deeply. I'd never longed to kiss her as much as I did at this moment. Her declaration wasn't much different than an acceptance to my proposal. Emily joyfully reciprocated till she heard her friends talking in the background. She pulled away and hid herself for a while trying to undo her rosy cheeks.

She let out a sigh for both of us at the thought of being apart. "I love you, Dr. Reid. Now go. Save lives." She nudged my arms away from her body.

"Hi, Jake," Sarah greeted me. "Did you have a good Christmas? How was Hawaii?"

"It was fantastic!" I gleamed. "How was your Christmas? You went up to Oxnard?"

"Yeah. It was great. What did you get Emily for Christmas?"

"You'll have to ask her. I tried to give it to her but she wouldn't take it. But, I got an unbelievable present from Emily last night."

I left it at that, knowing Sarah would put Emily through a rigorous question-and-answer session. I looked back at my girlfriend and smiled. She shook her head. I would be in trouble when she got back from Vegas. I'd be happy to be in trouble as long as she got back as soon as possible.

My day at the hospital was as crazy as expected. Being on vacation for almost a week, it was hard to get back into the routine. During a quick respite, I texted Emily.

Last night was even more amazing than our first night in Hawaii. Miss you. Love you.

You just got everyone in this car wondering what happened to us last night. Don't text personal messages!

Why did you let everyone read my message?

I didn't. Charlie stole the phone from me and read it out loud.

Ha! Ha! Ha! I'm OK with you kissing and telling.

I'm not. I hope you don't go around kissing and telling.

I wouldn't dare. I've got to go. They're paging me.

Of course they are. Bye.

Nick called to have dinner so I left work and met him and Doug near Nick's apartment.

"Why are you guys at your apartment during vacation?" I asked. "I'm actually glad you guys called. I need to move my stuff out of my house tonight. I'll buy dinner if you'll both help."

"We figured you'd buy dinner regardless. I can help but where are you moving to?" Doug asked.

"I'm moving back into Mom's. I want to be closer to Emily. They live near each other."

"She really doesn't have a sister?"

"No, Doug. She's an only child. She actually doesn't have any family. Her parents passed away."

"That's a bummer!" they both replied.

"How sad for sis not to have a family." Nick seemed really bothered. "I'll have to be even nicer to her."

"You do that, Nick. She'll appreciate it. As it is, she told me how much she likes you. She enjoyed spending time with you in Hawaii."

"Did she say she likes me too?" Doug eagerly asked.

"No, she thought you were creepy," I answered laughing at him.

On my way to the house, I called Emily to see what she was up to.

"Hello, Love. What are you doing right now?"

"Hi, Jake!" Her excited voice always made my heart thump a bit harder. "We're on our way to the stadium. Are you done with work already? How did morning surgery go?"

"I'm exhausted. I was in surgery almost all day. Then I had dinner with Nick and Doug, and now I'm on my way to my house in the Valley. I got Nick and Doug to help me move tonight."

"You're moving already?"

"Yeah. I want to be closer to you. Can I move into your house instead of Mom's?"

"OK. You can live in my house and I'll go live with your mom and dad."

"Can we both live with Mom and Dad?"

She quickly changed the subject. "Are you working New Year's Day? Sarah, Charlie, and I want to go to the parade. Will you go with us?"

"Thanks to you, the chief gave me the day off. Do Sarah and Charlie want to come to the tailgate party? I don't think I can get any more tickets to the game but they're more than welcome to come to the chief's party."

"We don't want to go to the party or the game. We don't like your team. We're coming back to my house after the parade."

"Emi…you have to go to the party. My whole family will be there. I'll buy you an SC outfit to wear," I laughed, imagining the scowl on her face.

"Yeah…real tempting…"

"When do you come home? I don't know that I like you being with Max as many days as you were with me in Hawaii. Can I come see you tomorrow? I'll be done with work early. I'll fly in and get a room, and you can stay with me instead."

"Stay home. We're here till Monday. I'll be home sometime in the afternoon. Come over after work and I'll make you dinner. I miss you. Good night."

With that, I was forced to hang up and start my move. Since Nick and Doug helped it didn't take long to move out my belongings. We drove back to Mom's, and they both stayed. All of us spent a good portion of the night playing video games in my room. Nick tried to convince Doug to spend the night but he opted to walk across the street to his home and sleep in his own bed.

The day started before the sun got up again. Today would be nonstop work so I texted Emily before leaving for the hospital.

I have a very long day today. I will not be able to call till late afternoon. Have a fun day. I love you.

Surprisingly my phone rang.

"Hi, Jake. Are you off to work already?" There was something wrong with my Emily.

"Emi. Why are you up so early? Are you all right?"

"I'm all right." The sullen voice told me she wasn't all right. Something had gone wrong last night. I could only guess who set her off again. "My back was hurting on this couch so I couldn't get a good night's sleep."

What was she doing on a couch? "Emily, why are you sleeping on a couch?"

She explained to me about their crazy back-to-college hotel scenario where everyone slept in one giant suite. I knew she would refuse but this arrangement didn't sit well with me.

"Emi, let me get you a room. Sarah can join you, or I'll fly in later and stay there with you."

Of course she wasn't happy with my suggestion. "Please, don't do that!" she begged me.

"All right but, Emi, are you sure you're OK? You sound sad. Did something happen with Max again? Do you want me to fly in today?"

She began explaining why she wasn't herself this morning but the moment her voice cracked I knew she was hurting about something. Regardless of her answer, I decided to fly in to Vegas later today and make sure nothing was wrong. She probably had another fight with Max. She really needed to stop seeing him.

Emi abruptly ended our conversation, and I left for work with a queasy feeling in my heart. Whenever she spent any time with Max, she reverted back to the Emily I first met. All our progress undid itself automatically. Even after Hawaii, her declaration of love, and spending a night together, I was unsettled about our conversation just now. Perhaps I was thinking too much into this situation. Once I got to Vegas, my jitters would hopefully be proven wrong.

None of the texts that were sent throughout the day got any response. It was unlike Emily not to answer back immediately. I got very worried. Thanks to the holidays, my schedule cleared earlier than normal, so I drove to Burbank airport eager to comfort my love.

Remembering Emily telling me everyone was staying at the Palazzo, I drove the rental car there but realized I didn't know what room they were staying in. I texted one more time, hoping she was able to pick up her messages by now.

Emi. I am here at the Palazzo but don't know where to go. Please call me or text back a room number.

#2260

Fantastic. She was here. I would be relieved as soon as I saw her. Sarah opened the door to greet me with a worried face.

"Hi, Jake. Does Emily know you're here? Have you spoken with her today?"

I was alarmed by Sarah's question. "No, I haven't spoken with her. You mean she's not here? Who just texted back?"

"That was me," Sarah answered.

"I've tried calling her all day. Where could she be?" Now I was really worried.

"We're not quite sure. She's been gone since early morning. I got up around seven and couldn't find her. She left her phone and wallet here. Ugh! I shouldn't have let Charlie fall asleep in our room. I'm so worried about her." Sarah looked like a mother who had lost her child.

"Sarah, I'm sure she'll be back soon. I talked to her early this morning and she sounded upset about something. Do you know if something happened with Max again last night?"

"I'm not quite sure. I didn't see her last night either." Sarah's face told me she was hiding something.

"Didn't you go to the game together?"

"Yeah…" She stopped talking.

"Sarah, please! What happened last night?"

"Well, Peter got all separate tickets and he sent Emily off with Max. Because we were so far from one another we all decided to catch a cab back to the hotel after the game. Emily was with Max the whole time, and I know I heard them come in at some point, but it looked like they were going back out somewhere."

"Why would she go out with him?" My voice rose, angry and frustrated. I couldn't understand why she felt the need to spend unnecessary time with her ex.

Sarah tried to defend her friends. "I'm not quite sure what happened, but it probably wasn't anything serious. Why don't you hang out with us? Emily should be back soon.

Suddenly, I felt a sick knot in my stomach. Sarah saw it on my face and feared having to answer my next question. "Is Emily with Max right now?" I asked slowly, hoping she wouldn't confirm my fears.

"We think they're together, but we're not sure."

"Sarah! What does that mean?"

She attempted an explanation, but fortunately for both of us, Peter came in the room and explained what had happened.

"Jake." Peter looked surprised. "When did you get here?"

"Just now. Do you have news of Emily?"

"Yeah. Max called to say they got stranded at the Grand Canyon. They can't get back tonight."

This was only getting worse.

"How come they hadn't called all day?"

"His phone wouldn't work down there. They're at the basin of the canyon. I'll call him back and let Emily know to call you."

"Thanks."

"Jake, it's not as serious as you think. Please don't be upset with Emily. Understand that they are still friends. I'm sure it upsets you that she's with Max, but the two of them together is really no different than Emily being with Peter."

I appreciated her comforting words though they didn't comfort at all. My phone finally rang.

"Jake? What are you doing in Vegas?" A guilt-ridden voice greeted me.

"Emi. Where have you been? I got worried when you didn't answer your phone all day."

"Well…I'm a bit stuck here in the Grand Canyon right now. A certain ex-boyfriend of mine brought me out to the canyon then got us stranded."

"Why can't you get back tonight? How did you get out there in the first place?"

"We got on one of those helicopter rides and we missed the flight out of here. We're stuck here for the night. I'm sorry. I wouldn't have come here if I'd known you were coming to see me."

"Let me get a helicopter to come and get you. I don't want you to be down there without me." I couldn't admit I didn't want her to spend a night with Max. I'm sure she knew what I meant.

"It's no use, Jake. They can't come down here without the Haulapai Indians' permission. Plus where we are, you have to walk at least another hour. It will be too dark by then."

I let out an annoyed sigh.

"Why don't you spend the night in Vegas and come into the Grand Canyon tomorrow morning? I'd love to go to the Skywalk with you. Can you do that, or do you have to work tomorrow?" She was trying to use that same voice she used on me last night before we ended up in bed together. It wasn't working its charm like it did last night.

"Emily. Where will you sleep tonight?"

"Right here on the ranch. Max and I will stay here, and then we'll take a mule ride first thing in the morning up to the Skywalk."

Even more aggravated at the thought of them being anywhere near each other during the night, I questioned, "Why are you there with him?" Then I quickly added, "Never mind, you don't need to answer that."

"I love you, Jake, and I miss you. I'll see you tomorrow morning?"

"All right. I'll see you then. Sleep well."

"Good night."

"Everything OK?" Sarah pierced into my eyes.

"Yeah, I suppose," I answered glumly.

Sarah asked Peter and Charlie to go have dinner with all the other guys, and she suggested we go and have dinner on our own. She said she wanted to talk to me. We walked into CUT Steakhouse and sat down to have our meal.

"Emily will be green with envy if she knows I'm here with you. She's been dying to come here," Sarah informed me. I'd have to dine here again tomorrow if that was Emily's culinary wish.

"Jake." I was still in my own world, worried about Emily and Max having spent too many days together. Sarah understood my woes. "Emily deeply loves you and only you. She hasn't loved Max in a long time." It was kind of Sarah to care about my feelings.

"I know she loves me but she gets in this weird funk whenever she spends too much time with Max. I don't want him to undo all the progress we've made. It wasn't easy getting this far with your overly cautious best friend."

Sarah started cracking up. "I wouldn't worry if I were you. She's head over heels in love with you. She told me you proposed after Hawaii?"

"Yeah, only to be rejected without a second thought."

"You are always so sure of yourself, and you come on so strong, it scares her. Though she hasn't admitted it, she regrets saying no." I was happy to hear Sarah's conclusion. "Do you know what it took for her to agree to sleep with you? Just the consent alone tells me she wants to be with you the rest of her life. She never once wavered with Max. Give her some time, she'll come around."

"Sarah, I don't understand why she's so scared all the time. Why does she always believe I'll leave her?"

"Because she thinks you're too perfect. You shower her with love and gifts and do whatever you can to give her everything she wants. Max was an introvert just like Emily. He could never express his love for her like you did. This really bothered her. She was never fully sure that he loved her as much as she loved him. Maybe because she had been alone for so long, she always wanted assurance from Max and he couldn't give that to her."

"But I give her that assurance continually and yet she's still not convinced."

Sarah laughed in the middle of chewing her steak. "When Emily used to describe her perfect guy to me long before you came along, she described you to a T. Her ideals have come to life, and it scares her. She just told me yesterday you were too good to be true in her mind. You're like a dream and she's waiting to wake up to her reality. But she loves you madly."

"So if she loves me so much, why do tears glisten in her eyes every time Max enters the picture?"

"Have you not seen how tenderhearted your girlfriend is? Max was her best friend, and she considered him her family. Someone this close to her betrayed her one day. If I or Peter or Charlie had done this to her, she would be just as hurt. Obviously, it's worse, because Max was her boyfriend. Don't take those tears so personally. She's just being Emily."

I felt much better after our talk. Prior to our talk, I knew Emily loved me. But now I believed Emily loved only me.

"Can you tell me about Max? Why did he leave Emily? I can't understand how Emily could have been so wrong about him. She thought he was going to propose to her but instead he leaves her...I don't get it."

Sarah's mouth twisted oddly and she stopped eating. Her silence scared me. "Do you really want to know?"

"Do you know something Emily doesn't know?"

She nodded yes.

"I'll tell you if you promise not to tell Emily. I guess it won't matter. Emily has you now." Her comment frightened me even more.

"Emily was right. Max was going to propose to her on graduation night."

"What?" I dropped my utensils. "What happened?"

"To make a long story short, he couldn't reconcile his desire to marry her with his lack of a future. He let her go, thinking it was the best thing to do for her. After all she'd been through with her parents, he wanted her to have a stable and secure life with someone... like you, perhaps. Maybe Max knew you were just around the corner. It literally almost killed him to be away from her. As much as you don't want to hear this, Max loved Emily just as much as you love her."

Sarah's words absolutely changed the way I viewed Max. While Sarah perused the dessert menu, my mind couldn't let go of Max's selfless act. Could I give up my love so she could have a better life? It was a gamble I wouldn't take, but for Max, he gave up Emily believing she would find someone better than himself. He truly did love Emily more than his own life. Did he love her more than I loved her?

A chilling thought crept into my mind. "Sarah, you don't think Max will try to win Emily back, do you? He wouldn't propose to her or anything like that, right?"

"I don't think so, and even if he did try, I don't think you have anything to worry about. Charlie and I were bowled over when we saw you and

Emily that first weekend you two met. She was a whole other person the way she flirted with you."

"That was a fun weekend," I agreed. "Thanks, Sarah. I feel much better."

"Thank you. What a fantastic dinner. I'll have to gloat when I see your girlfriend tomorrow. I promise you, she'll pout."

I chuckled, as I enjoyed watching my Emily pout.

Early the next morning, I left Vegas along with Sarah, Charlie, and Peter, who wanted to visit the Skywalk. Charlie rode with me while Sarah hung out in Peter's car. During the three-hour ride, we talked mostly about our girlfriends.

"So…can I ask if you and Sarah are getting married anytime soon?" Possibly it was too personal to ask this, but I felt comfortable enough.

"Well, can I trust you to keep this information from your girlfriend? If Emily finds out, there's no way I can keep it a secret from Sarah."

"I promise. I won't say a word."

"I bought a ring a few weeks ago and I was going to propose on Christmas but Sarah seemed suspicious so I didn't go through with it. After eight and a half years, it's hard to surprise her. She reads me like a romance novel." We both cracked up at this comment. "I heard you popped the question already." Charlie had an I-feel-for-you look on his face.

"Yeah. I think it was way too soon for my girlfriend. She rejected me even before I finished my question."

"Sarah told me Emily sounded like she regretted saying no to you. Since I divulged my only secret, will you tell me something?"

I looked over at him, wondering what he would want to know.

"The text message you sent while we were driving over to Vegas… there's no way you and Emily…not after she held out for four years with Max." His head shook automatically along with a "no…"

I laughed at him. "Emily warned me never to kiss and tell."

"No way! I don't believe you. Not our Emily."

"Correction, she's my Emily, and no…we didn't do anything to change your views of her. Her status hasn't changed."

"So what was the text all about?" Charlie wouldn't let it go. I had to tell him something.

"Emily was extremely tired in Hawaii after our first day, and I coaxed her into bed with me but nothing happened. We were probably both snoring away. It was an exhausting day."

"Oh…" He sounded disappointed there wasn't much else. "That's still huge you slept in the same room with her—in the same bed."

"Yeah, she was pretty freaked out when she got up in the morning." A silly smiled appeared on my face as I pictured Emily in that white robe, hair all knotted because it was wet from the night before, and unable to walk from all the exercise. "So when are you going to propose? Do you have another date in mind?"

"Yeah. We are supposed to go to Napa over the three-day weekend, so I thought I'd do it there on a hot air balloon."

"That sounds great. Maybe proposing in a car wasn't the best idea. Next time it'll be in a much more romantic setting."

"There's a next time already?" Charlie looked surprised.

"Oh yeah. We're going to Paris in February for a week and I plan to ask again. With that kind of setting, Emily's bound to say yes. If she rejects me again, I might keep her hostage there until she changes her mind." We both got a good chuckle.

Finally arriving at the Skywalk a bit after 8:00 a.m., we all walked over, looking for Emily and Max. There were so many people on the Skywalk it was hard locating the two of them. I scanned everyone who looked to be about Emily's build, and finally I found her right in the middle of the skywalk. Delighted to see her, I hastened my pace. Oddly, she looked frozen; she only looked down even though I continued to call out her name.

Following her eye, I stared at her view and saw Max on one knee holding on to Emily's left hand. If I didn't know better, it looked like Max was proposing to my girlfriend. Angrily I shouted her name. "Emi!"

All eyes peered her way and I could hear Sarah groaning. "What is he doing? Why is Max on his knee?" Sarah sounded as aghast as I felt.

"Sweetheart." I got to Emily as quickly as possible and turned her away from Max. "Are you all right?" She looked scared. "What just happened?" I angrily turned this question toward Max.

Charlie and Peter came and pulled Max away while Sarah made sure Emily was OK. Adding to my anger, Max put his hands on Emily's arms and told her, "Em, take your time, I'll wait." I didn't have to ask Emily to figure out what had just happened. He used his time with Emily to try to win her back.

But, I still needed Emily to explain what I had just witnessed.

"What happened, Emily? What was that all about?"

She stayed silent.

"Emi, please. Can you tell me why I saw Max on his knee?" She still wouldn't talk. Her silence agitated and infuriated me. To me this silence was no different than a confession. Something happened between the two of them yesterday and she was defending their actions. Frustration mounted, and I yelled at her. "EMILY!"

Tears brimmed to the edge of her eyes but she didn't cry. She kept her head down and quietly answered, "Max just proposed to me."

She confirmed my fear. "Why would he do that? What happened between you two yesterday? Did something happen last night?" I yelled even louder.

As soon as I said those words Emily's big brown eyes looked betrayed and the tears flowed. Initially I felt guilty for accusing her of something I knew she would never do, but my anger got the best of me.

"What happened last night?" I asked again angrier than I should've been.

She defended herself and Max and told me nothing happened. In my heart I knew Emily didn't love Max and I knew she would do nothing to hurt me but my words kept betraying me.

"Why would he be encouraged enough to propose to you, if nothing happened?"

Emily explained what Sarah told me last night at dinner and at this point, I wanted to apologize to Emily for being so furious with her and forget Max's proposal ever happened.

"So what did you say to him?" Of course I knew the answer, but I wanted to hear how she rejected Max's proposal.

"Jake..." She stopped and my heart sank. Was that fear or contrition in her voice? "I didn't get a chance to answer Max."

"What do you mean you didn't answer him? Emily, I don't understand." There must be something wrong here, I thought. This was all a serious nightmare.

Emily's face, full of sorrow and pain, explained it all. "Jake, I'm sorry. I don't know why but I went mute. I was in such shock when he asked me... and I knew the right answer was no...but it wouldn't come out. Then you came and...I don't know what happened."

Now, I was the one in pain. "How could you turn down my proposal without a second thought but give his proposal a second chance?" I couldn't believe my ears. The woman I wanted to spend the rest of my life with was contemplating whether she wanted to spend the rest of her life with not me—but Max.

She tried to defend herself again. "I'm not giving him another chance. I don't want to marry him!" This time she was angry and adamant.

"Then why didn't you tell him that?" I was even more incensed.

Deflated, she answered, "I don't know...but I will...I will as soon as I see him."

Emily then tried to talk to me and tell me how she loved me. The only words I could hear in my mind at this time were Emily saying no to me and yes to Max. After all I had done for her, after the abundant love I had given her, it ended with her choosing her past boyfriend of four years over me. I decided to walk away before I uttered something I might really regret.

Emily's cries echoed in the background as I walked into the crowd. With no more desire left to try persuading her to love me and me only, I drove the car back home. I figured she'd prefer to catch a ride with Max and her friends.

Everywhere I turned I saw bleakness. A life without Emily was not in my plans. I pictured us getting engaged at the Eiffel Tower in February and being married by the end of summer. We'd take a long passionate honeymoon on some island and spend time in those island huts she'd put on her bucket list. Rather than teaching, she could take cooking classes and enjoy the time till our first child was born. I imagined the joy of a first great-grandchild in the Reid family. He or she would be spoiled by every aunt, uncle, and cousin, not to mention the immediate grandparents. We would host Sunday barbeques. We'd raise the kids, retire, and love each other till we died. Emily, how could you not want this future for us?

Angry as I was I felt guilty walking out on Emily. I knew she was hurt, and I knew she'd be crying. I hoped Sarah would take care of her. Where would we go from here?

Next morning was New Year's Day, and I woke up to the sound of my phone.

Happy New Year, Jake. I'm alone in Texas right now visiting my parents. My parents would have liked meeting you. You three would've gotten along well. I thought this new year would bring us closer together. I guess I botched up my own hope. My new hope is that you find it in your heart to forgive me. I'm so sorry for hurting you. I would like to share with you what's in my heart right now. Please call me.

I was too angry to call yet heartbroken envisioning my girlfriend alone on New Year's Day. How lonely she must feel right now, by herself. I wanted to fly out and be with her and meet her parents. She sounded penitent in her text but I still couldn't rid my mind of Max, down on his knee, proposing. I decided to ignore her text and go to work.

To my annoyance, Jane came out of her room at the same time.

"Hey. Are you off to pick up Emily?"

I didn't answer her.

"Jake. What's the matter?"

"Jane, can you leave me alone?" my voice asked while my mind begged.

"Jake! What happened? Never mind. I'm going to call Emily to find out."

I stood next to Jane hoping to hear how Emily was doing.

"Hi, Emily," Jane said cheerfully. "It's me, Jane. Where are you? Aren't you going to the chief's tailgate party? Everyone will be asking for you."

Jane was silent for a while then she looked at me.

"Yeah, I talked to him but he wouldn't say much. He's such a grouch and a loner when things don't go his way. He's a bit moody right now." Relieved she was asking about me I wanted to rip the phone out of Jane's hands to make sure Emily was well. "OK. See you later."

Jane walked away from me, and I had to pull her back for an explanation.

"What did she say? How is she doing?"

"She's in Texas visiting her parents. Shouldn't you be with her right now? Her voice was hoarse like she'd been crying…a lot. Whatever happened between you two, let it go. Don't be your immature self. Call her and talk to her."

Jane made perfect sense, but I ignored her comment and walked down the hallway.

"Jake! It's New Year's Day and Emily's by herself. She has no family. Imagine how sad she'll be visiting her parents alone. You can be such a jerk sometimes. Let go of that stupid pride. Call her. Do you want me to call her for you?"

More than anything I wished Jane would take the initiative and force me to speak with Emily. This would be the only way my pride would allow Emily back into my life at this moment. Of course, Jane had no idea of what I desired, and I surely couldn't explain it to her.

"Jake, let me tell you something. Back in San Francisco and the other night on the plane, Emily confessed to me how much she loved you and how her feelings for you frightened her. She thought you were too perfect in her imperfect world. I tried to convince her that she was being needlessly paranoid, but deep inside I don't think she ever let go of the idea that you would walk away from her one day."

My heart ripped into even smaller pieces. I, a grown man, wanted to cry.

"You've now validated her fears. Don't you know how lonely Emily has been for so long? She might look and sound cheerful on the outside, but on the inside she's like a timid child at a new school—looking for a friend to sit with, to have lunch with, to be friends with. You were her best friend, and I don't know what went wrong, but she's crushed right now. Talk to her..."

Like a fool, I walked away.

Today was a day I would have begged for more work. Everyone's heart seemed to be well except mine. Eight hours of misery later I walked out of the hospital contemplating where I should go. My car drove itself to Emily's house. Parked outside her home, I thought about what I would do when she got home. Would I forgive her and continue with this relationship? Did she want to be forgiven? Perhaps she wouldn't want to continue our relationship.

I couldn't help recounting all the times I told her I loved her and showed her my heart. She had never fully reciprocated. But...there was Christmas night when she attempted to reciprocate. A myriad of conflicting thoughts filled my mind. Did she love me? Did she not? There was one conclusion that arrested all other thoughts—she turned down my proposal but was considering Max's. Once this entered my mind, I drove the car back home.

There was another text waiting for me when I got home. Apparently I hadn't taken my phone to work.

Hi, Jake. I'm at the airport coming home after visiting my parents. I'd hoped that you might have called by now—but you haven't. I know I messed up our relationship but I'd really like to try to work it out with you. Please forgive me. I can't imagine how hurt you must be right now. Believe me when I tell you I love you. Please call me.

It baffled me how she could be considering another man's proposal but tell me she loved me. I was livid reading this text. I couldn't think clearly; I had to turn in for the night.

Hi, Jake. School starts for me today. I'm quite relieved to have twenty-four kids clutter my mind from now on. I see that you haven't found it in your heart to forgive me yet. It makes me sad but I understand. I still have hope that your love for me will win over your anger toward me. I hope you are doing well. I miss you. I love you.

Today's text hit me harder than all the other ones I'd received. I knew my love for her was far greater than my anger toward this situation but I still couldn't get myself to call her. I missed her terribly and I too felt enormously empty and lonely without her. I hurt knowing she hurt, but there was also a part of me that wanted her to hurt. I had been so good to her all this time; I had loved her so much since the day we met and this was the way she was treating me. If there was any justice she would be just as miserable without me as I was without her—no, she should be even more miserable! I wanted her to appreciate me.

Still, I stopped by her house daily. Picking up the phone and calling wasn't an option, but I wanted to be near her. Possibly, I wanted to run into her and tell her just how empty my life was without her. With or without Max in the picture, I desperately wanted her to know how I felt. Today I stopped by early in the morning, but she had already left. On my way to work I got a call.

"Hey, Jake. Anything change between you and Emily?" It was Jane.

"Jane, I don't want to talk about it. Can't you just leave me alone?"

"I'm calling because I'm worried about Emily."

"Why? What's wrong with Emily?" I could never forgive myself if something happened to her because I wasn't around to take care of her.

"She's not answering her phone, and she won't return any of my calls. What's going on?"

"Jane, I don't know. We haven't spoken since Christmas."

"You haven't called her back? What could she have possibly done for you to not speak to her for so long? Did you two break up?"

"I gotta go. Let's talk later."

I heard Jane calling out my name, but I hung up on her.

Later that afternoon I stopped by again and she was still not home. I sat on her swing in front of her house when another text came in.

Hi, Jake. How are you doing? I hope you are not working too hard. What a silly thing to say, of course you are working hard. I too have been working hard at school. Today was an ugly day, as my student Jimmy got sick and threw up on me. It's been a while since we last spoke. Wow, you can hold a grudge. I thought you might have responded by now. I know I hurt you, and don't have a right to say this, but I hurt too, as you don't respond to any of my messages. Please call.

    I was disheartened to notice she didn't write that she loved me or missed me anymore. It pained me to think she had chosen Max over me and this was her way of trying to tell me our relationship was over. Next time we talked, could I be like Max and let her go, believing this was the best for her? I wasn't as selfless as Max. I didn't care if he wanted her and she wanted him, I wanted her and that's all that mattered. I would fight for her. This had gone on long enough. Jane was right. I was an idiot for not responding to Emily.
    I couldn't take it anymore. Right as my fingers punched in her number, the hospital called me back in to work. Figuring I could come back tonight, I went back to the hospital to take care of my patient.
    The next morning, I was getting ready to stop by Emily's house again when she texted again. I thought, "perfect." I would go over and beg for forgiveness. We would put this all behind us and start again where we left off.

Hi, Jake. I spoke with Jane a few days ago, and she told me you said we were no longer seeing each other. I don't know why it never occurred to me you didn't want to be with me anymore. I sent all those texts thinking you still cared for me. I understand, and I don't blame you. I'm sorry I've continually bothered you. This will be my final text. I want to say I'm sorry one last time and ask you to forgive me. You have been nothing but kind and loving, and I've only returned it with pain and uncertainty. I want you to know you are the only man I love. I wish I had figured this out sooner. Be well.

    Sick to my stomach, I dialed Emily's number but her phone went straight to voicemail. Racing to her house, I could only imagine how distraught she must have been all those days thinking I didn't love her anymore. How stupid could I be—just utterly selfish to think only of my feelings. All this time I blamed her and Max, never once thinking she was at home hurting. How could I have boasted my love for this woman when all I'd done was hurt her?
    Thoroughly relieved to see her car in the driveway I rang the doorbell. This nightmare was finally coming to an end.

Ding dong, ding dong. *Emily, where are you? I'm sorry, Sweetheart. It kills me you think I don't love you anymore. Please, answer the door!*

I went around back to look for her spare key and couldn't find it. Her car was here but she obviously wasn't. With a heavy heart I left her house. My life suddenly flashed before me and Emily wasn't in the picture anymore. All day I fought to rid myself of this horrid thought.

My phone rang and I jumped to answer it. It could only be Emily, I thought—or hoped.

"Hello?"

"Jake."

"Hey, Nick." Disappointed it wasn't Emily, I couldn't show any enthusiasm toward my brother.

"Are we leaving for New York tonight?"

"What do you mean?"

"Remember? We are all supposed to go to Masa this weekend. Where's Emily? Did she leave already?"

A refusal was on the tip of my tongue when it occurred to me maybe Jane could answer all these questions in my head. Emily said in her last text that she had spoken with Jane. Perhaps Emily confided in Jane what she was feeling all these weeks. I'd go talk to my sister and get some answers.

"What time is our flight?"

"Midnight."

"I'll pick you up at your apartment around ten. Be ready to leave."

Praying for a solution to this mess I created, we arrived at JFK and caught a cab to Jane's apartment. Much of me feared Jane would tell me Emily no longer wanted to be with me. Now my worries had nothing to do with Max. I clearly understood this was our problem, and I had masterminded this mess.

We walked into Jane's apartment, and before I got a chance to ask Jane any questions, she and Nick got into a fight about why we were here. Jane was unusually high strung while the two of them argued. Tired from not having slept at all last night, I walked to the sofa to sit down, when out of nowhere Emily walked out of the second bedroom.

EMILY! My heart swelled with joy. She had been with Jane all this time and that was why I couldn't find her. I could finally talk to her and beg her to forgive me. Whether it took a day, a week, a month, I wouldn't let her leave till she reconciled with me. Before I could utter a word, Nick greeted his future sister.

"Emily, when did you get here? It's so great to see you." Nick gave her a big hug and she looked pleased.

I tried to make eye contact, but she wouldn't look at me. Soon I would explain myself and retire the look of fear that still lived in her eyes since I last saw her at the Grand Canyon.

Emily finally spoke. "Um, I got here yesterday." Distressed, she headed to the door and said, "I was just leaving. It was nice seeing all of you."

No! Where are you going? You can't leave me again.

It was my hope to stop her, but simultaneously Nick called, "Emily, don't go. We're going to Masa for dinner. You have to join us!"

And Jane yelled, "Jake, you're such a jerk! How could you leave Emily stranded in Arizona? Why are you ignoring her when she's been trying to get a hold of you for weeks? How can you be so cold...?" Jane babbled on, but all I could focus on was Arizona.

Jane said I had left Emily stranded in Arizona. What was that all about? I turned to ask Emily, but she was gone. My eyes left her face for two seconds, thinking about Jane's accusation, and I'd lost my love again.

"Where'd she go?" I shouted at both my siblings.

"I don't know. She was just here," Nick answered back.

"Jane, what did you just say about Arizona? Why did you say I left her stranded there?"

"Go ask Emily!" Jane sounded disgusted with me.

I bolted out the door, ran down the steps, and came to a halt right outside the door. I searched to my left and scanned the block for Emily, she wasn't there. I turned to my right and found her running to the end of the block.

"*EMILY!*" I shouted from the top of my lungs. I wasn't going to lose her again. Not concerned with the events of the last few weeks, I couldn't live without her another day. Please don't leave me, was all I could think. She momentarily stopped at my holler then continued to walk away, flagging down a cab.

I caught up to her at the end of the block. "Emily. Please don't go." I held her hand and tried to grab her suitcase out of the taxi.

"I should leave. You three have a great time," she answered tacitly.

Emily. Look at me. Please forgive me. The pain in your eyes—how could I have done this to you?

"I feel terrible interrupting you and Jane, but I'm glad you're here. You didn't mention you were coming to see my sister." She looked even more hurt when I said this. "Regardless, we need to talk." I needed to ask her about Arizona among many other misunderstandings. I started with the topic of Jane's accusation as that bothered me the most.

"Emily, what was Jane talking about me leaving you in Arizona?" I feared her answer because deep in my heart I knew what I had done.

She only stared at the ground, silent.

"Emily, answer me! What was she talking about?" Though I shouldn't have been, I got angry again. I was angry at myself but took it out on Emily.

"What do you care?" she answered, shutting the trunk.

"Tell me!" I demanded, but then begged, "Please?" Please tell me I didn't leave you there that morning. *PLEASE* tell me you went back home with Max and Sarah.

"I waited for you to return."

Oh God. You waited just like that night you were leaving for New York. You trusted me to come for you no matter what the circumstance. What have I done? My heart bore down hard.

"What do you mean you waited for me to return? For how long?"

She wouldn't answer.

"Damn it, Emily, how long did you wait for me?"

"...Till it closed," she answered quietly. Even in this situation she was worried about my feelings. She gently told me of the atrocity I had committed.

"What? How could you have waited for me till closing time? Didn't you realize after a while I wasn't coming back? It was freezing that day. You didn't even have a jacket on. How stupid can you be?" That wasn't what I meant to say. Emily, please forgive me. How will I make this right?

In disbelief she stared at me with deep sadness in her eyes. But rather than breaking down and cowering, Emily angrily yelled back at me.

"Yeah, I was stupid all right. Stupid enough to believe you when you said you loved me and wanted to spend the rest of your life with me. Stupid enough to trust your words when you told me you would never let me be alone again. Stupid enough to think that the man I wanted to spend the rest of my life with wouldn't abandon me, that after he calmed down, would come back for me. That's how stupid I was."

I deserved the blame she put on me; every hurtful accusation had my name on it. I had let down my girlfriend—the woman I proposed to and promised many times to take care of for the rest of her life.

"Oh, Emily!" I groaned her name, anguished. "I left you by yourself at the Skywalk? You mean you didn't go home with Max?" How had this happened? "I'm sorry, Emily. I didn't mean to leave you there. You know I would never abandon you. I really thought you were with your friends. I can't believe I did that to you. How did you get home? Oh, Emi." I moved in to hold her for the first time in weeks. She shoved me away and glared at me. In her mind, I had betrayed her.

"I don't want your sorry or your pity. My breakup with Max was a walk in the park compared to what you put me through. You made yourself clear by not returning for me and by not returning any of my messages. I was right to doubt your love. There was no way you could have loved me as much as you said you did."

Please don't believe that. I love you. I'll prove to you I love you. I'll make it up to you.

Within seconds, Emily took off the eternity band and threw it at me. "Here! I don't think this belongs to me anymore." The ring fell onto the sidewalk and rolled. My first instinct was to chase down the ring and then talk Emily out of this misunderstanding.

My foot caught up with the rolling band, and I picked it up to take back to Emily and place on her finger. I ran back to her but found her nowhere in sight. Emily was gone. Never once did I think she would get in the cab and leave me. Just like that, I'd found the ring but lost my love. Frantic, I looked down the street but couldn't find her anywhere. Hoping Jane could help, I ran back to the apartment.

"Jane, where did Emily go?"

Jane looked at me disgusted again. "What do you mean? Weren't you with her? Did you push her away again? What is wrong with you?"

"Just answer my question! Where did she go?" Yelling wasn't going to bring Emily back but I had no one else to express my anger to.

"I don't know. She didn't know either. If you wait a little while, I'm sure she'll call as soon as she checks into a hotel."

"You sure she didn't go back home? Do you know what airline she came on? Call the airline or check the status of her ticket."

"Emily just left," Nick said. "Why don't you wait a little before doing anything? I'm sure she'll call as soon as she knows what she's doing. Right now, there's no use calling anywhere, Emily's in transit."

Nick made sense so I calmed down and hoped Jane could answer all my questions.

"Explain a few things to me," I appealed to the only person who had answers. "Why does Emily think we broke up?"

"Well, that was my fault. When you didn't answer any of my questions, I assumed you two had separated. I mentioned this to Emily just to confirm, and she took it to mean this is what you believed. I'm sorry, Jake. When she got here, I explained to her this was not what you had said, but since you hadn't contacted her in so long she didn't believe me. Why didn't you call her? Do you know how miserable she's been?"

I wanted to beat myself for making Emily so upset. I must have been out of my mind to have rejected all her appeals.

"What did Emily tell you while she was here with you? Can you please tell me everything?"

"Well..." Jane wouldn't continue.

"What's the matter?"

"Emily asked me not to tell you," Jane apologetically answered.

"Why would she do that? What doesn't she want me to know? Is she thinking of getting back together with Max? Is that why?" Maybe I was right not to call her if she had chosen Max. Maybe all this guilt and heartache was for no good reason. "Jane! Is she going to marry Max?"

"Who's Max?"

We both looked at Nick. He was so quiet we forgot he was still here.

"Jake. You think you have it all together but you are such an idiot. If Emily was going to get back together with Max, why would she try so hard to get back together with you? Didn't she write to you and tell you how much she missed you and loved you?"

"Yeah...What does that have to do with anything?"

"She doesn't love Max. She has no thoughts of getting back together with him. She loves you, you big dummy. She wants to marry you, but you've cut off all communication so she has no way to tell you this."

"She wants to marry me? Are you sure she told you this? Why didn't she say so before?"

"Ugh! Talk to Emily. These are feelings she wanted to express to you herself. She didn't want me to tell them for her."

Jane's revelations turned my foul mood into an elated one. I would go back home and find Emily, and we could work out this entire misunderstanding. We could still be married by the end of summer. For the first time since the Grand Canyon, there was joy in my heart.

"I have to warn you though, she was devastated when you didn't come back for her at the Skywalk." Jane burst my bubble.

The Skywalk—how could I have forgotten?

"Tell me what happened. I thought she went home with her friends. What was she still doing there?"

"She told her friends to leave, believing you would come back for her. She waited for hours then caught a ride with a park ranger to a car rental agency. From there she went to see her parents in Texas. Though she didn't say so, by the look on her face, you pretty much ripped apart her fragile heart. The crazy thing was, rather than blaming you, she blamed herself for being naïve and staying there too long. It broke my heart listening to her talk about you. She really loves you."

The room went dark and I had to sit. From the beginning of our relationship I had advertised to everyone this was the girl I would take care of forever. Last we spoke I made her promise to think of me as her best friend and her eternal love—the one who wanted to create a family with her. Emily would never trust me again. I needed to get home and be with Emily.

"Nick, can you see if we can go home today? Call the airline."

"We don't know if Emily went home. She might still be in town. Why don't we wait till she calls Jane." Nick too looked worried about his future sister.

"Knowing Emily, she went back home. She won't be roaming around this city. She'll want to be in a familiar environment. We'll come back next time with Emily and visit the city again. Right now, I need to find my girlfriend."

"Don't worry about it. Let me see what I can do about getting us home."

CHAPTER 13

Emily, Where Are You?

We didn't get home till early the next morning, and I went straight to Emily's. Again, she wasn't home. I racked my brain for the name of her school and couldn't come up with a name or an address. Then I thought of a contact number for Sarah or Charlie or even Max. I didn't have one. A call to Jane was a better option than throwing my phone against the wall.

"Jane, has Emily called you again?"

"No, not since she texted yesterday to say she got home. Are you at her house right now?"

"Yeah. She's not home. I don't know where she could be. She's never out this early on a Sunday."

"I'll call you if I hear from her. You'll find her, don't worry."

"Thanks."

I went home and tried to occupy myself while calling Emily over and over again.

Monday, I got an early call from Uncle Henry while I was at Emily's doorstep again.

"Jake, where are you?"

"Why?"

"You do know you have to be in Seattle tomorrow morning. The rest of your team is here getting ready for the trip."

I had forgotten. This surgery up in Seattle was a last-minute heart transplant. There was no choice but to go. A man's life depended on me.

"Chief, is there any chance you can go for me? I need to find Emily and clear up our misunderstanding." I probably sounded like a love-sick fool.

"I'll pretend I didn't hear that. Your team is counting on you as well as the team up in Seattle. Stop by the hospital and make sure all preparations are going well. I'll see you off tomorrow morning." There was no reasoning with the chief. He hung up on me before the conversation was over.

I stopped by Emily's throughout the day and one last time before I left for Seattle. She was nowhere to be found. During the week, I called, I texted, Mom dropped by, but Emily couldn't be found. Finally, I was home on Monday, and I went straight to Emily's house by late afternoon.

Ding dong.

Thank God…footsteps. She was finally home. This madness was done.

"Can I help you?" A strange woman answered the door.

"Is Emily home?"

"Emily doesn't live here anymore."

"What do you mean? She was just here a week ago. Where did she go?" My outlook on life got even bleaker.

"I'm not sure where she went, but I just moved in a few days ago."

"How long are you here for? Can you give me a contact number for Emily? There must be something wrong. I'm Emily's boyfriend, and I was away for a week. She couldn't have moved during that time. Please, can you give me her contact number?" Desperation engulfed me.

Emily, where have you gone?

"Well, if you're really her boyfriend, then you should already have her contact number, and it shouldn't be a surprise that she moved. Good-bye." Both hands, almost in a pleading manner, stopped the closing door. "Please leave, or I'll call the police."

"Can you please tell me where she went? Please!"

She took pity on me. "I honestly don't know where she went. We've never met. I'm supposed to route a check to her account every month and we have a contract till the end of summer. She won't be back here for at least six months."

"Thank you."

Defeated, despondent, wretched—all emotions whirling in my head, my heart, my entire self. I had no idea why this was happening. Why would she move out of her house, and where could she have gone? I called Jane again.

"Hi, Jake. Are you back from Seattle? Have you heard from Emily yet?"

"Jane, did Emily talk to you about moving out of her house?"

"No. She never mentioned any such thing. Why?"

"She's not here. I just talked to some woman who's living in Emily's house, and she told me Emily moved out for at least six months. Where could she have gone?"

"I have no idea. Do you think she went to go live with Sarah?" That was a possibility. "Have you called Sarah?"

"I don't know her number."

"What's her last name? Search her on the web."

"I don't know that either." I started to panic. Emily didn't want to be found. I had pushed her deep into a corner, because she was scared to face me.

"Jake, think about everything you and Emily talked about, and you might be able to come up with a last name or the name of anyone's workplace. Calm down and think things through. Go home and rest. You must be exhausted."

I went home and thought as Jane told me to do. No information came to me that would help me find Emily. I contemplated hiring a private investigator to find Emily but decided against it. All I could hope was for Emily to call me when her anger and hurt died down or for her to call Jane to give her a new contact address. That's when I would go and make amends.

A week had gone by and I had nothing. As hard as I tried, it wasn't easy hiding my despair from my family. Mom and Dad worried. The chief felt bad after I angrily told him what had happened while I was up in Seattle. It wasn't his fault—this was all a result of my selfishness.

Desperate for a phone call, I tried to go about my day without too much hindrance to my patients. I was done with morning surgery on Tuesday and thought about going out to lunch with the chief to break myself out of this dark haze. I walked toward the nurse's station to page the chief when I saw Emily's shadow darting into the elevator. I ran over to the elevator and caught a glimpse of my girlfriend on the verge of tears. That was her. Even though I saw her for a fraction of a second, there was no mistaking her beautiful face.

I turned to Linda, the head nurse. "The girl who just jumped into the elevator. Where was she going?"

"I'm not quite sure. Chief Reid brought her here but she left this and ran off when she saw you coming."

As fast as I could, I ran down the stairs to the lobby. I saw another glimpse of her leaving the hospital. "Emily!" I shouted her name but she didn't hear me. When I got outside, I couldn't find her. I had lost her again, but was encouraged that she had come to see me, and even more encouraged that she was communicating with me. Cheerfully I opened her letter.

January 27

Dear Jake,

I'm sorry we had such an abrupt ending in New York, but it makes me happy to know I saw you one last time. You're probably wondering why I'm writing you a letter all of a sudden. With much hesitation, I thought it'd only be proper to say good-bye. Since you don't answer any of my calls, I decided to send you a letter instead.

By the time you get this, I'll be on my way to Japan. I got a wonderful job teaching English in a small village. My principal was kind enough to let me take off the rest of the year.

Please accept my apologies one last time. You were truly the one person who understood me like my mom and dad. I will miss that sense of belonging. Please thank your family for their kindness toward me. For the first time in a very long time, I felt like I was part of a family. I will miss that as well.

I hope you found the eternity band. I'm sorry I threw it at you in New York. I'm also sorry I kept it so long. That ring made me feel like I was still a part of your life. I know now it was inappropriate to think this way. Although the band couldn't hold true to its name for us, I hope you will find someone who will wear the ring with confidence, knowing that you two can love each other eternally.

Thank you for loving me. You've touched my heart deeply. I take many beautiful memories of us to a foreign place. Be well.

Fondly,
Emily

My world went completely dark.

CHAPTER 14

This Must Be Hell on Earth!

A week since Emily left, I got home from my attempt to find her in Japan and found a letter waiting for me. I tore it open recognizing Emily's handwriting and prayed she would tell me all was forgiven and that she would come home to me.

February 1

Dear Jake,

Though you probably don't want to hear from me, I thought it would only be proper to write at least once and tell you that I am doing well. I finally got settled into Mr. and Mrs. Suzuki's home. They have two children named Yuki and Ryu whom I will be tutoring till June.

When I first got to their house, it made me chuckle to think that their entire house could fit into your bedroom. My room is a quarter the size of your bathroom. I guess everything here is compact.

The village is peaceful. There aren't too many cars here. We either walk from place to place or people scooter around. The school that I work at is nearby. Since all I do is go from school to tutoring, I do a lot of walking.

I hope that you are doing well. Please say hello to your parents and Chief Reid for me. And please apologize to Gram for me. Let her know I really wanted to meet her, and though I'd only spoken with her once, she made a wonderful impression on my heart. Take care.

Emily

It broke my heart to read Emily's letter but I knew she was safe and I would be able to find her one day. As fragile as her heart might be, she was a fighter and hopefully she would come around to accepting me again. Startled, I jumped when my phone rang.

"Hi, Jane."

"Jake, you're back. Mom said Laney called to say you were in Japan looking for Emily. Did you have any luck?"

"No." I sighed.

"Check your email. I just scanned and sent you Emily's letter. I can't believe she went all the way over there." Jane began crying. "You're such a jerk. You hurt her so badly, she doesn't even want to talk to me. She didn't send a return address."

"Yeah. She did the same on my letter."

"She wrote you a letter? What did it say?"

"She wrote just to say she was OK. I don't know if she's going to keep writing to me. If she continues to write to you, please send them to me. I'm going to go, Jane. I'd like to read her letter."

February 2

Dear Jane,

Please forgive me for not having called before I left. I couldn't get myself to talk to you after I saw Jake in New York. I'm in Japan right now teaching English. I don't know when I'll come back home. I hope you'll understand when I tell you I want to sever all ties with home for a while.

I've made such a mess of everything. I have so many regrets—turning down your brother's proposal so quickly, not turning down Max's quickly enough, but the biggest regret I have was never having shown Jake how much I loved and appreciated him. I always knew deep inside he was the one for me. Why was I so scared to admit this to anyone?

Even though I didn't get a chance to fully tell him about my love, I hope he got a good sense of it when he read my journal. I gave him my journal as his Christmas present. I hope my writing clearly illustrates these emotions.

Thank you for being such a good friend. When I get strong enough, you will be the first one I send a return address to. Until then, I'll write…you read. Take care.

Emily

The journal. How could I have forgotten about the journal she gave me for Christmas? Frantic, I thought through Christmas night and couldn't tear myself away from her consent to be with me that night. That consent alone should have told me she loved me and only me. Why was I so stupid? Where did she leave this journal? After tearing apart my room I found it on my bookshelf. Unwrapping the bow, I sat down desperate to hear her voice again.

November 7

I met a guy yesterday who made my heart go pitter patter for the first time in a long while. I met him while looking for food at a grocery store late at night. He stared at me with a curious eye, and I honestly wanted to stare back at him. He was so handsome. He was my absolute ideal—tall, dark hair, sparkling blue eyes.

I fell down at the market and this man—Jake Reid—was kind enough to take me to his hospital. I felt really lame. What a first impression. He took care of me last night and I felt so safe with him. I haven't felt that safe since Mom and Dad were alive.

He stopped by this morning to check up on my ankle, and we're supposed to have dinner tonight. He picked me up and carried me the moment he entered my house. The last time anyone did this was when Dad carried me around the house singing to me after I woke up from a bad dream. I think he likes me? I'm not quite sure. I guess we'll see. Sarah thinks I'm nuts for going out with a guy I met last night at a grocery store. She scolded me for letting him into the house this morning.

I told her how comfortable I felt with a guy I'd met less than twelve hours ago. Maybe I have gone off the deep end like Sarah said. I haven't had a date in so long I've forgotten what's normal and abnormal. We'll see. I'll write again after my date tonight. I hope my ankle cooperates. I'd really like to spend some time with this Jake Reid.

November 8

So A LOT happened since yesterday morning. Where do I begin? Jake and I went out to dinner—though I didn't eat much beyond chips and dip. He had to leave early. We talked briefly about me and my life up until now. I was stupid enough to mention Max the first night we met, so of course I had to explain more about him. Why'd I bring him up? He's the past. Hopefully, Jake will be the future?

After the date I couldn't stop thinking about this guy. He genuinely showed interest in me. He smiled a lot and many of the things I said made him laugh. When he brought me home, we had such an awkward good-bye. All he did was stare at me for a while, then he asked me out again. I was hoping he would kiss me, but I guess it was a bit early to kiss someone you just met. What is wrong with me? I actually gave him a kiss on the cheek the first night we met, but in all honesty, I wanted to make out with him in the car instead. Ha! Ha! Ha!

Anyhow, he came by again this morning and brought me breakfast. He asked what I liked to eat and bought one of everything from the bakery as well. I wished I hadn't promised Eunice I'd go to her birthday party. I thought of every excuse I could give not to go. I so wanted to spend the day with Jake. He had an entire day off and I was up in Oxnard. Ugh! That was frustrating. We could have been together all day and gotten to know each other.

Sarah sensed how anxious I was to be with Jake so she had me invite him to meet us for dinner when we got back to the Westside. That Sarah knows me too well, thankfully. We all met up at a bar and the second I saw him, he kissed me! Oh, I forgot—he kissed me this morning as well, but very lightly. We kissed several times at the bar. I tried not to show how much I enjoyed it. I don't think I fooled anyone. Sarah and Charlie looked completely alarmed. They'd never seen me so unscripted with a guy before.

Jake asked me to go away for the weekend, and as much as I wanted to go with him alone, I thought it would be best to take Sarah and Charlie along. Funny thing—It wasn't Jake I didn't trust. It was me! Ha! Ha! Ha! My promises of a virtuous life till I got married was going to be challenging with this guy around.

November 10

School has been crazy busy, and Jake too has been busy. I don't know that I like dating a doctor. I can't ever see him, nor can I just call him whenever I miss him. I text from time to time but even then I feel guilty I may be taking him away from his work. There are many more people who need his attention than I do.

I thought about Max today. I hope he's doing well. It's been almost a year and a half since we broke up and I finally feel like I can put this all behind me. I suppose much of this is thanks to Jake. In the short few days we've known each other, I've been able to do spring cleaning to so many parts of my heart. Isn't it strange? A few days with a new guy and four years start to erase automatically. Maybe it's not the four years I needed to erase. It's more the year plus of pain afterward I've got to let go of.

I hope I get to see Jake soon. I miss him terribly.

November 12

Yes! He came by tonight. He called to have dinner but ended up coming over around 9:30. I don't understand why this guy is so busy. Are there no other doctors but himself at his hospital?

Anyhow, I made him dinner, and he looked shocked that I could cook. I couldn't tell if he was just really hungry or if he thought the food tasted good. He was done eating within minutes. We talked about our day and I told him how much I despised eating alone. Though we didn't eat together tonight, it felt wonderful to have him home with me.

Watching him eat, I felt like I had a family again. I don't know when I last cooked for someone. Rather than going out, I'll have to try to cook more often. I hadn't felt that happy grocery shopping and cooking—ever! There was a purpose to what I was doing and someone to enjoy it with.

I had to kick him out earlier than either one of us would have liked. If he had stayed any longer, I really would have forgotten my promise to Mom. Yeesh! It's going to be a long courtship if I'm feeling like this already.

November 15

We had our official second date and our first fight. Maybe fight is a bit of a harsh word. Whatever it was I didn't like it. The morning started off great with us meeting Sarah and Charlie for brunch. I thought we'd have the whole day to get to know each other. WRONG! The hospital had other ideas. This chief of his can be a pain! He called at the onset of our date and told Jake to go to Atlanta.

Why Atlanta? I hope he comes home soon. I have no idea when he'll be back. We got into a disagreement because he thought I was going to his aunt's house for Thanksgiving, but I had already made plans. I waited and waited as long as I could before buying the tickets and agreeing to Sarah's plans. I so hoped Jake would invite me to spend Thanksgiving with him and his family. I was actually feeling down he hadn't done so yet.

Maybe he doesn't like me as much as I think he does?! Well, he asked me today but it was too late. He got mad at me in the car for making other plans. While driving to the airport, I thought about all of Jake's qualities—surgeon, good family, strong and secure, always so sure of himself, has the potential to be with anyone he wants. Then I thought about me—an orphan, insecure, unsure of life in general, not the most social person out there. We are so different.

I don't know if he and I can become a we. We'll have to talk this through when he gets back.

November 20

It's been five days since Jake's been gone and we haven't talked much beyond hi, how are you. He's been really busy filling in for his chief, and school was really busy this week as well. I miss him! This week wasn't much different than last week but knowing he's not down the street leaves a huge hole in my entire being.

I can't figure out why he has such a hold on me. I feel like his prisoner. He can make me happy and miserable all at the same time. Why am I so weak? How can a guy I just met have such a bearing on my life? I don't know how to answer this but what I do know is that I'm miserable right now. I want to call him but can't, knowing he's working.

How sad am I? I wonder what kind of hold I have on him...probably none! I think he likes me but we haven't really talked about us, and I don't know if he has any thoughts of where we are headed. I guess I'm not only frustrated but I'm also confused. We're not officially boyfriend / girlfriend but we're definitely more than friends.

Next time we get some time together, I hope we can talk about our relationship— if a relationship is what he wants.

November 22

It's Sunday and Jake is not going to make it up to Bacara. He's in town but working. Maybe he doesn't really like me? Maybe this is his way of telling me he wants to slowly end the little that we have. I'm really confused.

When I talk to him on the phone, he sounds so genuine. He's always talking about all the things he wants to do for me and how much he wants to be with me. But in actuality, we can't even spend an hour together. I'd like to believe it's because of his work but maybe I'm a fool to believe this. Oh goodness. I gave my heart too quickly and too deeply to a guy I just met and I'm going to be left hurting. Why do I do this to myself?

Whenever Jake talks about us and the future, half of me is thrilled he thinks we will be together for so long but the other half is scared to death he'll leave me. I guess this was a good lesson learned. I really need to guard my heart more and not let Jake or anyone else hurt me so readily.

Sarah and I leave for New York tonight. I asked Jake to come see me off and he promised to be there. If he doesn't come tonight, I'll consider all things finished and let go of my feelings for Jake.

November 22

He hasn't come. I've been sitting here at the airport waiting for him. I've delayed my flight twice, and this time I have to get on. Why did I trust my heart again? Against everything I thought—it's too soon, he's too perfect, Sarah thinks I'm crazy—I went with my emotions. Never again.

I thought he would come see me before I left. I guess my fears have been justified. I'll have to try to erase all that's happened with Jake so far while I'm in New York. What a bummer trip this will be.

UGH!!!

November 22

Jake came! He came to see me! He had to operate on someone, and it lasted a long time. He showed up right before I had to board. Like a fool, I cried when I saw him. My heart was so sad at the thought of having to end everything with him. I really wanted this to work more than anything!

I told him how much I missed him, and I want to believe him when he said he missed me more than anyone he's ever missed. I also confessed how he makes me so happy when we're together and so sad when we're not. Could it be that I love this man already? Perhaps I knew I would love him since the day we met. Whenever we're together I feel like I'm home. No one besides my parents—not even Max—ever made me feel this safe and loved.

I can't believe I wrote three times today. I am so exhausted. The lucky girl that I am, Jake upgraded my seat to first class (yay!) so I can sleep the next five hours into JFK.

Sigh! How will I go a whole week without him? I'll have to start thinking of ways to get out of this trip earlier. Maybe Sarah will tell me to go home if she notices how sullen I am. Then again, maybe not.

November 25

OMG! Can this week drag on any longer? I'm kicking myself for having agreed to come here. I feel so bad. Sarah went out of her way to be with me instead of Charlie so I wouldn't feel lonely, but I'm hating every moment of this trip. I want to be with Jake.

Thanks to Jake I've eaten at my dream restaurant on the East Coast—Le Bernardin. It was every bit as good as touted. And today, we leave our luxurious suite, thanks to Jake again, for Sarah's parents' home. Oh...I talked to Jake's sister, Jane, the other day. She sounded really sweet! I can't wait to meet her.

I wonder what Jake is doing right now. I think I'll call him.

December 10

Jake and I just got into another fight. He came over for dinner tonight, and I asked him to go to this stupid Christmas Ball and that's when everything went wrong. He got upset with me because I didn't ask him earlier. Well, in all honesty, he was upset because he thought I wasn't over Max. I told him I was, but he didn't believe me.

I don't think I like Max anymore…do I? I'm sure there's no more love in my heart for him but there is still a lot of hurt and there is a tie that I can't cut off just yet. I asked Jake to be a bit more understanding of my pain. He didn't want to be—he left me mid-dinner, mid-conversation.

I hate it when people leave me. I feel abandoned. I wish Jake hadn't left. My phone is ringing. It's Jake, but I don't think I can answer it. As it is, I can't stop the tears. If I talk to him, it will only get worse. UGH! Now he's texting. If I don't respond, he'll be worried, or worse yet, he'll stop by and see what a mess I am.

I wish Mom were around. I could talk to her about boys and she would tell me how I should react to situations such as this one. She would have all the right answers for me. She was always so savvy—something I am soooo not! I miss Mom and Dad.

December 11

Max is sleeping in the guest bedroom right next to me. What a shocking turn of events. We don't see each other for eighteen months and now only a wall and a few yards separate us.

Jake took me to the Christmas Ball and as always had to leave early. I drudged through dinner and festivities without him, but instead, with Max and his new girlfriend. After the event, Max and I ended up together—at Peter's scheming—and we went out for dinner. It was REALLY awkward at first, but soon we loosened up and had a wonderful conversation. We realized that we were not just exes, but friends, and dear ones at that. We went back to being friends and told each other about the last eighteen months.

Max told me he was in med school. I was so proud of him for figuring out what he wanted to do with his life. He also told me he was hospitalized the summer after we broke up. The minute he told me about the accident, tears came out uncontrollably. Again, I felt like an idiot! Why I wear my emotions on my sleeve, I just don't know. Max looked comforted. He actually held me for a while. It felt weird to be in his arms. It definitely did NOT feel right anymore. He didn't stir my heart or tug at my emotions. I can for sure admit I don't like him anymore!

Anyhow, Max got really mad at me when I told him how Jake makes me feel. He took it as a slam against our four years together. How could he think I believed there was anything wrong with our four years together? I loved him so much during those years. Looking back, I'm glad he was there for me during that time. It would have been hard not to have had Mom, Dad, and eventually Grandma and Grandpa without Max. He was there as my comfort during those times and I'm forever grateful for his love.

Tomorrow, or later this morning, I leave for a trip with Jake. I can't wait! He promised me a whole day together. I hope we can find some stability to this relationship / courtship / whatever is it that we're doing. I hope Jake likes me as much as I like him. I think he does but still I'm unsure…

December 12

Today was the most amazing day! No one has ever indulged me this much—EVER! We started on a flight up to San Francisco. No—we actually started off really awkward with Jake witnessing Peter, Jeff, and Max all waking up in my house. I've never given Jake an option of spending the night here, but he walked in to see three men sleeping in my house. Not fun! He didn't look like he was having fun either. Well, that got worked out OK, thankfully.

The first place we drove to when we got up north...FRENCH LAUNDRY! How did this man know this was my absolute dream destination? The food...heavenly! The conversation...wonderfully heartfelt. We got issues out in the open and learned a lot about each other. I told Jake everything I could about Max and hoped that he believed my honesty and sincerity.

Then we drove to their family apartment and I did something I hadn't ever done. I fell asleep with him on the sofa. It felt wonderful to wake up next to him. He also gave me this humongous diamond ring and asked me to be in a relationship with him—FINALLY! We are officially boyfriend and girlfriend. It made me happy that we were officially together.

I don't know what time it is right now, but I'm still here in SF and supposed to be sleeping in Jane's room. Jake gave me three sleeping options, and my heart wanted door #1 (Jake's room), but my mind spoke out door #2 (Jane's room). I would love nothing more than to snuggle into bed with Jake right now.

After getting to know the basics, Jane and I had a heart-to-heart tonight. I like her so much! She's genuine and kind and very similar to Jake. Both siblings are so confident. They set a goal and work to achieve it. Jane was valedictorian of her high school and graduated magna cum laude at Columbia. She thought about going into journalism but decided to go to law school instead. She said that one day she would love to write a book. She's so articulate and bright, she will most likely write a best seller.

Now that I've met Jane, I'm curious to know what Nick is like. Both Reids have told me he's the brightest in mind and personality. I can't wait to meet him as well as the parents who raised all three wonderful people.

December 16

I had lunch with Sarah today. She told me about her new project, and she also told me she thinks Charlie's about to propose to her. It is about time. They've been together eight and a half years. I don't know how she's waited this long. I guess it's not hard when you already know he's the one. They're really no different than a married couple. Charlie loves her so much! Maybe he'll propose on Christmas? Maybe that's too obvious. Maybe I'll call and see if he needs my help. Yeah, right. Like he's going to tell me about the proposal.

Jake came by again tonight and I told him about Mom and Dad and how they got together. He liked their story a lot. Who wouldn't like a happy ending? I wonder if we will have a happy ending. I'm beginning to believe we may be headed that way. It's early, but I think Jake's the one.

December 23

Jake's family is incredible. I must be dreaming. Not only is Jake the most amazing man, his family is just as wonderful.

Jake's mom, Sandy, doted on me from the moment we met at the airport. She's so affectionate. She reminds me of Mom. Mom used to hold my hand or put her arms around me all the time. She used to always touch me no matter where we were. Sandy does the same thing. From the moment I see her in the morning, she'll hug me good morning or she'll rub my back when she asks me a question, or she'll just put her hands around my arm and walk with me—that is of course when Jake is not all over me.

I love the attention. She's treated me no differently than any of her three kids. I feel like the fourth even though I'm not family. Most likely she's like this with everyone, but I'm sensitive to it because I haven't felt a mother's touch in so long.

Bobby, Jake's dad, is just as wonderful. He is quite verbally affectionate. He's always complimenting me or giving me choices on what I'd like to do. He does this in such a way where it doesn't come off as just being polite. Once I figured out he wasn't just asking out of courtesy, I started giving him my honest opinions. I even put in requests from time to time.

I don't know if it's right to feel so comfortable with Jake's family. I shouldn't unnecessarily put my hopes in a family who might never be mine.

December 25

Dear Jake,

Merry Christmas! The last two months have been a daily Christmas present with you in my life. I appreciate your unconditional love, your patience, but above all, I appreciate you. I love the way you smile when I say or do something silly, and I love the way your eyes twinkle when I say the right words. But most of all, I love the way I feel every time I'm with you. You know that feeling when you go away for a while and come back home and you think…Ahhh! It's good to be home? That comforting feeling, that, this is where I belong feeling? Well, this is what I experience whenever I see you. I am home when I'm with you.

    I'm sorry I spoke so soon today after you proposed to me. That wasn't really what was in my heart. I regretted my answer the moment it came out of my mouth but I was scared. I've never felt so sure about anything in my life as I do about you. How ironic. My absolute feelings about you frighten me.

    I've known for some time that I am crazy in love with you and want nothing more than to be with you the rest of my life. I guess I'm having a difficult time believing you will still want the same thing a few years down the road. I'm sorry for doubting you. Though I turned you down today, I hope you'll ask again, and I hope I'll be brave enough to speak what's already in my heart.

    You've made me look to the future with a smile and I thank you. I hope this book has given you a glimpse of how much you mean to me. Thank you for loving me.

I love You,
Your Emily

Emily, you silly, fearful, and crazy girl, how can you have been so unsure of us? No wonder you so easily believed I didn't love you anymore and left me. No wonder you could simply give up everything we had and go be alone in Japan. How many times did I tell you not to doubt my love for you? How many times did I tell you I loved you? Was it that difficult to believe me?

If there was anyone in this relationship who didn't show their true feelings, it was you. I'm overjoyed after reading this journal. I didn't know you loved me so much and for so long. I also didn't know you wanted to be kissed from day one. I would have obliged happily. I wish you had told me all your feelings. I wish I had read this journal sooner. If I had, I wouldn't have jumped to any wrong conclusions about you and Max.

I'm sorry for my terrible assumptions about you and Max. I know I hurt you badly. I can't believe how mean I was to you. What pains me the most is that I left you alone at the Skywalk. Like that night at LAX, I should have believed you trusted me to come back for you. What a fool I was. Once again, I only thought about how I felt, not about how you were feeling.

Oh, Emily, how lonely you must be right now. My heart grieves. Come home, My Love. Come back to me.

After reading Emily's journal, I got a second wind of hope. My life flashed before me again, and this time I saw Emily by my side. I didn't know when it would happen, but I knew I would find her and spend the rest of my life loving her.

I got back to the hospital and went about my routine. Morning surgeries continued, patients appeared happy to see me back after a week's absence, and most of all, the chief appreciated my almost cheerful disposition. Mom and Dad too stopped tiptoeing around me and we were back to being a family again. Jane called often and sent me Emily's letters weekly, and soon Nick joined in and drove over with Emily's letters. I had a good sense of how she was doing but soon spiraled back to my abyss, as she never wrote again after that first letter.

The chief found me at lunch one day and had a funny-looking grin.

"Are you excited to leave for Paris on Sunday?"

"Paris? What do you mean leave for Paris?"

"Jake. You were supposed to go to a conference for me in Paris. I guess you forgot? You're probably not in the mood to go, but the hospital is counting on you to represent us. Maybe it will be good for you to get away."

How could a trip to Paris—a trip that was originally planned for me and Emily—be good for me at this point? But, like the rest of my life right now, I didn't have a choice.

"Sure. I'll go."

"Thanks. And Jake?"

I wondered what the chief needed now. "Yes?"

"I'm really sorry about Emily. I feel terrible I sent you up to Seattle. But I know you'll find her soon. She can't stay away from a charming guy like you for too long." The chief laughed and walked away.

That was my initial thought when Emily first left. After her confessions in her journal, I thought there would be no way she could stay away from me for too long. There again was my overestimation of my worth. Emily had been gone for almost a month and she had no thought of keeping in touch me with ever again.

No matter my state of mind and heart, Paris was stunning. Chilly, but beautiful, this was a city meant to be shared with a lover. Never did I imagine I would be so depressed in Paris.

My phone rang during a lunch break.

"Jakey."

"Hi, Gram. How are you doing?"

"Have you had any contact with Emily yet? Has she called or written again?"

"No. She's been writing Jane weekly and she's also started writing Nick, but I haven't received anything since the first letter."

"How are you holding up?"

"I don't know, Gram. It doesn't get any easier as the days go by."

"I'm coming out to see you today. Let's meet for dinner."

"Gram, you don't have to do that. I'll come see you when the conference is all over."

"No, I think you need me there. My assistant will send you a time and place for us to have dinner. I'll see you later today."

"Thanks, Gram. I love you."

"I love you too. Cheer up."

Her call did cheer me up. There were so many people in my life who loved and cared for me. All worked to lift up my spirits. I couldn't help but smile when I thought of my almost-eighty-year-old grandmother flying in to see her grandson because he was distraught over losing his girlfriend.

The smile vanished the moment I pictured Emily alone in Japan without any family or friends. How suffocating it must be for her not to have anyone to talk to. I hoped she was at least communicating with her friends. Maybe it was just us she didn't send a return address to. Perhaps all her friends had access to her, and they were filling her emptiness. Thinking about her being alone, I would even welcome Max comforting her.

Dinner couldn't come fast enough. Gram and I met for an early dinner at L'Atelier de Joel Robuchon. A bit casual for Gram's taste, it would have been a restaurant right up Emily's culinary delight. She would have loved the prix fixe menu that included her favorite caviar and foie gras. There was even a chocolate dessert with Oreos that would have delighted her. There wasn't an item on the menu she wouldn't have wanted to try. Gram caught me as I let out a huge sigh.

"My favorite grandson!" She hugged me dearly. She knew I needed to be loved.

"Hi, Gram. Did you have a nice flight over here?"

"I took the Chunnel in. I can't stand the crowd at the airport anymore. It's easier for me to get around on the train. Have you ordered for us?" Even in her old age, my grandmother was stunning.

"I thought we'd order the prix fixe. Would that be OK with you?"

"Of course. I've always wanted to eat here. I usually end up at La Table. This is for younger people like you and Emily, so I thought we could check it out. You can come back here with Emily next time."

I sighed again at the mention of Emily.

"Gram, I screwed up badly. I don't know when or if I'll ever see Emily again. She's never coming back to me."

"Jakey, don't believe that. She'll come back once the school year is done. A break is always good for a couple. Look at how much you miss each other." Gram put her arms around me and hugged me again.

"I don't know if she misses me. She left thinking I didn't want her anymore. She's probably trying her best to forget me."

"Jakey...if she didn't love you as much as she did, she wouldn't have moved halfway around the world to try to forget you. This is the kind of love you can't let go of so easily. Jane tells me she writes about you in her letters. Emily needs some time to heal herself, but she won't stop loving you."

"Gram, what kills me is that Emily has cut off communication with everybody. She's living in a country where she can't possibly have a sincere conversation with anyone. She's hurting alone. Every time I think about this, it eats me up inside. And I pushed her to this. If I hadn't been so hard on her…If I had just called her…None of this would have happened."

"Jakey, don't be so hard on yourself. She wouldn't have gone away if she didn't think she could take care of herself. Let me tell you a story about your grandpa, and how we almost didn't get married. You'll enjoy it."

"What do you mean? You two were crazy in love. I don't think I knew anyone who loved each other as much as you and Gramps."

Gram smiled knowingly. Her eyes watered thinking about her husband who passed away too soon. "Jakey, you remind me most of your grandfather. You have that same passion and drive. My father was like that as well. That's probably why I favor you. You remind me of my two favorite men."

I never knew this. Our courses began to arrive, and knowing how much Emily would have enjoyed this food, I stared at all the plates set before me. Rather than eat, I sat back and listened to Gram's story. Since I knew it had a happy ending, I hoped to learn something from the story and apply it to my life with Emily.

"I met Jerry in college in London. He was attending medical school while I was in my junior year in undergrad. Your grandfather was so handsome. You look a lot like him, though I think your grandpa was even better looking than you." We both chuckled at her comment.

"Your grandpa courted me for a year then asked me to marry him. I thought as soon as I graduated, I'd be married and live a happy life."

"So what happened? It sounds like everything was going well."

"Jerry decided he didn't want to go into medicine; instead, he wanted to go to business school. Against his parents' wishes, he dropped out of medical school and decided to get his MBA in America."

"I assume you got married and followed him out to the States?"

"No!" she answered emphatically. My gram sounded as cute as Emily when she was upset. This time I put my arms around her and kissed her cheek.

"Gram, you can be so cute at times."

She answered back with another knowing smile.

"Jerry's parents cut him off financially and he didn't want us to get married till he was out of school. He didn't want me to suffer in America—heaven forbid I'd get a job and help support him through school. He told me to stay here for another three years while he got his degree, and he said he'd come back for me. I argued against the idea, but he up and left one day without a word. I was heartbroken. This to me was no different than him breaking off the engagement."

"Obviously you waited or I wouldn't be here today."

"I wrote to him and told him I was going to marry the next boy who looked my way. He basically laughed at me in his letter. I got so mad, I went to study fashion in Paris, and I told my parents not to give Jerry my forwarding address."

"No way. You went off by yourself? So did Great-Grandma really not tell Gramps where you were?"

"Both my parents were furious at Jerry for making me flee to Paris, so they kept to their agreement and wouldn't tell him where I was." Gram started laughing at this point. "During my time in Paris, I met another man, and he was crazy about me. I didn't love him like I loved Jerry, but I was so mad at Jerry I accepted this guy's proposal. And, as soon as I accepted his proposal, I sent a letter with my address, telling Jerry about my impending marriage. Well, he came across the Atlantic faster than I could pick out a wedding dress."

"Was he penitent or was he mad?" If I were Gramps, I would probably be a bit of both knowing the love of my life was willing to marry another man.

She cackled away this time. "Jerry showed up at my apartment, but I wouldn't see him. He begged me not to marry anyone else. He slept outside my door for almost a week. I would sneak out to class early in the morning when he was asleep, and my roommates would let him in the apartment to shower and change when I wasn't around. A week later, after I thought he'd suffered enough, I let him in the apartment and asked him why I should marry him instead of my fiancé."

"What did he say?"

Gram had a nostalgic look in her eyes. "He didn't say a word. Instead he kissed me passionately, and we spent our first night together."

"Oh, Gram!" I was a bit grossed out. "I didn't need to know that. Way too much information—though that was a beautiful story."

"I wanted you to know this story because I believe true love has a way of finding itself no matter how long the separation. You'll find her and when you do, don't ever let her wonder whether you love her."

"Thank you, Gram. I hope Emily has someone to comfort her during this time, as I have found comfort in you." Despair entered my mind as I knew Emily had no one to ease her pain.

March, April, and most of May went by much too slowly. As Jane reminded me in our many conversations, I waited for Emily's school year to be done. We both believed she would be home in June or at least let Jane know where she would be for the summer.

Against my wishes, Mom decided to throw me a birthday dinner, party, festivities, or whatever else it could be called. I woke up on my thirty-first birthday more depressed than ever. It was May 19 here, which meant it was the twentieth in Japan, and it was Emily's birthday as well. She was spending it by herself in a foreign land. I hoped she had made some friends, but knowing my love, even if she had made friends, she wouldn't let any of them know it was her birthday.

The chief and I came home early from work, and the party was in full swing already. There was a room full of family and friends, but I wished more than anything to be alone right now. I wasn't in a celebratory mood. Gram called and I talked to her for a while, and Jane walked in the door and surprised me as well. I walked over to thank Mom for helping me through these difficult days. It was bittersweet every time I appreciated my family for their abundant love, because I was reminded of Emily who didn't have any of this in her life.

The doorbell rang and I walked over to greet the mailman who delivered a couple of packages. One was from Gram, the other—it was from Emily! I ran up to my room and ripped open the package. She had sent me a letter and a gift.

May 10

Dear Jake,

Happy birthday! I did my best to have this reach you on your birthday. I hope I was successful. What did you do for your birthday? I guess it's silly to ask since you can't answer back.

I've been doing well here in Japan, and my Japanese has improved quite a bit. Have you ever visited Japan? It's absolutely gorgeous here. The food, of course is heavenly. Do you know people here don't eat as much sushi as they do in the States—though of course, I still eat it a lot.

I hope this has been a wonderful day for you. I'm sure your family has showered you with love and attention today. This probably wasn't the best idea, but I'm sending you a gift. I found these cufflinks during my trip to Tokyo last week. I was at a department store when I noticed these beautiful pieces with your initials on them. What were the chances of that? I thought these would look nice with that blue shirt you were wearing the night we met at the grocery store. They will both bring out the beautiful blue in your eyes.

If you don't like them, I understand. You gave me so many gifts while we were together I wanted to reciprocate in a very small way. I'm sorry I was always so selfish. I don't think I ever gave you enough—whether materially or emotionally. I was always on the receiving end. Lucky me!

I wish we had spent more time together before we separated. There aren't enough memories for me to think about when I'm here by myself. I guess we won't be celebrating our birthdays together, huh? I had looked forward to our back-to-back celebrations. It will be difficult to spend those two days without you.

I'm sorry to be rambling about. It's a bit tough being alone tonight. My mom died seven years ago today, and I wish I could be with her in Texas right now. I also wish you could be there with me. You always knew the right things to say to comfort me when I thought about my parents. I miss you, Jake.

Maybe when I return in a few years I'll be lucky enough to run into you or perhaps fall into you at the grocery store again.

I hope you have a wonderful birthday. Please say hello to your family for me.

Emily

Even before I put her letter down, I wept like a child. After all I'd done to her, she never once blamed me but always blamed herself for our separation. I knew she would be by herself today. How difficult it must have been for her the day she wrote me this card. Oh, Emily. Please come home to me. What do you mean you'll return in a few years? I can't last much longer without you. I miss you, Love.

CHAPTER 15

Is This Someone's Idea of a Cruel Joke?

My life—still barren from Emily's absence—trudged along. I worked longer hours and participated in every family function whether or not I enjoyed it. Hope was placed in the summer. A time when Emily might come back home. During my morning rounds, I got an unexpected call from Dad.

"Hi, Dad. Did you need something?"

"Son, come home now! Emily's here."

I couldn't believe what I'd just heard. I didn't ask any more questions but begged my dad to keep her there till I arrived. Without letting anyone know, I jumped into my car and got home within minutes.

"Where is she? Where's Emily?" I frantically searched for her once I got in the door.

Mom's face said it all. She had left already. "We tried to keep her here. We asked her to spend the night here with us, but she started crying and left. I'm sorry, Jake."

"How could you let her go?" Frustrated, I yelled at my parents.

"We're sorry, Son. We tried but we couldn't do much when she started crying. She looked so heartbroken, we had to step back and give her some room." My dad was visibly upset as well.

"Why is she here? Is she back home now? Should I go see her at her house?"

"She said she was only here till tomorrow. She's here for her best friend's wedding. This is why she stopped by." Mom held up a clock and a book. Emily must have bought these in Japan for my parents.

"Do you know about her friend getting married? Can you find her there?"

So Charlie and Sarah were finally getting married. I was happy to hear Charlie proposed to the woman he loved and was about to embark on the rest of their lives together. I would have to figure out where they were getting married.

"Mom, I need to get back to the hospital. Do you think you can call around to local hotels and see if they have a wedding booked for a Charlie and Sarah this weekend?"

"Sure. I'll call you the moment I figure out an answer."

"Thank you, and I'm sorry I yelled at both of you."

"That's all right. Emily still loves you, but you've hurt her deeply. Go make things right, Jake," Mom admonished.

I went over and hugged her. "I'm going to try the best I can." My voice didn't sound too hopeful.

Back at work, I tried to push my combined dread and excitement out of the way and worked hard to concentrate on my patients. Walking to the next person who needed my help, I saw a face I never in a million years thought I would welcome. Max. He was walking toward me and I about bowled him over with my enthusiasm.

"Max! What are you doing here?"

"I'm working here as of today till the end of summer when classes get back in full swing. How have you been doing? It's good to see you." He put out his hand and I shook it gladly.

"Do you have a moment? Can we talk?" I was sure Max heard the desperation in my voice.

"Sure. Have you talked to Emily? Max knew I hadn't but it was a formality he needed to respect.

"No. She hasn't allowed me to contact her. Do you know where she is? Have you talked to her at all?"

"No, I haven't talked to her either. She's only written me letters. She hasn't called nor will she send me a return address. She's hidden herself really well."

Comically, as much as I wanted Max to tell me he knew of Emily's whereabouts, I was glad he didn't know. It would have killed me if they'd been communicating while I was in the dark.

"Can you tell how she's doing? Has she written you a lot of letters?" That last question was a bit of a test. Secretly I hoped he'd say he only got a couple of letters like I had gotten.

"She wrote weekly." That was not what I wanted to hear. "She addressed it to me but often wrote about you. She misses you." Now that was what I wanted to hear. My hope resuscitated, Max continued. "I'm sorry I got between you two. I didn't understand how much she was already in love with you. I didn't think two months would solidify her future. I was wrong to think our past could revive our future. I should have realized earlier that it was long over between us."

"I think it's over with us as well. I hurt her badly. I don't know if she'll forgive me. Plus, she left believing I didn't love her anymore. She's probably let go of her feelings by now." I sighed again thinking about my grim future without Emily.

"If I read my letters correctly, she hurts but is still in love with you. Come to Sarah and Charlie's wedding tomorrow and find out for yourself. Em is the maid of honor. They're getting married at the Biltmore."

Finally! I would see her tomorrow. "Thanks, Max. Thanks for letting me know where she'll be. I'll return this favor one day. I'll see you there."

I went home, happy knowing this nightmare would be over soon. I was inching closer to finding Emily by the hour. I'd get to the wedding after the ceremony was done and accost her at the reception. Neither Sarah nor Charlie would be pleased with a crying maid of honor during the wedding ceremony.

Happily, I took my tuxedo and the cuff links Emily sent me for my birthday present to work and whistled my way through the day.

"Why are you so happy?" The chief found it weird that after almost six months I was smiling again.

"I found Emily. She's here for a wedding. I'm going to go see her after work."

"You found her? Where is she? Bring her to your parents' tonight and we'll intervene if you can't convince her to give you a second chance."

Giving him a funny face, I answered, "I don't want to be spending my first night back with her with the four of you. Leave us alone."

"All right. Don't mess up this time. Chain and ball her if you must, because I can't take your moodiness anymore."

It felt good to laugh again. As soon as work was done, I showered at the hospital, got dressed, and drove to the Biltmore. In less than ten minutes I would be back together with my love—or at least I hoped she'd take me back. With a nice gift in hand I walked up to the concierge.

"Hi, I'm looking for Charlie and Sarah's wedding reception?"

"Um, let me check, sir." The lady took unusually long finding their reception hall. "I'm sorry but I think their reception is over. I believe it was a noon wedding and they were done by six." This was not happening to me again.

"Could you please check one more time?"

"Sure." She made a call to the events coordinator and confirmed that Sarah and Charlie had gotten married earlier today.

I wanted to bang my head against the wall. Why hadn't I asked Max about the time of the wedding? Why didn't Max tell me about the time of the wedding? I looked at my watch and saw it was only seven. If they ended only an hour ago, they might still be around.

"Could I ask you a couple more questions?"

The lady looked like she would oblige.

"Are Sarah and Charlie staying here tonight?"

After typing it into the computer she answered, "No."

"What about Emily Logan?" She looked again.

"She checked out a couple of hours ago."

How lame could I be? When Max told me where the wedding was taking place, a light bulb should have gone off in my head. This was where she was staying. Without dwelling too much on my stupidity, I hopped in my car, headed toward the airport, and called Mom.

"Mom, could you go online and see what flights are leaving for Japan tonight?"

"Does that mean you didn't find her?" She sounded almost as disappointed as I felt.

"Long story…could you do the search and call me back?"

"Sure."

Mom called back and I got a short list of airlines I needed to run to and from. They ranged from times of 9:00 p.m., 10:30, and midnight departures. After parking my car in the lot, I ran to the first airline to purchase a ticket in order to get through the gate. By the time I waited in line to purchase a ticket that wasn't going to be used—as no one would let me cut in line though I begged and pleaded—I got to the gate too late. Everyone had boarded and the gate had closed.

"Please!" I begged the attendant at the desk. "Could you let me in or at least check and see if Emily Logan is on this flight?

"I'm sorry, sir. That's not possible. The gate has closed and the plane is ready for takeoff. Also, we aren't allowed to give the passenger list to anyone."

Since there was only a third of a chance Emily was on this flight, I went to the next airline. I purchased another ticket, searched, and waited, but didn't find Emily anywhere. Hope fleeting fast, I ran to the last airline and went through the same process. No different than my life had been the last five months, I had made the wrong choice and lost her again. Of course she was most likely on the first flight that I missed. Forty-five hundred dollars and three unused tickets later, I went home without Emily.

Putting my disappointment aside, I extended my search.

"Chief." He was my starting point.

"Are you with Emily now?" Having to undo Uncle Henry's smile made me cringe.

"No. I lost her again. Can you do me a favor? Can you look up a med student named Max? He's going into his second year of med school, and he just started working at the hospital. I need his phone number."

"I don't know if the hospital will give out his personal information."

"You're the chief. Don't you have any power?"

"Not really, but I will try."

The chief called back quickly.

"As I thought, they wouldn't give me his personal info, but he will be at the hospital in the pediatric department on Monday. You can find him there. Sorry about Emily."

"Thanks, Chief." I hung up the phone disappointed. I'd have to wait till Monday to talk to Max.

Morning surgery done, I ran up to pediatrics to talk to Max.

"What happened?" we asked simultaneously upon seeing each other.

I went first. "I didn't realize it was a noon wedding. I got there around seven and everything was done."

"I'm really sorry. I thought I told you it was a noon wedding. Sarah and I couldn't believe you weren't there. Here, I have Emily's address. I tried to relay this to you Saturday night but I couldn't find you at the hospital, and they wouldn't give me your personal information."

"How'd you get her address? How is Emily? How did she look?"

"Well…for as much weight as she lost, she still looked her beautiful Emily self." A rage of jealousy surged when Max talked so knowingly about her body and face. "She did her best to look happy for Sarah, but those sad eyes never left. Em almost cried when I told her you were coming to the wedding."

My heart lurched. Was she about to cry out of joy or sadness that I would be there? Five months later there were no more certainties as to where I stood in Emily's life.

"Here's her address." He handed me a sheet of paper with Emily's scribbling on it. "I think she's ready to face you."

"Thank you, Max. I will do my best to bring her home."

"Good luck!" he said and shook my hand again.

I got to my office and looked up the three airlines I had tickets to and booked the earliest flight out of LAX, which was Wednesday. I got a phone call from Jane while wrapping up my ticket purchase.

"Jane. I found Emily."

"You did? I was calling to give you her address. Check your email. I just sent you another letter and a copy of the envelope with a return address. I should've sent this to you sooner, but I was so busy I hadn't checked my mail in a while. How did you get her address?"

"I got it from Max."

"Max?" She was quite shocked.

"Long story, Jane. I'm leaving here on Wednesday. Wish me luck." I let out a huge sigh.

"She still loves you very much. Can't you see it in all her letters? She hurts because you're still so much a part of her heart. Remember, she believes you don't care for her anymore. Go find her and bring her home. Tell her we all miss her."

"Thanks, Jane. I'm sorry I've been so difficult. I won't come home without her, I promise."

"Call as soon as you reconcile. Bye."

"OK." Jane's encouragement made me almost believe everything would be all right once I found Emily. I proceeded to open up her email.

May 20

Dear Jane,

I sent Jake a birthday card and a small present last week. I hope he got it on his birthday. It's only been a month since my declaration of independence to you, and I feel like I've reverted back to the old Emily. Like a fool I rambled in Jake's letter about how lonely I was, and how I wished he were with me. Why do I do this to myself? I thought I had made peace with my heart. He probably laughed at my letter. Maybe he didn't even read it. (Oh, there go the tears again.)

Did you know Jake and I have almost the same birthday? He was born six years and one day before me. We had promised months ago to celebrate our birthdays for two straight days. I guess that didn't happen this year. I hope he had a good birthday. What am I saying? I'm sure he had a great birthday.

It is nighttime, and yesterday and today have been the most difficult days for me since arriving here. I didn't think I'd be alone today, especially not this year. I wished I hadn't trusted all the promises your brother made about our future. It hurts even more when those days come and go without him. I miss you, Jane. I feel so alone today. I tried calling you for the first time, but of course you weren't home.

By the time you receive this, I will probably be in LA for Sarah and Charlie's wedding. They're getting married this weekend. I assume you are in New York, so I won't bother calling you when I get to the States.

School is almost done here. Do you think you can visit me? I'm finally sending a return address so please write back. I can't wait to hear from you. Bye.

Emily

    I will be there soon, My Love.

CHAPTER 16

Emily? Can We Try Again? Please?

Landing in Narita airport my heart was heavy but hopeful. The chief gave me as many days as I needed to bring Emily home, so I contended only to look at the bright side. The cup would be half full from now on.

Asking for directions to Emily's village, my half-full cup all of a sudden toppled over and spilled empty. The person helping me explained it was too late to get to the village, so I would have to wait until tomorrow morning to continue my travels. Despondent but left with no choice, I stayed overnight at a tiny hotel and left first thing in the morning to find Emily.

With very few people speaking proper English, I had my share of difficulties finding Emily's host home. A kind lady walked me to the home, and I knocked, praying Emily was home. A cute little girl answered the door. This must have been Yuki.

"Are you Yuki?" I asked politely.

"Yes," she answered timidly, unsure she should be talking to me.

I heard a man speaking Japanese, most likely her father. He appeared at the door along with a little boy.

"Hello," I waved. "My name is Jake Reid and I'm looking for Emily."

"Ah, Jake san." Yuki and Ryu both repeated to one another, then giggled. It was a good sign that they knew my name.

"I'm Emily's friend, and I'd like to talk to her. Is she home?" I addressed the kids. They shook their heads no and quickly translated my message to their father.

"She is not home. She is…" Yuki started but her father stopped her from disclosing any more information. With a scowl on her father's face Yuki stopped talking all together. He said something to her in Japanese again.

"My father says I can give you no information. Please leave." She looked apologetic. I knew if I could convince Yuki who I was, she would convince her dad.

"Yuki, please let your father know I am Emily's boyfriend. I want to see her, but I don't know where she is. Has she ever talked to you about me?"

Depressingly, she shook her head no again. "But, I know who you are, Jake san."

By now Yuki's mom joined in the verbal ping pong. Yuki gave them a long speech in Japanese and I saw Yuki's mom urging the dad to do something. Next thing I knew, I had another address in my hand, but written in Japanese.

"I told my mom and dad Emily san writes to you every day and she cries. They tell me she is at a restaurant in Arayashima, Kyoto. I will go with you to the train station and help you buy ticket."

I should have known my girlfriend would be somewhere eating. Her first love would always be food.

"Thank you very much!" I bowed to everyone and waved good-bye. I walked through this quiet village with Yuki.

"Yuki, did Emily really cry every day?"

"Yes, Jake san. I don't know why. She write a letter to you, then she cries. Why you make her so sad?"

"After I see her today, I promise to make her happy from now on. Thank you, Yuki." I gave her a kiss on the cheek before getting on the bullet train. My spilt glass was back to being half full again.

Finding Kitcho restaurant proved to be much easier than finding Emily's host home. Each local who helped me with directions explained that Kitcho was the most famous kaiseki restaurant in Kyoto. A smile lit my face when I thought of Emily continuing her life with deliberation. Living in the land of kaiseki meals, she went out to cross off an item on her bucket list. I was proud of her.

When I got to Kitcho, Yuki's dad must have called in a reservation for me because the ladies knew me without any explanation.

"You are together with Ms. Emily Logan?"

"Yes!" I gladly answered knowing soon my glass would be spilling over with joy.

We walked down a long hallway, and as the server began opening the door, I saw a glimpse of Emily's back. I was suddenly breathing again for the first time since she left me.

"Finally!" I cried.

Hearing my word, Emily turned around faster than a speeding bullet. I saw tears of joy shine in her eyes. Oh, My Love. Why do you look so fragile? Why have you lost so much weight? It kills me to see you look so weak.

I practically ran and sat next to her. "Hello, Emily. Very long time no see."

Wanting desperately to hold her, I moved in toward her body but she shied away from me. I was hurt, but I understood. She was utterly befuddled to see me, and she probably didn't know what my intentions were for showing up here.

"What are you doing here?" Hearing her voice after so many months was like listening to an angel sing.

"Why do you think I'm here?" What kind of ridiculous question is that? I'm here for you.

"I don't know. Does the emperor need a heart surgeon?" Good to know she hadn't lost her sense of humor.

"Emily, I'm here to see you. We need to talk. Are you here alone or are you waiting for someone?" She continued to stare but couldn't speak. "Emily, are you not talking to me? I came all the way here to talk to you." It was like I was speaking to a wall. A little more deliberately this time, "EMILY, are you waiting for someone?"

"Yes," her voice raised, she answered with uncertainty.

What? I tried to talk to her again. "You are? Who are you waiting for? Are you waiting for a guy? Are you seeing someone already?" You can *NOT* be seeing someone already. Never once had I considered this scenario. "*EMILY*! I sound like a broken record. Are you seeing someone?"

She stared at me and asked, "Are you?"

This was going to be an irritating conversation if she didn't start answering some questions.

Frustrated, I answered, "Of course not! Do you know how far and wide I searched for you after you left me? Why did you make it so hard for me to find you? Why have you been gone for so long?"

She woke up with an unpleasant look on her face. "A bit bizarre you would try so hard to find me halfway around the world when you didn't bother looking for me when I was just down the street. And by the way, you left me."

Never had she used such caustic words with me. I suppose I deserved it. Nonetheless, her words burned.

The food kept arriving and I chuckled when I thought only my girlfriend would polish off her amuse bouche and move onto her second course, a piece of sushi, in the midst of a reconciliation. I had apparently placed below the food category again, as even our reunion could not stop her kaiseki meal. I ignored my meal and tried to talk some sense into her.

"How could you come into town last week and visit my parents but not me? How could you cut off all communication with me? Didn't you think I would want to see you…that I might worry about you? Didn't you want to see me?"

"How could you accuse me of cutting off all communication when you're the one who walked out on me after asking me to marry you? You're also the one who didn't communicate with me for weeks. I begged you to talk to me."

I was wrong to think this was going to be easy. I was going to have to be more powerful than a locomotive to win over my girlfriend again. What had happened to my meek Emily? We stopped our conversation as another course came in, and she concentrated only on the food, though I understood this was her way of protecting herself.

"Emily. Why didn't you send a return address to any of the letters you wrote? Maybe if you did, I could've resolved our issues sooner."

She stopped eating. She didn't know what to do—finally, a question that stumped her. Rage didn't fire back at me. I saw her upset expression fading. After much thought she gave a long but darling sigh. Perhaps I would soon be able to leap this tall building in a single bound.

"I didn't send a return address, because when I didn't get a response from you, I knew it was because you couldn't respond to me and not because you didn't want to respond to me." Her head dropped and the tears I was hoping for began. I believed now she still loved me. I just needed to convince her of this knowledge. Edging closer to her, I tried to touch her but she denied me again.

I spoke after she calmed down. "Emi, can I explain myself now? I'd like to tell you my side of the story."

"Jake, if you came all the way over here to apologize, don't bother. I don't want to hear it. You walked out on me a few days after you said that you wanted to spend the rest of your life with me and didn't explain yourself for months. How could you not know I would wait for you at the Skywalk? What happened to your promise of not letting me be alone? I have been so alone the past five months without you. I thought you loved me, that you really, truly loved me. Where were you all those days I begged you to talk to me? Why are you here now after all these months?"

Emily's tears were silent but damaging. I could hear her heart being shredded to pieces. I had done much wrong to her but I was confident I could convince her I still loved her, and after that, I would beg her to forgive me.

Hoping she was done I opened my mouth to speak but she pulled herself together and rolled past what I was about to say. "You can't begin to understand how much you hurt me. I don't want my heart broken anymore. You don't owe me any explanation. I have no claim on you. Please just leave."

Giving her more time to calm down and catch her breath, I slowly swept away all the hair that covered her beautiful face. I wanted to look into her eyes when I spoke. She didn't push me away so I brushed away the tears and left my hand on her face. It felt wonderful to touch her again. My Emily, my love.

When I saw my chance, I took it. "First of all, I'm sorry. I'm sorry I walked away from you that morning and I can never forgive myself for leaving you stranded. I can't believe I hurt you so much. You don't know how sorry I am that I left you alone. It was not my intention to not see or talk to you for this long. I came by your house many times trying to reconcile, but couldn't find you. This situation got out of hand." I hoped my words sounded as devastated as I felt.

"That morning when you told me about Max, you broke my heart." Tears glistened in her eyes again. My tenderhearted girlfriend hurt to see me hurt. "I have this bad habit of shutting myself down when things go badly. I know it's wrong and I know I've done this to you many times before. I'll work on that. I promise I will. I won't shut down on you or leave you anymore, I promise you. I'm sorry."

Emily struggled not to look in my eyes as I peered into hers. "I initially didn't answer your texts because I was angry with you. Childish, I know, but I couldn't get myself to return your messages. Eventually I calmed down enough to give you a few days to sort out your feelings and make you want to come back to me and me only. I knew I loved you, but this time I doubted your love for me."

That agitated look reappeared and I knew she was angry again. "Why would I try to communicate with you every day if I didn't want to be with you? I told you in every text that I loved you."

"I believed you cared. But you never affirmed to me that I was the only one you wanted. I guess I was looking for affirmation. When I didn't get this, I figured you had chosen Max over me and I let you go, though only for about half a second, thinking this was the best for you." I laughed a bit and thought it might lighten our mood. It didn't.

"Jake!" In the midst of her irritation, all I wanted to do was grab her and kiss her. I knew all would be OK after we kissed. "Did you read any of my texts? Every day I told you how much I missed you and that I loved you. Did you think it was all a lie?"

"I know. It was stupid of me. I couldn't trust you. I thought maybe you were letting me down easily. Every day I looked forward to your text but a part of me feared you would eventually tell me you had chosen Max." I did what she does so well and shrugged my shoulders apologetically. "When you sent me your last text, I realized I was completely wrong about your feelings. That's when I panicked. I saw these texts from your point of view for the first time. Maybe you still loved me but my lack of response would make you believe I didn't love you anymore. I couldn't assuage the sick feeling in my stomach. Since I couldn't get a hold of you, my only solution was to see Jane in New York. I hoped she could give me some answers."

She was nowhere remotely convinced, so I had to juggle from offense to defense back to offense.

"I came looking for you at your house as soon I received your last text. I wanted to tell you what was in my heart, but you didn't answer the door. Little did I know that I would see you in less than twenty-four hours."

"OK, so you finally saw my point of view, but you still didn't say anything to me in New York to resolve our situation." She moved her face away from me. "If you still loved me, why did you send me away again? You could've stopped me."

"When I saw you in Jane's apartment, I was dumbfounded. You were the person I most wanted to see but the last one I expected to see. At first I said nothing out of shock. Then Nick started talking, Jane started yelling, and next thing I knew, you were gone. Even before I reached you at the cab, Jane's words about Arizona haunted me. In my mind I could picture you standing at the Skywalk waiting for me to return. I was angry with myself but took it out on you instead. Please forgive me. All those hurtful words—I meant none of it."

"Jake…I'm too scared to do this again. My heart is beyond repair. Did you have so little faith in me that you would believe one night with Max would lead to something improper? Did you really think so lowly of me? If that wasn't bad enough, you left me without giving me a chance to explain myself. How can I trust you again? All these months I hurt, believing you didn't care anymore—that you coldly cut me off."

Up until now my attitude and words exhibited confidence. I put behind all those dark months of struggling and brandished a fearless look. After Emily's confession, it was time to beg for forgiveness. My confession, my mea culpa, my declaration of love needed to be spoken.

"Emily, you must believe me when I tell you I love you! I never stopped loving you. I don't believe I can ever not love you. I'm sorry I broke your heart. I'm sorry I abandoned you. I will never do it again. I absolutely cannot live without you. When I read your letter at the hospital, my world collapsed. It was like falling into some dark abyss. I couldn't function for weeks. I took a sick leave and searched for you everywhere. Only when I received your first letter from Japan, did I think that there might be a chance we could meet again. That maybe we would love again. That's when I decided to get my act together and go back to the hospital and wait for you to return to me."

Emily only sat there and nodded her head. I took that as a good sign.

"I will work to earn your trust again. Just please don't tell me we're over. Oh, my sweet Emily, how did we go this long, apart? I've missed you so much."

I leaned in and touched those lips I'd been longing to kiss since our last night together. She didn't move away this time. She froze with our touch. We both savored this kiss we'd desired for so long. I tasted Emily's tears as I refused to let go of her lips. No different than what she had written in her journal, we were home—this was where we belonged.

"Emily?" Penitent and deliriously happy to be with her, I confirmed, "You still love me, don't you?"

For the first time since we reconnected she held me tightly and admitted, "Jake, of course I do. I never stopped loving you. I'm sorry too for hurting you. This was my fault as well. I've missed you so much."

That was my girl. We would be OK—no, we would be better than OK. We would love each other forever.

Emily broke out of our embrace and cast her doubting-Emily look, "You really still love me? We're back together again?" With these questions, I knew my Emily was here for good.

"Emily. I love you!" I reassured her.

"You're not leaving me anymore?"

"Never!" I answered and placed her back in my arms.

Her beautiful smile back in place, she asked me how I found her. The long version started from Sarah's wedding, to LAX, to Yuki's house, and then to finally finding her here at Kitcho. She laughed at my irritation.

"I'm glad you're here. Are you done, or am I still in trouble for hiding myself so well?"

Though there was much more to say, an apology took precedence. "Emily, I've said so many hurtful things to you. My actions were inexcusable. Please forgive me."

"Jake, I created this mess. You had no choice but to feel insecure because I wavered. My actions were hurtful as well. I forgive you as you have forgiven me. Let's not dwell on this anymore." Her answer, always gracious, made me feel better.

"I can't let go of the image of you waiting for me at the Skywalk. You've always been so trusting of me to take care of you. All the months we were apart, the thought of you losing faith in me tormented me. It scares me you won't ever completely trust me again."

"Frightened? Yes. But I don't think I can stay separated from you anymore. Right now and maybe even forever, my love for you outweighs any fear of getting hurt. I want to trust you again. Just please don't break my heart."

I kissed her lips as a seal of my commitment to her. "I'll make this up to you the rest of our lives together. Please don't doubt my love for you anymore."

She agreed with her head bobbing up and down.

We hashed out our misunderstandings about how she could so easily believe I didn't love her and I explained again why I didn't contact her. It dawned on me during our conversation that I had not given her a belated birthday present.

"What did you do for your birthday?" Emily inquired first.

"I was so depressed the last five months, Mom threw me a party. All was going well till I got your card and present, and that depressed me even more thinking about you being alone." I showed her the cuff links she'd sent me. "Thank you for your gift. You don't know how much these meant to me." Then I asked her about her birthday, though I really didn't want to know.

"Did you celebrate your birthday at all?"

She had tears in her eyes when she shook her head no. I was hoping to be wrong about her birthday. I had hoped she had made some friends and had gone out for a fun day.

"Sarah called me and sent me a gift, but that was it."

"Oh, Sweetheart, I'm sorry. Of all the days we were apart, those were the hardest days for me as well. Come here," I pulled her as close to me as possible. "I have your birthday present. I didn't know when I'd be able to give this to you but I had it made regardless."

The flat-shaped sapphire pendant Gram handed down to me along with diamonds added around this stone—my own personal touch—illuminated Emily's neckline. Her smile shone even brighter.

"Jake, this is beautiful! Thank you. How is Gram?" she asked fondly.

I explained to her how disappointed Gram was to see us separated then told her about my visit with her in Paris, retelling all the details of my grandparents' separation and reunion.

"I'd like to meet her one day," Emily chimed in. "Maybe when I'm back in the States we can go see her."

"Emily, let's go home. My family misses you too. I promised them I'd bring you back. Can you leave with me tomorrow?"

Through her silence she spoke her unfavorable answer.

"When is school over?"

"In two weeks. It's not much longer."

I let out a huge sigh. I'd have to go another two weeks without her unless I decided to stay here for the next two weeks. The chief wouldn't be too happy about that.

"As much as I don't want to leave you, I'm going to allow it on one condition."

"And what would that condition be?" she asked.

"When school is done, pack a bag of clothes but Fed-Ex the rest of your belongings to Mom's house."

"Why?"

"Because, you're going to meet me in Paris. We're going to take that romantic trip you promised me. If you agree to meet me in Paris, then I'll let you finish out the school year." This was more than a fair deal.

Her huge grin said it all—no answer necessary.

"Also, I have one more request," I added. "I'm going to buy you a laptop with a webcam. I can*NOT* go another two weeks without seeing you—not after having endured five months. We will set up a time to talk each day."

She grumbled. "Is that necessary? It's only twelve days. What a waste of money."

I gave her a don't-argue-with-me look and she yielded.

We left the restaurant and walked around the streets of Kyoto behaving like two people in love. We held hands, we smiled, we kissed. It was most important to me that Emily understood how much I loved her. Walking around and catching up on the last five months, we finally stopped at a park bench, as we still needed to resolve a few unfinished issues.

"Emi?" I needed to close out Max from our lives. "What happened between you and Max?" I explained to her it was Max who encouraged me to pursue her, and that he was instrumental in helping us find each other. She looked happy to know he had helped.

"Let me tell you what got us into this whole mess," she began. "When I turned down your proposal, I knew it was temporary. It was just a matter of time before I accepted your offer of marriage. My love for you was already there. I just couldn't take that last leap of faith. Ultimately I couldn't trust that you wouldn't wake up one morning and stop loving me."

Her lips deliberately found mine before I could voice an objection about her lack of faith in me. I happily accepted.

"As for Max, I knew the moment he proposed, he was not the person I wanted to spend the rest of my life with. You were too deeply embedded into my heart. 'No' was the correct answer but I was too much in shock to say anything. And then I saw you running toward me, and I was terrified you might be mad. I froze. I didn't know what to do. I hope you can understand these were words I desperately wanted to hear at one point in my life, and I didn't know how to refuse Max but still keep our friendship. Max will always be like family to me, no matter what. Can you handle that?"

I nodded slowly but assuredly. Before I found Emily, I had promised myself that when we got back together again, I would not let my insecurities get in the way of our relationship. Finally, I could accept this man who cared for Emily till I found her. In many ways I needed to thank him for loving her and protecting her during some of her most difficult years.

After Max, we laughed over our disastrous reunion in New York.

"You know what hurt me the most in New York?" Emily asked me.

"That I asked you how stupid you could be for waiting for me at the Skywalk? I was such an idiot that day for saying all those things to you."

She laughed wholeheartedly. "I'm glad you know. No, that's not it. I was most hurt you chased after a ring rather than chasing after me. That's the main reason I got in that cab."

"Emily! Never in a million years did I think you would get in that cab. It was pure instinct that made me run down the block looking for the ring. It wasn't an issue of importance. If I knew you were going to leave, I couldn't have cared less what happened to the ring. How could you think I'd choose a ring over you?"

She did her cute shrugging of the shoulders.

"So I'm confused about something." I wanted to know about her tenant. "You hadn't left for Japan yet because I didn't get your letter at the hospital till a week or so later. Where were you all that time?"

She explained she lived with Sarah then had a sudden fit of anxiety.

"Jake. What am I going to do?"

"Why? What's wrong?"

"I don't have a home to go back to. My tenant is staying in my house till the end of summer."

"Fantastic!" I whooped. "Move in with me.

"Correction, move into my parents' home with me. You can take up occupancy in the guest room, unless... you get scared on the third floor by yourself and want to sleep in my bed with me."

"You're incorrigible." Her lips curled into a wanton smile.

Emily started calling friends and family to spread our news of reconciliation. She bothered Sarah and Charlie during their honeymoon, and I got a threat to my well-being from the newlyweds if I hurt Emily again. Then there was the call to Jane who also threatened to disown me as a brother if I screwed up again. Then Emily had to call Max. She thanked him, then handed the phone over to me, so I could do the same.

"Hey, Max."

"I'm glad you found Em. I can only imagine how big her smile must be on that pretty face. Keep her happy." Something in his voice didn't sound right.

"I want to thank you for your sacrifice. Sarah told me why you let Emily go, and I don't know if I could've been as selfless as you. Thanks to you I've found my happiness. I will do all I can to return the favor one day.

You would be the kind of guy I'd be proud to see my sister date. Thank you again."

"Take care of her. She's a special girl." He sounded sullen saying these last words. He was finally forced to let my Emily go, and I thanked him for this sacrifice as well.

Next Emily asked me to call my grandmother. Though they had only spoken once, there was a familial bond that had formed on Christmas night—not much different than the one Gram and I shared. I called as my love asked me to and handed the phone back to her. It sounded like the two of them shared love and tears, then Gram asked to speak with me.

"Jakey, are you going to propose to Emily in Japan?"

"Yes, Gram."

"Why don't you wait till Paris? Emily tells me you're meeting her in Paris."

"Yes, but why?" I tried to be as vague as possible so Emily wouldn't catch on.

"I want to hand down my mother's diamond to you two. You can get it reset while you're in Paris, then propose to her. Stop by London before going to Paris. Can you do that?"

"Definitely, Gram. Thank you."

Gram had one of the most incredible Asscher cut diamonds. It was handed down to her from her mother, and we all believed it would be handed down to my mother. Ecstatic she wanted us to have her most loved jewel, I would wait a few more weeks before sealing our future.

"What did Gram say?" Emily of course was curious.

"Not much," I tried to sound nonchalant.

"When can I see her? Can we visit her after Paris?"

"That's very possible." I ended our Gram conversation, changing the topic to one I knew she'd be interested in. "Aren't you hungry? I'm starving."

"Wait, we have to call your parents and tell them I'm coming to stay with them. Are you sure they won't mind me living at their house?"

I couldn't believe how unsure she sounded. She still didn't understand my entire family considered her a Reid already. To relieve her worries, we called Mom and Dad and, as expected, they welcomed her with open arms.

We sat ourselves on a plastic picnic-like table at a noodle truck parked nearby and ordered a late-night snack. With all misunderstandings figured out, I still had one last bone to pick with her.

"Emi?"

"Yes?" She had an enormous grin on her face.

"What's the smile for?"

"I love hearing you call me Emi. This is something no one else calls me."

I too smiled and continued. "Didn't you say you were waiting for someone back at the restaurant? You made it sound like you were seeing someone already. What was that all about?"

Her sly grin came back. "Yes, I said I was waiting for someone, but I never said I was seeing anyone."

"What does that mean?" Not being above ranting like a five-year-old, I needed a clearer answer. "Have you dated anyone since you got here? Have other men asked you out? If so, how many?"

The only movement from her mouth was of her chewing her udon noodles. I grabbed my girlfriend and tickled her weak spots—which included about every part of her body. She started with a laugh and ended with a fit of coughing, as a noodle must have gone down the wrong pipe.

"All right! You play dirty," she accused, but I didn't care as long as I got my answers. "You, no, yes, and many," she answered.

Who were you waiting for?—You

The first answer confused me till Emily explained she had been waiting for me since Christmas to come back for her.

Have you dated anyone?—No

I was definitely good with this answer.

Have other asked you out?—Yes

How many—Many

Yikes. I had forgotten about her appeal to other men.

"What do you mean many men have asked you on dates? How many single men could live in that tiny village of yours? And why would they ask you out? Didn't you tell them you were taken?"

"Why on earth would I tell them that? There's no ring on my finger that says I'm taken. And, I didn't stay in the village the whole time. I traveled throughout Japan. You're not the only man to find me attractive."

She was right about that. I wasn't the only man who would love my Emily. I reached into my pocket for her eternity band. Emotion overwhelmed me at the thought of placing this ring on her. Perhaps I would propose to her now and propose to her again in Paris with Gram's ring. Emily watched the ring come out of my pocket and her face lit up this dark night. She believed I was going to propose again. Oh, how I would disappoint her. I hated that thought.

Deliberately placing the ring on her fourth finger, I fought against myself and my promise to Gram, and I swallowed a proposal. All I could utter was, "I don't ever want to see you take this ring off unless I replace it with another one, OK?"

Emi's face fell from the heavens down to the pit of the earth. I could read her disappointment in clear English. I'm sorry, My Love. I'll propose soon, I promise. Hating and yet somewhat enjoying her disappointment, I held back my pleasure.

"What's wrong?" I questioned her so casually. "Were you expecting something else? Do you not like this ring?"

Very matter-of-factly, she voiced her opinion. "I love this ring."

Arriving at the hotel, I walked up to the front desk to get a room. Emily, a little jittery, asked about my suitcase.

"They're holding it for me here. I haven't had a chance to check in yet," I told her.

By the hue on her cheeks I could tell something good might be coming my way.

"Why don't you have them bring your stuff up to my room?" She couldn't look me in the eye, and I didn't care. I grabbed her hand and bolted up to her room before she could change her mind.

My dream turned into a nightmare when I saw the double beds in her room. There was no way I was going to sleep two feet away from her. She had to make a concession.

"Love, I've been apart from you for too long to be satisfied sleeping in a bed next to yours." Please, please, please, say yes.

She gave me a half smile and spoke slowly. "Would it satisfy you to sleep in a bed..." she paused while I prayed, "with me?"

"*YES!*" I cheered and picked up my girlfriend and plopped her on the bed.

She giggled in delight and I had her dress unzipped in a New York minute. Our kiss got quickly suspended as Emily laughed uncontrollably.

"What is so funny and why are you pulling away from me?" I begged for an answer.

"Oh, Jake. I'm sorry. It's been so long I forgot you would connote sleeping in bed with me much differently than I denoted those words." Her body came over to embrace me but I rolled over onto my back.

"You've got to be kidding me! Emily! What else would I think when you ask me to spend a night with you?"

"I'm sorry." She pleaded with her body partly on mine and her lips showering my face. "The best night's sleep I ever had was with you on Christmas night. Since then there hasn't been one night where I've slept peacefully. That's one of the reasons why I lost so much weight. I've been sick a lot since we separated, because I couldn't get enough rest. Can I just sleep in your arms tonight?" she asked with caution.

What could I say to that? Through the course of the next few months I would most likely hear many more heart-wrenching stories about Emily's trials. Securely holding her body to mine we relished a quiet moment.

"Emi, can I ask you something?"

"Sure," she answered pulling away slightly.

"When did your mom put in this crazy request about you saving yourself for your husband?"

"Oh gosh, a long time ago. She and Dad both had a talk with me sometime in junior high. Mortified that both of them were talking to me about boys and sex I agreed to everything they asked. I just wanted them, especially my dad, out of my room. Then, right before Mom died, she had me promise her again." She crinkled up her nose and gave me a what-can-I-do look. "There was no turning back after that last promise."

"So do you know if your mom practiced what she preached?"

Emily went into a guffaw. "I don't think she did. She would never give me a straight answer."

"How frustrating!" I answered half-jokingly and half-seriously.

"Jake, I'm sorry I frustrate you." My love suddenly turned very serious. "But if forever is what you still want with me, then we will have a lifetime to be together. Would you be willing to wait a bit longer?" From cackles to tears between a few sentences, I lifted up her sullen face.

"Love, can we make a few promises to one another?"

Her tears dropped with every nod.

"I promise you that I will never walk out on you or give you the silent treatment no matter what the situation. We will talk through any problems we may have. Even if you don't want to hear them, I will tell you about my feelings."

"OK. I like that promise. What do you want me to promise?"

"I want you to promise me that you will never be afraid of me in any way. I don't want you to fear hurting my feelings or fear losing me. That's not going to happen ever again. I want you to completely trust me again even though it might be hard. It still kills me that I left you stranded in Arizona.

Will you share with me what you were doing and thinking all those hours you waited?"

Were these answers I wanted to hear? Probably not, but I thought if I shared in her pain it could be cathartic for both of us. Our day at the Skywalk possibly traumatized me more than it did Emily.

"I will answer you if you will promise me this will be the last time we talk about the Grand Canyon. You can't keep beating yourself up about what happened there. Can you let it go after tonight?"

"I'll try..."

"Well, the first couple of hours I was busy walking back and forth looking for you. I believed you would come back. There were so many visitors I searched carefully, not wanting to miss you. Then the next several hours I sat in the middle of the Skywalk reliving what had happened that morning and wondering why I hadn't turned Max down right away. First I got upset with myself for not being able to make a quick decision, then I got mad at you guys for hurting me so much."

Now, I couldn't look at her. I was ashamed at my behavior and angry for making Emily suffer through such misery.

"If you were there that long, why didn't you call me? I believed you were with your friends. You know I would never abandon you, don't you?"

"Of course I do. Jake, I know you would never intentionally hurt me. I didn't call initially because I knew you needed to cool down. Then I didn't call because I was angry with you and Max. Eventually I didn't call because I knew it was over between us and that you wouldn't want to see me anymore. Then, sometime after, I sat in the middle of the Skywalk and fell asleep from emotional exhaustion. Only with the help of a kind park ranger was I able to rent a car. Afterward I went to go see my parents and then I came home. The rest you know."

Hearing the story from Emily didn't make it any better. In fact, I felt worse. Emily was smart to make me promise her to let go of this day. I laid back and couldn't speak for a while.

"Jake." Emily brought her face right up to mine and forced me to look at her. "You promised to let this go. Forget about this day, or I'm going to start feeling guilty about the fact that none of this would've happened if I had turned Max down from the onset. Do you want me to start wallowing in my guilt?"

"No...I don't want you to put this on yourself. Let's change the subject. Why did you come all the way up to the OR that day you were leaving for

Japan but run away when you saw me? That was you I saw in the elevator, right?"

"You saw me?"

"I saw you about to cry in the elevator and I ran down the stairs to catch you but couldn't. Why didn't you stay?"

"Well, the chief spotted me downstairs in the lobby when I stopped by to drop off your letter, and he urged me to come up. Against my better judgment I followed him up like a sheep about to be slaughtered. When I saw you walking down the corridor, thoughts about our crazy meeting in New York sprang to mind, along with the fact that you hadn't called me in three weeks. All that combined, I didn't want my heart broken if you were to reject me again, so I got scared and ran…into an elevator." She laughed. "If you would've caught me downstairs and asked me to stay, I would've dropped all my plans to have had one more chance with you. I guess that's what I was secretly hoping for when I followed the chief up to the OR."

"But why Japan? Why did you come here and so suddenly?"

"It's actually not as spontaneous as you think. I applied for a teaching position before I met you. They happened to have an opening in January. Timing-wise it just worked out."

"So all this time you wrote letters to everyone, but no one was able to write back to you? Did you make any friends here? It sounded like you traveled quite a bit in Japan."

"Sarah had my contact info. If you would've found Sarah, you would've found me much earlier."

"Yeah, I tried. Without a last name, it wasn't easy. What is her last name by the way?"

"Well now it's Charlie and Sarah Abner. Before, it was Jenkins, and Max's last name is Davis. Anyhow, I didn't have too many friends here because we had a hard time communicating. But I did get to see a lot of this beautiful country. I used to go into Tokyo all the time."

"By yourself?" I couldn't imagine my timid girlfriend traveling the country alone.

"Yup, by myself. Aren't you proud of me? I did a lot of things by myself. While we were apart, I became a more independent person by choice. When my parents died, I survived out of sheer necessity. But out here, it was more out of a desire to learn about this country. I had a good time by my lonesome." "I am very proud of you, Sweetheart. Every time I read one of

Jane's or Nick's letters it brought a smile to my face knowing you were living a full life despite my absence."

"So tell me some of the things you did while I was away."

"Well, I waited and waited for letters that never came," I lamented.

"Am I back to being in trouble?"

"No." I quickly kissed her lips. "I read your journal over and over again, attempting to make myself believe you still loved me. Did you know I forgot all about your journal till after you left for Japan? Only when you sent your first letter to Jane was I reminded. I was giddy for weeks after reading your journal. I didn't realize you wanted to make out with me from day one."

"Oh, no. You can't use my journal against me." She started laughing. "I think I was in love with you from day one."

I held her even closer to me. "I know I was in love with you from day one. Anyhow, I'm not using your journal against you. I'm just stating a fact. Did you keep a journal while you were here?"

"Yeah, I did." There was a note of apprehension.

"Will you let me read it? I'd like to share what was in your heart during the months you were away from me."

"You don't want to read it, Jake. Of course there's a part of me that enjoyed being here and appreciated living with the Suzukis, but there was another part of me in that journal that struggled through each day. I don't think I want to read it again for a while."

"Whenever you're ready to visit that life, I'd like to do it with you, OK?"

She nodded with a smile.

With that we stopped talking and after a long and passionate embrace, I encouraged Emily to get some sleep. I could see the sun coming up. If my arms were what she needed to get a peaceful night's rest, I would become her pillow for the night.

I couldn't sleep. Just content holding my long lost girlfriend, I caressed her like a father holding his newborn. I could've held her and watched her sleep for days. She woke up mid-morning with a dazzling smile.

"You're still here," she spoke whimsically. "It wasn't a dream."

"I'm still here, Love, and will be with you forever." I kissed her head before we got up to get ready for the day.

With half the day gone, we grabbed a quick lunch and went to the Sony store to buy her a laptop.

"When does your flight leave, Jake?"

"At midnight. I have some time. What do you want to eat for dinner? Let's go have a nice dinner, then I'll catch the Shinkansen to Osaka and fly out of there."

"Didn't you say you came in through Narita?"

"Yeah, but once I got there, I realized it would be easier to get home via Osaka from where you were. They say it's about an hour and a half train ride. What do you want to eat, My Love?"

"I'll give you one guess," she answered excitedly.

"Sushi?"

"Yup!" She jumped up and down. "It's expensive to eat sushi here. A lot more expensive than the States, so I didn't eat it too often. Now that you're here, I'll have to take full advantage of you." It was good to hear Emily giggle again.

A VAIO for Emily, a PSP and Nintendo DSI for Yuki and Ryu, and a multicourse sushi dinner for both of us, and it was time to part. As the night wore on, so did the frown on Emily's face. It was going to be hard to separate again.

"I don't want you to go. It feels like a dream to be back together with you. I don't want to say good-bye anymore." I had never seen Emily cry so hard. Impossible to believe, but I was the stronger one.

"Love, it's only for twelve days. We'll see each other soon. After that, we don't ever have to say good-bye. Make sure you log on to your computer at 9:00 p.m. your time. This will serve as a substitute until Paris."

What I really wanted to say was I'll stay here till your school year is done. I'll take a sabbatical and you can sleep in my arms nightly, but I didn't.

"OK," she sobbed. "I'll miss you."

"Me, too, My Love. Me too."

We said a quick good-bye and got on our trains.

Back at home and back at work I crossed off each day with a thick black X till the twelve days were done. I started the mornings, 5:00 a.m. to be exact, on the webcam with Emily. Many of the days I had to keep our conversation G-rated due to Yuki and Ryu eavesdropping or outright participating in the background.

"Hi, Jake san!" Both kids greeted me before Emily got to the computer. "Emily go to the store for making breakfast tomorrow. Can we talk to you?"

"Sure. How are you two doing?" I greeted them warmly.

"We are fine. Jake san, you marry Emily soon?" Yuki asked.

"Can you keep a secret?" Perhaps I shouldn't entrust my deepest secret to a couple of elementary students.

"Yes. Please tell us." Yuki was the talkative one today.

"I am going to propose to her when I see her in Paris."

Both kids looked at each other—mouths wide open—and yelled, "Okasan, Otosan!" Next thing I saw were four faces looking back at me on my computer. Yuki rattled off what I assumed was my secret to her parents and both their faces lit up with joy. Yuki's mom proceeded to say, "Good luck, Jake san," and left the conversation.

"Hey, what's going on in here?" I heard my love walk into the room.

Both kids giggled and left the room. I should have made them promise me one more time to keep my secret. I trusted they would.

"Good morning, Honey. How are you? I'm sorry I'm late. I had to run to the neighborhood store."

"Hi, Love. What's for breakfast tomorrow?"

"I learned to make these glutinous donuts filled with an from Mrs. Suzuki. I'm going to try them again tomorrow."

"What's an?"

"It's sweet red beans. It's delicious. I'll make them for breakfast when I get back home."

My heart tingled when she referred to living in my parents' house as home. It would absolutely be her home till we got married and created our own home.

"Do you know we only have three more days till we see each other?"

"No…I haven't been counting down the days at all," she answered nonchalantly. "I've only been counting down the minutes."

She made me laugh this time. "Did you get the ticket I sent you? Are you packed and ready to leave?"

"Thank you for the ticket, and I already sent most of my stuff to your parents' house. I will send the last box the day I leave. Honey, I have a request."

"What is it?"

"Do you think I could leave this laptop here with the Suzukis when I leave? They've been so kind to me the last five months. They've treated me like their family, and though I've given them a gift already, I'd like for the kids to have this computer."

Always a sweet soul, I loved her more with each act of kindness. "Of course, you can. I'll buy you a new computer when you get home."

"Thank you, Jake. The kids will be thrilled. Isn't it time for you to get to work?"

"Yeah," I answered, my voice full of regret that I didn't stay in Japan with her.

"I'll see you in Paris, Dr. Reid."

"Bye, Love."

CHAPTER 17

Will You Marry Me? Part 2

The plane landed in Heathrow on time, and Gram had sent her driver to pick me up. I never understood the appeal of London, as weather was always drab and everything was so overpriced. We pulled up to Gram's flat, and she was waiting for me at the door.

"Good morning, beautiful Grandmother." Her wide smile told me she liked this address.

"Hello, favorite grandchild. How was your flight?"

"It was fabulous. Gram, nothing could possibly spoil this day and the rest of my life, as a matter of fact. I'm going to be with Emily again."

"Follow me, Jakey." She led me up to her room. From a safe in her huge closet, she pulled out the most stunning diamond. I couldn't believe she was willing to give this to me and a girl she's never met. "This is for you and Emily."

I hugged my Gram for a long time. "Thank you, Gram, for loving Emily so much. She will be very touched to know you gave this to us."

"My only requirement…hand it down to your daughter. That was my mother's request, and I failed her by having five sons."

"We'll try, Gram. We'll come see you after Paris, and you can finally meet your newest granddaughter."

"I can't wait," Gram said, sending me off to Paris.

I checked into Hotel Ritz, a stomping ground for my family when we were younger, and thought long and hard before deciding to get two rooms instead of one. I kept telling myself Emily would want me to hold her to sleep every night like she did in Kyoto, but I knew if I slept with her for six straight nights, sleep would be the last thing on my mind. In fact, Emily would lose sleep again. Against my better judgment I got adjacent rooms.

"Bonjour, Monsieur Reid." The concierge recognized me from my youth.

"Bonjour." I didn't know whether I should speak French or English since the concierge was actually an American expat. My French was a little rusty so I decided to speak English. "You still remember me? I haven't been here in years."

"Oh yes. How could I forget? Your family came here yearly. What brings you here this week? Are you here on business or vacation?"

"Purely vacation—actually I need to go pick up my girlfriend at the airport soon."

"Ah, you're here with an amour?"

"Yes. Do you think I can ask you for a few favors?"

"Of course, Monsieur Reid. How can I be of help?"

"My girlfriend arrives at noon. Could you ask housekeeping to draw a bath for her? We should be back here in an hour. Also, would the chef do a cooking class for us at the Escoffier sometime in the early afternoon?"

"Bien sur! I will take care of it for you, and I will get you a car and driver for the week. Anything else?"

"Do you think we'd be able to get a reservation for dinner at Le Jules Verne tonight?"

"I don't see why not. I'll take care of that as well."

"Merci!"

"Your car will be ready in about twenty minutes. He will meet you outside."

"Thank you very much," I repeated.

While waiting for the car, I walked past the posh shops and noticed a striking outfit gracing the window of Chanel. Emily would look gorgeous in this outfit. I'd have to have her try it on and buy it for her even if she refused. A nice sales gal greeted me.

"Bonjour, monsieur."

"Bonjour." I answered. "Could you put this outfit on hold for me till my girlfriend can come and try it on?"

"Of course, sir. What is your name?"

"Put it under Jake Reid. Thank you."

This day was turning out better than expected. Emily probably had no expectations of this day except to be with me. I was sure she would be delighted.

My driver was waiting when I got back to the hotel and we left for Charles de Gaulle airport ready to pick up my future bride. Emily came out early with one compact suitcase and ran into my arms. We couldn't let go of one another. Her longing, no different than mine, expressed itself in a borderline wanton kiss that I thoroughly enjoyed. Sooner than Emily expected, I pulled away, not wanting to get carried away with our embrace. I was inches away from calling the hotel and canceling that second room.

Trying to shake off her kiss, I held her hand and took her to the car.

"This is not our car, is it? You got us a driver too? Aghast, Emily stared at me and wouldn't get in the car.

"Yes, it is, and yes, I did." I didn't see why she looked so embarrassed.

"You have got to be kidding me. We cannot ride around Paris in this limo. How embarrassing. We're not rock stars."

"Get in," I commanded.

Emily was in awe with the sights of Paris. Her eyes didn't leave the scenery even with me by her side. At one point during the ride, I had to coerce her to look at me, so I could embrace her. Indubitably, her face got red and told me to hold off till we got to the hotel. With all that was intimated since my love landed in Paris, that second room looked more and more unnecessary by the minute. Still, I would respect her—or better yet, her mother's wishes—a little while longer till we got married.

We walked up to her room and disappointment streaked across her face when I led her into her room. Little did she know how hard it was to see her want me this much. Was this reverse psychology she was using on me? Why was I the one now trying to preserve her purity? I kept reminding myself I wouldn't have to wait much longer.

"This room is amazing, Jake." I led her into the bathroom for her bath. "What's all this?" Her lips formed an appreciative semicircle, and she came over and placed her arms around my body.

Housekeeping had done a fabulous job of drawing my love a bath. Hundreds of rose petals covered the water and scented candles lit up the room. Hot water flowed from the mouth of a gold swan, and I encouraged Emily to relax before we began our many excursions.

"Why don't you unwind a bit and we'll start our trip after your bath."

"Thank you, Jake. You know, you're spoiling me. I can really get used to this." I wanted her spoiled and loved. The theme of this trip would be to assure her of my love.

"It can all be yours if you like, My Love. No one is stopping you." She looked like she was considering taking my offer.

As I headed to the door to run my errand, Emily stopped me.

"Where are you going?" Was this a trick question? Wasn't she about to undress and take a bath? Did she want me to join her?

"Um...out to give you some privacy. Do you want me to stay?" Staring into her face, I saw her contemplate that thought. Absence truly had made the heart and body grow fonder. It was unreal—no, it was perhaps my dream come true—to witness such desire in her eyes.

She changed the look on her face and casually asked, "No, I mean where will you be while I'm taking a bath?"

"I need to stop by Boucheron. I'll be right back."

"What's Boucheron?"

"It's a jewelry shop." Before shutting the door I peeked at her curious expression.

To build up to my proposal, I wanted to drop hints along the way and maximize interest. I only hoped I could hold off till the end of the week to propose. Boucheron hadn't changed since last I visited with Mom about ten years ago. Henri, her favorite jewelry setter continued to work here for the last thirty plus years. Unsure whether he would recognize me, I began to speak in French.

"Bonjour Henri. Vous souvenez-vous de moi?"

"Of course, Mr. Reid. I remember you from when you were a little boy." Henri spoke graciously, as if he were my grandfather. "What brings you here? Is Madam Reid here in Paris as well?"

"No, I'm here with my girlfriend, and I need your help."

"You have finally found your mate?" He chuckled.

"Yes, I have! I can't wait for you to meet her." Henri had known all of us since we were born, so introducing Emily to him would be like introducing her to one of my family members. "Gram gave me her diamond, and I'd like to reset it for Emily." I handed the Asscher cut diamond to Henri.

"Ah, yes. I remember this diamond. Your grand-mere has had this ring reset several times. You are a very lucky man to receive such an extraordinary diamond." He took out his magnifier and began inspecting the diamond. "It's an exceptional quality jewel. How do you want it set?"

"I'm not quite sure. How do most people set it these days? I want to propose to my girlfriend by the end of the week."

"You can leave it alone; it can be set with micro bezel diamonds around the Asscher cut; or you can add trillants or traps on the side. With a diamond of such magnitude, I would leave it alone. It needs no addition."

"I'll take your advice. I also have this two carat solitaire that I'd like to turn into an earring. You'll also have to find me a matching one for the other ear."

"Anything else?"

"Is it possible to do this all by Thursday or Friday?"

"I will make sure it gets done right away. We will need your amour to come in for a sizing. You will have to bring her in somehow without letting her know what your intentions are."

An obstacle—I'd have to come up with a story to throw her off. After Kyoto, Emily was probably on high alert for a proposal so I'd have to think of a good story.

"One more thing…Emily has an eternity band I need slightly enlarged. I will bring it to you when she comes in."

"D'accord, Monsieur Reid. I will call when the ring is ready for sizing."

"Merci. Au revoir."

"Au revoir."

Feeling good about my trip to Boucheron, all I needed now was to hatch a good explanation as to why I needed Emily to go into Boucheron with me. Knowing without a doubt Emily would be hungry, I stopped by the boulangerie and picked up a strawberry and butter cream crepe.

Excited to start the week with my love I hurried up to her room.

"Emily?" I caught her mid-bite. Her eyes looked up but her mouth kept busy on the crepe. "Tell me some of the things you want to do in Paris. We can go out of Paris as well, if you like."

Emily explained she had been to Paris with Sarah before, and she wanted to visit all the usual places most tourists wanted to visit. I'd have to ask Francois, the manager, to add a twist to all of our excursions.

While she added to her list of places to see, she shared bites with me, and once she was done, I led her to the Escoffier. I couldn't wait to see her face when she saw the cooking lessons that were ready for her in the kitchen.

Emily's eyes almost popped out of their sockets when she saw the huge kitchen she would cook in. This kitchen, at least five times that of French

Laundry, contained kitchen equipment beautiful enough to place in any gourmet cook shop.

"Are we really getting cooking lessons?" She could hardly contain her excitement.

"Yes, Love. Put on the apron and let's see what Chef Daniel wants us to make."

I donned an apron with no thoughts of cooking. My satisfaction and pleasure would come from watching Emily enjoy herself. She followed the chef around like a little puppy and did everything he asked her to.

"Amily," the chef gave her name a French pronunciation, "Recevez s'il vous plait lets oeufs, le beurre, le lait et le crème du refrigerateur."

Her French was better than I thought. She took out the eggs, butter, milk, and crème from the refrigerator as the chef had asked. Then she found bowls and mixers and knives and cutting boards and went to work. Several times I served as translator for both parties while I grabbed a seat and drank my cafe. Emily was in her element. When all was done, we had more desserts than we could possibly eat. Of all the sweets my sweet created, the croissants were the winners.

Stomachs filled and hearts content, we walked toward the Tuileries Garden for a stroll in the park. Emily, lips spread with joy, was in deep thought.

"What are you thinking right now?" I wanted to share what was so important on her mind.

"I was thinking that our private lesson at the Escoffier was about the coolest thing I've ever done in my life!"

I knew she cooked well but I didn't realize she enjoyed cooking to this extent.

"If life would have turned out differently for me when I was younger, I probably would've gone to cooking school after undergrad. I feel most comfortable in a kitchen. Maybe one day when I'm retired, I'll enroll in a cooking school just for fun. Thanks to you, I've checked off another thing I've always wanted to do. Thank you."

Whenever Emily shared with me about her earlier years my heart broke. These stories never got any easier to hear. But, I had the rest of our lives to spoil her rotten, in every which way my heart desired.

"What's next?" She pulled me down the block. "This is so much fun! I might never want to leave."

I led her to Chanel and forcefully nudged my thrifty girlfriend into the store. She positively refused to buy a dress here but I didn't take no for an answer. She followed the same saleslady and tried on the dress and boots I picked out for her. By the smile on her face I knew she loved the outfit. It was a sleeker, night version of the outfit she wore up to San Francisco. She looked hot. We purchased the outfit and walked back toward the hotel.

I noticed that the smile had left Emily's face.

"Do you not like the dress?" I asked, concerned. "Are you upset I didn't give you a choice in the matter?"

"No, no. I love the dress. It's beautiful and practical as well. I can wear it multiple times."

"Then why do you look unhappy?"

She gave me a crazy apology for not having given me enough—emotionally and materially—since we started dating last October. Could she still not comprehend the depth of my love for her? Back to the theme of this trip, I had to assure her of my feelings.

"Emily. Back in New York when I was stupid enough to go chasing after your ring rather than stopping you from leaving, then back at home when you left me nothing but a letter and ran off to Japan, I promised myself that if we ever got a chance to be together again, I would spare nothing of myself." Her lips slowly motioned upward. "Whether material or emotional, what I have is yours. And I know that materially, if our situations were reversed, you would do the same for me. So please let me dote on you the way I dreamed for so many months while you were away."

Her face appreciative, her lips showing contentment, she answered, "I love you, Jake."

"I love you too. Now let's get ready for dinner."

Emily went into her room and I hopped over to mine and called Francois.

"Allo?"

"Francois, this is Jake Reid."

"Bonjour. What can I do for you?"

"Could I sign Emily up for cooking classes the rest of this week while we're here?"

"But of course! The classes are held at the Escoffier at 6:30 a.m. every morning. There are two other mademoiselles signed up."

"Thank you. I'll let her know."

"Au revoir."

"Good-bye."

Suiting up quickly, I used Emily's card key and walked in on her as she was finishing. With her dress not fully zipped in the back, I took the liberty of helping myself by unzipping it and allowing my hand to travel up and down her body. Emily turned around and feigned a feeble attempt at loosening my hands. My lips carefully enjoyed parts of her body that weren't covered in makeup.

"Jake," she said, in a tone of gentle admonishment I chose to ignore, "what about dinner? I need to finish getting dressed."

"Let's skip dinner. We can go to the Eiffel Tower tomorrow."

I could feel her inner battle as she pushed me away only to pull me back in for a kiss full of lust. She was so ready to be with me. I tested her struggling willpower even further and tugged off her dress. Quickly glancing at her almost naked body, my lips and hands reached parts of Emily that had never been explored. It felt amazing to touch her.

"Jake?" She let out a weak plea. "Jake? Honey? Please don't…"

She continued pleading but I wasn't listening. I was a few caresses away from sweeping her off her feet and making love to the woman I wanted to spend the rest of my life with.

"Jake…" She was letting out another round of pleas. "I'd really like to honor my mom's wish and stay a virgin till I get married. Please?"

UGH! I stopped immediately and walked away. "I gotta get this done," I thought and spoke a little bit too loudly. I needed to get this ring on her, and then maybe then she would be willing to be with me, knowing we had promised to spend the rest of our lives together.

Leaving the temptation of a bedroom, we went and had a delicious dinner at Le Jules Verne, then drove through the city. Around midnight we found ourselves back in front of Emily's room. Our lips locking again, I let her go, knowing if we stayed together any longer, I wouldn't be able to yield to her wish.

Sometime in the morning I was woken up by a phone call.

"Bonjour, Monsieur Reid. Can you come in this morning with votre amour and try on the ring?"

"It's done already?"

"Oui." I knew Henri was a master jewel setter but he exceeded my expectations.

"Of course. I'll be there this morning."

"Bon."

I had to get up and think of an excuse as to why I needed Emily to try on this ring. What would I say to her? Hopping in the shower, I hatched a devious plan to make her believe she was trying on the ring for Mom's sake, as the ring was supposedly going to be handed down to her. Yes, that was a good idea. Then another thought came to me—I figured out how I would propose to my love.

Quickly getting dressed, I went down to see Francois and asked to meet with the head chef. I asked the chef if he could make five petit fours with pictures on each of them symbolizing our relationship. Each petit four would be placed in a ring-size box with the thought that I'd put the engagement ring in the sixth box. He would also pack a picnic basket for us so I could cross off the last line item on her bucket list—to picnic in the Tuileries Garden with someone she loved. The chef would have everything ready for me on Friday. My plan was set and I raced back to my room.

It was almost time for Emily to get back from her class, but I was still a bit jet lagged so I decided to close my eyes till she got back.

"Hi, Beautiful," I mumbled as Emily woke me up snuggling into my body. "How was class this morning?"

"Excellent!" She sounded happy. "I have breakfast for you, if you like."

Hungry, but liking the feel of Emily in my arms and in my bed, I held her a little longer.

"Why are you dressed but asleep? Do you want me to leave so you can sleep some more?"

My body perked up to the idea of placing Gram's ring on Emily's finger this morning. How would I do this without proposing? I kept telling myself I just needed to wait a few more days.

Emily's curious eyes didn't leave my sight as soon as I told her we were headed to Boucheron this morning. Her senses were on high alert. Walking hand in hand I spoke about our scheduled trip to the Louvre, lunch at Laduree, and a France vs. Italy soccer match in the afternoon. I could tell Emily was waiting for an explanation about the jewelry store, but I didn't say a word. Later, I'd have to explain this was done not as a punishment, but as a defense mechanism. If I started talking, I would end up proposing on this very sidewalk.

Henri and Emily greeted each other, and I finally gave her an explanation.

"So Gram is about to hand down her mother's diamond to my mom. It was my great-grandmother's desire to see this ring handed down from daughter to daughter. Gram wants Henri, our family's favorite jewelry setter, to reset this ring so she can pass it down to her. Gram nor Mom will have anyone touch their jewelry, except Henri."

With only a baffled look on her face, she continued with her questions. I answered all her questions, but in her mind I was giving her all the wrong answers. After her many attempts at a different answer, she stopped talking. A chuckling Henri in the meanwhile brought the reset Asscher cut to me. My entire being began to shake at the thought of putting this ring on Emily's finger. I handed over Emily's eternity band and Henri walked out to give us a moment.

Emily was just as nervous as I was. She stared at the ring then looked into my face and eagerly awaited the question I wasn't going to ask. I tried to smile, though I was sure it was an awkward one. Like the scene in Kyoto, I held her left hand and took a deep breath before holding the ring at the tip of her fourth finger. More than life, I wanted to get on my knees and propose to her this very second.

I'm sorry, My Love, was the only thought that echoed in my mind while pushing the ring on her finger and watching the brilliance on her face. The look in her eyes—a euphoria, a trance, an almost delirium of joy—paralyzed me. I had to remind myself to breathe or I'd buckle from a lack of oxygen. If Henri hadn't interrupted our moment, I would have gotten down and proposed to Emily at the jewelry store. Before caving into my heart's desire, I quickly took the ring off Emily's finger. Her discouraged eyes turned away from me. I caught a flicker of tears in her eyes as she walked outside and pretended to look at the jewelry in the store. It was at this point I decided to pull up the proposal to tomorrow if possible. I called the chef and begged him to finish the petit fours as soon as possible and walked out to see my love. I held her in my arms for a while, knowing how hurt she was at this moment.

The inner workings of the Louvre held no interest for Emily. Sadness wouldn't leave her disposition no matter how hard she tried. I took her to Laduree, a beautiful tea shop specializing in macarons and hoped food—her biggest passion—would bring my girlfriend back to life.

"Emily." We had conversed so little since this morning. She only played with her food. "Emily!" I called again.

"Huh? Yes? Did you need something?" She finally looked at me.

"What's wrong with you? You've been zoned out all morning since Boucheron. Is something wrong?" *I'm sorry, Love. I know what's wrong, but I can't undo your sadness just yet.*

Comically, jet lag was her excuse for her behavior.

"OK," I responded, trying not to laugh. "Have you tried the macarons?"

"Yeah," she answered unenthusiastically.

We left behind more macarons than we ate. Even food was not bringing out an animated response from Emily. This was going to be a long day for both of us.

Our third day in Paris, and to my chagrin, the chef called to say the petit fours would not be ready till tomorrow morning. Bummed out, I headed for Emily's room.

"Why are you here by yourself? Is everything all right?" I was worried she might still be moody from yesterday.

"It's perfect! I came in to call Sarah. I was just headed your way." She reached over to kiss me good morning. Emily appeared to be back to normal, to my relief.

We headed out for a long day of shopping. From flea markets to antique shops to specialty boutiques to a group of book stalls, Emily bought presents for everyone back home. I knew my Emily was back when she told me she was starving.

"What shall we eat?" As always, I left the food choices up to her.

"I'll probably regret this, but let's eat at Moule et Frites. It's right there," she pointed to the restaurant just steps away from us. "Then I want to go eat ice cream at Berthillon."

"All right."

"Did you know," I said while chewing on a mussel, "that there are 250 bouquinistes in the Left Bank? Most vendors have to wait eight to ten years to get a spot to open up a book stall."

"How do you determine who gets a spot and where?"

"It's all based on seniority. Some of these people have been there longer than we've been alive."

"Fascinating," she answered while finishing off her last french fry.

"Are we really eating ice cream now after such a filling lunch?"

"Are you kidding me?" She had an incredulous look on her face. "You can't come all the way to Paris and not eat at Berthillon."

"If you say so." I was stuffed, but I guess my girlfriend still had room in her stomach.

The rest of the day flew by between dinner, opera, and another round of dessert.

I got up early on our fourth day to get ready for our big day. I hurried over to Boucheron and picked up the rings and earrings and safely put away everything but the engagement ring. Once Emily got back, I'd pick up the picnic basket and the blanket, and we'd go have our picnic. Jittery but thoroughly excited, Emily would finally and officially be mine. I waited anxiously for her to arrive.

We left for the kitchen as soon as Emily walked in the door, and I was too nervous to talk to her. Her big brown eyes stared at me and shadowed my every move without a word. We got to the garden, and I found a pretty spot near all the flowers and laid out the huge blanket.

I could see anxiety written all over my love's face because of my silence, but I let it be since this would all be over soon. I quickly took the ring out of my jacket pocket and put it inside box number six. Then I looked through the basket to see what I should bring out first. Searching for the appetizer and wine, Emily spoke.

"Jake, I'm sorry but I don't really want to eat any more French food. Can we just skip to dessert?"

I panicked! If she wanted dessert first, that meant I'd have to propose in the next few minutes. I hadn't even considered how to propose—how would I ask her to marry me? Feverishly I searched through the basket for my six ring boxes and placed them in the correct chronological order.

"What's in all these fun boxes?" Emily stared at the boxes with her beautiful smile.

"Open it." Giving her the first box was cathartic in an odd way. Our crazy courtship was almost done. Emily would be mine forever. I would love and protect this woman for the rest of my happy life.

Emily opened the first box, and I was disappointed that she still had that same look of wonder.

"I guess you don't remember how we first met?" I couldn't hide my disappointment.

"Oh!" Now she got it. "Of course. This was the cereal I was reaching for when I bumped into you. Oh, this is so sweet. Do all these boxes contain a memory?"

I nodded yes while she took a bite then gave me a bite. This petit four tasted no different than Captain Crunch cereal.

"I want the next box," she demanded with her hands out.

I moved myself to face her so I could clearly see her expression when she opened the next five. Emily opened box number two, looked at it, took a small bite, then closed it back up.

"Why are you leaving half the taco in the box, and don't I get a bite?"

"No. Don't you remember? You had to leave halfway through our dinner because you got called away by the hospital. The story of our life! This one doesn't deserve to be eaten beyond the halfway mark. I should've known then you were a workaholic…Next!"

I tried to get a sense of whether she was serious or kidding. My silence must have scared her.

"Please?" she asked angelically and threw in a kiss for good measure.

She opened box number three and thought about it for a few seconds.

"Oh, I get it. This is an opera cake. This must symbolize the opera we saw in San Francisco, right?"

I rang a pretend bell to signal that her answer was correct.

"This is loads of fun!" She clapped her hands like a little girl opening up gifts, and I was Santa who brought her everything on her wish list.

The chef had decorated the fourth dessert with a blue fondant and tiny orange Nemo-looking fish covering the petit four.

"This must be Hawaii. Too easy. Let's see what this one tastes like."

The fifth petit four was an Eiffel Tower, which we both agreed was too intricate and beautiful to eat. We saved it. Though I came up with the memories, the chef outdid himself on the artistry of each item.

Emily leaned over the opened boxes and kissed me. "Thank you, Jake, for coming up with such an elaborate trip down memory lane. And thank you for crossing off another item on my bucket list. You are just too wonderful." There was deep appreciation in her eyes.

"OK, I'm ready for the last one."

Handing her the last box, I calmed my nerves the best I could, and this time, I was the one who examined her every move. She too moved slowly—like she wanted to savor the last surprise. Nowhere did I notice any signs of her realizing what was about to happen.

There it was—the look of pure bliss as I saw her open up the ring box. Her face then trickled from an overwhelming joy to a contained joy to a not very joyful face at all. I couldn't tell what was going on in her mind as her smile completely disappeared. She then finished opening up the box with no enthusiasm at all.

"Why is your mom's ring here? Where's my eternity band?"

So that was why she had shown no enthusiasm. She thought I'd place the eternity band back on her finger. Boy was she in for the surprise of her life. I took the ring out of the box.

"Emily, I can't imagine anything I would like more than to spend the rest of my life with you. Will you marry me?"

That was my simple yet heartfelt proposal. Sooner than I could look to her for an answer, she threw herself at me and answered a definite "*YES!*"

Bliss, elation, and above all, love—that's what we both felt at this moment. We were now officially engaged to be married.

Finally. Tears I wouldn't mind wiping off her face. She held me so longingly I couldn't get Gram's ring on her.

"Why did you wait so long? You know I've been waiting." She asked in between the tears.

"Have you been waiting? I hadn't noticed." I couldn't help the laugh that followed. "I rather liked the disappointment on you face each time you thought I might propose but didn't. Your anticipation put me on an emotional roller coaster every time." Surprisingly my laugh turned into a guffaw.

She got upset—in a cute, Emily-like way. "I can't believe you did that! How mean are you? You knew I was waiting, but you kept it from me purposely and poked fun at me in the meanwhile?"

"No, of course not…well, kind of." Formed into a giant pout, I could help myself to her lips. Since we were close to being married I figured my fiancée wouldn't mind being tangled up with me on the blanket. She still pulled away from my lips sooner than I'd liked, and I had to explain why I didn't propose sooner.

"Many times I wanted to propose, but I kept thinking of reasons why it wasn't the right moment. For instance, I wanted to ask you to marry me at Kitcho, but it was a bit too soon after we had reconciled. I wasn't sure you were ready, and we still had many issues to resolve. Then when we were at the park, I thought about proposing with the eternity band, but I knew that if you had said yes, I wouldn't have let you stay in Japan, not even for two weeks."

"Yeah, I probably would've had a hard time leaving you if you had asked that day. But, I was sorely disappointed when you didn't."

"I know. I wish I could have taken a picture of your expression when I put the ring on your finger without much more than a warning for you not to take it off." I had to laugh again when I thought of her sour expression that night. "Although I felt terrible, I didn't propose. But Tuesday was the most difficult. I desperately wanted to propose to you at Boucheron. The look on your face when I placed this ring on your finger was magical. You absolutely glowed. I used every ounce of self-control not to ask you to marry me that day."

"But why? You could've asked at Boucheron. That's why I was so sad that day. I couldn't get this ring and your would-be proposal off my mind. I was really bummed out. I even called Sarah to grumble."

"I didn't go through with it because I had this picnic in motion already. Also, I didn't want to give you another haphazard proposal like the one in the car on Christmas morning. I planned a deliberate expression of my love and forced myself to wait another few days. I was actually going to wait till tomorrow but couldn't hold out any longer."

"I'm glad you didn't wait till the last day. You would've pushed me into depression if this didn't happen soon. As it was, I was giving myself pep talks in the morning."

Gently, I pulled out her hand and placed the engagement ring on my love. It looked stunning on her.

"Wait. Why am I wearing a substitute ring? Did you not bring my ring with you?" I'd forgotten she still thought this was Mom's ring.

"This is your ring, My Love."

"What do you mean?" Her eyes, wide open, she looked back and forth from me to the ring. "What about this whole story about your grandma's ring? Did you make it all up?"

"No, it's all true. This ring belonged to my Gram's mother, and she told her to pass it down from daughter to daughter. As you know, my dad does not have any sisters so there's really no designated heir to this ring. It probably would've gone to my mom and then to Jane. But, Gram offered it to us. When I talked to Gram in Kyoto she asked me to wait on the proposal till we got to Paris. She wanted Kyoto to have this ring. She was most impressed with our love for each other and is elated to welcome you as her granddaughter."

I kissed the teardrops that were forming again.

"Gram loves you too. Let's call her. She's been waiting to talk to you. I wouldn't let her talk to you, because I didn't think she could keep my secret."

I dialed Gram to tell her of our good news.

"Hi, Gram. I'm calling to let you know that Emily accepted my proposal, and we're getting married."

"Congratulations, Jakey! I knew you two would end up getting married. Come see me. I want to meet my new granddaughter. I'll have my assistant send you two tickets on the Chunnel. Can you come right away?"

"Of course we can. Thank you for everything, Gram. I love you." With that I hung up the phone.

"How come I didn't get to talk to her?"

"She wants us to Chunnel into London right now. Do you mind if we cut Paris a day short?"

"Of course not. I can't wait to finally meet Gram."

In deep thought Emily started packing up all the uneaten food. "But Jake? Shouldn't this ring be handed down to a Reid?"

"Sweetheart, you were a Reid the moment I laid eyes on you. You just went about in a circuitous way of becoming one. Mom and Dad have known for a while that Gram had plans to give me this ring. They were pleased it would be handed down to you. And as for Jane, she won't care that she didn't get the ring. Her future husband can buy her a new ring. But…this does mean you need to bear a daughter so you can pass it down to her. Speaking of, how many kids are we going to have?"

"Five."

"Five? I'll be paying college tuition the rest of my life. I'd like to retire one day."

My love, my future wife, the future mother of my kids—I marveled at that thought.

Gram and Emily met, bonded, and loved each other all within their first hug. Gram didn't even look my way the first twenty minutes we were in her house. Her favorite grandchild had been replaced by a total stranger in under a minute. That had to have been a world record. Of course I knew Gram loved my Emily so immensely because she knew of my deep love for her.

"Emily, why are you so thin? Has Jake not been feeding you?" She scowled at me. So she was finally talking to me after looking Emily up and down.

"Are you kidding me, Gram?" I had to defend myself. "She eats like a horse. And, she's got tremendously expensive taste."

"Did you take her to nice restaurants in Paris?"

"Yes, Gram. Jake has spoiled me all week. He's always taken good care of me—starting from the day we met." My fiancée was defending me. I liked this feeling. We were a team.

I smiled at Gram, and Gram nodded with satisfaction.

"Gram," Emily spoke again, "thank you for giving us your ring. It's stunning."

"Jakey told me that you refused his proposal the first time because the two carat diamond wasn't big enough. He came and begged me for a bigger diamond so I had to pass down my most treasured heirloom so you would finally marry my favorite grandson," Gram accused.

Emily looked at me in horror.

Stuttering, she spoke, "No, Gram. That's not true. Oh my gosh, I can't believe you told her that." She gave me a nasty look I didn't know she possessed. "Gram… Jake…"

Gram and I howled. My eighty-year-old grandmother pulled a fast one on my sweet and naïve fiancée. "Gram's just kidding, Love."

"Oh!" She let out a breath. "Funny, Gram." Ha, ha, ha was what I expected to hear next but Emily held Gram's hand and walked into the next room for tea.

"When's the wedding?" Gram asked us both.

"I don't know. We haven't discussed it." Emily looked to me for an answer.

"How about the Fourth of July?" I asked Emily.

"Next year, Fourth of July?"

"No, I mean, July Fourth, as in three weeks from now."

"In three weeks?" Gram and Emily both answered in an *are you insane* tone.

"Yup." I didn't know what the big deal would be. Mom and all my aunts would be more than happy to help us. We wouldn't invite too many other people beyond family. A wedding could absolutely happen in three weeks.

"What's the rush, Jakey? She's agreed to marry you. She's not going anywhere."

I needed to finally get around that block. "Gram, Emily won't have sex with me till we get married. I need to get married right away."

Gram lauded Emily's purity, but by the look on Emily's face, I knew I would be in trouble. While Gram called Mom and Dad, I pulled Emily next to me and tried to make amends.

"I'm sorry, Love. I didn't mean to embarrass you. Are you mad?"

"Yes," she whispered.

"How can I make it up to you?" I whispered suggestively in her ears.

She jumped in horror. "You can start by sitting next to your grandmother instead of me. I'm not letting you touch me till we get married."

"I have this feeling you won't be able to hold out for that long." There was something to think about.

"I've waited this long. What's three more weeks of complete abstinence?" Now she was threatening me.

"We'll see…" I faked a confident voice, but I had a feeling she would win if she was determined to keep me at bay. I prayed she wasn't being serious.

We talked to everyone back at home, and I pitched the idea of getting married at the house; Emily loved it. Mom and Aunt Babs would start on wedding preparations till we got back, and we went shopping for our wedding attire. After a quick trip to the dress and tuxedo shop, a bowl of noodles for dinner, and a more than exciting trip to the department store to pick out lingerie for my bride, we were all exhausted.

The three of us slept in Gram's room in three separate beds. As soon as Gram conked out for the night I lunged into Emily's twin-size bed.

"I knew this would happen. The minute her head hits the pillow, Gram is out. We finally get some alone time. I don't think I've touched you since we got to London."

"Is this why you wanted to sleep in this room? I'm still upset with you for your indiscreet confession about my lack of experience. I told you I'm not letting you touch me till we get married."

As soon as my lips touched her neck, it was game over. She lost.

"Your grandmother is five feet away from us."

"We're engaged to be married in three weeks. Are you still going to hold out on me? Should we go back to my room and sleep on the floor? Or, there are many more rooms in this flat with larger beds."

"Like you said, we have three weeks left. I didn't wait this long to break my promise to Mom with three weeks left. You can stay here for a bit, but you need to move back over to your bed," she admonished.

I laughed.

She slept in my arms like an angel.

CHAPTER 18
Mom and Dad?
Pleased to Meet You!

Rather than visiting Jane in New York, we chose to visit Emily's mom and dad in Texas. Emily couldn't contain her excitement as we bought some flowers and walked toward their grave. As we got closer, excitement mixed with sorrow colored her face.

"You are in such deep thought. What are you musing over?"

"Even with you by my side, I was wondering whether I would still be sad when I saw them."

Aside from the obvious, I couldn't understand why she would be sad.

"I'm usually elated to be with them but sometime during the visit, I get sad knowing I have to leave them here. They can never go back with me...I can't ever bring them back to life."

I hugged my future wife to comfort her pain. I realized now I could never fill that void for her no matter how hard I tried. It needed to be filled with parental love. Possibly my parents could try a little harder to fill her emptiness.

"Mom. Dad. I want to introduce you to Jake. This is the man I want to spend the rest of my life with." Emily introduced me to my future parents.

"Hello, Mr. and Mrs. Logan. My name is Jake Reid and I am late but here to ask you for Emily's hand in marriage. I'm sorry I didn't come earlier to ask for your permission. I should have been here back on New Year's Day with Emily, but I was a fool. I've hurt Emily a lot since Christmas, but I promise you I will love your daughter as much as you love her if you'll allow me to marry her. I'll take care of her and protect her. I'll make sure to love her so fully and completely that when she comes to see you in the future, she won't leave you sad, missing your love. Thank you for bringing her up so beautifully. Emily has an incredible warmth and sincerity I'm sure she learned from both of you."

I proceeded to give them our dramatic story from the day we met at the grocery store.

"I'm sure it comes to you as no surprise that Emily stunned me with her beauty and kindness from the day I met her. I think I fell in love from that first night, but it took her a long time to admit she loved me. Mom, I'm sure you're thrilled to know your daughter has kept her promise to you till the very end. She won't let me get too far, though I still try. Sorry, you probably didn't want to know that."

I chuckled to myself till I heard Emily cry.

"What's the matter?" Circling my arms around my soon-to-be beautiful bride, I thought, "I really should carry a pack of tissues with me. You cry way too easily." I kissed her forehead.

"I was just asking my dad who will walk me down the aisle."

"You know my dad would love to walk you down. You can also walk down on your own, and that would make a beautiful statement of how strong you have been, coming this far on your own. We have a few weeks. Let's think about it."

Once I saw that Emily was OK, I continued telling Mom and Dad about our courtship.

"So your daughter doubted my love for her and left me with nothing but a letter and traveled all the way to Japan. I didn't see her again for almost five months. She wrote me two letters, while Max got weekly letters, and when she came into town for Sarah's wedding, she saw everyone but me—her future husband. Can you believe her? After my many confessions of love, she couldn't trust me."

I glanced over at Emily to make sure she wasn't crying again. She was in her own thoughts with a smile on her face. She must have been talking to her parents about us.

"I'm going to assume you love me like my parents love Emily and are giving us your blessing to get married. I know it broke your heart to leave her so early but I promise to make up for your absence. I will take good care of her. Thank you for Emily."

I waited for Emily to be done, and before I could say a word, of course the first thing she said was, "I'm hungry. Let's go have steak."

CHAPTER 19
Should We Just Elope?

We got home to a flurry of hugs and kisses—actually, Emily came home to a flurry of hugs and kisses. My parents outright ignored me, their son who was trying to bring in two large suitcases by himself. Last I remembered, we started with one compact suitcase into London, and about thirty-six hours later, I had two large suitcases. Gram and Emily went on a buying binge during those short hours.

Once all the love was shared between all my family members but me, I led my fiancée upstairs to my room to unpack. We walked in to find all her belongings from Japan sitting neatly in one corner of my room.

"Why don't you take my room and get yourself settled? I'll go all the way down to Nick's room and sleep in his twin-size bed while you sleep alone in my king-size bed." Maybe she got the hint.

"There's no reason to leave your own room." She actually uttered these words.

"Really? Since we're getting married soon, can we start living together as of today?"

She laughed. Of course, she laughed.

"No, silly. I can sleep in Jane's room or go upstairs to the guest room. You don't need to be displaced because of me."

"Forget it. I'll sleep in Nick's room. Good-bye!" I proceeded to march out of the room.

"Where are you going?"

"To rest. I'm tired."

"Oh." She frowned. "I thought we could hang out after I got laundry started."

"We could take a nap together," I suggested.

"Never mind." She rolled her eyes at me. "Go to Nick's room, and I'll come by when I'm done unpacking."

I angrily marched to Nick's room and hopped into bed—alone—to rest before dinner. After I rested, I'd help Emily do laundry and we'd go have a nice meal with my parents.

My eyes opened and it was dark outside. I looked at the clock and it said 4:30. I couldn't tell which 4:30 it was. It looked too dark to be p.m., but I couldn't have slept for over twelve hours already! Dazed, I couldn't understand why I was sleeping in Nick's room. I did a quick replay of my last coherent memory, and I remembered that Emily was living in my room while I temporarily took refuge in Nick's. I ran over to my room.

"Emily?" She wasn't in bed. Actually the bed looked no different than when we first got home. "Emily?" I walked into my closet and still no Emily. But, yikes! Did my closet look clean. All my ties were color coordinated. Belts precisely hung up on the belt rack. Every watch and cuff link were lined up on my drawer tray. My scrubs had been washed, ironed, and folded in a neat pile. I opened up all my drawers, and every piece of clothing had been refolded and replaced according to type—underwear, socks, shirts, shorts, jeans, and sweaters. My closet was scary looking. I didn't realize Emily had a neat-freak side to her.

Emily. The sight of my closet made me forget why I came in here to begin with. I ran downstairs and there she was...my Emily, in the kitchen with an apron on. It was a dream to see her here playing house.

"What's the matter?" Emily asked.

"I came looking for you in my bedroom but you weren't there so I got worried. By the way, is today Monday morning or Sunday afternoon?"

"It's early morning Monday." My soon-to-be bride giggled. "Did you think your bride got cold feet and ran away?"

Wrapping my arms around her, I pulled her into my body. "Good morning, Beautiful."

"Good morning. You fell asleep at 4:00 in the afternoon yesterday. I trust you are well rested?"

"Yeah. I feel good. Did you sleep at all last night? I noticed that you ransacked my room then put it back together in a scary way. Are you normally this neurotic?"

"No. I hope you don't mind. I couldn't sleep so I kept myself busy between your room and these croissants."

My life was only getting better. It appeared Emily made croissants from scratch last night as well. Money was well spent on those cooking lessons at the Escoffier.

I ran back up to my room to get ready for the day and zoomed back down to find a vegetable omelet, French press coffee, and three kinds of croissants waiting for me. I couldn't wait to get married and make this woman my wife.

"Love, what else did you do last night?"

"Um, I did many, many, many loads of laundry by myself even though I recall someone promising to help me." Her lips looked like a right-side up macaroni. I grabbed her cheeks with my hand and smacked my lips on hers.

"Sorry. That was payment for not helping with laundry."

"Ooh. I like those kinds of payments. Then, I unpacked all my stuff and put it away in your, I mean, soon-to-be our mansion-like bedroom. Then I answered a slew of emails—most of them from Japan. And lastly, I chatted with Sarah and Max, and we are all having dinner tonight in Santa Monica. Can you make it?"

"Probably not. I'll call the chief and see what the schedule looks like today."

"What is this delicious smell?" We both looked up to find Nick walking into the kitchen. Emily and Nick exchanged hugs and more love while I sat by my lonesome. He sat and ate breakfast with us and woke up Mom and Dad in the meanwhile.

Emily and I asked Mom and Dad if they'd mind us living with them for a whole year instead of just this summer, as Emily's tenant needed to lease her house another year. Nick also talked of moving back in the house. This was an extremely joyful time for me having all the people I loved under one roof again. We hadn't all lived together in over ten years. To make it even sweeter, I'd be with the person I loved most.

Time sped by and Emily walked me to my car. Her smile turned into a frown, and she sighed.

"I'm sad to see you go. How am I going to go the whole day without you? When will you come home?"

I placed my hands on her face. "Probably not till late—maybe some time after midnight. I'll know better as the day progresses."

"Midnight?" Her whine grew louder.

"The chief told me I've got a tough three weeks before the wedding. You're OK taking care of this wedding without me?"

"Yeah, I'll be fine. I'll just miss you!" I loved it when she whined.

"I know, Love. I'll miss you too."

We kissed, we tried to part, then we kissed some more. It would be a long day without my love.

"Congratulations, Dr. Reid! We hear you're getting married." A group of nurses at the station chorused. "When's the wedding?"

"Thank you. We're getting married in three weeks on the Fourth of July."

"Why so soon?" Jeffery, our youngest intern, asked, "and who's the crazy girl?"

"It's Emily, the girl you asked out and the same girl who turned you down."

"No way! You're getting married to her?" There was a look of incredulity on his face.

"Why do you speak with such wonder? What about this story surprises you?"

"Why would she want to marry you when there are younger, better-looking doctors in this world—like me?"

"Why don't you shadow me today, Jeffery? As a matter of fact, why don't you stay with me all week? Be in OR 1 in ten minutes."

"Maybe I shouldn't have said anything."

Everyone on the third floor laughed at Jeffery.

The morning whizzed by and on my way to the cafeteria, I called Emily.

"Hi, Honey!" Emily sounded ecstatic to hear from me.

"Hello, My Love. What are you and my parents up to right now?"

"We're eating a grilled veggie salad, and after lunch we're going to the Christian Dior store for another fitting. Your tuxedo is here and they want you to come in for another fitting."

Emily gave me a detailed summary of all that had been accomplished for the wedding. Having been with her an entire week after a five-month absence, I missed her intensely. Going home from work had a whole new meaning with Emily living with me. I couldn't wait to be with her.

"Jake?"

"Yes, Love. What's the matter?" She sounded sad.

"I really miss you. Can't you come home any earlier than midnight?"

My heart delighted to hear her sorrow. "I miss you too. I'll be home as soon as I can, but don't wait up for me. It will probably be very late."

"OK." She sighed.

"Do you want me to bring home anything? Are you craving anything?"

"Just bring yourself home. You are all that I crave."

I chuckled at her answer. "All right. There goes my pager. I'll try to call again later. I love you."

"I love you too. Bye."

The next number of hours sped by, and I was more than ready to go home. Tired but happy at the thought of seeing my fiancée, I headed toward the elevator and ran into Max.

"Hey." We shook hands. "I heard you had dinner with Emily tonight."

"Yes. Congratulations. That's some ring you put on her finger."

"Thanks. It's all due to a generous grandma."

"I drove your fiancée home, and she wanted me to tell you she'll be pining away for you. She wants you home immediately."

We both laughed. "Yeah, I'm headed home right now. It's been a long day without her. Have a good shift. See you soon."

"Bye."

I committed every traffic violation to see my Emily that much faster. As soon as I got home I was greeted by a body lunging at me, almost knocking me off my feet. I picked up my love, and we walked up to our room, lips attached. Practically falling on the bed Emily showed me what she meant when she said she was pining away for me.

She responded to my lips, my tongue, my hands. I wondered... did we get married already and I'd forgotten about it? It was unreal the way she was letting me touch her as freely as I'd liked. I took off her pajama top and she allowed me. My hands caressed body parts that usually stayed hidden, and my mouth quickly went south and explored newfound territory. Unknowingly, my hands began pulling down her pajama bottoms, and even with her mouth free to admonish or even weakly complain, she only moaned with pleasure. This was too weird. I had to stop.

Staring at her, I asked, "Are you going to stop me? This is unusual that you haven't said no yet."

Her wide brown eyes stared innocently. "Um, I wasn't ready to stop but I guess we should, huh? Sorry I got carried away." She started to giggle.

"You've got to be kidding me. I stopped us?" She might have gone till the end if I hadn't pulled away. What an idiot I can be at times. "I can't win." I shook my head in fury.

"Yup, I guess I have you trained better than I thought." While she guffawed I walked in to take a cold shower.

"Emily, when do you want to take…" I stopped my question when I noticed she was soundly asleep. Wrapping the blanket around her, I kissed her lips one last time and slept in Nick's uncomfortable bed.

The next morning, Emily wasn't in our room again. She was probably downstairs making breakfast for me. I got dressed as quickly as possible, thinking she might allow me to have my way with her again before I left for work. Looking irresistible in her apron I waltzed into the kitchen and showered her with love till I got rudely interrupted.

"Ahem! Hello, nephew. Don't I get a good morning kiss?"

"What are you doing here, Chief?" As if I didn't see my uncle enough at work, he was in my kitchen interrupting my cuddle time with Emily. "Hi, Aunt Babs. Good to see you." I reached over the island and gave her a peck on the cheek.

Uncle Henry explained he needed a ride to work and while I noshed on my crepes, Emily gave me a rundown of all that needed to be accomplished today. I chimed in and asked her to go to the bank and get her name on all my accounts. She sweetly recited the name on her ATM card that read Emily Reid and smiled.

"Emi, can you deposit my paychecks into our checking account while you're at the bank?"

Instead of a simple yes, I got a shocked, "Do you really get paid this much? Is this a monthly or every other monthly paycheck?"

"Emi, this is a two-week paycheck. You do know that I save lives by operating on hearts, daily. Sometimes it's multiple hearts. Anyhow, we need my paychecks if we're going to enjoy trips like Paris. We probably spent at least one paycheck in Paris."

"Are you kidding me? We spent that much money there? We cannot vacation like that anymore."

"It shouldn't be as bad next time since we won't have to get two rooms."

I attempted to kiss her again when Aunt Babs interfered this time.

"Why did you have two rooms at the Ritz?"

"Don't ask. I got into big trouble for telling Gram that Emily's a virgin."

Aargh! I shouldn't have said that. Emily's head went down, and she gave me that shooting daggers look again. Just when I thought I'd paid for my mistake in London, she would be upset with me again for a while.

"You mean you're not pregnant?" The chief yelled out. "That's not why we're having this shotgun wedding?"

Crap! Only the chief would come up with such asinine ideas to get me into more trouble. I looked over at Emily and couldn't help but laugh. She was mortified at the accusation of being pregnant when she hadn't been anywhere near sex. While everyone at the table apologized for their major faux pas, I took my flustered fiancée upstairs to make sure she wasn't too upset.

"You OK?" I gently pushed her against the wall and undid the tie on the apron.

"I'm fine." She once again flashed her trooper smile.

"I'm guessing," my mouth was all over her ear, "you won't let me," my hands went under her shirt, "finish where we," I unhooked her bra, "left off last night?"

"You're guessing correct," she answered but left my hands and lips alone. "Jake?"

"Hmmm?" I couldn't talk. My mouth was busy.

"Can I come visit you at the hospital and have lunch with you today?"

"I'd love that, Emi. My colleagues keep asking when you're going to stop by. When do you want to come?" Her news was exciting enough to make me stop what I was doing.

"Maybe around 1:00? Will you be done with morning surgery? I'll make you something yummy for lunch."

"I should be. If I'm not done, wait for me in my office and I'll meet you there."

"OK. You should go before Uncle Henry calls for you."

Too late. He yelled my name, but I left only after giving my future bride another round of passion.

The chief and I went our separate ways after surgery, and I ran to my office eager to see my bride.

"Emily?" I walked in to find her asleep on my couch. I knelt down and kissed her lips till she woke up. After calling Uncle Henry to the cafeteria, I introduced my beautiful bride to everyone. All the nurses greeted her warmly—well, almost all of them did. And Emily charmed my fellow doctors with her looks as well as her wit.

"Ms. Logan!" We heard as we entered the cafeteria.

Emily gave me a who's that, look.

"Ms. Logan, do you remember me? I'm Jeffery."

"Umm…"

"Jeffery from the ER, genius young doctor?"

"Oh. I remember you. It's so nice to see you again." Emily unnecessarily greeted him kindly. "You're not in the ER anymore, Dr.…What should I call you?"

"Just Jeffrey is fine," Jeffery answered, first trying to get Emily to be on friendlier terms with him.

"Dr. Collins," I answered soon after trying to separate any niceties between my fiancée and my subordinate.

"Dr. Collins, have you been well?"

"I turned twenty-one, so now we could go get that glass of wine, if you like."

"That's really sweet. After the wedding we'll have you over for dinner and we can have that glass of wine then. Would you like to join us for lunch?"

Before Jeffery got too excited, I told Emily he needed to get back to work and shoved him out the door.

"That wasn't very nice, Dr. Reid," she reprimanded.

"And that wasn't very nice of you to get his hopes up. He's a young kid. His heart is probably racing at the thought of having dinner and a glass of wine with you."

"With us, Dr. Reid. I don't think he misconstrued my words like you did. Did you call Uncle Henry?"

"He sure did. What's for lunch, Niece?" The chief walked in as we grabbed our table.

"Sushi!" she answered.

Emily proceeded to lay out large round boxes filled with food. One box had all tempura, another had an array of sushi, another had salad and pickled sides, and there was also a box with only sashimi, and the last had all kinds of fruit with cream. My bride outdid herself.

"Thank you, Sweetheart. This looks amazing." I thanked her with a kiss. "Emi, what fish is this? I've never seen it before."

"Oh, it's my new favorite fish. I discovered it when I was in Japan. It's called Kinmedai. I think it's a cross between a red snapper and a sea bream."

"What did you do to it? It has a delicious smoky taste to it."

"You're supposed to either take off the skin or sear it. I used the pastry torch I bought in Paris and torched the skin. Isn't it yummy?"

The way her eyes lit up…I could never compete with this joy, though I believed now I came a very close second to food.

"It's all excellent, Emily," the chief complimented while stuffing his face.

"Thank you, Uncle Henry."

"Emi, have you thought of what you want to do after the wedding?" I asked her.

"What do you mean? I'll enjoy married life till school begins mid-August."

"Would you consider quitting school and going to culinary school? We have a top notch culinary academy five minutes from our home. Why don't you enroll there in the fall?" I wanted to realize this dream for her immediately. She didn't need to wait till the kids were gone and we were retired. If this was one of her dreams, she could have it now.

After doubting her desires, her ability, and even our finances, she promised to consider this option. An amazing lunch gone, I went back to a full day. The chief and Aunt Babs found me on my way to their dinner.

"Don't you look beautiful, Aunt Babs."

"Thank you, Jake. Am I almost as beautiful as your fiancée?"

"Not even close," I said with a smile.

"Did you two enjoy your lunch today? Sandy, Bobby, and I were also treated to a wonderful lunch. Jake, you did really well with that bride of yours. She's kind and pretty and she can cook. I hope Doug will find somebody just as sweet."

"Thank you for the nice words. Now would you put in a good word for me with your husband, so I can go home to my Emily before midnight?"

"Henry, if the hospital isn't too busy, let Jake go home early. Emily was moping around the house this afternoon after seeing Jake at the hospital. That girl has no interest in the wedding. She just wants to say I do and be married to our nephew. If it weren't for the family, I could see her agreeing to elope and be married tomorrow."

"That's how I feel. How'd you figure out Emily so easily?"

"It doesn't take much to read her. I don't know how she stayed away from you for so long. She is very much in love with you."

"I love her even more, Aunt Babs."

"Enough with the love…you can go home if there isn't much else going on," the chief pretended to be exasperated.

"Thanks, Aunt Babs." I gave her a wink.

Grabbing the flower arrangement I picked out during my dinner break I broke every traffic law again and raced home. I walked in the door to find Sarah walking out.

"Hi, Sarah." I gave her a peck on the cheek. "How was the honeymoon?"

"It was wonderful. Thank you for the fabulous wedding gift. Charlie and I use the cappuccino maker every morning."

"My pleasure. I'm glad it finally reached you."

"You sent them a wedding gift?" Emily asked.

"Of course I did. I gave it to Max when I saw him at the hospital right before I came to find you in Japan. I would have gotten them something even nicer if Sarah had let me know sooner where you were hiding." I tried to give her a mean smile.

"I think it's time for me to go."

"You're leaving already? Stick around."

"Look at Emily. Does she look like she wants me to stick around? I have to go. My hubby is waiting for me. See you soon."

"Bye," Emily answered quickly and shooed her out the door.

I picked up my delighted fiancée again, and hoping for a repeat of last night, kissed her all the way up to our bedroom. Rather than fulfilling my fantasies, she jumped down and had me sit so we could talk wedding.

"I thought I deferred all the decisions to you." This was my way of getting out of talking about the wedding.

"You did, and I gave your mom our proxy but there are a few matters I'd like for us to decide. First, where are we going for our honeymoon?"

"I don't care. What do you prefer?"

After a back and forth on city vs. island honeymoon, we compromised on five days on an island, then the next week all throughout Japan.

"What's next?" I got up from my designated corner, trying to get closer, but no such luck.

"Dinner menu…what do you want to eat?"

This one was an easy one, as we could hire chefs from our favorite restaurants to come cook at our wedding. The doubting Emily look resurfaced but I convinced her this was the best way to go. Of course she agreed, and I lunged at her with thoughts of frolicking with her on the sofa. She held me off again.

"I need to talk to you about…Never mind. I'll talk to Mom tomorrow about it."

"Emily. Speak now or we're done talking for the night. I didn't come home early just to talk."

Her face flushed. "What do we do about birth control? Do you want to have a baby right away?"

Finally. "Are we actually talking sex?" A conversation I was interested in.

"Yes, we're talking about sex. What do you want to do?"

I told her I was fine with any decision she made. My preference would be to start tonight but she wouldn't go for it. Instead, I promised to make an appointment for her with the OB at the hospital.

"Are we done now?" Wanting to get back to last night's passion, I hurried the conversation along.

"I need to talk to you about Max."

Max himself didn't bother me anymore but whenever Emily brought him up, it bothered me. She told me he was upset she was marrying someone other than him, and I told her he would soon forget her and find another girl. This truth irritated Emily, though she didn't express it.

"He can't ever forget me," she shot back at my statement.

"Does that mean you can't ever forget him as well?" I'd see how she'd get herself out of this one.

"No," she began to stutter. "It just means that…well, you should know…it's not easy to forget me." Her laughter echoed loudly in our room till I covered her lips with mine and carried her onto our bed. To my dismay, she didn't let me get too far and kicked me out of bed.

Saturday came and I made reservations at Urasawa for us, Jane, Nick, Sarah, Charlie, Peter, and Max. While Emily, Jane, Nick, and Sarah left for wedding shopping, I went back to the hospital. Undoubtedly, it would be another busy day. Hurrying home, I showered and drove into Beverly Hills, eager to see my bride.

Emily entered minutes after I sat and greeted Hiro, and she hastened over to a seat next to me. We embraced amid many unnecessary comments from my siblings. As everyone sat down, our courses began. Charlie sat on the other side of me and told me about his latest project. Emily and Sarah chatted about the wedding, and Peter and Nick got along famously talking about their undergrad years.

To my delight, I noticed Jane and Max absorbed in each other. They noticed no one else at the bar. Comically, I could tell my fiancée was not happy with this situation. She and Sarah whispered about the new couple, and all I could hear was Sarah saying, "Be nice." I rubbed Emily's back, and she turned to glance at me.

"Everything good?" I knew it wasn't, but thought I'd ask anyway.

"Uh-huh." With a curt answer, she turned to face Sarah again. I held back a laugh.

After a four-hour dinner, Emily and I got into my car and drove out of the garage. With good foresight, I had brought my two-seater, so Jane caught a ride home with Max. By the looks on both their faces, they were glad to have more time with one another. The only unhappy person was my bride.

"What are you laughing at?" she asked very annoyed.

"You sound a bit agitated." I couldn't help the guffaw that came with the answer. "I don't think you have to worry about Max. He obviously isn't as devastated as you think he is about losing you."

She didn't appreciate my comment and gave me the silent treatment the rest of the way home. Once home, I noticed Emily not so nonchalantly looking to see if Jane was home. I picked her up and told her, "She's not home yet. We don't do bed checks in this house."

Now Emily was really irked. She got down from my arms and took her pillow upstairs to the guest room. I made fun of her a bit more, against my better judgment. After much mockery, I ran upstairs and grabbed Emily from the bed and put her over my shoulders like a little child. Once we got into bed, I went about my business as though Emily had given me consent for my every move.

"Jake?" she called me with very little force.

"Hmm?" I knew she'd give in if I pushed her just a little more.

"If you are planning on sleeping here tonight with me, you need to behave." She sounded so unconvincing.

"Can I sleep here?" I was only too happy to have her in my arms tonight.

"You can if you promise to behave. My wall of defense is crumbling by the day. You need to help me at this point."

Here it was again—reverse psychology. With two weeks left till the wedding, I decided to honor her request. Although...my hands had a mind of their own and went exploring without permission from either one of us.

I woke up sometime in the late morning to find Emily still asleep. She jostled around, then pushed herself closer into my body and fell back into a deep sleep. Putting my arms around her, I realized my presence was really her Ambien. Lazily, I too decided to sleep some more.

"Good morning." She smiled when I woke up.

"Good morning. What time is it?"

"I think it's almost noon." She stretched out her arms. "I feel so good right now. Finally, I'm caught up on sleep."

"If you let me in your bed from now on, I'll help you sleep well every night."

"Yeah, if only we could just sleep together. It wouldn't be like your hands or lips would go on parts of my body in the middle of the night without my permission," she kidded.

"You're practically my wife. Do I need permission?"

She didn't answer me.

"Do you want me to bring up something to eat?"

She shook her head yes and I went down in my pajamas, surprised to find Max in our kitchen.

"Hey, Max. Did you spend the night here?"

Max and Jane looked at me horrified.

"What?" Their aghast look caused me to laugh.

"No, Jake. He's here to take me to the airport. Where's Emily? I want to say good-bye."

"Why don't you call her later? She finds this situation," I pointed back and forth to Jane and Max, "a little weird. I'll tell her you left already when she asks about you."

"Is she OK?" Jane and Max asked simultaneously.

"She's fine. Don't worry about Emily. I'll take care of her. You two enjoy yourselves."

Both parties blushed and left without saying much other than good-bye. While fixing breakfast I called Tony, a dance instructor, to come and give us ballroom dance lessons today. There were still way too many items left on Emily's bucket list.

Emily was dressed and ready for the day when I brought up a hodge-podge of food.

"I called a dance instructor to come and teach us ballroom dancing for later today."

Looking up from the computer, there was excitement in her eyes. "Thank you, Honey. That'll be a lot of fun."

"Is that the doorbell?" I asked, getting off my seat.

"I'll get it. You finish eating," Emily suggested.

She came back up with Sarah and Charlie, and we enjoyed their company until Emily kicked them out, promising to meet them for dinner and a movie later.

"I can't believe you and Charlie today." She complained about us talking about private matters such as our sleeping arrangements.

"He asked," I defended myself. "Are you mad? I didn't tell them about last night. Can we try it again tonight?"

I got kicked back into Nick's room, and she ran off without saying much more.

Tony showed up right on time and wanted to teach us all the popular dance steps today. Emily was willing; I wasn't up for that much dancing. We started with the foxtrot then moved on to the waltz. My fiancée was not as graceful with her body as I imagined her to be. In fact, she had two left feet.

Not able to learn the dance steps, she gave up and asked, "How is it that you are getting all these moves so easily, when I can't memorize any of them?"

"Oh, that's because I took..." I slowed down my train of thought as I saw Tony feverishly shaking his head as well as crossing his arms into a large X. "...Dancing...lessons with...Kelley."

Immediately I saw why Tony put up blinking lights and practically lunged at me to cover my mouth from saying any more. Emily's expression went from eager and willing to despondent and conflicted.

"Tony, I think I'm going to stop for today," was Emily's response. "I'll have Jake teach me the rest. Thank you very much for taking the time out of your Sunday to work with us." With that she shook his hand and went upstairs.

"What did I do?" Thoroughly confused, I hoped Tony could help.

"Jake, dancing is intimate. No woman wants to hear that her man practiced all these moves with another woman. Didn't you see me warning you?"

"Yeah, I did, but I didn't get why you were warning me. I guess I need to go up and explain myself. Thanks again. Bye."

After walking Tony out, I didn't know what I should say, since I didn't believe I did anything wrong.

"Emily?" I called out, running up the stairs. "Emi, where are you?"

"I'm changing for dinner. Can you give me a few minutes? I'll meet you downstairs."

"All right."

Nervously I waited for my fiancée, who took an unusually long time getting dressed. Since the Grand Canyon, I thought our disagreeing days were over, but apparently they weren't. She finally came down.

"What's wrong?" I tiptoed around her to assess her mood.

"Nothing." She didn't sound fine. "Sarah called to say they're on their way to dinner. Let's get going."

"Do you want to talk about what's bothering you?" I stopped her from walking away.

"No, not really." She gave me her *I said no, but I really meant yes*, tone.

"Emi. Talk to me. Didn't we promise to talk through any issues? I'm not quite sure what the issue is right now but we can't go to dinner with you pouting the whole night."

Her lips shut even tighter.

"Emily! You are driving me crazy with this silence." I implored.

"...I feel like nothing I ever do with you will be a first. There's always been some other girl who's been there before me."

I wanted to answer, *"Are you kidding me? This is why you're upset?"* But, attempting to be as thoughtful as possible, I brought her into my arms and consoled her.

"Emily. You are the first girl I proposed to and the only girl I've ever wanted to marry. Isn't that enough? If someone had told me you'd show up in my life when I turned thirty, I'd have hidden myself in the hospital till then." I hugged her tighter and kissed her head. "Ideally, I'd like to have met you when you were in high school so I could've gotten to know your mom and shared in your pain when she died. I would've married you right out of high school. We could've commuted to school together—you in undergrad, me in med school."

My words softened her instantly.

"I'm sorry I'm so lame sometimes," she apologized. "My cup is brimming over with joy, and I have to go and spoil it with my stupid jealousy. Do you forgive me?"

How could I stay mad at my bride? "Nothing to forgive. Let's go, Mrs. Reid."

CHAPTER 20

Are We There Yet?

The chief let me start my two-week vacation early and gave me Friday off to go run errands with Emily. We got up early and went to the Westside for our final fittings and to do a little shopping for our honeymoon.

"Jake, after your fitting at the Armani store, can you bring the car around so I can put my dress in the car?"

"Can't I walk into the dress shop with you? I'm dying to see what you look like in your dress."

"Are you serious? I don't want you to see it yet, and Mom and Gram would have a heart attack if they knew you saw me in the dress. I'll meet you there in half an hour."

Emily dropped me off at my shop first to make sure I didn't follow her to hers. After a quick fitting, I picked up my outfit and on the way out found a great dress for Emily to wear tonight to our dress rehearsal and dinner. Knowing she would frown at spending so much money on a dress, I bought it for her without her knowledge.

With our wedding outfits safely tucked away in the car, we went to lunch.

"What are you craving today, Love?"

"Let's just have a salad. I don't want to feel heavy or bloated for the wedding. Can you believe we'll be married in two days?" Her grin made my face smile as well.

"In two days I get to sleep with you."

"Is that all that's on your mind?"

"Is that not all that's on your mind?" I asked.

She only stared in wonder.

Home felt like an airport with people coming and going with their suitcases. Gram and her staff took up the entire third floor and several of my cousins decided to stay in Nick's and Jane's rooms even though their homes were only steps away. Emily was busy greeting my cousins, and I walked over with all the guys and helped Aunt Barbara get her backyard ready for our Moroccan Riad-themed dinner.

Before our rehearsal I took Emily up to our room to have her try on the dress I bought for her.

"Why did you spend so much unnecessary money?" I knew she would complain. "As it is, the wedding will be expensive enough."

"Because I thought you'd look beautiful in this dress." I pushed her into the closet with her dress. "You need me to help you take your clothes off?"

Her glower gave way to a chuckle.

We finished our rehearsal and walked over to Aunt Babs'. Her backyard was completely transformed into Morocco. My aunt had a treasured talent for throwing imaginative theme parties. During a delicious dinner, musicians played while belly dancers danced all around us.

"This is so amazing, Honey. Did you know about this dinner?" she whispered in my ear.

"I had some idea but I didn't know to what extent. Aunt Babs throws great parties." I saw the chief walk up to the mic. "I have one more surprise for you, Love. Watch and listen," I whispered back while planting a kiss on her lips.

"Thank you all for coming to this festive event. We want to celebrate Jake and Emily, as this day was a long time coming for them as well as for those of us who had to live with Jake during Emily's absence." The chief rolled his eyes and shook his head. The crowd laughed. "Jake, come on up and continue our Reid wedding tradition."

Kissing Emily one more time, I walked up with my fiancée's wedding gift in my pocket.

"Most of us in this tent know that we Reids have a tradition at our dress rehearsal dinner. This tradition is started by the first child of his generation to get married and all the other children in that generation must follow the same tradition he chooses. Since I am the first among the cousins to get married, you all must follow my lead when you get married."

There were a few unhappy faces in the audience. Wait till they saw what I got for Emily. There would surely be more unhappy ones.

"The chief informed me I needed to pick from one of the wedding traditions of something old, something new, something borrowed, or something blue. Gramps apparently chose something old and gave Gram a pearl necklace that his mother wore on her wedding day. Gram?" I looked around for my grandmother. "Will you be giving this pearl necklace to my Emily as well?" She chuckled while everyone booed.

"Gram, I demand a recount. Who voted to give Jake the six carat diamond?" Doug, the contentious one, asked.

Before Gram could answer I ordered him to sit down and continued my speech. "The chief continued the tradition by picking something blue and he gave his bride a measly blue garter. All of his brothers had to do the same for their brides as a wedding gift. Now I must say, that was a crappy wedding gift."

I made my mom and aunts proud with that declaration.

"Now it's my turn and I chose to pick something old and something new."

"Show off!" Cousin Glen yelled.

"The only way to outdo a six carat Asscher cut diamond ring is to shower my bride with more diamonds."

This statement got every woman, including Gram, cheering for me while every unmarried guy rushed the stage and tried to hurt me. The guys picked me up and threatened to throw me off the stage till they saw Gram's unhappy face. As always, I was saved by my grandmother.

Walking over to Emily, I could see the tears forming in her eyes. I wanted to carry her to my stage, but knowing how embarrassed she would get, I only held her hand.

"Emily," my confession began, "after our first date, I knew you would be the girl I would marry. What I didn't know was how deeply I would fall in love with you and still I grow to love you more each day. I cherish your warmth, your honesty, and the way you trust me to take care of you. In turn, I strive to be your shield and protector and make you the happiest woman in the world. In short, my life is only complete because you are here with me, I love you."

Her tears of joy fell along with those of all the other women in the tent. I caught a glimpse of my mom, and she beamed a proud expression. She approved of my future wife and knew I would be well taken care of.

"Emi, give me just a second." I excused myself and walked over to Mom.

Hugging her, I expressed, "Though Emily is my new love, you will always be my first love. I love you, Mom. Thank you for accepting Emily like your own daughter, and thank you for my thirty-one years of life. I promise I will continue to make you and Dad proud."

"I love you, Son," was all she could utter between the tears.

Back on the stage, I held out the same box I proposed with on Christmas morning. "Here is your something old."

"I don't have any fingers left to wear another diamond ring," Emily said with both her hands up in the air in an attempt to be funny.

She opened up the box with one diamond earring and looked confused. "Jake, this is gorgeous but how does it become something old and something new and why is there only one?"

I explained that this was the first diamond I proposed with back in December.

"The other diamond," I pulled out the matching pair, "is a new one I picked up from Boucheron in Paris."

Emily was quick to put them both on and thanked me.

The party done, everyone helped clean up, and we all headed for our separate quarters. Emily was more than upset we wouldn't see each other till our wedding day, to keep in line with our last Reid wedding tradition of keeping the bride and groom separated till they met at the altar. Trying to change her pronounced frown I aggressively kissed her till she could do nothing other than smile.

"I'll see you at the altar," I said, walking my fiancée to her door.

I slept another uncomfortable night in Doug's room and we all left early morning for a ranch.

"What's on the agenda?" I asked my brother.

"I'm not at liberty to tell. You're supposed to do everything as planned, and Doug and I are your shadows till the wedding."

Rolling my eyes, I called my bride.

"Hello?" I didn't recognize this voice on the other line.

"Who's this?" I questioned.

"Jake, you're not supposed to have any contact with Emily till you meet her at the altar."

"Aunt Deb! Is this really necessary? You are holding on to Emi's phone?"

"We all went through it. Bye." She hung up on me. I was thoroughly annoyed.

At the ranch many of my college and medical school buddies waited for me to arrive, and after an elaborate BBQ lunch, we got into teams and went hunting. Not having done this since med school, my shooting was rusty. I was told there was a prize for the group and the individual with the most game hunted. Competition on, my roommates and I, who used to hunt regularly in college, went after the prize with gusto. We were the first team to reach a team record of twenty-five birds with me having shot ten birds—an individual high.

Our team won a full-day shooting trip and I personally won a rifle, which I didn't think Emily would be too happy to have in the house. I asked Uncle Henry to keep it for me at his home instead. It was nice spending time with my buddies, whom I had all but forgotten since Emily entered my life.

"So tell us about your fiancée, Jake. You haven't been to any of the get-togethers in so long we know nothing about the woman you're marrying tomorrow. Only through Nick did we hear bits and pieces," my old roommate Steve said.

"She is phenomenal. She's gorgeous, kind, loving, sweet, bright, funny…"

"Never mind. It was stupid of me to ask you. What do you think, Uncle Henry?" Steve asked the chief instead.

"I have to say everything Jake mentioned is true. My soon-to-be niece is pretty special."

I high-fived my uncle.

"Hey, I saw Kelley the other day in Chicago." My buddy Ron started talking. "I was there on business, and I ran into her on the elevator."

"How's she doing? I heard she got married soon after we broke up."

"She was pregnant with her third kid already. She looked great, and she said she and her family lived in the suburbs somewhere near Chicago."

In the middle of our conversation, I got a text from my love.

Just got home. If you are able, call directly to our room. Missed you very much. Can't wait to become Mrs. Reid. Love you even more.

"Sorry guys. The missus is texting. Need to call her." I dialed our number immediately.

"Hi, Honey. How was your day?"

"Hi, Beautiful. I had a fun but lonesome day today without you," I answered.

"Where are you and what did you do all day?"

"We're about an hour north of home and we're up at someone's ranch hunting pheasant, quail, and chukar. I shot a Reid record ten, beating the chief's old record by two."

"That's great but what's a chukar?"

"It's a type of bird in the pheasant family. What did you do all day, My Love?"

"We went to the spa and enjoyed every treatment, thanks to Gram, but I really missed you."

"I missed you too."

Listening to my bemoaning, all the guys made fun of me as some pretended to be me, crying, some mimicked my words, and others pretended to throw up. Emily laughed on her end.

"Who are all those people in the background?"

"My college and med school buddies along with the rest of the family. You'll meet them tomorrow."

"When do you get home?"

"I think we're spending the night up here and then we have appointments at some spa tomorrow. I don't exactly know. No one will give me a clear answer for fear I may bolt on them. The cousins are all seeking revenge because I gave you diamonds for your wedding present."

"Oh, I see. What would they do if I came to see you?"

"I wouldn't be surprised if Jane is guarding your door right now." We both laughed. "I guess I'll see you at the wedding."

"Yes, you will, Dr. Reid."

"Good night, My Love. Sweet dreams."

"I love you. Good night."

Talking to her made me want to drive home and be with her tonight. Not wanting to fight with the uncles and cousins, I decided to wait a few more hours when no one had a right to separate us anymore.

CHAPTER 21

FINALLY! Mr. and Mrs. Reid

I got Nick up early in the morning and forced Uncle Henry to let us go home to pick up my tuxedo. This was a brilliant idea to see Emily before the wedding, or so I hoped. Driving like a speed demon, I heard the phone ring.

"Hello?"

"Good morning, Handsome." Ah, there was my sweet bride.

"Hello, my beautiful bride. You're up early. Did you sleep well last night?"

"No. I can't wait to have you in bed with me." I liked the way her mind was working. Tonight would be all that I'd dreamed of.

"Aw, Sis! I don't need to hear this kind of stuff so early in the morning. It's making me nauseous."

Emily giggled. "Nick, go find something else to do. Don't listen in on a soon-to-be newlyweds' conversation. What did you expect?"

"We're driving and you're on speaker so we're going to have to keep this conversation G rated, although I like the way you're thinking."

"Where are you off to so early in the morning?"

"We're coming home briefly to pick up our tuxes, and then we have to meet everyone at the spa for haircuts and grooming."

"Does that mean we can see each other this morning?" Her excitement couldn't be contained.

"I will try to sneak into our room, but Nick is supposed to be my guard. He promised the chief to keep me away from you."

"Nick, if you give me thirty minutes with your brother, I promise you a meal at Masa when we get back from our honeymoon. What do you think?" she begged my brother.

Nick wouldn't change his mind—actually he didn't have much of a choice.

"Sis, if I let Jake see you, the chief promised to torture me on my wedding day. He threatened many times."

"Nick, we won't tell him. I promise!"

"They'll read it on Jake's face. He'll have a stupid grin instead of this scowl he's had since Friday night."

I picked up the phone to have a private conversation with her.

"What will you promise me if I sneak into our bedroom for half an hour?"

"What can we possibly do with all these people in the house? There's no privacy right now."

"We can always lock the door."

I saw Nick look away and hum a tune to himself.

"Why don't you get into the room first, then we'll talk."

"All right. I love you."

Emily wasn't exaggerating about the house being a zoo. Women were inside the house getting groomed and men were outside the house building our wedding. I snuck past Aunt Babs and ran upstairs. Almost in the clear, our door in sight, I tiptoed past Jane's room, and out came Laney.

"Mom, Gram," she hollered.

I tried to muzzle her with my hands. "Laney, come on. Let me see Emily. I'll remember this when you get married."

It was no use. The cavalry showed up within seconds. I pleaded to see my bride. "Just a quick hello, Mom. I promise, I'll be right out."

"Laney, carefully go into Jake's room and grab his tux. We need to get him out of here. And make sure Emily stays in her room," Aunt Babs ordered.

"Gram, let me see my bride. We haven't seen each other since Friday." I begged again.

"Jakey, you'll see her soon. Now get going," she commanded.

Without a choice I yelled through the door, "Emi, I'm off to the barber. I'll see you tonight, Sweetheart. I love you."

"I love you too." She called right back. "I feel like a prisoner in my own house."

Leaving the house I understood the reality of today. Excitement was not an exact enough definition for what was going on in my head and my heart. The girl I loved from the moment I saw her in the grocery store would soon be mine. We would never have to part; we would never have to say good-bye. I would finally be with her daily, sleep with her nightly, and love her eternally.

My head was in a cloud the rest of the day. As soon as Nick and I were done, we headed back home and I watched the backyard metamorphose into a wedding garden. Two tents went up and as I started walking out to see what was in the tents, Nick and Doug stopped me.

"What's the matter now?" I asked.

"Emily is watching from your room. We can't let you out there." This had gone far enough. I was about to go out when Nick mentioned, "Sis looks gorgeous. Don't you want to wait just a little longer and see her when she walks down that aisle? She will take your breath away."

Liking what he said I sat in the living room and tried to calm the butterflies. The phone rang and it was Jane.

"Hey, Jane. How's Emily?"

"Hi, Honey." It was my bride!

"Emi! Hi, Love. My gosh, I've missed you. Can you believe we're finally getting married?"

"I'm so excited." She sounded like she was walking on cloud nine. "Are you home? Do you see how incredible the house looks?"

"Yeah, I'm home but they won't let me outside because they see you watching from our room. This has gotten ridiculous. But, it's almost over. I'll see you soon."

"Sorry, Jake, time's up. She's starting to tear. See ya later," Jane explained tersely then hung up.

I waited some more till Uncle Henry came and told me it was time. Though extremely nervous, my feet practically ran to the altar. Nick and Doug stood as my groomsmen while Gram, Mom, and Dad seated themselves. Jane was next to walk down and lastly I saw Sarah getting ready to walk. I peered around Sarah to find my bride but she was hidden behind the french doors.

The moment I'd dreamed of for many months arrived. Wagner's *Wedding March* began and I watched Emily step out to the door with her head down and body paused. It looked like she needed a moment before starting down the rose petal aisle made just for her.

When her head lifted, our eyes met, and I was blown away by the sight. I had to force myself to breathe, she was so stunning. While she slowly walked down the aisle, I reminisced on our first meeting at the grocery store, to the heart-wrenching day she left me for Japan, to our loving reunion in Kyoto. So many highs and lows marked our relationship. Those days were done. Our slate was clean now—ready for new adventures, new mistakes, and new ways of making up for those mistakes.

I walked out to Emily as she reached the altar and took her hand. Pushing back her veil, I was overcome by her beauty. Today, I understood the definition of beautiful to mean Emily Logan Reid.

"You look beautiful," I whispered while kissing her shiny red lips."

The crowd chuckled.

Unable to focus on anything the minister had to say I eagerly awaited the vows and the exchanging of rings. Emily stubbornly refused another ring so I placed the same eternity band on her finger as a symbol of our eternal commitment to one another.

He finally pronounced us and we kissed for the first time as man and wife.

"I love you, Mrs. Reid," I said while kissing my bride a few more times.

"I love you too." She glowed.

We took our obligatory pictures alone and then with the family and Jane annoyingly tagged along as Emily's helper. When we got to the reception everybody appeared to be having a great time.

"The food smells so good, Honey. When can we eat? Jane only let me eat a small salad today."

"Let's go eat now. What do you want me to get you? There's an array of Mediterranean tapas, and all kinds of pizzas."

"You're not eating yet. We can't get food on your dress," my pesky sister discouraged. "I can get you some water if you like."

"Never mind," Emily moaned. "Let's ditch her," she whispered. I laughed at my wife.

"Congratulations, guys!" All of our cousins came to greet us. "What an amazing wedding and reception."

"Thanks," we answered. "Wait till you see the dinner tent. They're opening it now," Emily announced. "Let's go in."

The dinner tent showcased a variety of sushi and steaks and pasta, which all looked appetizing.

"Honey, I want to show you something." My wife led me to the cake table. "Aren't these cute?"

Emily had petit fours made with our caricatures on each one of them.

"These are a tribute to our Paris trip and your proposal. I'm going to see what you taste like," she said and popped one in her mouth. "Yum." She smiled like a little child.

After much pleading Jane finally allowed us to sit and eat our meal. Jane brought us a large platter of everything the party had to offer and I fed my radiant bride. Toward the end of dinner, Nick got up to the mic and started our toast.

"Jake and Emily are the only married couple I know who were broken up longer than they were together. I think they technically dated less than three months. Due to my brother's stupidity, Emily left him for Japan for four months, and they finally reunited with the help of Emily's ex-boyfriend of all people." Emily's friends all laughed at this comment.

"Jake had a chance to reunite with Emily in New York in the middle of their separation, but due to his stupidity again, he went chasing after a ring my sister threw at him instead of chasing after her. They finally got back together in Kyoto and he proposed to her in Paris."

Nick turned to my bride, "Emily, you're the coolest sister anyone could ask for. I love you as though you've been a part of our family since the beginning." He then turned to me. "Jake, you've been a role model to me since we were kids, and I wish you and Emily a lifetime of happiness." Turning lastly to the crowd he said, "I'd like for you all to help me cheer my brother and sister, Dr. and Mrs. Jake Reid." We both got up to hug Nick.

Next on the to-do list was the cake cutting, and Jane gave me a stern warning to be a gentleman and not smear any frosting on my bride. I didn't know what would possess her to think I would do such a thing to my bride. I fed Emily her piece while being blinded by the photographers.

Emily grabbed a huge piece of cake and before I knew what was happening, she mashed it on my face to a throng of cheers.

"You want to play naughty?" My devilish tone must have scared her. She tried to run away, but not before I grabbed her and came down hard on her lips. Jane wasn't happy with me ruining Emily's makeup. Emily didn't seem to mind, as she kept coming back for more kisses and cake.

The majority of the guests moved back into the other tent to dance, and we followed along. Once we got on the dance floor, we noticed no one else. Our lips didn't part, our bodies moved as one.

"Excuse me, may I cut in?" I heard someone say but didn't care to look up. Our embrace continued.

"Excuse me, may I cut in?" Whoever this was, I was irritated.

"Yes?" I asked.

Max wanted to dance with my wife and after a quick hesitation, I told him, "Briefly. I'll be right back to claim my wife."

"Honey?" my wife whispered, "can you bring Jane over here in a couple of minutes?"

I nodded my head OK and went to look for Jane.

"Hey, Jane. Emily's looking for you."

"I can't believe you two are separated."

"Let's go. I want to get back to my wife." I pulled her along.

We got to Emily and Max and I found Max a little too close to my wife. Emily looked up at me in delight. "Um, Jane?" Emily asked her new sister. "Do you mind changing partners with me? I'd like to be back in my husband's arms."

Jane and Max couldn't help their huge grin as Emily leaned over and gave her ex-boyfriend a final hug and kiss. He would always have a teeny tiny piece of her heart, and I was OK with that.

"You are the most incredible woman in the entire world. Thank you for putting a smile on my sister's face."

"She's our sister now." Emily answered.

I didn't let anyone else dance with my bride. I monopolized her the whole evening. When night fell upon us, all the chairs were set up on the lawn to watch the fireworks.

"Ladies and Gentleman," the DJ announced, "please grab a seat and watch for a most special fireworks show. I'm told that the groom's wedding present will happen sometime during this display."

"What's the present?" I kept asking while trying to kiss my bride.

"It's coming up. You need to pay attention or you'll miss it."

I watched intently but saw nothing that resembled a present so I started playing with Emily's neck. Emily pointed to the sky and called out, "Here it comes."

I looked up and saw the letter I. Then came the shape of a heart. Then came the letter U. Then I saw a letter J explode, then an A, then a K, and lastly an E.

While they shot off more hearts, I contemplated what I just saw. I, heart, U, JAKE. That spelled, I love you Jake!

"How did you do that?" In awe, I stared at my wife. "That was the coolest present ever!"

Emily explained the difficulties she went through to get my present, and my family and I were amazed. With fireworks done, I tried to convince my bride to start our wedding night a bit sooner but she wouldn't budge. I begged, pleaded, and implored but to no avail. Walking away, pretending to be sore, I hoped she would follow me, but instead she went and danced with every guest who came to the wedding. I too got abducted by my aunts and girl cousins and was separated from my wife for hours.

Finally, my wife conceded she was ready to leave. We said our thank yous to our family, and I rushed Emily into the car.

"Which negligee did you bring?" was the first question I asked when we got into the car. I couldn't wait to see her in a negligee—or better yet, nothing at all.

"Oh my gosh! I forgot to pack the negligees. I only brought my flannel pajamas." She started yawning. "I'm exhausted. I couldn't sleep a wink last night. Aren't you tired?"

My face could not have looked happy. She turned away. I hoped she was kidding.

"So which negligee?" I asked again. "Is it that red one I picked out in London? It's not that boring white one Gram picked out, is it?"

"I'll give you two clues. Tonight's outfit was not purchased in London but you've seen it before."

Fantastic! I thought. "You kept that one from Paris? The one that was supposed to go to Sarah?" I had begged her to keep this skimpy teddy she had purchased as a gift for Sarah. She must have obliged.

My bride looked out the window and was in deep thought. Perhaps all this talk about tonight was making her nervous. I forgot at times that I needed to be sensitive to the fact that this would be her first time.

"Are you OK?" I asked, reaching over to hold her hand. "Am I making you nervous about tonight?"

"I'm fine—a bit scared but happy to be here with you."

"Sweetheart, you have nothing to be afraid of. Although it was frustrating at times, I'm thrilled you have been with no one else. I consider it a real honor to be your first and only man."

Even in the wee hours of the morning, there were many guests who congratulated us as Emily, still in her wedding dress, and I walked up to our honeymoon suite. Placing the Do Not Disturb sign on our door, I carried her over the threshold, and we began our life as Mr. and Mrs. Reid.

CHAPTER 22
Baby…x 2?

"Good Morning." Emily shyly looked up from the covers as I was packing up our belongings.

"Good Morning, Mrs. Reid. How do you feel?"

"Happy. How do you feel?" She smiled a radiant smile.

"I feel like I'm walking on water. Is your body OK? Are you sore at all?"

My wife stretched herself this way and that way and answered, "I think I'm OK. Why do you ask?"

"Well, I thought since this was your first time…I wanted to make sure I didn't hurt you in any way. Did…you…like it?" I asked awkwardly. I felt lame asking these questions but I didn't know how better to say it. "Did you enjoy yourself?"

"Of course! What would make you think otherwise? I worried you might not have enjoyed yourself, with me being so inexperienced and all."

"Emily, our first night together was nothing less than perfect. I don't think I understood what it meant to make love to a woman till we made love. It was the most incredible feeling being with you."

"I felt the same way. Last night or this morning—whatever time it was—was amazing. By the way, what time is it? I should get up, huh?"

"It's around two. You don't have to get up yet if you don't want to. Our flight leaves at nine tonight so we have some time."

"I should get up and get ready." My wife stared at me.
"What?" I wondered out loud.
"Can you turn around?" Her cheeks flushed.
"What for?"
"I need to go in the shower but I'm naked. I don't want you to see me."
"Emi. I saw all there was to see last night. It's all in my memory now. If you can't get up on your own, I'll come over and pick you up." She yelped as I picked her off the bed and took her in the shower.

We got dressed and Emily dialed my parents at the house.
"Hi, Mom. Yes, we had a good night. Jake told me you were coming here to pick up our car and wedding attire and I was wondering if you, Dad, and Gram would like to join us for an early dinner. Our flight doesn't leave till nine. OK. See you then."
"Are they coming?"
"Yup. What shall we do till they get here? It will be about an hour and a half before they can get here."
"Should we get a massage? We can call for an in-room massage."
"That sounds great. After your attack in the shower, now I'm sore."
I laughed at her accusation. She enjoyed it just as much as I did.
After a relaxing massage, we waited for my parents at the restaurant.
"I'm starving. I haven't eaten at all today and you've put me through way too much exercise. I'm running on negative calories." Emily's stomach started growling.
"I didn't hear any complaints from you early this morning or in the shower."
She giggled and our lips locked until we heard a voice say, "Get a room." That could only be the chief.
Emily got up and hugged everyone. She and Mom whispered a quick conversation, and I saw Mom hold Emily's cheek in her hand and hug her like a little child. Emily went over and gave Dad a kiss as well.
"I assume all was good last night?" Only the chief would ask such a loaded question.
"It's none of your business," I answered back.
"Emily," Aunt Babs joined in, "you know that Estelle and Sandy both had honeymoon babies. Watch out or you may carry that Reid tradition as well."
"How fascinating," Emily added. "My mom had a hard time conceiving me and a really rough pregnancy, so I don't know if I'll get pregnant that easily."

"A bit premature to be talking about babies," I said. "Although I don't mind the making process." I added grinning. "Where's Gram?"

"She was too tired to come out. We all went to sleep sometime this morning. Everyone was just getting up as we left," Mom explained.

"Why didn't they go to their own house?"

"We asked one of the chefs to stay behind, and he made breakfast for everyone. While the cleanup crew took everything away, all your cousins were too tired to walk home. They crashed in the ballroom."

"What does that mean to walk home? How can they walk all the way home?" With a baffled stare, Emily looked to me for an answer.

"Have I never told you that each of my uncles owns a home on our street?"

Emily shook her head no.

Dad added, "The house across the street from ours…"

Emily thought hard and answered, "The huge one?"

"Yes. That's your Gram's home. You know where Uncle Henry and Aunt Barbara live, and next to them is David's house, in between Henry and our home is Billy's home, and Roy has a house on the other side of our house."

"Are you kidding? How come I never saw any of them while living in our house?"

"That's because only Henry and I still live in our original homes. David, Roy and Billy ended up finding homes elsewhere but they kept the homes on our street." Dad finished telling our fun story.

"This Reid family saga gets better and better. How fun. So who lives in these homes now?" Emily wondered.

"No one lives there, though they're kept up nicely. Those three homes and maybe even Gram's house are up for sale to any family member who wants to buy them. Grandpa wanted his family close together so these homes will stay in the family."

Emily had that twinkle in her eye as soon as I finished my statement. "Do you think we could afford to buy one of these homes if we sold both of our houses?"

"It's possible…would you like to, Emi?" Knowing my bride, this idea thrilled her.

"That would be ideal if we could live near Mom and Dad. And as an added bonus, Uncle Henry and Aunt Barbara will be nearby as well." I saw my aunt and uncle's appreciative smile.

"Let's mooch off Mom and Dad for a while then discuss it again when your tenant is about to move out. We have some time."

"Jake, I got a call from the university and they accepted your application to teach." This was fantastic news. My bride would be ecstatic when I explained to her what was happening.

"I applied for a teaching position at the med school after I found you in Japan," I explained to Emily. "After being separated from you for so long, I wanted to spend as much time as possible with you when you got back home."

My Emi looked thrilled. "How many days do you teach?"

"He'll work Monday through Thursday at the hospital and teach on Fridays. We hired another doctor so Jake will be on call one night a week and he'll work only one weekend a month." Emily hugged the chief in response to his answer.

"We can have a normal marriage." Emily declared. "Yay!"

Emily and I enjoyed our six-some dinner and Mom and Dad drove us to the airport. Dad and I took out our two carry-on suitcases and I marveled at how efficiently my wife packed.

"Oh no, Honey." She shook her head. "I have another suitcase inside my suitcase for all the shopping we're going to do."

My parents laughed.

"What happened to my frugal girlfriend?"

"I became a Reid," she announced with a teasing smile. "I'm only joking. I brought another suitcase for all the presents we need to bring back. It's not for me. You're such a spender; one of us has to be the thrifty one."

I joined my parents in the guffaw.

Mom and Emily had another private conversation, Emily hugged both my parents, and we walked onto the plane.

"What do you and Mom keep talking about?" I asked once we were comfortably seated.

"Oh. Um…Mom came and talked to me right after we got engaged about our first night together and she tried to answer any questions I might have."

I was sorry I asked. My cheeks got hot and I was embarrassed. "You mean Mom had a sex talk with you?" I whispered so no one in our cabin would hear.

"Well, kind of. Since I don't have a mom, and knowing that I was a virgin, she thought I might need someone other than Sarah to talk to. It was really thoughtful of her. She's treated me no differently than Jane. She almost feels like my mom. I'm sure with time, I will love her just as much as my own mother."

I knew Mom would love Emily no less than she loved the three of us. If anything, Emily would receive even more attention than the three of us combined, and that would be fine with all of us.

"So Mom wanted to make sure I was OK after our first night."

"Got it."

Exhausted from the wedding and our post-wedding activities, Emily and I slept through much of the flight into our island.

Four days in a beautiful hut in the middle of the sea, and ten days exploring Japan, my bride and I were happy to be home.

"Emily! Jake!" Our family greeted us.

"How was the honeymoon?" Nick asked.

"It was marvelous." My bride glowed. "We brought presents for everyone."

It took Emily longer than expected to settle back into our time zone. She slept more than usual and her body couldn't handle food like it used to. I was a bit concerned about her.

"Honey," she called me from bed, "what am I going to do about school? I start in a couple of weeks and my body still feels unsettled from our trip. What do you think is wrong with me?"

"Tell me your symptoms, Emi. We've been back almost two weeks. It can't still be jet lag."

"My equilibrium is off, I feel vertigo when I get up too quickly, I feel queasy at the thought of all food except ice cream. And, all I want to do is sleep," she complained.

"Maybe there's an issue with your blood pressure. Or...you could be pregnant, but since we just got married, I doubt pregnancy symptoms would show up so quickly. Have you told Mom and Dad about what's going on with you?"

"No, I didn't want to worry them. Mom and Dad are busy getting Gram packed to go back to England. I wanted to go with them to England but I don't think that's going to be possible with the way I feel."

"Emi," I argued, "what about me? I can't be alone in this big house. What will I do?"

"I'm here by myself all day when you're working. It's not too scary. You'll get used to it." She giggled. "Once Gram leaves I won't see her again for a while. I thought I'd spend a little more time with her."

"No, you can't go." I jumped into bed with her and we both knew Emily would have to catch up on sleep while I was at work tomorrow.

Another full day at the hospital came and went, and I was only too happy to drive home to see my wife. Beyond ideal, I'd walk into a home where my wife greeted me with enthusiasm—dinner on the table—and the rest of the night filled with all new kinds of fun.

"How was your day, Beautiful? What did you do?"

"Not much. I had lunch with Sarah then went to the farmer's market."

"More salted caramel ice cream?"

"Yup. I can't get enough of that stuff. I have no desire to eat anything else so…" Her eyebrows arched and shoulders shrugged. "Guess what? I have exciting news!"

"Sarah's staying in town?"

"How'd you know already?"

"I ran into Max at the hospital, and he told me. Did you know Max and Jane have been spending a lot of time together?"

"Uh-huh. I talked to Jane today when she got home. They seem to like each other very much. Do you think it's serious?"

"It may be headed that way. Are you OK with it?"

"Of course. Anyhow, back to Sarah…Her staying in town is part of the excitement. But there's more." My wife's face filled with color for the first time since we got back from our honeymoon.

"Are you going to tell me?"

"Sarah's pregnant!"

"What? Already? What happened? I thought she didn't want a child till she was thirty. It's five years too early."

"I know. She was bawling at lunch because life wasn't going the way she planned, then she pulled herself together and got excited by the end of lunch."

"How far along is she?"

"Not far. She's only about six weeks. She's due in early April. Isn't that exciting?"

By the excitement in her voice, I wondered if Emily wanted the same thing. I was about to ask when we got interrupted by Gram.

"Hi, Gram. Did you have a nice day?" Hugging and kissing my grandmother simultaneously she looked pleased.

"I had a good day. I went and met some friends for brunch and a garden tour, then Bobby, Sandy, and I had a wonderful dinner prepared by your wife while she sat and ate ice cream. Emily, dear, are you sure you don't want to go see a doctor? Your face is pale all the time and you've lost too much weight from lack of food."

"I'll be fine, Gram. Since leaving Japan, my body hasn't had a chance to catch up to my life. From Japan to Paris, to London, then back here to a wedding, then back to Asia. I'm exhausted."

"If you say so…I want to talk to you two about something."

We both looked at her, as Gram had a serious but smiling face.

"Your parents told me you wanted to live on this street to be near them."

Emily said yes with her head but she stayed quiet, waiting for Gram to finish her thought.

"When your grandfather passed away," Gram said to me, "his will stated that this house was to be left to you after I died. Since I don't live here anymore, I thought it was time to let you have this house, since you've started your own family. Would you two want to live there?"

I was in shock with the news. In my mind, the house I most wanted to live in was my grandparents'. I'd spent much of my childhood in that house. That house to me was part of my happy childhood. Before I could say yes, Emily surprisingly answered, "No." Gram and I couldn't believe her answer.

"Gram, I don't want to live there unless you live there with us."

"But Emily, my home is in London."

"Gram, I know you were born in London, and I understand that Grandpa is buried there, but you have no family there. While you're still here, why don't you spend the rest of your days with us?"

"But what about my husband? I go see him often. I won't be able to do that if I live here."

"We can go visit him together. Many years from now, you will be back together with him forever. Let's us have you until then. Please, Gram? Will you live with us? I want to share as many days with you as possible and I want our kids to grow up loving their great-grandmother."

As much as I loved my Gram, never once did I think of asking her to live with us. I only envisioned Emi and our kids living together. My wife's love for my grandmother put Gram at a loss for words. Never could I catch up to my wife's kindness. Touched, Gram told us she'd think about Emi's offer or demand.

"In the meanwhile, I want you to start redoing the house," Gram told Emily. "Let's go there tomorrow morning and you can keep what you like and discard what's not to your taste. There's a lot of furniture stored in the basement that you can look through."

"Does that mean you will live with us?" Emi asked, holding Gram's hand.

"I will seriously think about it. You can redo a room for me on the first floor if you like." Gram answered with a smile.

"I'm going to take that as a yes, and I'll start tomorrow. Maybe we'll stay here while you're getting your affairs in order in London then we'll come pick you up." My wife went off making her own plans without Gram having agreed to anything. Gram only laughed at all of Emi's suggestions.

"Love, let's let Gram get some rest." I meant this for my grandmother's well-being but I also wanted to get upstairs with my wife for our own well-being.

"Good night, Gram. We love you." Emily and I kissed her good night, and as soon as Gram was out of sight, I picked up my wife and took her to bed.

"Oh, my phone is ringing." Emily hopped out of my arms to reach for her phone.

"Hi, Sarah…No, not yet. I'll get to it soon, I promise."

The two friends were having some cryptic conversation, which I couldn't decipher.

"No, I'll do it…I don't think that's necessary. I promise. I'll get to it. I've got to go, Sarah. Jake is waiting for me. Bye."

"What was that all about?" I asked with much curiosity.

"Um…" Emily couldn't answer me. Now I had no choice but to pursue this conversation.

"Emi, you know I don't like it when you don't give me a straight answer."

"Sarah was just checking up on me since I haven't been feeling well. She wants me to…um…go see a doctor."

Emily said this with enough hesitation to make me question her honesty but since there'd be no reason for her to lie to me about any of this, I let it go.

"Do you want me to make an appointment for you at the hospital?"

"No, I'll go see my regular doctor. I'm fine. Everyone is making a bigger deal than necessary."

"If you say so, Love. Let's get ready for bed."

The next week was a busy week at the hospital and Emily appeared back to her normal self—actually, she was happier than usual. I couldn't tell whether her joy came from remodeling our new home or the fact that she said she felt better. Her face was still pale and she still ate nothing but ice cream but she was in high spirits.

"Jake, I have a surprise for you." Emily exclaimed after I finished dinner tonight. "Let's go."

She led me out to our future home and walked me up the stairs.

"I want you to close your eyes and I'm going to hold your hands and walk you into your surprise."

"What is it? Are you showing me our new bedroom? Did you get it fixed up already?"

"You'll see. Are your eyes closed?"

"Yes, Love. They are closed. Is it much farther?" I asked, as she stopped walking.

"You can open your eyes, Honey."

I opened my eyes to see a room painted in a soft yellow. In this dainty room I saw my old crib on one side of the room with an animal circus mobile hanging above it. Next to the crib sat a rocking chair and an ottoman. On the other side of the room was a huge dresser with a changing table on top of the dresser. In the armoire next to the dresser, there hung baby clothes and booties. I still didn't get it.

"You set up a nursery now for whenever we might have kids? Isn't this a bit premature? Also, where'd you find my old crib?"

She just looked at me and smiled. "Look over by the dresser."

I walked over and saw nothing but a bunch of diapers in a box and a framed picture. I opened up all the drawers and there was nothing in them. Looking at Emily to ask what was going on, I slowly turned back to the framed picture. Something stood out. I picked up the frame and saw an ultrasound picture with a little dot inside it. The picture was titled "Baby Reid."

I yelled, "You're pregnant?"

Emily beamed. "We're having a baby, Jake. You're going to be a daddy."

With a sudden rush of joy, I went over to hug my wife. Something about this revelation made me even happier than our wedding day. Could this be considered blasphemy?

"When...How...I don't get it. What happened?"

"Are you bummed out it happened so quickly?" She totally misread my comments. Ecstatic would be an understatement.

"Are you kidding me? This is more exciting than our wedding day." Perhaps I shouldn't have said that. I looked at Emily to make sure I wasn't in trouble.

"Weird, but I thought the same thing. Your baby is inside me." She marveled, rubbing her stomach. "If I'm this happy now, what a mess I will be when the baby arrives."

I picked up my wife, and she read my intention correctly.

"Our bedroom is next door. It's all fixed up already."

Laying her on our bed I asked her again when this all happened.

"From what it seems, I think I got pregnant on our wedding night or some time right after. I'm about six weeks right now."

"I thought we were going to wait. Didn't you want some time alone before you got pregnant? Did you not go see Carole at the hospital and get on the pill?"

"I saw Carole but decided not to get on anything."

"Why? Not that I'm complaining."

"After much thought, I figured if I wanted to have a lot of kids, I needed to start sooner rather than later. I also thought about Gram and how I wanted our kids to get to know her before she passed away. Do you think she'll be happy?"

"Sweetheart, this news is going to turn this whole family upside down. When should we tell everyone?"

"How about this weekend at Gram's birthday party? No one knows yet. I went to a doctor just to confirm that I was pregnant, but I'd like to go see Carole at the hospital with you, and you can see our baby."

"I can't wait. Thank you, Emily. You've added even more joy to my already amazing life. I love you so much."

"I love you too."

Walking on air, it was hard to contain our excitement in front of our family. Mom kept asking about all the smiles, and we couldn't keep it from her any longer.

"Mom," Emily started, "we're having a baby!" I ended the sentence.

"What?"

Emily nodded her head yes as affirmation to my statement. "You're going to be a grandma."

Crying, Mom went over to hug Emily. "When did this happen?"

"I've known for about a week but kept it from everyone, so I could surprise Jake. I set up a nursery in Gram's house and showed Jake yesterday. Then, we went together to see the doctor today, and here are the ultrasound pictures. We were going to keep it a secret till this weekend's birthday party but I couldn't keep it from you any longer."

"This was why you were so pale and tired...the salted caramel ice cream?"

"I think so." Still in my mom's arms, my wife turned to me. "Jake?"

"Yes, Love?"

"Would you mind if I stopped working? My mom was really sick when she was pregnant with me, and I have a feeling I'm headed that way myself. The doctor says it's unusual to be experiencing all these symptoms so early in the pregnancy."

"Of course I don't mind. Emily, you do what's best for you and the baby."

"What shall we do about Dad and Gram? Should we tell them before the party?"

"Tell us what?" Dad and Gram walked in right as Mom finished asking this question.

"Well...Dad...Gram...Emily's pregnant!"

Nine months and many pints of ice cream later, my beautiful girlfriend, turned radiant wife, became a proud mother of twins. Elizabeth Logan Reid and James Logan Reid, named after their maternal grandparents, became the center of our universe. After a quick trip to London to pick up all of Gram's essentials, Mom, Dad, and Gram came back home to be with Emily during her difficult pregnancy, and they have become the most doting grandparents. Uncle Henry and Aunt Barbara also spoiled our children to a point where their own children complained about the lack of attention in their own lives.

"Hello, Beautiful!" I called out to my girls, rushing through the front door to see my kids before bedtime.

"Which one of us are you addressing?" Emily chuckled as my baby squealed once she saw me.

"Hello, Ellie. How was your day today?"

She responded with the most dazzling smile. I picked her up to more squealing and delight.

"Where's James?"

"Upstairs, asleep—where this little one should be right now. You were a naughty little one today. You are so lucky your daddy is home early," Emily warned with a smile and kisses to our daughter.

"Were you naughty today? How could a cute little three-month-old like you misbehave? What did you do today?" I couldn't stop kissing my daughter. She and James had my hair, my eyes, and my coloring but looked exactly like their mother. In all honesty, Ellie was even more beautiful than my Emily. Though, I'd take this information to the grave with me.

"Are you talking to me?"

"Uh-huh. What did you and the kids do today?"

"Let's head upstairs and put this little one down, and I'll tell you. You mind if we have dinner after Ellie falls asleep?"

"Not at all. Let's go, Cutie. I'll rock you to sleep."

"Please don't do that. Both kids—this one in particular," Emily said, pointing to Elizabeth, "gave me a hard time today because they've been so spoiled. Gram, Mom, Dad, and all your aunts and uncles went to some function all day today so I thought it would be a perfect time to start training them to sleep on their own."

It drove Emily crazy that neither Ellie nor Jimmy had ever slept in their bassinets or cribs during nap time. Mom, Dad, and Gram, along with the other four aunts and uncles who dropped by on a regular basis, fought over who got to hold either child during nap time. There weren't enough babies for the arms waiting to hold them. Neither child had been on the floor to practice tummy time, and we were sure they'd never crawl since they were always lying comfortably in someone's arms.

"After everyone left, I fed and changed the twins then put them down in their bassinets for their naps. They both hollered! So I held them at the same time, rocked them a bit, and placed them separately, Ellie in our room in the bassinet, and James in his room in his crib. They both hollered again but James eventually got tired and napped. This little one refused to sleep. I would pick her up and she'd quickly fall asleep; I'd put her down, she'd wake up, and scream. We battled for a couple of hours until it was time for James to wake up and for both of them to be fed again."

"After another round of feeding and changing I needed a change of scenery, so I strolled them to the park."

"You walked all the way over there with the kids?"

"Yup. I hoped Ellie would sleep. She didn't! She stared at the scenery, stared at me, then stared at her brother, who fell asleep again after a bit of crying."

"So what did you do with our Elizabeth?"

"I told her about our entire courtship and all the drama it entailed. The funny thing—I think this girl understands English already."

"Do you understand what I'm saying, Elizabeth Logan Reid? Do you understand Daddy when I tell you I'm madly in love with you?" My daughter squealed in delight again.

"You see what I mean? Hand her to me. Let me feed her one more time." Though our little ones had worn out their mother today, Emily couldn't help her continual embraces to our daughter. She hugged and kissed this little one, who demanded attention from anyone within a smile of her.

While Emily nursed Ellie, she went on with the story. "When I got to the part where you left me at the Grand Canyon, Ellie cried. And this cry wasn't an—I need something—kind of cry, it was a sad sob. I think she felt my pain. Her cry woke up James, and I picked him up while pushing Ellie and finished our story up until Japan. Once we got to the park, I put them both in the infant swing and I pushed them for a long time."

"Did you love the swing?" I reached over and held my baby's hand.

"They both loved it. Maybe we should get one of those play structures in our backyard and add a couple of infant swings."

"Sure. I'll look into one tonight. So did this little one nap at all?"

"Nope, she listened intently to the rest of our indelible memories of love while walking back home, then hollered some more while I made your dinner, and here she is dozing off again in my arms. I'm going to change her one last time and you can put her down. Oh, I hear James whimpering. Can you get him? He's probably hungry. He didn't eat before going down for the night."

Ellie's eyes opened the minute Emily put her on the changing table. "Mommy loves you so much, Elizabeth Reid. Now please, go to sleep!"

I walked over to pick up my son, the calmer and more reserved child. Emily had compared James to her father since the day he came out of her womb, and Ellie was the spitting image of her maternal grandmother. In a strange but happy way, the children have filled Emily's void of losing her parents. Many times I'd watch her staring at the babies with tears in her eyes. But now all traces of sadness disappeared when she thought about her parents. Elizabeth and James reminded her of the parents she missed, and for that she loved them doubly.

"Hello, Son. I missed you today." When I picked up my son, he welcomed me with a smile almost as bewitching as his sister's. "Shall we change your diaper?"

James didn't squeal and coo like his sister. Instead, he liked to watch the room and the people in it. His smile was no less dazzling. Both kids seized my heart in a way I couldn't explain with words. When together with my family, nothing mattered but them. The love and protection I wanted to give Emily while we were dating seemed trivial compared to the love and protection I felt for my family now.

James began to whimper again. He looked so much like my wife when he cried. "Are you hungry? Do we need to go see Mama?"

I walked back into our room and we traded off babies.

"I changed his diaper already. By the familiar Emily-look in his eyes, he's hungry. Come here, my princess." I took Ellie in my arms as Emily finished kissing our daughter and saying good night to her.

"Hi, James." Emily cooed to our son. "Do you need to be fed? You're hungry, huh?"

I rocked Ellie to her room and saw her big blue eyes staring at me. She had that same look of unconditional trust that her brother and Mama had, and I would work hard to keep this look forever. Emily and I would also work hard to unconditionally love all our children and help them to reach their fullest potential.

"I know your mommy told me not to do this, but I'm going to rock you till you fall asleep, OK, Princess? You are even more beautiful than your mother, but don't tell her I said so, or I'll be in big trouble," I whispered.

Ellie sounded her version of a giggle and her eyes gently closed to sleep. I kissed her tiny, soft lips one last time and laid her in her crib for the night.

"You're done, already?" Emily looked surprised when I came back in the room.

"Piece of cake. I don't know why you struggled all day. She fell asleep immediately." Chuckling, I talked to our son. "You're a super fast eater, aren't you?"

"I think he's exhausted from the park. Will you lay him down as well?" Emily embraced our son. "I love you, James. Sweet dreams."

"Of course."

I kissed my son on his tiny, soft lips as well, and we were finally done for the night. All this craziness would begin again early tomorrow morning.

"Are we alone now?" I picked my wife up off her rocking chair and laid her on our bed.

"Don't you want to eat dinner?"

"Let's eat later. It's been a while since we've been alone with everyone making pit stops at our house. The chief would've shown up here tonight if it wasn't for the hospital meeting he had to attend."

"It's been crazy but I've loved every moment of it. Your family's been wonderful with the kids. Do you know your cousins come by often as well? Doug and Laney practically live here when they're not in school and Glen has been by at least once a week. This is what I imagined family life to be—bustling with people, overflowing with love."

I couldn't help but kiss my wife. Something about motherhood—she oozed confidence and sensuality.

"Should we try for another baby tonight?"

"Already? I can't keep up with the two we have right now. Let's give it a little more time," she answered with advances of her own.

"Emi?"

"Hmm?"

"Do you know it's our one-year anniversary next week?"

"Yeah. I can't believe how quickly the year has gone by. We became an instant family in under a year. How crazy."

"I was thinking maybe we should go up north and relive our San Francisco date. Do you want to go up to Napa?"

"It sounds ideal but what about the kids?"

"Let's take the kids up to the apartment along with Mom and Dad. Once we set up a room for the kids and get them settled, we can leave them for the night with my parents. We'll go have dinner at French Laundry and spend a night in Napa."

"I don't know, Jake. That's a lot of work for your parents."

"Sweetheart. My parents can give them a bottle right before bedtime then do what they normally do—hold them to sleep. Ellie and James both sleep through the night, and we'll be back before their first feeding—or maybe after their first feeding. Don't you have a lot of milk stored in the freezer?"

"Yes, but…"

"No buts. We're going. I'll make sure no one is up there next weekend."

And this is how our life would be. In between Emily's hectic days with the kids and my overscheduled days at the hospital, Emily and I would find time to love the children daily, love each other nightly, and live a lifetime of happiness eternally.

Thank you for reading *Indelible Love—Jake's Story*. I hope you enjoyed reading both novels as much as I enjoyed writing them. Though *Emily's Story* has a special place in my heart as my first novel, I love Jake and his tremendous love for his girlfriend and eventual wife. He's the type of hero I'd like to bottle and save as a future husband for my little girl.

Jake's Story has been a favorite of all the Reiders from around the world. This book has sold equally to all my other books, combined. I decided with this print version to add a bit more of the reception and their first night together. It's a bonus I wanted to write for those of you who've loved Jake and Emily's story.

If you haven't already, I highly encourage you to read *Indelible Lovin'—Max and Jane's Story*. This story revolves around Max and Jane, with surprise appearances from all members of the Reid family.

Thank you again, and I hope to see you in Max and Jane's world.

(Bonus reading from Jake and Emily's reception and wedding night)

"Who the hell is that stunning blonde laughing with your bride?" My buddy Donovan would always have a weakness for beautiful women, but who this beautiful woman was would shock him.

"That's the little girl you called your fifth sister."

"Shut the fuck up! That is not Delaney Reid!"

"That is. She's all grown up, huh? While you were screwing around with Kate and all the other women in between, our Laney grew into quite a beauty."

"She was always beautiful, and bright, but was she always that well-endowed?"

"Hey. That's my little cousin you're talking about. Uncle Henry would kick your ass if he knew you were ogling his daughter in such a way."

"Speaking of kicking your ass, I see that Jane and your bride's ex have become an item. Shit, you knew I wanted to ask Jane out, and you wouldn't let me. What the hell?"

Donovan was unhappy. "Buddy, I've always told you. She's not the girl for you. I say this not because she's my sister. You and she are too fickle, too alike, too selfish—the list is endless as to why it would never work. But I think this match with Max is a good one. And Emily is thrilled with the two of them getting to know one another."

"When the hell did you become a matchmaking mama?"

"What's wrong with the woman you have in your arms right now?"

"Nothing's wrong. She's just not right."

"And Kate?"

"Kate and I are done. I'm tired of us."

"What happened to living in wedded bliss with her for the rest of your life?" I jabbed at him. I knew he and Kate were not in a good place right now.

"That wedded bliss ended the moment I got out of my early twenties. I don't think I'll ever find my Emily."

"Don't look too far. She may be closer than you think." I laughed. "Buddy, I've spent way too much time with you, and not enough time with my bride. You done with all your questions?"

"No. I have one more."

"Make it quick!"

"You ready for tonight? It's not every day you come across a virgin bride."

"I was ready the night we met at the grocery store. I can't wait to get out of here." I started walking away from Donovan but thought I'd do one last round of matchmaking. "Go say hello to Laney. I'm sure she'd like to see you again. It has been a long time."

"Yeah..." The way he answered me made me think he wasn't going to go see my cousin. I wondered what would stop him from reacquainting himself with his favorite Reid.

Damn! Another interruption. Max stopped me before I could reach my beautiful bride. "You have a moment?"

Um...no! "Sure. What's up?"

"I wanted to make sure that you and I were OK. I know I've apologized about coming between you and Em, but since it looks like I may be hanging around you a bit more often, I'd like to know you don't disapprove."

"Don't disapprove? Is that the same as approve? Is this a trick question?" Damn, I was getting snarky from being kept away from my wife.

"You know damn well what I mean. Do I have your blessing to date Jane?"

"Do you normally ask the girl's brother?"

"No, but when the girl's brother marries a girl I dated for four years, I thought it prudent to ask."

Was Max getting snarky with me now? "You're starting off on the wrong foot, pissing me off." I smiled to show him I wasn't being serious. "I'd like to get to my wife, and I don't give a damn what you and my sister do. Just please don't give me any details!"

Max chuckled. "You found a good woman in Emily. She will make you very happy."

"I know," I answered confidently. "It's rare to find a woman whose inside beauty outdoes the stunning outer shell. You were stupid to let her go," I teased.

"It was the best thing I could do for Em at the time. Knowing now who was coming after me, I'd do it again for her. Be good to her."

This guy was all right in my book. Jane needed someone to love her unconditionally and selflessly. She was spoiled, selfish, and wild. She needed a good man to channel her energies in the right direction. And Max looked like he needed a feisty girl to keep him on his toes. These two would be a perfect match.

"You have my blessing. Be good to my sister and don't come complaining to me when you find that life is more complicated with Jane than you bargained for—but trust me, my little sister will be worth the pain."

Before he could thank me, I walked off and attempted to reach my enchanting bride, who was dancing with Uncle David.

"Congratulations, Jake. Your Emily is wonderful!"

"Thanks, Laney." *Seriously?* My wife is just steps away from me and I've now been stopped by three well-wishers. "You enjoying yourself at the wedding?"

"My mom did another fantastic job, huh? Your wedding is perfect, just like the bride and groom."

"Laney, you're pretty perfect yourself. I heard you kept my bride entertained while she was trapped in her room, yesterday and today."

"We had such a good time talking about Japan, and Emily and I have so many things in common. She's the sister I've always wanted."

Laney was always the sweetest Reid. "You and Jane can get your fill of Emily once we get back from our honeymoon."

"What a great honeymoon you will have. If you get a chance, go visit Tokyo University and take her to eat sushi at Jiro's."

"Good idea, Laney. I forgot about Jiro's. We'll send pictures when we're out there and we'll send pictures of our hut in the ocean. I don't think the waves are big enough to surf, but Emi and I will try to get in a few water sporting activities."

"You'll have a blast."

"Thanks, Laney." I wanted to walk away, but I could tell she was not finished with me. Her expressive face showed some frustration.

"Um...Jake...?"

"Yes, Laney?" And can we please make it quick? I have a wife to get back to and a wedding night to begin.

"Was that Donovan you were speaking with earlier?"

"Yeah. Has he come up to say hello to you? He said he would." Perhaps I shouldn't have raised her hopes up.

"He did?" Her face brightened enough to make me feel guilty now. "Should I...I mean maybe I should just wait till he comes by and says hello."

"Laney, I think it's fine for you to go up to him and say hello first. Sometimes, guys don't know what to do in certain social situations and need a little help getting reacquainted. Donovan would be more than happy to see you." *Go, talk to him, and let me be.* That was a mean thought, but I was that desperate to have my wife back in my arms.

"I'll think about it. I'm sorry I've kept you from Emily for so long. I just wanted to congratulate you and to tell you how much I like Emily."

"Thanks, Laney. We'll all catch up when we get back."

"Sure thing."

"Jake!"

Damn family of mine, they won't let me be! "What's up, Jane? Make it quick. I have a bride to reclaim."

"What's the hurry? You've got the rest of your life to claim her."

"And the rest of my life still won't be enough time."

"When did you become such the romantic?"

"Since I met Emily. Now can I go?"

"No! Wait up. I wanted to talk to you about Max."

Groan! Not this again. "Max is great, I approve, your sister is over the moon about you two, what else do you need?" I desperately tried to move this conversation along. I was dying to see my wife.

"Are you sure Emily's not weirded out by us dating?"

"Nope. Not weirding out at all. Only happiness for you both."

"Is...Donovan still seeing Kate?"

Here we go again. My damn best friend will be the death of me.

"No more Kate but who knows with them. He's not right for you. I know you think he's dreamy, but he's not. He's no dreamier than the rest of us." I looked over my sister's shoulders to see the back of my bride. She was now dancing with Donovan, and it pissed me off that they physically looked so good together. "Are we done, Jane?"

"You're so curt today." Jane was annoyed. "What's got you in such a foul mood? It's your wedding day. Lighten up!"

Aargh! "I'll lighten up when I can have my wife in my arms again."

"Damn! See if I ever come to you for advice again."

"Yeah, yeah..." I left my sister before she said anything else that would keep me from my bride.

Almost there. We were just a table away from one another. I would tap my best friend in the shoulder and kick him off the dance floor. How dare he slow dance with my bride? There were more than enough women here who would fall over each other if he asked them to dance. Why did he have to pick my bride?

"Emi..." The call out to my bride disappeared with Nick's voice topping over mine. Another sibling—why did my parents have to have so many kids? "Hey, Nick."

"Am I bothering you?"

Oh no. You and the entire family have only been a pain in my ass. "What's up?"

"I just wanted to congratulate you and Emily again. She's really the coolest gal. I can't imagine ever meeting someone that great."

"Thanks, Nick. But trust me; you'll meet someone just as wonderful as my wife. And if you'll excuse me, I need to reclaim my wife."

I decided it was my wedding night. I could be a little rude to my sibling.

"Well, hello there, husband. Long time no see."

"Don't I know it. I had so many damn well-wishers, when all I wanted to do was be with you. Can we leave now?"

"I think I'm ready to go."

Finally! The reception was over for us and we were on to the good stuff. Emily agreed to leave but it was so late, and I feared we'd both end up asleep on our wedding night. We got to the hotel, and the manager had upgraded us to their Presidential Suite. I needed nothing more than a bed and this bride of mine, but I'd take it.

"Jake?" my bride asked shyly. "Would it be all right if I showered right now? I have so much makeup and hair product on, I feel a little gross."

"Should we shower together?" I dared to ask.

"I honestly wouldn't mind, but, I want you to see me in the negligee. If we got in the shower right now, that whole surprise element would be gone."

"Whatever. Just go and get it done." This wait was killing me.

After what seemed like an eternity, Emily got out in a robe and asked me to get lost for a few minutes while she dried her hair and got ready for bed. If I didn't know the woman so well, I would have sworn she was trying to kill me by ways of torture. As a courtesy, I jumped in the shower, got myself all clean, and burst out of the bathroom with the anticipation of a man with the worst case of blue balls.

"You ready, Love?" I called out to give her a small warning that I was ready. There was no answer, as I expected. I could picture her under the covers, nervous. "Emi?" I called her again.

What I saw made me wonder if I should laugh or cry at this situation. My bride was fast asleep with the duvet completely covering her. I slid into bed with her and brought her into my arms and thought a couple of hours of sleep couldn't hurt.

Exactly two hours to the second, I could wait no longer. As I undid the covers completely, this virgin bride of mine was in the most scandalous nightie that showed everything and nothing simultaneously. Lying flat on her back, she gave me easy access to slowly trace her leg and kiss her shoulder and neck. Comically and sadly, my bride was still dead to the world. If I wanted her up and participating, I'd have to take more drastic measures.

Slowly peeling off the nothing-there negligee, I took a moment to appreciate her spectacular body. I knew I'd be in for a treat, but what was in front of me was even better than dreamed.

"Emi?" I laid on top of her and started kissing the side of her breast. "Love, I can't do this on my own." I suckled her nipple, and that jolted her awake.

"Jake?"

"Yes?"

"Did I fall asleep?"

"You sure did."

"I'm so sorry!" She sounded apologetic enough for making me watch her sleep.

"Emi. It's all good as long as you start participating."

She started to giggle. "Did you undo my clothes? I'm feeling a bit violated here."

"Really?" I slid my hand between her legs. "How do you feel now?"

"Aroused." She moaned. "That feels incredible."

"If you'll help me get out of my clothes, I can make you feel even better."

My sweet bride unbuttoned my pajama top and peeled it off while my fingers were still between her legs, but I had to help her with the pajama bottom. "Are you ready?"

She nodded with sweet innocence.

Gently placing myself on top of her, Emily opened herself and welcomed me. Poised right at her juncture, I went in slowly and about killed myself with the excruciating pleasure that continually beckoned me. Emily whimpered with each push.

"Am I hurting you?" I was doing my best to love her as gently as I humanly could.

"Jake," she complained.

"What?" Shit, what was I doing wrong? "What's the matter?" I worried.

"Finish it up. You're making me wait and I can't stand it. Please make love to me."

I chuckled. Here I was thinking I needed to be careful with this woman for fear I may hurt her. If she needed for me to finish, that's what I'd do.

Emi let out a whimper when I initially thrust into her, but quickly moaned with pleasure and learned to meet my every movement.

Neither of us lasted very long. I was surprised to find her heading toward the end so quickly but I wasn't complaining. After months of foreplay, I knew I couldn't hold out. Our next round would be longer. As we both reached our climax together, it was absolutely incredible. My bride's beautiful face glowed with contentment and pleasure.

"How was it?" I had to ask.

"Well...I don't know..." she said demurely. "Can we try one more time so I can give you a definitive answer?" She giggled again.

"We can try as many times as it'll take for you to come up with a definitive answer," I teased and kissed her lips.

"I love you, Jake."

"And I love you, my sweet bride."

BLOG STYLE

Indelible Lovin'
Max & Jane's story
d. w. cee

12-04-2012 A Harley Man?

I looked out my window as a loud roar of pipes rolled up the driveway. Max pulled up on a sleek new motorcycle. At least I thought it was new. I hadn't seen Max in about six months so I couldn't be sure when he got the bike.

Max was *so* not the Harley type of guy. He was the straitlaced, straight-A, straight-shooting type. The boy next door, as my sister-in-law, Emily, described him. Those monikers, as well as Max's ex-girlfriend, and my new sister, Emily, were the reasons why we took a break for a while.

I stared at the good-looking brown-haired, brown-eyed guy. With more ease than I preferred, he gave Emily a hug and a kiss.

"Max! What a wonderful surprise. What are you doing here…and so early in the morning?" Emily greeted.

"Hi, Em. I see motherhood agrees with you. You look beautiful even at this early hour." *Really?* Did he always need to find her so enchanting?

"Hey!" Of course, where Emily was, my brother wasn't far behind. "Get your hands and lips off my wife!" he demanded.

"Lighten up, Dr. Reid. I was just saying hello to my beautiful ex-girlfriend."

"Must you always bring up the fact that you and my wife once dated?"

"We didn't just once date; we were together twice the length of time you and she have been together."

The irritation in Jake's eyes was cracking me up. He was so easily riled. Though, the conversation outside was making me feel a little snarky myself. *Relax…* My new mantra, as we were going to try again. I needed to get over my "hang-ups," as Max called them.

"Cut it out, both of you," Emily warned while giving her husband a loving embrace. "Good morning." Now she was addressing only Jake. "I brought the kids out so they wouldn't wake you. You got in so late last night from the hospital."

"It was lonely in bed without you," Jake announced loudly, so the whole neighborhood could hear. "I wanted to be out here with my family." My brother's voice got louder with each word, but not as loud as his twin son and daughter—Elizabeth and James.

"Da! Da! Da!" the twins screeched. The four of them made a gorgeous family and the smile on Max's face warmed my heart. For a change, he didn't look like he was still in love with Emily; instead, he looked like he was in love with the idea of a happy family.

Time to make my grand entrance!

"Hey," I greeted.

"Hey..." His voice was soft as he locked eyes with me. Had he thought about me in the past six months? Had he missed me? Had he been dating around? Would we be able to make it work this time?
"Is this what you meant when you said you wanted to go for a ride?"

"I thought we'd ride up the coast for a while."

"OK, I guess..." What would happen today? Things had ended so abruptly between us. One day we were, then the next day we weren't.

"I can't wait to spend the day with you. I've been looking forward to it all week."

Really?

He somehow heard the doubting Thomas question in my head.

"Hey." He gently tugged my chin up with this thumb and forefinger. "I guess you haven't missed me as much as I've missed you. Can we try this again and see where it takes us?"

Twenty+ words was all it took to melt away the bitterness of the past year and make me want to start again. I smiled. *Pushover!* Yeah...pushed over and falling again. I was such a LOSER.

"Don't let go of another good one!" my brother sarcastically yelled as Max tried to muffle his words with the roar of the bike.

"Hold on tight!"

Ominous and yet very promising words…

12-09-2012 Well…That Didn't Go So Well

"You're back!" My sister-in-law smiled with more enthusiasm than totally necessary. "You spent the night?"

"No," I cut her off, "I mean yes, but no."

"Explain, Sister." The thing about Emily—as sweet as she is—she's ruthless when she wants something from you. Whether it's the dazzling smile she throws your way, or her sweet innocent pleading look, you can't say no. Does this woman have any negatives in that beautiful frame of hers? I love her, but *ugh*!

"We rode up to Santa Barbara and were having brunch at the Four Seasons when everything went downhill."

Emily didn't need to know that the ride sucked. There was too much wind, the seat was uncomfortable, it was cold, and we didn't say one word to each other for an hour and a half, but did I complain? No! I was accommodating—as accommodating as Jane Sydney Reid was ever going to be.

"And…?"

"Max's cell phone kept ringing. After about the fifth ring, I kinda yelled at him to pick up the phone, and guess who was calling him?"

"Who?" Emily's big brown eyes were bugging out. It was cute, in a freakishly bugging sort of way.

"Some *GIRL*! He was so uncomfortable talking to her and he couldn't—no, he wouldn't—tell her that he was out with me. I was so pissed, I felt like walking out on him, but I sat through his awkward conversation to get some answers."

While I was pining away for him the last half of the year, apparently, this jerk was dating around.

"He explained that he had 'group-dated' this girl, another doctor at his hospital, briefly." Emily's mouth opened but I didn't give her a chance to start. I had too many things to say. "And though it bothered me, all would have been OK except…his last date with her was just 'a few days ago.'"

Those were the jerk's words, verbatim! What kind of man tells one woman that he misses her and would like to try for a relationship with her one day, then goes out with a totally different woman the next day? Am I wrong to want someone to love me and me only? Forget love—way too soon for that concept. I just want someone to want me and me only. Maybe it's an LA thing. Perhaps I should move back to New York and work a hundred hours a week and be on track to become the youngest partner at our firm.

"No!" Emily was horrified, then mad. She pulled out her cell phone and before she could call Max, I took it away from her. "Let me call him and yell at him. He can't treat you like that! Oh, Jane…" Then, she hugged me. I think she was more hurt than I was. No matter what I thought or said about my sister, I loved her and she genuinely loved me. The rivalry was only on my part and solely in my head. "So where were you all yesterday?"

"I left Max, got myself a room, then a rental car. After calling around, I got a hold of my girlfriend Hilary, and we hung out the whole day. The thought of sitting in the hotel room and gorging on ice cream was tempting, but I spent a boatload of money on clothes and shoes instead."

"Oh, sweet Jane! Your knight in shining armor will come around. Max just needs to sort out his life and grow up some more."

At this point, Max ≠ a knight in shining armor. Well…back to the drawing board!

12-13-2012 Another Date...and His Initials Aren't MD

This was the text that greeted my morning.

Can we meet for a quick lunch? You need to give me a chance to explain.
I *need* to give you a chance?
OK, sorry. Not the right thing to say. A lunch for a chance to grovel?

That made me laugh. Since I left without hearing the full explanation, I suppose I needed to give him a chance. Ha! It was more like I was dying to know who this Joyce girl was that he had been dating. From what my brother Jake told me, she was this brilliant doctor from Stanford who had been after Max for a while. When I asked what she looked like, he shrugged, saying that he hasn't paid attention to another woman's looks since he met Emily. Whatever... *Dork!*

OK but you've gotta come my way cuz I only have thirty min.
Perfect. See you soon.

The morning flew by between meetings and prep work for a case I was assisting.

"Jane, you have a moment?"

"Um, sure."

Donovan, the head lawyer in mergers and acquisitions, waited for me to get up from my seat and practically held my hand into his office.

"What's up?"

He handed me an envelope and gestured for me to open it.

"I just got these tickets to a Laker game, and I was wondering if you wanted to go with me."

"Like... as in a date?" I sounded so sophomoric, or better yet, so moronic, asking this in a high pitched voice.

"Yes, as in a date. Dinner at the Palm, floor seats to watch Kobe, Pau, and Howard in action? Unfortunately your favorite player is still injured."

Damn!
Double Damn!

Floor seats, Laker game, hot successful lawyer... Why couldn't he have asked me out just a few days ago? Do I go? Do I need to explain about Max? What would I say? *Um... I'm kinda re-seeing this guy who had been dating around while I thought about him constantly?*

"Hello. Earth to Jane?"

"Wait, how'd you know Steve Nash was my favorite player?"

"I heard you mention it the other day and bought these tickets with you in mind."

A man who listens to what I have to say even when I wasn't talking to him? Was he for real? Was I an idiot for letting this one go?

"Sure. I'd like that."

"Great! We'll take the company shuttle. I'll pick you up at 6:00?"

A goofy smile crossed my lips. "See you at 6:00."

That high didn't last long as the speakerphone buzzed. "A Max Davis waiting for you in the lobby..."

Triple Damn!

entwined

CAN LOVE REALLY CONQUER ALL?

DW CEE

OLIVIA 2010

"Olivia!" Shocked would be an understatement for what I felt right now as Jamie approached me. "Oh my gosh! What are you doing here? I mean, it's great to see you again." He grabbed me, hugged me, and wouldn't let go. I felt like I was breathing again for the first time in many years.

It had been a long and hard six years without him. Last we saw each other, he asked me to leave his life once and for all and never to contact him again. I choked at this memory and worked to control thinking about that night. All those times I needed him while raising Ollie. All those days I missed being loved by him. I shook my head and rid myself of these thoughts. After all, I should consider him no different than any other acquaintance—except for the fact that Oliver bound us for life.

My heart pained at his release. "Hello?" Jamie waved his hand over my face. "Are you there?"

"Sorry. I'm surprised to see you again. How are you? What brings you to New York and Central Park of all places?"

"I was going to ask you the same thing. I've been so stressed out with work—with it being tax season and all, I've been running during my lunch breaks."

"Are you here on business?"

"No. I live in Manhattan now. I moved a few years ago."

Here he was, in a neighboring state, and we run into each other at the park of all places with Ollie just a few steps away.

"What are you doing at a kiddie play area and in New York of all places?"

"I live in Jersey. We moved here five years ago."

Jamie's face looked like I just solved a riddle for him. "So that's where you went. I went looking for you at your house after we last spoke and I couldn't find you. Did you come here to be near your mom?"

"Yes." My voice sounded monotone. I wanted to hide my true feelings. "It was nice seeing you again, Jamie, but I have to go." I wanted to get away before he saw Ollie. Though I wasn't as anxious as I thought I would be, I wasn't ready for him to meet our son.

"Wait!" Do you have a number or an email address? Can I contact you?" There was some desperation in his voice—maybe that was more my wishful thinking.

I probably had a half smile on my face, wondering why he wanted my info. He was happily married with at least a couple of kids by now. His first child would be just a month or two younger than our Ollie. I didn't need to complicate his life with our presence.

"I don't think that would be a good idea. I really have to go." Walking away, my heart broke as he let me get away from him again so easily. Deep down, I wanted him to beg me for a number. It wasn't right of me to desire a married man. My pace hastened.

"Mommy." Ollie called me over. "Can you push me on the swing?"

"Sure. Let's go."

I picked up our son and plopped him on the swing and pushed him gently.

"Mommy, that's not high enough!" Ollie yelled. "Higher...Faster!" he yelled even louder.

I did as I was told and my son's cackles of delight echoed through the park. I kept my head down, not looking back at where I was just a minute ago. He had most likely left. There was no need to check. Jamie was not mine anymore. He had made himself clear the last time we spoke.

"I'm hungry. Can we eat, Mommy?"

Slowing down the swing, I picked up Ollie and left the sand area. "What shall we eat?"

"How about pizza?" My four-year-old could eat pizza every day if I let him.

"Again?" I kissed his nose. "All right. Let's go eat pizza again for the third time this week."

I looked up from Ollie's smiling face and nearly had a heart attack when I bumped into Jamie again.

"Hey," he called hesitantly.

"Hey," I called back.

"Who's this?" Jamie asked both of us.

I had no idea how I was going to explain Ollie to his father.

"I'm Oliver and I'm four, almost five. I was thwee last year." I guess I didn't have to say a word.

"Hi, Oliver. I'm Jamie. What a great name. My middle name is Oliver."

Ollie stared at this stranger who should have been his closest friend. "Who's this, Mommy?"

I saw the surprised look in Jamie's eyes. I knew what he was thinking.

"Mommy?" Both Hutchison boys asked simultaneously—one out of shock, one out of curiosity.

"He's an old friend of Mommy's. I knew him when Dani and I used to live in Los Angeles."

Ollie leaned over and whispered in my ear. "Could he be my daddy? Is he the one?"

Tears formed unwillingly. Lately, Ollie had been asking more frequently about his father. His father stood just a step away and I couldn't tell him the truth.

"Olivia, I thought you couldn't have...Are you married?"

Words halted, his eyes immediately darted to my ring finger. What were the chances that he'd recognize this generic gold band on my ring finger to be the one he gave me on our last night? It was scratched up and worn through since I never took it off. Though our relationship broke, the ring stayed on my finger to keep other men from paying any attention to me...or so that was the reason I gave myself and all those around me. Painfully I had to acknowledge now that I wore this ring as a constant reminder of what I once had with Jamie.

"I'm hungry, Mommy."

"OK, Sweetheart. We'll go now." I stepped around Jamie without answering his question. "Good seeing you," I said, walking away.

"Wait, can I join you?"

Before I could answer no, Ollie spoke for me again. "Sure, Mr....What do I call him, Mommy?"

"My name is Jamie Oliver Hutchison. You can call me Jamie."

"Hey, that's my name!" My heart skipped several beats. Ollie knew that his last name was Hutchison but I had told my son many times he could never tell anyone this information. He usually told people his name was Oliver Maize.

"I told you we had the same Oliver name." Jamie put out his hands ready to shake Ollie's. Instead, Ollie gave him a high-five. "Where are we going for lunch?"

"We're having pizza!" Ollie shouted into the air and ran off ahead of us.

"What happened? I mean, how did Oliver happen? Didn't the doctor tell us you couldn't have kids? Isn't that why we had to break up? And when did you get married?" Jamie sounded anxious for an explanation. I wanted to tell him that it wasn't me who ultimately broke off the relationship. He was the one who didn't want to see me anymore. He chose having kids and living a life with Melinda, his ex-girlfriend, over me.

I wanted to tell him the truth about Oliver but I didn't want to disrupt his idyllic life.

"Ollie's adopted." The words just popped out of my mouth. Why had I said this? What a mistake.

"Huh? That doesn't make sense. Why? How random. Ollie seems wonderful, but you never mentioned wanting to adopt. What happened?" He sounded frustrated now.

"I wasn't looking for Ollie. He came looking for me. It's a long story, Jamie. Maybe one day when we're in a different place I'll explain it to you."

Dumbfounded. That's how Jamie appeared.

"Liv, he looks just like you. And, where did the name Oliver come from?"

I chuckled at the inside joke. Only if you could see that your son is a mirror image of you. From the day he was born, I understood I would never forget your face.

"I guess we've lived together long enough to start looking alike," I answered with slight laugh. "As for his name...he came with the name." I was on a roll with these lies.

Jamie looked to be buying every misinformation. We stopped talking as we sat in the booth with pizza in hand.

"Ollie, what's your favorite food?"

"Pizza."

"What about your favorite toy?"

"Firetwucks," he answered with his mouth full.

"Are you in school yet?"

"I'm going to start kindergarten soon, Mommy says. Right, Mommy?"

"Yes, Sweetheart," I answered, wiping down his mouth.

"Any favorite places you like to visit?"

"The zoo—that's my favorite place in the whole wide world. I like sleeping in my mommy's bed a lot too. That's my favorite place, but I can only do that on special days, Mommy says."

Jamie and Ollie looked smitten with one another. Blood was thicker than water.

"I used to love the zoo when I was little. That was my favorite place too. Maybe we can visit the zoo in Central Park? Would you want to do that with me, Ollie?"

Our son looked up at me with expectant eyes. He wanted to go but didn't know if I'd let him. My silence kept Ollie quiet as well.

"Oliver, if you are almost five, when is your birthday?"
"Tomowow."
"Tomorrow? Happy birthday. I'll have to get you a present. What would you like?"
"To see my daddy. Mommy says I'll see him one day. I hope it's tomowow."

Ollie's request left us both speechless. I pulled our son from his chair and brought him onto my lap.

Hugging him, I reassured, "Ollie, your daddy is missing you too. You will see him soon. If you're done, let's say thank you to Mr. Hutchison and go home. It's time for a nap.

"Thank you, Mr. Hutchison." He yawned and was ready for a long nap. I picked him up and carried him out the door.

"Thanks for lunch, Jamie." Without saying much else, I walked toward the subway. I felt Jamie walk behind us but neither of us uttered a sound. As I shifted Ollie's drowsy body, Jamie came up from behind and carried our child to the subway. Silently we waited for the train to approach.

"Olivia, can we go somewhere and talk? I have so many questions for you. Like…where you've been the last six years. Why you've never tried to contact me. Did our relationship mean so little to you that you could abandon it after one argument? And, where's your husband? Did you two separate?"

My words and the tears stayed hidden.

"Are you going to disappear again without a trace? Will you at least take my number and call me? I've missed you. It's been so long…too long." He laid a heavy burden on my heart. I wanted his number, his heart, his commitment to me and Ollie. This could never be.

I took Ollie from his father and stepped into the train.

"Wait!" He held my arm. He slipped his business card into my purse and said, "Please call me. We need to talk." He sounded desperate now.

"You made yourself clear to me the last time we spoke. I don't want to be your 'burden.' Hope Melinda is well."

With perfect timing the door shut and I sat with my back against Jamie's face. I heard the banging on the window but my crying eyes didn't turn around. Hugging our son tightly to my chest I cried all the way home.

Carrying Ollie from the station to my mom's house, I was lost in my own thoughts of what had transpired today.

"Olivia!" my mother yelled. "Wait up." I turned to see her hastily walking toward us. "Have you been walking with Oliver this whole time? Here, give him to me."

My mom looked up at me in fright. "What happened to you? Why have you been crying?"

"Ollie and I ran into Jamie at the park today. What am I going to do, Mom?" The tears fell even heavier.

Printed in Great Britain
by Amazon